TRADER
JACK

THE STORY OF JACK MINER

D0040215

Acclaim for *Trader Jack*

Neil Behrmann has pulled off a literary coup with *Trader Jack*. He has crossed the frontier of financial commentary – where his penetrating analysis has earned a global reputation for exceptional quality – into the world of fiction and created a gem. This is not just a financial thriller which keeps the reader spellbound through a roller-coaster ride in market speculation. It deeply stirs the emotions – in particular anguish for the lead character, Jack. Some may see in him the alienated outsider, but he is also a descendant of Voltaire's naive, gullible ingénue. Jack journeys through the global financial markets, populated by villains, but he also encounters goodness.

This gripping story which I couldn't put down, is in its deepest sense a scathing indictment of shallowness, greed and hubris, interspersed with humour of the absurd. *Trader Jack* will bemuse and entrance all those lucky enough to find their way to it.

— Brendan Brown, author of *Euro Crash*, is Executive Director and Chief Economist of Mitsubishi UFJ Securities International.

TRADER JACK

THE STORY OF JACK MINER

NEIL BEHRMANN

Copyright © 2010 Neil Behrmann

The right of Neil Behrmann to be identified as the author of this
work has been asserted by him in accordance with the Copyright,
Designs and Patents Act 1988. All rights reserved. No part of this
publication may be reproduced stored, or transmitted in any
form, or by any means electronic, mechanical or otherwise,
without the express written permission of the publisher.

First published in Great Britain by
HandE Media Production and Publishing 2011

Second Paperback Edition published by New End Books 2011

A CIP catalogue reference for this book is available from The British Library

ISBN 978-0-9533843-1-0

New End Books Ltd, London, UK

www.newendbooks.com

This is a work of fiction. All characters in this publication are fictitious
and any resemblance to any persons living or dead is entirely coincidental.
Names of real world media such as The Wall Street Journal, Bloomberg,
Daily Telegraph, Daily Mail, Financial Times and other companies such as Nestlé,
Maxwell, Lavazza, Sarah Lee, Kraft and Illy have on occasion been used solely for the
purpose of creating the illusion that the story occurs in the real world, but their inclusion
does not imply any endorsement by those companies. The names of the companies
mentioned are registered trademarks and the rights of the proprietors are acknowledged.

Cover Design by Ruth Mahoney

Typeset by Avon DataSet Ltd, Bidford on Avon, UK

Printed and bound in UK by TJ International Ltd, Padstow, Cornwall, UK

To Joy, Anna & Amy
For all their help and encouragement

In Memory of my parents, George and Anne
and my brother Tony

1

THE WITNESS

About fifty people were sheltering in the open parking space under Queen Elizabeth Hall. A few were in sleeping bags, but most were under blankets and cardboard boxes. The moon and streetlights helped us see what we were doing and we settled down next to a pillar. Before long we were asleep.

The girls slept well, but I kept waking up. The hard, cold concrete floor penetrated my sleeping bag. My bones were aching and I was feeling stiff. I lay there with my eyes open, observing the others. Some slept soundly, others shuffled about. Further into the darkness, I could see the red tip of a cigarette.

Jazz stood up and pawed me, demanding a walk. I put on my jacket and left my stuff with the sleeping girls. It had stopped raining and the moon was full. We passed the Royal Festival Hall and a pier and walked alongside the river. The reflection of the moon was on the water and Big Ben, on the other side. Its bells chimed and I glanced at my watch; 3am. Waterloo Bridge was on our right. On the left, a railway bridge with a pedestrian crossing. The London Eye, the huge Millennium Wheel, was about two hundred yards away.

We began our walk on the south bank towards the Eye when I heard a thud and a choking cry. It came from the pedestrian bridge. A man must have jumped, but instead of falling into the river, he had come to a halt in midair. He hung from the end of a rope, kicking and struggling.

I rushed to the bridge, my dog alongside me and sped up the stairs towards the rope. It was tied to a railing about halfway across the bridge. The man was kicking and shaking; the rope swaying. I reached for the rope and managed to catch it. The knot fixed to the balustrade was thick and I struggled to untie it. It was too tight. I dug into the knot with my pocketknife to loosen it, so that he could fall into the river. It was his best chance. No use. The man was now twitching. Time was running out.

Jazz started growling and I looked up. There were two of them. They were at the other end of the bridge and were beginning to turn back and come towards me. The first was about six foot four with a burly body and thick beard. The other was wiry and small. I called them to help me relax the stranglehold. Jazz bared his teeth and barked; made me feel uneasy.

The yellow light of the moon, shone on them. Both were in black and they had covered their faces with balaclavas. The big one had a rope in his hand. They were coming to stop me, not to help. I felt the rope with its heavy burden. The twitching was beginning to stop and the poor man was no longer lurching furiously. It was too late. I could be next. There was only one thing to do. Run!

They tensed up like runners on a starter block and sprinted after us. Followed us from the bridge to the walkway, past the

Royal Festival Hall. We turned towards Queen Elizabeth Hall where the girls were. Maybe we could hide there, but there could be a gang of them and they would find me. Better keep going. They were getting closer; their panting, louder. We ran up the stairs to Waterloo Bridge. The small wiry guy reached out to me and as I turned, I saw his small black eyes and a snake tattoo on his arm. Lucky. He tripped over a homeless guy lying in the corner of the stairs. The big man lunged at me, but missed.

I was now on the bridge and was too far ahead of them. I looked around, the men, hot from the chase, had taken off their balaclavas. Under the light of the streetlamp, the small guy was bald and had a scar across his cheek. The big guy, with the beard had a large flat nose. It looked as if it had been broken. They cursed in a language that sounded Eastern European.

I stepped up the pace and managed to get further away from them. A police car drove by on the other side of the road. I shouted for help. The police didn't stop, but it was enough to make my pursuers hesitate; allowed me to widen the distance between us. At the end of the bridge, a car was waiting for the traffic lights to turn green.

'Can you take me to a police station?' I called.

The guy closed his window, but pointed to the left. We ran across the road ignoring the red lights. I quickly turned around. The two men had suddenly stopped chasing. They were gone, but where? Maybe they knew a short cut. They could still get me. I turned left and jogged up The Strand, the road that leads to Trafalgar Square. We raced past pubs, restaurants and theatres; past other homeless people, who were lying in shop doorways. At last a sign: Charing Cross Police Station. I rested a bit, caught my breath, tied Jazz to a pole, climbed up the stairs between two big columns and went inside.

An officer was working behind a small window to the left of the reception. In front of me was a notice board with a poster of a missing girl. Another poster sought information about a man with a thick beard. Under his picture was the warning, 'Dangerous'. I went to a desk under the notice board and took a pen out of my jacket. On the back of a pamphlet about crime prevention, I wrote: 'Man hanging from railway bridge. Opposite Royal Festival Hall. Happened at 3am.'

I folded up the note and passed it to the officer behind the window. He opened it, just as I walked out. No way was I going to get involved in the murder. Me, the only witness. They would ask too many questions. I would be news. The killers could find me.

'Hey you, come back!' the officer shouted.

But I was gone. I untied Jazz quickly and we ran around the corner. We wandered through Covent Garden and eventually found an entrance to a shop. Huddled together and got some sleep.

When I woke up, it was light. We walked to Trafalgar Square, tired and hungry. My backpack was at Queen Elizabeth Hall and the girls would be wondering where I was. But I couldn't go back until there were lots of people around.

Later during the morning, we went back to the Hall. From Waterloo Bridge, I could see the ribbon cordon at the entrance of the railway bridge. They had cut the man down. The police must have taken my note seriously. There was quite a big crowd there. Using people as cover we made our way towards our sleeping place, next to a wall covered with graffiti. The girls had disappeared. I looked around to see if they had put my stuff in a corner or something. The homeless and cardboard boxes were gone. Empty. The police must have been around asking questions. They could have my bag. Fortunately my passport and letters were on me. But my fingerprints were on that rope, the hanging rope. That was scary.

A large dustbin van was in the street, between the Queen Elizabeth Hall and the Royal Festival Hall.

'I'm looking for some bags. Did you see any?' I asked.

They didn't bother to answer. There was no point in staying there. Best to move on. Get out of London, but with no money, how?

*   *   *

It's five years since it happened, but I still can't get it out of my head.

And now I'm writing about it. Not once. Not twice. The fourth fucking time!

Mrs Small keeps crossing out swearing: 'Broaden your language. Dig deep. Find new words. Write. Rewrite.'

Lights still on. Jim down there snoring. How the hell can you sleep in this place? Hot, noisy and stinks. Had enough of writing. Don't feel like reading.

Two months since I've been banged up. Fraud! Not small

stuff! Big time! Lost seven billion. Seven years for seven thousand million.

Twenty one in June. Twenty eight when I'm out. Must cut time. Keep my head down. Mrs Small's Creative Writing Group. It has to get me out. It must! Problem. Mayfair murder. They still think I did it. Don't believe me. Keep coming back. Questions, more questions.

Can't sleep. Going nuts in here. Memories. What I did. What I should have done.

Thoughts, round and round. OK, take it easy. Write them down. My story. Everything. The truth. Make them understand. From the beginning, when Bill died . . .

2

THE FUNERAL

I still remember the coffin. The big knot in the pine wood. The circles around that knot. The vicar droning on. I wasn't listening. Just looked at the plain wooden box; the knot.

They began to sing but I didn't join in. My throat was dry. Nothing came out. Then silence and the conveyer belt began to move. The coffin slid further away, through the curtain. Gone.

The vicar pointed to the door and I walked out without looking around. Outside, the sun was blinding. I shielded my eyes and through the gaps between my fingers, saw red, pink, yellow, orange and white roses. I walked over to the bushes, snatched a few yellow petals, crunched them in my hands and read some memorials: 'James McNaughton. Darling Husband and Father. Rest in peace.'

Then another one: 'Timothy Kane . . . Darling Brave Tim. God's always with you. Died October 1998 aged Thirteen.' It was bad enough losing a dad, but imagine a son!

I turned to face them. They were now out of the chapel; about thirty of them huddled in a group. I was hot and itchy as they shuffled up to me, one by one. I stuck my finger into my collar and loosened the button and tie. Felt a bit better. Dad had bought the second hand blue suit nine months ago. But I had grown a bit and it felt tight.

Aunty Peggy was first. Short and fat with dyed blonde hair, a red blotchy face and grey sunken eyes, Peggy planted a kiss on my cheek. I can still smell her sweat through her sickly perfume; her breath an ashtray. Uncle Martin, her husband, was next. He put a wet palm in my hand. A drop of sweat fell from his nose on to his thick grey beard. About six foot three and one and a half foot wide, his stomach sagged over his trousers. Both of them were in black; all of them dressed in black. They kept on coming; a long line of uncles, aunts, cousins and Dad's drinking mates.

The only ones I wanted to be there were at the end of the queue. They were in their navy blue school blazers.

'All right then?' asked Tom.

He was sixteen, but bigger than me. Tom, then Joe, touched my shoulder before moving aside. Joe was small. He had thick glasses and lots of spots. He looked like a geek, but wasn't that clever.

'See you later,' mumbled Joe. 'Beach football. Same place.'

'See you,' I said with a grin; then hid it. The vicar was nearby. The vicar came up, glanced at my friends with a false smile and wiped his brow with a handkerchief. About six foot tall with a black and white silk gown, he was hot and needed a shower badly.

'I know you aren't religious, but feel free to visit me any time,' he said, clasping my hand with a sweaty grip. 'Come to Church. It will comfort you.'

He continued to hold my hand limply as I slowly tried to withdraw.

Reverend Cook peered through his smudgy glasses. He knew what I was thinking.

'I can see you want to be alone. We'll keep the urn for you. When you're ready.'

Relief. I was on my own again. That's where I wanted to be. I watched them chat to each other in small groups, some glancing at me. At last they made their way to the car park. I was about to wander through the rose beds again, when someone tapped me on my shoulder. It was Mrs Derby. Her eyes were red from crying; her mascara smudging her plump, pretty face. She hugged me and I could smell the plain soap on her pale white skin. For the first time I felt myself choke.

*　　*　　*

Our flat was crowded with so-called mourners and other hangers-on. Some wake! I was supposed to be the host, but hardly anyone spoke to me. They stood around or leaned on chairs and the table, drinking and snatching crisps and nuts. Some asked me about myself. Most of it was a load of rubbish about school. GCSE exams, what AS levels I would take, football and cricket. They finished their drinks and left after shaking my hand and wishing me good luck. A few remained, but the bitter, lager and coke were almost finished and the wine bottles were empty. Hopefully they would soon be gone. I stroked Jazz and he rubbed against my leg and licked my hand. Other than Mrs Derby and

I, the wheaten terrier with his soft, wheat coloured coat, seemed to be the only one who really cared about Dad.

I grabbed a bottle, snatched a few peanuts and walked to the window. Summertime. Hundreds of people down there – a long column from the Captain's Table at the edge of the harbour to the pier below our flat. The tide was out and from where I was looking, the boats seemed to be stuck in the mud. Directly down below, Dave was doing an active trade in spades, buckets and sandals.

If Dad were still alive, we would be having a great day in our fish and chip shop. Taking orders, frying, wrapping and ringing the till. He always said that Bridlington had a future. If only the Council would develop the town. If only it didn't rain so much.

I looked back at the guests in our small two-bedroom flat. Mike, Sheila and Sharon stood next to my other cousin, Alan. They were Martin and Peggy's kids; Mike and Sheila were at University and Sharon worked at Tesco. Alan, sprawled on the sofa, was dozing. His long legs dangled on to the floor, a glass of lager and a sandwich plate next to them. Jazz sped to the half-eaten sandwich and gobbled it up. We watched him sniff the lager and sample a bit. Froth was on his nose. Mike clapped his hands and Alan woke up, startled. He bent down and sipped his lager. We burst out laughing.

That was more like it. The wake was livening up. I put on some CDs of Louis Armstrong, and Ella Fitzgerald, some of the old-time favourites of Bill, my Dad. He was so mad on jazz that he named our dog after it. The five of us began dancing. Jazz lived up to his name. He jumped up and joined in, allowing each of us to hold his paws.

I was hot and sweaty and needed to change, so I slipped out of the living room. Bursting, I ran to the loo and afterwards washed my hands and face. Looking at the mirror, I noticed a spot on the side of my nose and picked at it. I was still quite skinny with short brown hair, light blue eyes and a small nose and mouth. My front teeth overlapped.

I made my way towards my bedroom. Uncle Martin, Dad's brother, was speaking.

'Look we hooven't seen 'em for yonks,' he said in his thick Yorkshire accent. 'Hardly know laad. I'm skint. Really. Wish we 'ad room for 'im.'

'One of us must take him in, we have to,' whispered Martin's wife Peggy. 'Bill went bust before he died. Left him with nowt.'

'Not us, wish we could,' said a voice that sounded like Uncle John from Mum's side. 'We're also short . . . It weren't easy to chip in for this lot.'

'Nice people! Paid a few quid for their party!' I whispered to myself, deciding whether I should walk in.

'Look, 'e's just turned sixteen, 'e'll find soomething . . . maybe fish and chips,' said Martin.

I slipped quietly into the room and they turned to face me, smiles sheepish. Martin was sitting on my chair sipping his half pint of bitter, his black striped suit jacket, behind him. A button was missing on his white shirt. Through it I could see his fat hairy belly.

'We're wondering where you should live,' said Peggy, puffing away.

She looked dazed from the heat and booze and threatened me with a hug. I carefully avoided her. John, with his bad skin, mean face and skinny arms and hands, managed to catch my arm and ruffled my head. My Mum's brother! Very different. Him ugly, her pretty. I wondered if we were related.

I pushed him away and stared at them, not bothering to answer. The room was full of smoke. I went straight to the window, opened it a lot wider, leaned over and watched Dave down below. They waited and shuffled about embarrassed. Martin said stupid things such as 'Bill was a reight good sooart' and 'pity mother no loonger with you'. I ignored them. Jazz trotted in and came straight up to me. I patted him, saw his lead on the table and put it on. I just stood there, saying nothing; not bothering to look at them. It seemed forever, but at last they took the hint and began to leave the room. Peggy, about to leave and looking guilty, pressed twenty pounds into my hand. Then she kissed me on the cheek and went. I just stood there. Didn't thank her.

At last I could get out of my hot tight trousers. I threw them on to the suit jacket that was lying on the bed, took off my shirt and put on some shorts and a T-shirt. I felt a lot cooler and was about to put on my trainers when Mrs Derby walked in. She handed me an envelope.

'Bill gave it to me a fortnight before he died,' she said.

About fifty, and plump with curly brown hair, Gill Derby had a kind face and a soft voice. She lived upstairs and was our landlady. Gill started crying again and hugged me. Good old Gill. She really loved Dad. I wondered if they had anything going.

'Look I know Bill was behind. Don't worry,' Gill insisted.

'Stay here until I find another tenant. If the worst comes to the worst, you can move in with me.'

Jazz started barking. Like me he wanted to get out of the place. Mrs Derby provided the cover and we managed to escape. I waved just in case some of the others were looking. We ran down the stairs on to the harbour pier, forcing our way through the crowd. We reached the boats at the far end of the harbour and looked back at all the shops and stalls. "Our Plaice" fish and chip shop was boarded up. Next door, Dave was swamped with customers.

*   *   *

It was hot, steaming hot. Hundreds of people were pushing their way down a long wide harbour gangway towards the beach. The past few summers had been wet. That was one of the main reasons why "Our Plaice" and Dad went down. It was a hot July; few clouds, burning sun. Beaches were full.

Reaching the beach at last, I kicked off my trainers, threw down my shirt and took off Jazz's lead. He sprinted ahead of me and I followed. The tide was right out. I felt my feet sink into the wet sand and the shells and mussels crunching under me. We raced across shallows towards the sea, until the water was up to my knees. Then I dived in, Jazz swimming alongside me. The water was cold, numbing cold, despite the heat from the sun. It was the North Sea current that came from Scandinavia, all the way down to the eastern English coast. There were hardly any waves; just the freezing swell. We headed back to the beach, running zigzag alongside the shallow water for about half a mile. Close to the shore and on fairly dry land, Tom, Joe and two other guys were playing football on our beach pitch. Tom kicked towards the opponents' goal but the wind carried the ball away from the pitch and it landed near me. I dribbled on to the pitch, dodged a couple of opponents and took a shot at goal. The ball was light and as I slammed it and misjudged the weight, the breeze from the sea lifted it way past the goal.

Jazz chased after it, but unlike other dogs, used his brain and didn't puncture it. A couple walking past, were amazed. The dog could dribble with his nose and feet. We played for about a quarter of an hour. My side, even with Jazz's skill, was down a goal.

Sue, Jodie, and a girl we hadn't seen before, showed up and watched the game. We stopped concentrating and missed lots of goals as we sneaked glances at the new girl. She was really pretty, with a great tan and long straight, shiny brown hair.

The game was getting so bad, we decided to stop playing and have a dip. It gave us the opportunity to meet her. She was Sandy Swann and was from Australia. We hardly spoke to the other two. Sue, with black frizzy hair, was fun, but a bit silly. Jodie had nice blonde highlights but her teeth stuck out a bit. Sandy's tiny bikini barely covered her breasts. She noticed us make a rush for her and smiled. She was used to guys chasing her.

Sue and Jodie didn't have swimming costumes, so Sandy had five of us all to herself. We charged into the sea and dived into the shallow waves.

'What you doing in Yorkshire?' I asked.

'Visiting my cousin Sue. We're going to London.'

'When do you go back home?'

'Got another two weeks. Then school.'

'Where?'

'Perth.'

'Western Australia?'

She touched my shoulder by mistake and I felt a tingle. She smiled and swam ahead. 'Think she fancies you?' asked Tom.

'Dunno.'

'Come out with us tonight,' said Joe. 'It'll stop you thinking about your Dad.'

'Some relatives are still at the flat,' I said. 'I better go.'

'They've probably left. Let's go deeper,' Tom said.

We swam out towards Sandy. She was hanging on to a red and white buoy. The water was much colder there. Sue and Jodie, paddling in the shallows, were a long way back.

'What do you do around here?' shouted Sandy.

'The usual stuff. Movies, fairs, snooker, clubs,' replied Tom.

'What your clubs like?'

'Much the same as others.'

'There's a comedy show tonight,' said Joe. 'In Whittington's basement.'

'I'm not so sure I feel like it,' I said.

'What's his problem?' asked Sandy.

'His Dad died two days ago. The funeral was today.'

She looked embarrassed.

'Sorry, I'm really sorry.'

'Come on, it will do you good. No point in sitting alone at home,' said Tom.

*   *   *

I took Aunty Peggy's twenty pounds out of my pocket and used some of it to buy tokens. There were six of us at the fair and we went on the Whip, the Big Wheel and the Helter Skelter. Afterwards, we walked to the Whittington Pub. The basement was full, but we managed to squeeze around a table near the front of the stage. John Dimes, the comedian, was trying to be heard above the noise. He was only five foot tall and could easily have been a circus clown. He suddenly went silent and eyed the audience with sad eyes. The tactic worked and the chattering died down. He told jokes; some good, some bad. The audience was so drunk that they laughed at everything. Some jokes were about death. St Peter's Gate, that sort of thing. Tom and Sandy kept looking across at me to see how I was taking it. I wasn't bothered. The comedian now had the audience's full attention. Except for an occasional clatter of glasses and some giggles, they listened to his story routine. He winked at Sandy, tried to pull her on to the stage to help him juggle some balls, but she managed to get away from him.

Sandy touched my hand: 'Want to go for a walk?'

We squeezed through the gaps between the tables and made our way to the promenade. She grabbed my hand and guided me towards some stairs down to the beach.

'How coom, you doon't taalk with Yorkshire aaccent,' she asked, nudging me.

'Because, me moom woos teeecher; taught bairn elecootion,' I laughed.

We took off our shoes and walked in the thick sand. The tide was in and we felt the spray of the breaking waves. It was almost 10pm and the sun had set only minutes before.

The sand was cool and through the dusk I could see her dark eyes, longish nose and full lips. She edged closer to me.

'I heard that your Mum also died.'

'Yes, when I was eleven.'

'What did she teach?'

'English and maths.'

'Can't imagine what I would do if I lost my Mum and Dad.'

'You get used to it.'

'Who are you going to live with?'

'Not relatives. They're measuring straws. Short one gets me.'

We laughed and held hands.

'Can't stand mine either. When's your birthday?'

'Turned sixteen, on June 1.'

'I'm sixteen in July. Gemini and Cancer. Do you think we're suited?'

I felt myself blush.

We sat down at the bottom of a sandy mound, well away from the water. No one was around. I put my arm around her. She snuggled up close. I looked down at her and she stared up into my eyes and touched my forehead. I kissed her cheek, then clumsily tried to find her lips. There was a grain of sand there as we began to kiss. It hurt me a bit, probably her too. I tried to slip my hand under her sweater. She pushed me away.

Darkness was beginning to close in. Through the gloom, I could just make out the froth from the waves. She kissed my cheek, grabbed my hand, pulled me up and dragged me towards the promenade.

'Amazing. It's just got dark and it is almost the middle of the night,' she said.

'Come here in winter. Pitch black at four,' I whispered into her ear.

3

THE LIQUIDATOR

I was dreaming about Sandy. We were kissing, but she was slobbering all over me. I half opened my eyes. Red tongue, black nose and fur. I pushed away Jazz and looked at the clock. It was about half eight. The sun was streaming in and the dog wanted his food and walk. Jazz ate some leftover sausages and bread from the wake and nibbled a banana. I brushed my teeth, looked in the mirror and felt good. We charged down the stairs on to the pier, down the long gangway to the beach. The port was virtually empty and the desolate Bridlington beach seemed to go on for miles. I thought of what Bill used to say: 'Magnificent North England beach. Pity the town's tatty.'

Filey is only about ten miles away. No comparison. A wood overlooks part of its beach and it has quaint cottages, hotels and shops. Tourists pour into the town. If only Dad had opened "Our Plaice" there, we wouldn't have been broke. He might have lived.

The tide was going out and the waves were tiny. We ran in the shallows for about half an hour, the sweat trickling down my back, the sun getting hotter. Only my feet were cool. Jazz found a stick and I threw it and followed him into the water. I ducked under a medium sized wave; felt free, completely free.

About a hundred metres out, I glanced back towards the shore. A few pretty houses were on the outskirts of town. They were the exception. Far towards the right, overlooking the harbour, was the shabby, crumbling building where I lived.

A dark cloud appeared and it turned cold, so I raced out of the water and jogged at a fast pace towards home.

*   *   *

Mrs Derby called me when I passed her flat on the way up the stairs. A man in a grey suit was in her living room. He stood up stiffly, put out his hand and introduced himself: 'Mark Baton, Bailey & Baton.'

He shook my hand tightly: 'We represent your father's creditors.'

The accountant, in his late forties, was balding, with thin lips and a narrow mean face. Must have come from years on the job. Baton was patronising and I took an instant dislike to him. When he smiled, he couldn't help but sneer.

'I gather you know that your father's business was failing,' Baton continued in a posh accent. 'Did you know that the bank called in his loan?'

'When?'

'A week before he died?'

Gill Derby winced and turned away to pour me some tea. This guy wasn't exactly tactful.

'I'm afraid I have to value his remaining assets. The equipment in the shop, stock and investments, that sort of thing,' he said. 'Help the creditors recover their money.'

'Suppose that's what a liquidator does!' I snapped.

He looked at me self-righteously.

'I can understand your feelings. But he did borrow the money, you know. Good people and companies are short.'

'Like the bank,' I murmured sarcastically.

'Yes, but there are others too. Mrs Derby is one of them. Your father was about three months behind on her rent. Almost two thousand pounds.'

Gill interrupted him as she passed me a cuppa and a biscuit: 'Look, I don't really care. They've lived here for a long time. Bill always paid. It was only recently . . .'

She looked at me sympathetically and shook her head: 'I don't want to be part of this. The lad's got enough problems.'

'Yes, I realise that, Mrs Derby. You've already told me. But it must be done,' he continued pompously.

'Now, young man, please show me where your father kept his papers and his computer; the keys of the shop.'

'OK,' I said and took him up to our flat.

I had meant to clear up the mess from the wake. Empty bottles, dirty glasses, crisps, peanuts, cigarette ends and bits of bread were all over the place. It was a rats' paradise. Jazz slammed his paws on a small living room table and gobbled up a congealed sausage. Baton shuddered. He walked around the room, making sure that he didn't touch anything. He made notes of the table, chairs, the battered telly and other bits and pieces. Baton followed me into Bill's bedroom and he quickly examined the dressing table and a cupboard.

'Did your father make a will?'

'Dunno. He used to put all his papers in this,' I said, pulling them out from the dressing table and piling them on top.

Baton tried to ignore the mess on the bed, the banana skin on the floor and Jazz's dirty dish next to his basket. He shook his head in disgust.

'Well? Anything more?'

I went to the cupboard and clutched the box file of the shop's invoices, expenses and bookkeeper's accounts. Baton double-checked to see that nothing was left. He found a small leather case and a bag with some more papers.

'Where's the computer?'

'In my room.'

He followed me there. My small second-hand laptop was on my unmade bed; the printer on a table.

He examined it with a sneer: 'Isn't this obsolete. Do you manage to connect to the Internet?'

'Use it for school. Not for broadband. Get that at Internet café,' I said biting my lip.

'Where do you go to school?' he asked peering down at me. 'Done your GCSEs? Do you think you'll pass?'

'Bridlington. Yes, I think I've done OK.'

I was getting irritated with this idiot. I felt like punching him on the nose, but he was the type who would call the police.

'Are your father's records on it? Emails?'

'Some stuff about the shop.'

'His mobile?'

'Can't find it. Must have got lost when the ambulance took him to hospital.'

'Any investments?'

'Don't think so. Don't think he had any. Never spoke about it.'

'Where can I work?' he said huffily.

We went into the kitchen and I cleared the table and wiped his chair. He waited impatiently as I went to get the laptop, files and papers. I dumped the papers on to the table in a messy pile. Baton flushed.

He took a laptop out of his bag, pushed some papers aside to give him some working space, sat down and began to work. I connected the laptop to the power as he began to sort out the papers. I was tempted to blow a fuse and crash his computer. But he watched me suspiciously and was soon itemising an inventory of junk.

I grabbed a broom, a pan and some black bags and went into the living room to clean up the place. After about three hours or so, Baton came into the living room with the envelope that Mrs Derby had given me.

'What's this?'

'Dunno, I haven't read it yet.'

'It could be the will. Could you open it please.'

I glanced at the letter: 'Doesn't seem to be a will.'

'Can I see it?'

'It's personal.'

'I must read it.'

Losing his patience he snatched it from me and read it quickly. For some reason, which I couldn't understand, he went into Bill's room and directly to Jazz's basket in the corner. He took the cushion out and picked it up, examined it carefully and placed the basket back in the corner. I put back the cushion and looked at him puzzled. For the first time, he was embarrassed. He even softened a bit.

'My apologies . . . Sorry . . . I had to read the letter . . . It's my job, you see.'

I put the letter in my back pocket and turned away. I didn't want to show him that I was upset.

'Can I have the key of the shop?'

It was hanging on a hook behind the kitchen door and I handed it to him.

'The shop's downstairs, almost directly below the flat. That's why we moved here,' I said. 'The equipment is still in good condition.'

'Doubt if it's worth much. We'll see when we sell the business.'

He half mumbled to himself, but in a spiteful way, making sure that I could hear: 'Doubt if the creditors will get 5 pence in the pound.'

Baton put the papers that he needed in his briefcase, took the box file and my computer.

'I'm sorry, I'll have to take this; I'll return it as soon as possible.'

'But that's got all my personal stuff on it; my addresses, my emails.'

'Sorry we have to do a proper search.'

He gave me the small leather case and shook my hand: 'I think you'll want this.'

At last he was gone. I continued to clean up the flat and filled lots of large black bags. After making my bed, I lounged on the battered sofa and opened up the case. There was a knock on the door. It was Gill.

'What a thoroughly unpleasant man,' she said wearily.

She glanced at the landscape print on the wall and Mum and Dad's wedding picture on the mantelpiece.

'Make sure that you don't leave anything personal. He's going to have an auction.'

'Won't get much money for this lot.'

'The creditors will get nothing. Not even the bank. All of this will go to Bailey & Baton,' she said.

'They don't call them liquidators for nothing. What do you think of the flat?'

'Tidy . . . clean! I'm impressed . . . I meant what I said . . . You can stay here until I find another tenant.'

'Thanks. I'm not sure what to do.'

'Is one of your relatives taking you in? Martin? John?'

'Don't think so.'

She was silent, obviously disgusted.

'If the worst comes to the worst, you can move in with me.'

I gave her a cup of tea and offered her a few of the leftover biscuits from the wake. We sat on the sofa and she noticed the open leather suitcase filled with photos and letters. She picked up a picture of me as a baby.

'Sweet. Can I take a look?'

'Sure.'

We laughed as we sorted through the old family pictures, especially me as a kid. I opened a letter that Mum had written to Dad.

Darling Bill,
Thanks for your letter, which I received this morning.

Cornwall is lovely and we miss you. Yesterday, we were at the tip of Land's End and looked out towards the sea. It was a beautiful day, not the drizzly weather you're having in Yorkshire.

The letter went on and was signed, *Much love, Jane. Lots of kisses from Jack and I.*

I passed it to Gill: 'Nice handwriting. Pity mine's not the same.'

Gill read it and looked up at me. Her eyes had tears in them. I felt my eyes getting watery. I tried to stop, but I couldn't help myself. It just came, like a sort of coughing fit, on and on, my shoulders up and down. I wiped off the tears on my forearm.

'Thirty nine when she died, now Dad at fifty two,' I managed to choke out.

Gill put her arms around me and hugged me tightly. I could hear her heart beating underneath her big soft bosoms.

'Let it out Jack . . . Don't try and stop it . . . Nothing to be ashamed of . . .'

I was angry with myself: 'Sorry, I'm being stupid.'

'No you're not . . . You've been very brave . . . Just turned sixteen and both parents gone. Who do you think you are? Superman?'

We were both crying by now. She kissed me on my cheek.

'I was depressed for months after my parents died . . . I'm also an only child . . . Don't bottle it up . . . Let it out Jack . . . Just let it out.'

She went into the kitchen and put the kettle on: 'No arguments . . . I'm taking you out for lunch.'

* * *

After lunch with Gill, I began thinking of Sandy again. My mobile had run out of credit. So I stopped at a phone box and found her cousin Sue's number. One of Sue's brothers answered. He told me that Sue and Sandy had left for London. Sandy had managed to get tickets for the Lord's cricket test. Her cousin was playing for Australia. He thought that they were staying in Hampstead in north London, but he didn't know the address. Wouldn't give me Sue's mobile number. I kicked myself for forgetting to ask Sandy about her plans.

Jazz and I hadn't eaten so much in a long time and were feeling full, so we went for a walk along the promenade. We reached a paddling pool, close to the beach below. It had been raining. I found a *Yorkshire Post* under a beach hut, put the newspaper on the wet bench and sat on the sports pages.

The cloud had lifted and it was getting light again. A little kid, wearing just a T-shirt and a nappy, was in the water. His mother and father looked on proudly as he paddled from one end to the other. I tried not to laugh when the boy slipped and nearly fell.

While I was watching, I felt some paper in my back pocket. I had forgotten about Bill's letter. I hadn't read it properly. For the first time, I realised that Dad had been an outpatient at the hospital and was waiting for a heart bypass operation. He had decided to write to me just in case.

They told me to stop smoking and lose weight, he wrote.
You know those pills that I've been putting under my

tongue . . . They're Glyceryl Trinitrate. They help me through the chest pains.

It was a pity that Bill had kept all his problems to himself. I knew that he had angina. I just didn't know how bad it was. I read on: *I've cut down on smokes and sweets, but it's bloody hard. I think it's mainly stress. The shop's been losing money for a long time. You've been a great help, but we're not making enough to meet the bills. I don't know if I can hold out until the end of the year. I owe rent on the shop and flat and the bank is threatening to call in the overdraft.*

The kid fell and began to howl. His mum picked up her dress, waded in, dragged him out and dried him. After he was dry, she changed his nappy and he quietened down.

The letter continued: *I'm fifty three next birthday, so it's going to be a battle to get a new job. I hope that it will be some years before you read this, Jack. All I can say is that I've been thinking of your lovely Mum.*

I turned away from the family and wiped my eyes with my sleeve.

Look after yourself. That's why I shouted at you when I saw you smoke the other day. Give it up! OK! Don't chuck in school. Make something of yourself. You've got it in you.

Take care of Jazz. I can see him now. Snug in his basket. Always sleeps in the same place. Keep him there. He likes it.

Love Bill.

If Dad's somewhere up there, he needn't worry. I stopped smoking when he died. That stuff about Jazz, his basket and his sleeping place. Why was Baton so interested in it?

* * *

We walked up the stairs to the flat and bumped into Gill. She offered me a bed for the night. That puzzled me a bit until we were inside. I couldn't switch on the TV. They had cut off the electricity. It was still light enough to go through all the letters and photos in the small leather case. I kept some and threw out others. I went to Bill's cupboard and put his clothes into two black bags and carried them to the living room. That would be for Oxfam or some other charity.

I kept thinking about Dad's letter as I walked around the flat, putting some photos, a few family things, jazz CDs and a few books in his large brown suitcase.

Bill's favourite Louis Armstrong CD, a photo of Dad and Mum and her engagement ring were put in the side pocket of my backpack. My passport and birth certificate went in my inside jacket pocket. There was nothing for me here. Might as well go to London. Far more opportunities there. Try to find Sandy. There was just enough money to get there. I could be a waiter, get a job in a shop or something. Had plenty of experience selling fish and chips.

When I was finished, I felt much better. I had made a decision. The backpack and sleeping bag were on the bed, with a towel, trousers, shirts, socks and a few other things. It was beginning to get dark. After feeding the dog, I had a lukewarm bath and got into Dad's bed. It made me feel close to him.

The early morning sun woke me up. Jazz was fast asleep in the corner of the room. I thought of Dad's letter and remembered Baton examining the battered basket. By mentioning it in his letter, Bill had obviously made the liquidator suspicious. Jazz woke up, jumped out of the basket, stretched and wagged his tail. I went over to the corner where he slept, picked up the basket and took out the dog's cushion. I felt the basket to see whether there was a false bottom or hidden compartment or something. Same as Baton, I found nothing.

Just when I was about to put it back in the corner, I noticed that the floorboard wasn't nailed down. I knelt down and touched the board. It moved slightly. I took out my pocketknife, pushed it into a crack and started loosening the floorboard. It came out. The gap was about a foot long and about four inches wide. A crumpled newspaper was inside. I pulled out the paper and found a black metal box. It was locked. I lay flat on the floor, put my hand in the hole and found the key. Jazz cocked his head when the box opened. Inside were two envelopes. The first was another letter from Dad.

The letter was dated June 17, about a fortnight before Bill died. It said that there was a document in the other envelope. I was the owner of 600 OilFinder Global Ltd and 500 MineDeep World Ltd shares, which Dad had transferred into my name. He wrote that he had once saved a mining prospector from drowning. The grateful geologist gave him the shares. They were worth around ten thousand pounds, the letter said.

I opened the second envelope and found the document. It said that the shares were registered in the name of Jack Miner. Bank Gorde, Amsterdam was holding them in safekeeping. I couldn't understand why Bill was banking with a Dutch bank, but I suppose he wanted to keep the shares a long way from the creditors. If he knew that he was bankrupt and owed people money, he should not have given me the shares. Baton was looking for his investments.

The letter added that if there were any further questions, the bank should call Fred Carrender, the prospector. Carrender lived in Johannesburg, South Africa. His address and telephone number were in the letter. A folded paper napkin was at the bottom of the box. I picked it up and notes fell on to the floor. They came to £250. I put the empty box back into the hiding place, found a hammer and some nails and nailed down the corner plank. Knowing that Baton was bound to investigate further, I decided that I had better leave Bridlington soon. I didn't know anything about the stock market, investing and that sort of stuff and had to find out what I should do about those OilFinder and MineDeep shares.

I looked through a few of Dad's old books and found: 'Investing In The Stock Market'. Before putting the book in my rucksack, I paged through it. People could buy and sell shares through any bank or stockbroker. They could be sold in London.

After Jazz helped me finish the remaining milk, bits of cereal and a half loaf of stale bread, I wrote a note to Mrs Derby.

Dear Gill,
I've decided to go to London. Thanks for all you have done for me. I'll keep in contact.
See you,
Love Jack

P.S. Here's £50 towards your rent. I'll try and pay it all some time. Please don't tell Baton where I've gone and look after Bill's suitcase. You can give the bags to Oxfam.

With the backpack and sleeping bag strapped on, I struggled downstairs with the suitcase. I left it with the flat's keys outside her front door and put the letter through the letter box. It was around 6.30am that Friday when we made our way towards the station. Only street cleaners were around.

4

THE BROKER

I was thinking about Sandy as the train entered King's Cross Station. Dreamed that I would bump into her on the street and we would hug each other. I could still taste that kiss and feel the grain of sand between our lips.

The Tourist Office gave me some maps. I bought a guidebook and worked out how to get to Hampstead. My backpack and sleeping bag were dumped at 'Left Luggage', but I kept my passport, documents and cash. I had only been to London twice with Dad. We went to tourist places like Oxford Street, the Tower of London and best of all, Chelsea football ground. The score was Newcastle United 2 Chelsea 1. We, the Newcastle supporters, went wild.

Jazz edged close to me on the escalator on the way to the underground. The air was stale and hot. Down below the place was grim. All those people crowded on a narrow platform, fighting for space, pushing us towards the edge. We waited and waited. The crackling sound system blared out something. No one could make out what the announcer was saying. Probably explaining why the trains were late. About half an hour later, we heard what had happened. A woman had fallen on the line and a train had hit her.

'Another suicide!' complained a commuter. 'Why here? Why don't they just take an overdose?'

Men, women, children and a dog stepped back, cramming each other towards the back wall. Better to be squashed and safe.

A train arrived at last. We shoved our way into the packed carriage. Passengers, like cattle, crowded into the narrow space between the doors. It was remarkable how the long aisle between the seats was virtually empty. The crowd had no common sense. I headed for the aisle, keeping the dog between my legs. Relief. After a few stops a seat was vacant. Just after Camden Town, midway to Hampstead, the train coughed and spluttered and came to a halt. The coach was boiling hot. An old guy opposite me looked as if he was about to faint. I offered him my bottle of water. He shook his head.

A man next to me was reading a newspaper and I glanced at the story. Moscow Narodsky, a Russian bank, had crashed because of fraud. British banks that had loaned money to the Russians could lose money. I leaned over, trying to read the sports pages. The Ashes Test was starting. England against Australia. Cricket at Lord's. Mike Swann, Sandy's cousin was playing.

We sat in the train without air conditioning. Waiting and boiling. Nothing happened. Twenty minutes passed by, but it seemed much longer. At last the train began to move. First a jolt, then slowly forward. The doors opened at Chalk Farm, the next station. Relieved passengers escaped. Then on again until we arrived at Hampstead. The guidebook said it was the deepest station in London, but only one lift was working. The queue was long and the lift slow. Fed up, I decided to walk and Jazz and I panted our way up the narrow winding stairs in semi-darkness. They went on forever.

*　　*　　*

We were outside at last. It was a beautiful day and Hampstead looked great. According to the guidebook it was one of London's 'villages', but was only about four to five miles from the West End and the City. McDonalds was near the station and I bought two hamburgers for Jazz and myself. I wondered where Sandy was staying as we slipped into Flask Walk, a quiet street with quaint little shops. I sat down on a bench outside a pub and shared the hamburgers with Jazz. The dog was so thirsty that he lapped up all the water in the pub's bowl.

Afterwards we went back to the high street, down the hill past some banks and restaurants and shops. I couldn't believe how much everything cost. Ties for forty pounds and Polo shirts for a hundred. Cars including a Porche and Ferrari were trapped in a traffic jam on the narrow street.

A community centre, near a post office and next to a flower shop, was across the road. I saw a notice board and went over to see whether I could find work and somewhere to stay. There was nothing for me, just cleaners, nannies and typists looking for jobs and leaflets about meditation, fitness and art classes.

Stalls selling second-hand clothes, jewellery and bookstalls were inside the community centre. A dark blue tracksuit cost seven pounds, with a T-shirt thrown in.

At a second-hand bookstall, I paged through a National Geographic magazine. 'Russia's Icy Wealth' was the cover story. Inside there were pictures of oil fields and gold, diamond, platinum, palladium, nickel and aluminium mines in icy Siberia.

'This isn't a library,' snapped the bookstall owner who had stubble on his chin and a black ponytail. I put back the National Geographic and was about to leave when I noticed a tattered paperback: 'How I made $5 million in the stock market.'

The book's pages had turned light yellow. It was published more than forty years ago. On the back cover was a faded picture of the author, James Manson. He was an actor. Bill and I used to watch a lot of old movies. I remembered James Mason, but had never seen or heard of James Manson. If some unknown actor called James Manson could make money from stocks, then anyone could. The book cost 50 pence and I put it in my jacket pocket.

A flower shop was next to the community centre and I thought of Sandy again, but was in and out quickly. No way was I going to buy roses at those prices!

I decided to take Jazz for a walk on Hampstead Heath and examined a map on the notice board. Further down the High Street, we turned into a road that led to the Heath. A few yards down the road, next to some posh restaurants, was a shop with a sign 'Wardle & Co – Private Client Stockbrokers'.

A stockbroker in Hampstead? Thought that they were in the City. It was a good opportunity to sell my shares. I tied up the dog and walked inside.

Five desks had computers on them, but only two men were working. Both were wearing blue shirts with white stripes and their ties were similar. They looked as if they were in some sort of brokers' uniform. The one sitting close to the window was on the phone talking in a heavy Scottish accent: 'Bank shares are down . . . Market's bad . . . Not a good time. OK we'll sell . . .'

I stood there behind the chair opposite him, waiting for him to invite me to sit down. He ignored me and picked up another phone: 'Sell 500 Barclays and 1,000 Lloyds at best.

Book them to Mrs Thistle.'

He turned to me: 'If you're looking for a job, there's a community centre up the Hill.'

'I don't want a job. I want to sell some shares.'

'What shares?' he asked looking me up and down. 'Shouldn't we be speaking to your father?'

'He died last week. See . . . I own 600 OilFinder and 500 MineDeep shares,' I said, passing him the share registration document and my passport.

The guy at the other desk had stopped working and was listening. That wasn't really surprising. A large mirror was on the back wall. I looked a mess. My light blue shirt was creased and my trainers were dirty. I looked like someone who was living on the streets.

'What's a stockbroker doing in Hampstead? Aren't you guys supposed to be in the City?' I asked, seating myself in the chair at last.

'We serve HNWs,' grinned the young man sitting nearby. He was an Asian guy, well built, with silver rimmed glasses.

'HNWs?'

'High Net Worth individuals.'

He pointed to a woman parking a convertible Merc outside the shop: 'Designer car, dress, watch and pram. Matching baby. Maybe VHNW.'

'VHNW?'

'Very High Net Worth. Seriously rich!' he said, smiling.

'Wait here,' said the guy opposite me. He took my documents and went into an enclosed office at the back of the room. An older man, in his late fifties with short grey hair came out. He didn't have his jacket on and was more casually dressed than the younger guys. I stood up.

'Mr Miner, we don't normally deal with minors,' he said with a deadpan face. The other brokers grinned.

'Name's Jim Wardle. Haven't run away from home have you?'

'I come from Yorkshire. My father left me the shares before he died,' I said, showing him Dad and Mum's death certificates and my birth certificate.

He glanced at them. 'Both dead! Where in Yorkshire?'

'Bridlington.'

'Bridlington? I'm from Filey . . . My Dad and Mum are still there.'

That cheered me up. Wardle chatted a bit about Filey, the town near Bridlington and then introduced his staff. The guy who had asked all the questions was David Drummond. He was from Glasgow. The other was Shri Khosler, a Londoner. David was really well groomed with a silk paisley tie and matching handkerchief. His hands were manicured and he wore a gold signet ring. He fixed his gaze on me and I turned away. Jim let me sit in front of a terminal. The screen kept changing, showing hundreds of shares and prices, mostly in red. Only a few were blue.

'Red means losses,' explained Drummond. 'Bad market. Bearish.'

'I've worked that out,' I said. I had read Bill's stock exchange book on the train. I knew that the bears were the sellers and the bulls, buyers.

Jim looked at Drummond and Khosler and began: 'All potential clients should be taken seriously. Let me tell you a story. A long time ago, when I started in this business, a man walked into our office.

'He was Asian with a long white beard, tattered kaftan and stained white skullcap. Our secretary tried to turn him out, but before she could do so, he slammed a bag on to her desk. He tipped the bag and dumped bundles of dirty notes and coins. There was such a large heap that some of the cash fell on the floor.

'When we'd finished counting the cash our hands were black. The pile came to more than a hundred thousand. We chose a selection of shares. My boss came back from a long lunch. That's how it was in those days. He told us that Mr Sutie was one of his richest clients. The shares eventually made Sutie another million.'

'Can't do that now. Guys like that could be terrorists laundering money,' said Drummond. 'We must contact the companies. Make sure this young man is a bona fide registered shareholder.'

'Come on David, give us a break,' said Shri.

'Who are your guardians? Is there a trust? Any brothers or sisters?' insisted Drummond.

'No guardian. No brothers and sisters.'

Shri picked up a remote control and switched on a TV behind us. He groaned when he saw the cricket score.

'Oh no! England a hundred and thirty for six!'

'Who's taken the wickets?' I asked.

'That West Australian fast bowler, Mike Swann.'

I moved closer to the TV. Swann was bowling. He was big, about six foot four, tanned and lean with broad shoulders. Close up, he looked a bit like Sandy. The same brown hair. He was very fast, sometimes pitching the ball right up, others bumpers. England's batsmen were ducking and weaving, but some of the balls reared up and hit them.

'Swann is a cousin of my friend. She's also from Perth,' I said.

'That's it! Proof! He's no terrorist, David,' laughed Wardle. 'Come with me Jack.'

We went into his small office where I showed him Dad's letter. I decided that I had better be straight and told him about the bankruptcy and Baton.

'Liquidators! Know all about them. If you're on the company register, don't worry. We'll check with Bank Goede that you're the shareholder,' said Wardle.

'How long will it take.'

'Since the bank is in Amsterdam, it could take a few days. Maybe by Tuesday or Wednesday. But that should be a formality. If you wish, we'll be your brokers.'

I looked at his terminal screen: 'What's the price of OilFinder and MineDeep?'

'OilFinder is Britain's biggest oil company, a wonderful company. Don't sell it at 600 pence. It's cheap.'

'And MineDeep?'

'It's dropped 50 pence to £1300 in the past few days. It's one of the biggest mining business in the world, produces copper, aluminium, gold even diamonds. Don't sell!'

I calculated that at those prices the shares were worth £10,100.

'Can I sell now, they're going down?'

'Think about it. It's only two years since 9/11 and now this Russian bank failure. The market downturn has nothing to do with OilFinder and MineDeep . . . They're blue chips . . . Top companies,' said Wardle. 'See you on Tuesday. Enjoy your weekend'.

I watched the cricket for a bit. Swann had taken five wickets. England were almost out. Made only 160 runs and were bound to lose. I was just going through the door, when I had a strange feeling; a sort of premonition and turned around. Wardle was talking to his secretary.

'If it's OK Mr Wardle, can I sell them today?'

'They're your shares, Jack, you can do what you want.'

'Great. Please sell all the shares now.'

'We should first check with the companies that he's the shareholder,' said Drummond.

'I'm sure he is,' said Wardle. 'If he wants to sell now, let him sell. Where can we reach you, Jack?'

'I'll come in on Tuesday or Wednesday,' I said and walked out feeling important.

It was Friday and with £165 in my pocket, I could buy a ticket for the cricket test and try to meet Mike Swann. Maybe he could tell me where I could find Sandy. Jazz and I continued walking down the hill until we reached the

Heath. We then broke out into a run past some ponds and up a steep hill. It was a clear day and at the top, there was an amazing view of the centre of London several miles away.

A map on a copper plate showed me what I was seeing. My marker in the far distance was the round dome of St Paul's Cathedral. Further south was Canary Wharf, the highest building. In front of Canary Wharf to the east, were the buildings of the City, the financial centre. The tallest were Natwest Tower and a building that looked like a gherkin. Further to the right towards the west, I could make out the Houses of Parliament and the Post Office Tower. London, my future, was in front of me.

5

DOWN AND OUT

Back in central London, I found the YMCA. It was in Tottenham Court Road and was full. I had to find somewhere else to sleep. The road had loads of mobile phone and computer shops. I walked into one, bought some credit for my mobile, surfed some sites and played a few games until they kicked me out. Jazz who had waited outside patiently with his tail down, was happy again when we walked towards Oxford Street. A Burger King was on the other side of the road. Jazz, tugging at his lead, pulled me down some stairs into a smelly dark subway. Some guys were huddled up against a wall filled with graffiti. They were under dirty blankets and cardboard boxes.

'Pound for a cup of tea,' one of them pleaded. I put 50 pence in his cap.

A mongrel snarled at Jazz and went for him. The owner, pale, eyes dull from drugs and with bandages on his arms, didn't take any notice. I pulled back Jazz to avoid a fight.

We hurried upstairs to Burger King. I managed to push Jazz under the table before anyone saw him, tied him up and went to the loo. It was fairly clean, given the amount of

people who used it each day. After washing my hands and
face, I bought two burgers, chips and a coke and got some
water for Jazz. We were eating our food when I noticed two
girls, a couple of tables away. They were drinking water. The
younger one was skinny with dark circles under her eyes.
She had greasy brown hair tied back in a scrunchie. She
looked as if she hadn't eaten for days. She came up and
patted Jazz. He wagged his tail.

'He look like my dog,' she said in a heavy accent.

'Is your dog outside?'

'No, at home. Moscow.'

The older girl, also looking weak and tired, joined her,
stroked Jazz and helped him drink his water from the paper
cup. She was more curvy with bigger breasts and short black
spikey hair. Both wore dirty T-shirts and stained tracksuit
bottoms. Jazz was enjoying the attention, but I had to push
him back under the table. Luckily a guy cleaning the tables,
didn't notice the dog or chose to ignore him.

'Where you from?' asked the older girl, also in a Russian
accent. She looked about nineteen and her friend a couple
of years younger.

'North England. Are you also from Moscow?'

'Yes.'

'Why don't you sit down?' I suggested, putting the Burger
King boxes in the bin. 'I'm Jack.'

'Me Sasha. She Natasha,' said the older girl. 'We cousins.'

They sat down, their eyes on a couple enjoying their
hamburgers.

'Hungry?'

They nodded their heads.

'Hamburger? Milkshake?'

'Thank you. You good to us,' said Natasha, her stained top covering small breasts with no bra.

Leaving Jazz with them, I stood in the queue, bought hamburgers, chips, a strawberry and chocolate milkshake and a coke. It was getting crowded around the till. Two guys and a girl kept pushing and shuffling against me.

Back at the table, Sasha and Natasha gulped down their food and milkshakes. The chocolate milkshake looked good, so I thought I would get one. I went back to the counter and felt my pockets for money. Couldn't feel any notes. I stepped back from the queue. The money was gone. I had forgotten to put the notes in my inside jacket pocket. Must have been the people who had shoved and pushed me. They stole the money from my back pocket. My mobile was gone too.

Panicking, I rushed to the table, grabbed Jazz's lead and sprinted into the street. Didn't recognise anyone from the queue. We ran down into the subway. Not there! By now the girls were also helping me search for the thieves. Waste of time. I frantically searched through my jacket, shirt and pants, shaking the James Manson and London guide-books again and again. The notes were gone, £150, gone! Just a few coins. I counted them. £9.83. I still had to pick up my backpack and sleeping bag at King's Cross station. That would cost me five pounds. I had almost nothing for the weekend and I couldn't collect from the brokers until Tuesday or Wednesday. I didn't know what to do.

'We know place to sleep. You want come?' asked Natasha.

'I have no money. Just this,' I said, showing her the coins.

'No problem,' said Sasha. 'You good to us. We help you.'

'Strong man and dog protect us,' laughed Natasha.

'You must be joking,' I said, as they stroked Jazz. 'What you doing in London?'

'We finish school in Moscow. We must learn good English. Helps get good job,' said Sasha. 'Me want to join police. They looking for people who speak Russian and East European languages.'

'Policewoman? Interpreter? But . . . but, how?' I asked, observing her dirty top and hair. 'You can't apply looking like . . . What happened to your money?'

'We come visit friend. Stay with friend. But friend gone.'

'When did you come?'

'Tuesday. We meet man. He says he has room for us. We go into house. Room empty. We like it. Give him money for rent. He gives us key. We go get our things and come back, but key doesn't fit,' said Sasha shaking her head.

'We can't get into house. We wait for man. He doesn't come. Other people arrive and open door. Don't know man. Never seen him. We go up to room. Key doesn't fit. Can't get in. We wait and wait but man doesn't return,' said Natasha.

Bigger idiots than me, I thought. Now they were homeless, sleeping on the streets. I would have to do the same.

'I'm going to King's Cross to pick up my baggage,' I said.

'King's Cross bad place. Bad girls,' said Sasha.

'We meet you here,' she said, showing me a piece of paper with Lincoln's Inn Fields written on it. 'Van comes. Gives us soup, bread.'

I looked up Lincoln's Inn Fields on the map. It didn't seem that far away from King's Cross. They picked up their bags and walked with me past the bookshops in Charing Cross Road and into Covent Garden. Then we split up.

*   *   *

King's Cross to Lincoln's Inn was much further than I had thought. It was a long hard walk. Luckily the map I had was OK and it was still light when Jazz and I arrived there. Eighteenth century houses surrounded a large square with a garden and tennis courts. I searched for Sasha and Natasha and saw them waving to me from a queue near the iron gratings of a large grey building at the end of the square. A van arrived and a man and a woman in white coats handed out soup in paper cups and some bread, butter and jam.

Just before the gates were locked, we sneaked into the park, went to the toilet and hid in some bushes. When it was dark, we laid out our bags between the bushes. Jazz slept between us. Luckily it didn't rain that night and we were soon asleep.

I was dreaming when I suddenly felt someone prodding me. Two cops were shining their torches in our faces. They told us to move on.

We quickly packed up our stuff and left the park.

'I know place,' said Sasha.

It was around midnight and bleary-eyed we trudged across Waterloo Bridge, the Thames below us. St Paul's Cathedral and City buildings were on our left, Houses of Parliament and the Big Wheel, on our right. We were so tired that London's tourist sites didn't impress us. All we wanted to do was put down our bags and sleep. We walked in silence towards the south bank of the river. It began to drizzle so we raced to some stairs, down to the river. A man was huddled under a blanket, his open cap next to him. If I didn't get a job this weekend, I would have to do the same. Sasha led the way along a wide pedestrian pathway. Then into the sheltered open space under Queen Elizabeth Hall.

*   *   *

That's how I came to be there and saw the poor guy hanging from the bridge. How I escaped the murderers.

I avoided the police and didn't know whether they had my things. No way was I going to let them talk to me. My DNA was on that rope. They might think that I did it. Fortunately my passport and other documents were at Wardle & Co. It was time to move on. I had to get a job and get out of London. Go to the seaside. Brighton, perhaps.

*   *   *

It was Saturday morning and I wandered over to Oxford Street and walked into a shop that sold cameras and TV's. The cricket was on. Australia were one hundred and thirty for one; their batsmen hammering our bowlers. I watched for a while, hoping that I would spot Sandy in the crowd.

The shop had no vacancies and others didn't want me either. Jazz pulled at the lead as we turned into Regent Street on the way to Regent's Park. It was sunny and hot. In the park we came across a duck pond next to a rose garden in full bloom; a fusion of dark and bright red, yellow, pink and white colours. I sniffed their scent and remembered the funeral. It was only a few days before, but it seemed much longer. I lay on my back under a tree and fell asleep, Jazz beside me.

The dream was bad. I woke up with a jolt, feeling my neck and remembered them. Would they recognise me, the only witness? It was 6pm in the evening. We had been there for hours. I had to get away, far away, but there wasn't enough money.

I walked further north through the fields and playing grounds of Regent's Park, the dog running and sniffing ahead of me. There was a drought and the grass was brown. At a café, not far from London Zoo, I went into the toilets, washed myself and looked at myself in the mirror. I badly needed a bath and my clothes were dirty. Hungry, so hungry, but didn't even have enough money to buy a sandwich. A biscuit would have to do. Lucky! An unopened ham sandwich pack in the bin. One sandwich for me, the other for my tired dog.

In the distance I could hear a crowd cheering. We walked towards the noise. By the time we arrived at Lord's Cricket Ground, the crowd was coming through the gates. I still had this crazy idea. Would meet Mike Swann and find out where Sandy was staying.

There was a long queue at one of the gates. Play was finished for the day and it was puzzling why people were queuing.

'What's the score,' I asked a guy at the end of the queue. He looked about forty. He was unshaven and his black denim jacket was faded and torn.

'Don't understand,' he said in a thick foreign accent. 'We come clean ground.'

I went up to an official who was wearing a fluorescent yellow jacket.

'Can I have a job?'

'Stand in the queue, it's five pounds an hour.'

Most of the cleaners seemed to be from Africa and Eastern Europe. Few were speaking English. There were about eighty of us, waiting. Spectators were still coming out of the ground. They hardly gave us a glance. When they did, they quickly turned their eyes away. I was one of the invisible people, the people who clean the streets and public toilets. The people who aren't people.

I was near the back of the queue and was glad that they chose me. Others who came later were rejected. Eventually the line began moving. Security officials searched our bags and bodies. They then passed us black bags, divided us into groups and sent us to different stands. I asked an official if I could tie up Jazz inside the ground. Luckily he agreed.

Dad was keen on cricket and we often watched games together on TV. Football was my favourite sport, but in the summer I played and watched cricket. It was strange being at Lord's for the first time alongside immigrants and asylum seekers who didn't have a clue about the game. Lord's is the Mecca of cricket. The ground is more than a hundred years old. When England plays Australia, Lord's is bursting with almost 30,000 spectators. Cricketers in England, Australia, India, Pakistan, South Africa, West Indies, Sri Lanka and New Zealand dream of playing at Lord's. Dad once tried to explain cricket to an American. He couldn't work out why a Test Match went on for five days and that sometimes it ended in a draw. Recently they introduced Twenty/20 cricket, a fast, compressed version of the game that finishes in three hours with a result. They are going to stage games in the US hoping that cricket will catch on there, but it can't compete with baseball.

For us cleaners it was just work. Picking up rubbish and empty bottles on a stand named after Dennis Compton, a famous cricketer. Directly above the stand was a white building that looked like a rectangular space ship. This was the centre for TV, radio commentators and the press. Through the darkish windows, a few reporters were typing their stories on laptops.

Across the green field, directly opposite my stand, I spotted the famous Lord's Pavilion, a Victorian building more than a hundred years old. Above the Pavilion in the players' dressing rooms and balconies were the English and Australian teams. I attempted to climb over the fence and run across the field to the dressing rooms to find Mike Swann, but a security guard stopped me. That stymied my chances of making contact with Sandy's cousin; made me feel gloomy. No chance of seeing her again.

The scoreboard in the corner of the ground showed that Australia was almost two hundred runs ahead of England. Our side was likely to lose. It was a hot day and the crowd had drunk a lot. We worked silently along the rows of seats throwing empty bottles and cans into recycling bags and rubbish into others. I found some wrapped sandwiches that hadn't been touched and put them in a supermarket bag. That would be supper.

We finished just after 8.30pm, but since it was only weeks after midsummer, the light was only then beginning to fade. They paid me ten pounds. That would keep me going for a while.

* * *

After resting in a small park near Lord's, we walked down St John's Wood High Street, where there were fancy shops and restaurants. Further on, the streets were wide and the houses large.

It was then that I saw her. She was sitting in the garden of a pub on the corner of the road. Sandy, my Sandy. She wore a silky blue top and her brown shiny hair was in a high ponytail. She was sitting alone at a table drinking a beer. Jazz pulled the lead and rushed towards her. Before we could get near, a guy came out of the pub with a packet of peanuts. He was much bigger than me and at least two years older. Seriously good looking. I watched them as he put his hand on her shoulder. She looked up and kissed him. It wasn't just the kiss that got to me. It was the length of time. The way she held his hand.

I was at the entrance of the garden and was about to walk away, when she noticed me. I felt myself blushing.

'Jack . . . Jack Miner. What are you doing here?'

I noticed her puzzled expression as she looked at me. Unshaven, sweaty, dirty.

'I had to do some bu . . . business here,' I stuttered.

I could see that they didn't believe me.

'Are you OK?' she asked. 'Why don't you sit down?'

She stroked Jazz who was panting and wagging his tail madly.

'I think he's thirsty.'

There was a bowl of water nearby. I picked it up and put it in front of the dog. He gulped it down.

'Sit down,' Sandy's friend said. 'Want a beer?'

'Half a pint of lager,' I mumbled, thinking that I might as well have a drink. I was trapped.

'Jack Miner . . . Friend from Yorkshire,' said Sandy introducing us. 'Peter Taylor.'

Taylor shook my sweaty hand firmly and went inside to get the drink. Through the open door, I saw him take some ice, rub his hands and wipe them with a paper napkin.

'Are you sure that you're OK, Jack?' asked Sandy. 'You don't look it.'

'I'm fine. Lots of things have happened. I'll sort it out,' I said.

She told me that she was staying with her uncle in Hampstead. That Taylor had taken her to Lord's. They were going to a party. Before I could ask her for her address, he was back with the beer.

Taylor touched her hand. I was pleased when she withdrew it. He glared at me.

'How long are you staying in London?' he asked.

'Not sure, I'll know next week.'

'When do you go back to school?' he asked, patronisingly.

'Not sure I'm going back. Thinking of starting a business,' I countered. 'My Dad left me some shares. I'm selling them.'

'Maybe I can help. My father works for an investment bank,' said Taylor with a disbelieving sneer.

'No thanks, I've got a broker.'

He didn't bother asking any more questions. We finished our drinks and walked into the street.

Sandy touched my elbow: 'Need a lift anywhere, Jack?'

'I'm going to Hampstead,' I said hoping they were on their way to the West End. I felt so small and upset that I wanted to get away from them.

'Off to the concert at Kenwood?'

'Yes,' I lied, not knowing what she was talking about.

'Our party's in Highgate. We can drop him there, can't we Peter?' she said.

'You can walk from there to Kenwood,' said Taylor unenthusiastically. 'What about your dog?'

'He'll be OK. I'll put him on my lap.'

Taylor's open Golf convertible was parked near the pub. I climbed into the back, with Jazz next to me. He drove through side streets to avoid the traffic and eventually reached Highgate Village. At the top of the hill, the car was caught in a traffic jam and became almost stationary.

'Kenwood's down there,' said Taylor, pointing towards the bottom of the hill. 'On the way to Hampstead. About half a mile.'

'Thanks. It would be good to see you, Sandy? Where did you say you were staying?'

'I told you. With my Uncle. I'm going back in a few days,' she replied impatiently.

She scribbled down an address on a piece of paper, allowing Taylor to glance at it. It was Perth, Australia. Obviously she didn't want to see me again.

Jazz jumped out of the car and we started walking

towards Kenwood. I was feeling low. By some miracle I had found Sandy, but had cocked up. I kicked a stone in front of me. Had felt like an idiot in front of her boyfriend. Despite what happened in Bridlington, she wasn't interested. I was a loser. Worse still, she was probably sorry for me.

Jazz became excited when he spotted woodland on the left. The evening was beginning to close in. We turned into a narrow gate and heard music. It was Dixieland Jazz and had to be the Kenwood concert. A narrow path through a small wood ended up in a field. In the distance there were lots of parked cars. It was now quite dark, but the moon had risen, helping me to stumble along a pathway towards the music.

A crowd of people were in front of Kenwood, a huge stately home. In the distance, down a hill, was a white stage. I tried to get closer to the performers, but there was a fence surrounding the concert area and plenty of guards. Friends and families were sitting on the grass, eating and listening to the music, within and outside the enclosure. The band was playing furiously and some people were dancing. We sat down next to a family who were sitting on blankets and watching from outside the fenced concert area. The kids were keen on Jazz, my Jazz. They gave him some scraps, pulled him up by his paws and danced with him. The family gave me some chocolate cake and I felt much better. We stayed there for a while and I began thinking of Dad. He would have loved the concert. I began to feel depressed again as I watched people enjoying themselves. All I had was Jazz, an old watch, a book and a few pounds. I didn't think about any of the positives. The money I would get from selling the shares. What I could do with it. That money was abstract. Not the here and now.

The concert ended with an amazing firework display. Rockets soared into the sky and burst into multicoloured patterns. When it was all over, the audience rolled up their blankets and ground sheets and packed up their rubbish. Shadowy figures wound their way home in the moonlight. Jazz and I forced our way against the tide of people coming out of the concert area. We slipped inside. The audience had cleared most of the rubbish and the cleaners were placing the remainder into large black bags and huge bins. I asked for a job, but the cleaner who was in charge, just patted Jazz and shook his head. The leftovers from the food and drink stalls went to the staff or were sold at very cheap prices.

I managed to get a large bottle of coke, a packet of crisps and some chicken and bacon sandwiches for a pound. Jazz managed to find some cold meat, some bread and other scraps of food. Luckily someone had left a blanket. Closer to the pond that overlooked the empty stage, I found a ground sheet. We left the concert area and joined some people who were walking in the darkness up an avenue lined with trees. A road to the right led to a clearing. Helped by moonlight I walked to some thick trees, laid down the groundsheet, covered Jazz and myself with the blanket and fell asleep.

*   *   *

I woke up suddenly. Jazz was snarling. A black retriever was sniffing us. It was a bright summer morning. The place was full of dog walkers and joggers. I was starving and gobbled up the crisps and shared the sandwiches with Jazz. Afterwards, I covered the blanket in the groundsheet and hid them in the bushes. Then we wandered down a winding hill until we came to some ponds. We walked past the first pond with swans and ducks. Fishermen were trying their luck, but it didn't seem as if they had caught anything. We ambled on until we came across a second pond, fairly close to the first. Men were diving off the steps of a wooden platform into the brown water and several were sunbathing on a large raft in the middle of the water.

I tied Jazz to the fence and tread the narrow path that led to a changing room without a roof. A few men were sunbathing naked and some were changing for their morning swim or having a shower. At last I could have my first proper wash in two days. The water was ice cold, but it felt good.

Breakfast, a walk and shower had stopped me thinking about myself. But as we continued our walk, I thought of Sandy and the gloom came back. I was a complete and utter failure. People walked past us, but I didn't even notice them. I was clean, but still felt uncomfortable in my smelly clothes.

A cafeteria, near some tennis courts and a children's playground with large carved wooden animals, wasn't open. So we kept on going, southwards, out of the Heath, towards Central London. After aimlessly crossing a few streets I came across a market with lots of stalls and customers. A T-shirt and two pairs of boxers cost £4.80, leaving £4.20. Every penny had to be counted. That's how tight it was. I bought a couple of dog biscuits for Jazz in a pet shop on the corner of the road.

For some reason I was mesmerised by the goldfish and the tropical fish swimming in the glass tank. Up and down, backwards and forwards in their small aquarium. I must have been there for ages until a shop assistant shouted: 'Either buy some fish or leave. You can't hang around here.'

I looked at her blankly, ran out and shuffled through the market feeling depressed and lonely. My life was awful.

Even if I was going to get £10,000 for my shares, Baton would probably find me, take the money and leave me with nothing. I was so down, that I forgot that Jazz was walking alongside me. Didn't even notice him foul the pavement. Dad had taught me to pick it up, but this time I couldn't be bothered.

It was late morning. I was getting hungry again and bought a loaf of bread and some milk at a small supermarket. There were some newspapers there. The *Sunday Telegraph's* front page headline was: 'Russian Banker found hanging from Charing Cross Bridge.' It was getting hot, but I went cold. I picked up the newspaper and quickly read the story.

The article said that in the early hours of Saturday morning, the police had found a body dangling over the Thames. He was Boris Yapolovitch, chief executive of Moscow Narodsky, a Russian bank. It had collapsed with estimated losses of at least £4 billion. I read further and shivered. The story continued that a witness had reported the hanging, but had disappeared. The police were searching for a boy who was about sixteen or seventeen. They were investigating whether Yapolovitch had committed suicide.

Moscow Narodsky was one of Russia's biggest banks, the article said. It lent money to Russian companies producing oil, gold, nickel, platinum, aluminium and other resources. Yapolovitch, a leading Russian banker, was well known in financial and business circles. He was married with three children and had houses and flats in Moscow, London, Paris and New York. He owned a football club in Moscow.

I began to panic, held Jazz's lead tightly and ran across several roads, dodging between cars. I wasn't looking properly and we were lucky that we weren't knocked over. I tried to think logically and calm down. Had to make a decision. I could go back to the police and give them more details, but they would find that my finger prints and DNA matched those on the rope. I could be a murder suspect. If they let me go, I would be in the newspapers and the killers, who were probably Russian, would try and get me. Baton, the liquidator, would find me and take the 10K from the brokers. Better to hide on Hampstead Heath for a few days, collect my money at Wardle and leave London. I felt my cap and realised that the murderers saw me wearing it, when I was running away from them. So I took it off and threw it in a dustbin.

We headed back towards the Heath and reached a station called Gospel Oak. Nearby was a large red brick wall. It surrounded a swimming pool and a long queue of mainly parents and kids were waiting to get in. There was no way I wanted to be with people in my mood. So I did my best to avoid them. We walked around the wall, following the path that led to the cafeteria that I had seen in the morning.

A little later we came across a pond where dogs were barking and swimming. Jazz ran in, chasing after another dog's stick. Both of them were swimming towards the deep water. Some swans were nearby, but I was so involved in my problems that I didn't notice what was going on.

'That swan is going for your dog,' shrieked a woman. 'It will drown him.'

I looked up and saw the large white bird swim rapidly towards Jazz. The swan was on him, pushing him down with its wing. Jazz was a strong swimmer but he couldn't escape. There was only one thing I could do. I threw off my jacket, waded in and swam towards them. The swan was on top of Jazz. If it pushed him under water, the dog would drown.

I grabbed some sticks in the water and threw them at the swan. Missed. At last I reached the bird, but by now Jazz was under. Keeping my face away from the vicious beak, I touched a wing. The bird was startled and withdrew from me. It then took off and flew across the pond to the other side. Thankfully the other swans kept their distance. Jazz was underwater. I couldn't see him because it was muddy, but I felt for his body, found his hind legs and pulled him up. Then I put my arm around his neck, lifesaver style, and swam back to shore. By then a big crowd had gathered. I shook Jazz, but he didn't stir. Then I hugged the dog, feeling helpless.

'Jazz, Jazz. Come on boy, come on!'

I shook and pumped him. Jazz my friend, my only friend. What would I do if he died?

6

FISHING FOR GOLD

I'm sitting on the sofa in a large room. A beam of sunlight filled with tiny particles, crosses the room. It comes through a dirty window and reaches a dusty bookcase. Books. Lots of books. Sigmund Freud, Carl Jung, Melanie Klein. Nearby, 'The Criminal Mind', 'Dangerous Severe Personality Disorder'.

The psychiatrist opens the door and walks in. He's about fifty with owl shaped glasses. He's short with a fat tummy. Floppy, black hair. Dandruff on navy blue jacket.

Walks over to desk. Takes out a brown file, notebook and pen. Sits down on large leather chair. Silent. Observes me. Then talks softly. Yellow teeth match nicotine-stained fingers.

'I can see that you've made yourself comfortable.'

'There wasn't much else to do.'

A hollow laugh. Must have heard that line umpteen times.

'I'm Dr Klugheim. Did Mrs Small tell you about me?'

'She told me that you're her boss. Asked me whether you could read my notebook. I said it was OK, provided no one else did.'

'Very interesting . . . Looks like the beginnings of a book. Who taught you to write?'

'*Dunno . . . Not school . . . Teachers were useless. It just comes out.*'

He waits. Says nothing. Me sullen. Staring him out.

'*You've been here three months. Mrs Small thought that it might be a good idea if we met. Talk things through.*'

No reply.

'*The wardens report that you don't mix much. Keep to yourself.*'

'*I'm OK. Just keep my head down. Count the days until I'm out of here!*'

He opens up the file and reads some pages. I notice they're typed.

'*It says here that you were feeling down. How about now?*'

'*I feel great. What do you expect? It's a holiday camp. How do you feel?*'

'*The bridge. Those nightmares. Still having them?*'

No response.

'*Are you finding that writing helps you?*'

'*I just think about the past and write stuff down.*'

'*Good!*'

Silence again. Eyes on the minute specs in the sunbeam. Away from him.

'*Your parents. It must have been hard . . .*'

Begin to lose my cool. Doesn't take a genius to understand why I'm here. The Governor, screws and doctors are panicking. Ernie Shiren managed to hang himself. Happened last week.

'*A kid of eighteen dead. Did you have little talks with him?*' *I snap.*

Klugheim winces: '*We're here to talk about you, not Ernie.*'

I'm silent again. Thinking, calculating. Better play along with him. He's the best chance I've got. Could get me out of this place. Recommend me for good behaviour.

'If you think I'm going to top myself, you're mistaken . . . I've got better things to do.'

'Good. Sometimes things can overwhelm you,' he says.

I sit there. He waits. I wait. Wonder what he's thinking.

'You were depressed. But you still jumped in and saved your dog,' he says after a couple of minutes. 'Brave, but reckless.'

'I can swim.'

'You cannot believe how many people die trying to rescue animals.'

'It's a funny thing . . . That swan attack got me going.'

'Go on. Tell me what happened.'

I don't know why, but I feel relaxed with this guy. My head slips back on to the sofa and I let go. Talk freely. Will write it down later.

* * *

An old woman held Jazz down while I pumped him. She was the owner of the dog that had been swimming with Jazz, when the Swan attacked. We thought that it was all over. He just lay there as I pumped and pumped his tummy, pushing down on the soft fur. Jazz stirred, coughed and slowly lifted his head. A mixture of water and vomit dribbled from his mouth. He rose and stood unsteadily on his feet, his tail down. Then he shook himself. The crowd clapped and cheered and began to move away. The old lady gave Jazz a treat and his tail began to wag. Then another treat.

'I think he'll be OK,' said the lady, touching my hand. 'Let's go and have some coffee.'

I picked up my jacket and we followed a path towards a gate at the corner of the Heath, near some tennis courts. The lady was seriously strange. She talked to her dog as if the animal was a person. 'He's getting better all the time, Pattie. You watch over him OK?'

My wet clothes chafed me while we walked, but the sun was hot and my shirt was drying quickly. Dogs have amazing powers of recovery and Jazz managed to keep up.

We sat outside an Italian restaurant, near the Heath gate.

'Two cappucinos. Lots of chocolate,' shouted the lady.

'Pizza. Plenty of ham,' replied the waitress, who obviously knew her.

Couples nearby, observed us without a word. Me, in wet muddy clothes, covered with weeds from the pond and the short, dumpy old lady with straggly grey hair. Her blue jumper had several holes in it and her shirt, a frayed collar. The black skirt was creased and blue and red odd socks protruded from her muddy shoes.

'You sir? Anything to eat?'

'No thanks.'

'Two pizzas. You're not Jewish are you?' asked the lady.

'No, I'm not Jewish.'

'Lots of ham.'

As we waited the lady introduced herself as Martha. She asked me about my parents and where I came from. Where I was staying in London. I told her how I had lost my money and that the Heath was my temporary home. The large and flat pizzas, covered with ham, arrived. Martha picked off her ham and held up some pieces. The dogs, in sitting position, waited obediently and caught the meat when she threw it.

'Pattie! Stop! Give Jazz a chance. Be good now!'

I piled into my delicious pizza, while she snatched some ham from it and gave it to the dogs.

Martha was strange. She spoke loudly, maybe because she was a bit deaf. The waitresses and owner of the café seemed to like her and didn't mind the dogs. She joked and patted the dogs and I began to feel a lot better. The bill arrived and I searched my pockets for money.

Martha pulled out some coins and put them on the table: 'I'll pay. They give me a discount. Now you and Jazz come home with me to have a nice bath.'

'Are you quite sure? I can go to the men's pond and have a shower there.'

'No! I can tell that you're a respectable lad. You saved your dog. That's good enough for me.'

We walked up the road past some restaurants until we came to her place. It was a cottage. The white paint on the walls had turned grey and was peeling. Inside, the room was cluttered with dusty furniture. The curtains hadn't been cleaned for years. Books were piled on shelves around the room.

She took me to the bathroom, which was decorated with faded floral wallpaper.

'Just relax and have a bath,' she said, as she passed me a towel, a shirt and trousers.

'You're about the same size as Tony,' she said.

'Who's Tony?'

'My husband. He died twelve years ago.'

I looked out the bathroom window. Pattie and Jazz were in the small back garden, overrun by weeds. He was following Pattie happily, making his mark on bushes. I scrubbed the bath before I got in, reckoning that Pattie must have been in it, many times. The water was hot and I lay there. It felt good.

I had almost fallen asleep when Martha called: 'You ready? I've got some tea for you.'

I came out wearing her husband's suit trousers and blue striped shirt.

'How long have you lived here?' I asked.

'About forty years . . . Estate agents pester me . . . Offered me nearly a million. But I don't want their money.'

'Million for this place? Wow! Live here alone?'

'No, with Pattie. We meet friends in the park. We're never lonely. What about you?'

I don't know why, but I started telling her things about myself. How I came to London, looking for Sandy. How I had lost my money and my things.

'What's this?' she asked as she went to the table and brought me my coins and the battered James Manson book, "How I made $5 million on The Stock Market".

'Dad left me some shares. I want to find out what to do,' I said.

'Have you read it?'

'Not yet . . . Bought it at the Hampstead Community Centre. Just saw it there.'

She opened it and looked at the inside page. 'Published in 1960! Don't you think things have changed since then?'

'Maybe. Maybe not.'

'Maybe that book was there for a reason,' she said. 'Just lying there waiting for you. Why don't you finish your tea and read it.'

* * *

The first part of Manson's book was about his life story. His father was English and his mother, Russian. She was an actress and she taught him 'method acting'. Becoming the character he was going to play. Thinking and feeling like the character. It was something like a personality change for the part. Manson was short, stocky with average looks. He didn't become a star, but managed to get good character parts.

One day some guy offered him a job in a small theatre. It was a strange deal. Instead of cash, the theatre owner paid Manson shares in oil companies. The oil shares soared and from that time onwards, Manson was hooked on the stock market. Manson acted in all sorts of places. He travelled from London to Paris, Frankfurt, Vienna, New York, San Francisco, Hong Kong, Tokyo, Johannesburg and other cities. He never got the big roles. He remained a character actor, managing to earn enough to enjoy travelling and experiencing different countries. Even when he was thousands of miles away from the New York and London stock markets, he continued to buy and sell shares. Communications were bad in those days. Since there were neither mobiles nor the Internet, he had to go to the post office to telex orders. Long distance phone calls were very expensive. Sometimes he did well and other times badly.

Brokers and friends gave him tips on what stocks to buy. He made money on some, but he mostly lost.

To try to stop losing money, Manson decided to find out everything about shares. He gave some examples. An oil company like OilFinder has its shares quoted on the stock market. Manson would read the news reports about OilFinder and ask his stockbroker to send him all the information about the company. Whether it was doing well or badly. Then he would study the oil industry to see whether the oil price was going up or down. If the oil price rose, OilFinder's profits would increase and vice versa. But despite all this research, Manson still found that he rarely made money. Even if a company's profits soared, its shares could go down.

It was all about fashion. If the big pension funds and other investors liked the shares they would buy them. On the other hand, a share could go unnoticed for a year or more because it was unfashionable. There were other complications. Regardless whether an individual company's profits rose or fell, a change in economic, business, geopolitical and other events, would influence its share price. Shares were small boats in the market sea, sailing happily in good weather and struggling or capsizing in a storm.

Manson concluded that it was all about the market mood. Whether investors were confident or worried. Bullish or bearish in market speak. Share prices would either lurch upwards or slide, if participants in the market became optimistic or pessimistic. It didn't matter if the reasons were logical or illogical.

In the end Manson decided that shares behaved like live

beings. They did their own thing. If they wanted to rise they would rise. If they wished to fall they would fall. There had to be an easier and more profitable way to play the stock market than studying company and brokers' reports. That was the start of Manson's first million.

*   *   *

After studying Manson's book for more than two hours, I felt like a break.

'Want some scrambled eggs, Jack?' asked Martha, who sounded like my Mum.

I stretched and smiled: 'Later, thanks. OK if Pattie joins us for a run?'

Martha went to her bedroom and came back with some running shorts and a white T-shirt that had belonged to Tony.

It was just after six and we ran up the hill towards the west into the evening sun. It was tiring up and down the heath hills, but I felt great. Jazz led the way with Pattie behind him and raced towards some trees near the centre of a hill. They sniffed a couple who were snogging under a blanket, then scampered further up the hill. I followed puffing and panting, onwards and upwards, hamstring and calf muscles straining. The soles of my trainers were digging into the uneven sandy path when I finally reached the top. The dogs were waiting for me and led me towards a clump of trees. From then onwards we followed a much easier downhill route and the path wound towards a pond where people were swimming.

Both dogs were panting and needed a swim badly, but they were barred from entry. I wanted to cool down. So I put on their leads, tied them to the fence, threw off my shirt and sprinted for the water in my shorts.

The pond, with dark brown water, looked dirty.

'Is the water OK?' I shouted.

'Quite safe,' replied a lady who was swimming near me. 'It's running water. Feel the current?'

We chatted as we swam and she told me that the pond was near the source of the River Fleet. From there it flowed underground to the City of London.

'Hundreds of years ago, the Fleet flowed through the City into the Thames,' she said. 'The City grew and roads and buildings were built above the river. It is now below a road known as Fleet Street. London's newspaper offices and printing plants used to be on that street, but they moved to other parts of London. The Corporation of London is in charge of the City and looks after Hampstead Heath. It's because the source of the River Fleet is here.'

I wasn't really superstitious. But wasn't this another sign that I should play the stock market? First Manson's book, second my Hampstead brokers and third the City controlled the Heath.

I couldn't wait to finish Manson's book. I put on my trainers, picked up my shirt, untied the dogs and still dripping ran towards the eastern part of the Heath and Martha's house.

* * *

Martha gave me a lovely surprise. She had tidied up the house and made up a bed in the spare room.

'I don't want any rent. Just make yourself at home,' she insisted. 'Pattie enjoyed the run. We want you to stay with us.'

'Wow, thanks Martha. As soon as I get some cash, I'll pay my way.'

'Shut up and finish reading your book,' Martha said. 'I'm not sure that money will make you happy. But if that's what you want . . .'

I ate some bread and cheese while Martha fed the dogs. Afterwards, I sat down on a rickety chair alongside a round antique rosewood table. It had two books on it. The first was by Manson and the second, *The Crowd* by Gustave Le Bon, belonged to Martha's husband.

'Tony was a psychoanalyst,' she said. 'Markets are all about people. Clever individuals invariably become fools in a crowd.'

Martha was a bit strange, but certainly not stupid. She gave me some paper and a pen and I made notes and drawings to adapt Manson's methods so that I could understand how they worked and to picture them in my mind.

Manson believed that investors should ignore brokers' tips, news, profits, interest rates and all that stuff. They should just concentrate on the share prices. Watch and see if the shares keep rising or fall back again. The shares themselves would signal when you should buy or sell them.

It was as if the shares were alive. I remembered the fish in the pet shop earlier in the day. How the fish swam up and down in their tanks, just like shares. I imagined a large aquarium. My aquarium was divided into several compartments. Thin membranes separated the divisions in the tank. Fish swam happily up and down and sideways in their own space. Small blue fish swam at the bottom. Gold fish swam in the second compartment and black fish were in the top part. I imagined that I was throwing fish food on the water. The black fish ate the food, leaving hardly anything for the gold and blue fish in the lower parts of the aquarium. So I threw more food on the water. Hungry gold fish burst through the membrane towards the top where the black fish were swimming. The blue fish followed into the second part of the aquarium swallowing the remaining morsels. After the food was eaten, some of the gold and blue fish returned to the lower parts. Others remained at the top.

Manson explained that the behaviour of shares was similar. For some time a share would fluctuate up and down at the bottom between 100 and 200 pence. All of a sudden there would be a sudden increase in trading. The share would burst into a new range of 200 to 250 pence. That's when Manson would buy. On the other hand, similarly to the fish, the share could force its way to a new 251 to 300 pence trading band and rise even further. This would be a signal that it was going to soar to even greater heights. Manson would keep holding the share for as long as it kept rising. He 'allowed his profits to run'. On the other hand if the share fell to a lower level, he would sell quickly.

I read and re-read the book that was less than 200 pages long. Went to bed at about 2am in the morning and fell into a deep sleep, dreaming about fish in a mammoth aquarium.

The dogs woke me early in the morning, but I was so

excited that I wasn't tired. Martha was still sleeping so I took them out for a short walk and then came back again and paged through *The Crowd*. I knew that dictators like Hitler could influence crowds and encourage them to do terrible things. But as Martha said, the crowd also pushed the stock market up and down. Anything could influence the broking and investor crowd. A cure for cancer, an oil discovery, bank crashes or war. If the crowd of investors noticed that certain shares were going up, they would follow and buy. During a panic the crowd would dump shares. The book helped me understand that if I played the stock market, I had to move fast. I had to buy and sell before the crowd. Manson warned that mistakes would be made, but I would be OK if I sold my shares quickly and cut losses before they became worse. The first loss was the smallest loss, he wrote.

I was ready to act, but how?

'The market opens tomorrow and I want to catch some fish,' I told Martha.

'It's a waste of time fishing in Hampstead ponds. Hardly any fish. There's a good fishmonger in Kentish Town,' she said.

'No, I mean shares . . . I want to study the stock market. See which shares to buy.'

'Try Swiss Cottage Library,' grinned Martha. 'It's about two miles from here.'

* * *

There were several computers inside Swiss Cottage library. I browsed the Internet to find out what was happening on the London Stock Exchange. Some sites displayed shares on charts. Most shares had peaked recently and were now falling.

I had a pencil and paper and drew an aquarium with units from bottom to top. I didn't bother with the numerous shares that were slipping towards the bottom of the tank. But the charts showed that gold shares were behaving differently. I followed Manson's instructions and examined the charts of gold share prices over a period of three to five years. During most of this time they had done virtually nothing. The gold fish had swum calmly up and down at the bottom of the tank. They were virtually asleep. But suddenly in the past week, gold shares had risen. This was a sign that something was happening. I found that there were lots of gold mines in the United States, Canada, South Africa and Australia. Sure enough, their shares were beginning to rise. A friendly little girl came up to me with her mother and gave me some crayons. She watched me take an orange crayon and draw a gold fish pushing though the membrane. She took the crayon and drew a few more rising from the bottom to the top of the lowest compartment. Some went halfway through the membrane. I looked at the drawing with a child's imagination. My drawing became the aquarium in the pet shop. Gold fish were desperate for food. They were bumping their heads against the membrane of their compartment. I thought about it. The food of the gold mines was gold. If the gold price rose, profits of gold mines would increase and their shares would rise. I searched for a chart on the gold price. The price was hardly moving. That puzzled me until I discovered from the charts that gold shares tended to rise before the gold price began to increase. They also rose much faster and much more than gold. I knew that there must have been some sort of explanation, but I didn't care. From what I saw, if the gold price rose by say ten per cent, gold shares would soar by thirty per cent. If gold bullion jumped by a third, the price of gold shares would double. If gold fell, the shares would come down with a bigger bump. Huge amounts of money could thus be made and lost in gold shares. The charts also showed that a gold share boom could happen within weeks, let alone months!

It seemed that the crowd playing the stock market had become bored with gold and gold shares in the past year. They had decided to leave them alone. Gold fish had swum aimlessly for many long months near the bottom of the tank.

Something had aroused gold fish in the past week. I was so excited that I went to the water tank at the edge of the room and downed two cups. I peered at the tank and imagined my gold fish swimming to the top.

Back at the front desk, I asked the librarian whether there were any chart books on the stock exchange. I wanted to feel the charts in my hands and write down the prices. It would give me an even better understanding on what was happening to gold shares. Manson had done that before the Internet, PCs and laptops were invented. If it worked for him, it would work for me.

The librarian took me to the reference library and luckily there were several chart books with the price history of all sorts of shares. I looked up gold shares with charts going back twenty years.

Five shares interested me. In past gold booms and busts,

they had gone up the most and fallen the most. Back in the library I saw a pile of *Financial Times* newspapers. I found the pages of share prices and wrote down the prices of the gold shares, going back a month. I drew another aquarium. Using an orange crayon, I plotted the path of my five gold fish. All had broken through the membrane. I had never traded in the stock market before, but I was sure that the shares were giving a signal. The price of gold was about to rise. If gold dust fell on the water, my gold fish would quickly swim for the food at the top of the tank.

I searched for articles about gold and gold shares in the *Financial Times* and other newspapers. There were hardly any reports. Gold wasn't news. The crowd was ignoring it. The charts and prices indicated that only a few investors were expecting something to happen. I had to move fast. It was too late to buy the shares today, but I would make sure that I was at the brokers at the opening of the stock market tomorrow.

I found out why bank shares had fallen to the bottom of the tank. On the front page of the *FT* was a report about the collapse of Moscow Narodsky bank. Several British banks and companies that had dealings with Moscow Narodsky were caught. They had combined losses totalling billions. According to Nostrum Krebs, an *FT* columnist, the Russian banking collapse had turned into an international financial crisis. He predicted that the stock market would slump. Investors were going to lose fortunes. I hoped that Wardle had sold my shares on Friday.

I glanced at another newspaper and saw: 'The Russian Banker Mystery'. I paged through the paper and found the article in the features section. It was about Boris Yapolovitch, the poor guy who I had found hanging from Charing Cross Bridge. The article wondered if the Russian mafia was involved. It said that there were several other murders during the past year. The men and women who had died were involved with Russian gangsters.

I shuddered and wanted to get to Martha before it was dark. As I was leaving I saw a huge guy walking ahead of me. From the back he looked just like one of the men who I had seen on the bridge. I freaked. But he turned around suddenly and a small child rushed up to him. He was Jewish, with a long black untidy beard. The man picked up the boy and gave him a hug. He was certainly no murderer.

I touched my brow and felt the sweat. After going to Wardle & Co tomorrow, I would get out of London. The question was, where?

7

A Russian Scam

When I arrived back at Martha's place, my jeans and shirt had been washed and neatly folded on my bed. Martha was not only giving me shelter, but was mothering me! We sat down for dinner and had egg and chips.

'Want to make lots of money, Jack?'

'Yes. I'm going to show them.'

'Show who?'

'Them!'

I didn't want to tell her that I was talking about Sandy and her rich boyfriend. It would sound silly. But that was the truth. I couldn't help thinking about her. One day I would have a sports car. Cool clothes. Big flat. Then I would meet her and tell that Taylor guy to get lost. That's what kept me going at the library. That's why I wanted to win. No way was I going to be on the streets again. I had done my bit for the homeless!

'If you put your mind to it, you'll become rich, Jack. But don't forget your true self.'

'What do you mean? I know who I am.'

'Why do you think I gave you *The Crowd*?'

'The book's a bit boring, but I read a few pages. Learnt a few things.'

'I wanted you to read it because it was one of my husband's favourite books. I was his secretary. That's how I met him.'

I couldn't believe it. Martha was nice, but nutty. A secretary? Her house was a mess. Sure, she cleaned it up for me, but her things were still all over the place.

'As a psychoanalyst, Tony believed in the individual. That we're all unique. He warned that individuals lose themselves in the crowd.'

'Your book gave me some good tips about the stock market.'

'It's not about getting rich, Jack. Those celebrities. Their parties . . . They're just another crowd.'

'So what. They have a great time.'

'Really? Tony had lots of celebrities as patients. They weren't too happy. They were depressed. On drugs.'

I nodded my head, but wasn't concentrating. I was thinking about Sandy. Was fed up with being poor. Martha's book had showed me that the crowd was powerful. If you knew how to take advantage of it, you could make lots of money.

The next morning I put on fresh clothes and Martha gave me a battered old briefcase that belonged to Tony. Inside were my papers with gold share prices and drawings of the aquarium, a pencil, pen and crayons. Jazz and I began our walk across the heath to the brokers. It had rained during the night and the dew on the grass glistened in the sun. We climbed Parliament Hill and looked back towards the city. The atmosphere was hazy in the early morning light. I could just make out the buildings in the far distance. It was 8am in the morning. Thousands would be arriving at their offices to start work. Jazz, nearby, was licking the dew off the fresh grass. I felt the coins in my pocket and held the briefcase tightly against my side. It was my big day. I was going to show Sandy that I was a winner.

*   *   *

When I arrived at Wardle & Co, Jim Wardle, David Drummond and Shri Khosler were huddled around a desk. They were looking at the screen on the terminal. I could see from the doorway that virtually all the figures were in red.

'It's a bad market,' muttered Drummond. 'Last week we told them to hold on. Now what?'

'Good morning . . . Nice day,' I said.

Drummond looked up: 'Nice day? You must be joking.'

He turned his eyes towards the red prices on the terminal. Drummond was calm the previous week, but now his hand was shaking. He struggled to light a cigarette, had a few puffs and put it out quickly when Khosler glared at him.

'What do we say to our clients now?' asked Khosler.

'It's a bear market,' said Wardle. 'Prices could go down a lot further. But we don't want them to panic. Just tell them it's a small setback. That it won't last. Try and calm them.'

'It's going to be one hell of a day,' mumbled Drummond softly.

The words were barely out of his mouth when the phones started ringing. They rushed to their desks, ignoring me.

'It's a market correction,' Khosler explained to a client

as he scrolled down the screen. 'The market's down five per cent. Yes I know I told you not to sell last week . . . Sorry. I can't get it right all the time . . . OK . . . OK, I'll do my best.'

He picked up another phone: 'Sell at best 2,000 M&S, 5,000 BAE . . .'

'Want some coffee?'

I looked up at Tracy, Wardle's secretary. She seemed to be the only one who wasn't worried.

'Thanks, white, two sugars please,' I said observing the hectic dealing. 'Can you ask Mr Wardle if they sold my shares?'

Tracy with a black bob and bright red lipstick, sauntered up to Wardle in her short black skirt and plain white blouse. He glanced at me and nodded while he was frantically selling shares. She went into his office and brought me some papers.

Wardle half waved to me: 'You're lucky . . . you're out!'

Tracy showed me two separate pieces of paper. One of the broker's notes said 'sold 600 OilFinder at £5.90' and the other, 'sold 500 MineDeep at £12.95'. I added the sums. After brokers' commission and stamp duty, I was left with around £9800.

'What is the price of OilFinder and MineDeep today?' I asked.

Tracy went to a screen: 'They're falling like stones. Wow! Everything!'

I finished my coffee and patted Jazz on his head. They were so busy shouting and making excuses that they didn't notice that a dog was in the office. Their clients were very angry. They were blaming their brokers, not themselves.

'No boom can last forever,' Wardle was explaining down

the phone. 'Yes I know the market peaked a fortnight ago . . .
It's almost impossible to sell at the top . . .'

He looked exasperated as he picked up his other phone
and shouted out more sell orders.

Another phone rang and Wardle answered: 'Yes I know
that your shares started falling a week ago. Yes, I told you to
hold on. No one expected a panic.'

'I hope it's a correction and the market will settle down,'
Drummond was saying. 'Yes it could be a bear market.'

They were all jabbering at the same time. Then I heard
Khosler: 'That Russian bank failure is turning into a full-
scale banking crisis. Yes some of our banks are badly exposed.
Their shares are well down. All down. Yes, maybe the Bank
of England will step in and support the banks. We can only
hope.'

There was no point in doing anything now. They were
far too busy. Tracy was typing on her computer. I sidled up
alongside her and asked her to search for the price of gold
and Ajax Gold Mines, Downtown Mining, Golden Fish
Mines, Playdon Discovery and Raven Creek.

It was remarkable. Despite the general stock market
slump, gold and the gold shares were steady. On the
terminal screen, almost all the shares were red and falling
but the gold shares were blue. Amazing! They were up
slightly. I wrote down their prices and went and sat down
in the reception area. I took out my aquarium drawing and
my orange crayon and worked on the coffee table. I drew
my gold fish swimming in the second compartment of my
aquarium. Despite the stock market slump they had not
fallen back to the bottom division of the tank.

I looked up and noticed that a tall man with silvery white hair and a white moustache had sat down nearby. He was reading a newspaper, but was peeping at me from time to time, trying to see what I was doing. When he saw that I noticed him, he quickly lifted his newspaper. I could see the headline of the main story on the front page: 'Bank Crisis: Yapolovitch in Russian Mining Fraud'. Further down the page was a photo of a woman and a headline: '*Telegraph's* Moscow Correspondent dies'.

I nervously went across to Wardle and asked if I could speak to him privately.

'I don't have time to talk,' he snapped. 'OK, I suppose I need a break. Tracy can you get me some coffee?'

'Thanks for selling my shares. Can I buy some others?'

'What? In this market?' sighed Wardle. 'You can't be serious.'

I had written down my order: Buy 1,000 Ajax, 1,000 Downtown, 1,000 Golden Fish, 500 Playdon Discovery and 500 Raven Creek. At the latest market prices they would cost about £9,600, including brokerage charges.

'OK if you want to lose your money, don't blame me,' said Wardle, sighing. 'I've learnt over the years not to argue with clients. It's your money. If that's what you want to do with it . . .'

I watched him as he picked up the phone and asked the dealer to buy my gold shares. I sat down in the reception room to wait for confirmation. The silver haired man was still sitting there.

'Did I hear you say gold?' he asked.

'Yes that's right.'

'Do you think it's going up?'

'Maybe.'

'Those drawings of yours? Are they telling you to buy gold?'

I didn't reply. There was no way I was going to tell him why I was buying gold shares. Tracy came up and gave me my broker notes. They had bought me my gold shares leaving me with cash to spare. I asked for the money and she gave me nine crispy twenty pound notes.

'Did you just buy gold shares?' insisted the man.

Now that I definitely owned the shares, I was happy to talk.

'They're going up while the rest of the market's going down,' I said. ' I don't know why, but it could mean that some people expect gold to rise.'

He smiled: 'I hear that Moscow Narodsky has been selling gold.'

I shuddered. That bank again! He looked at me closely with sharp eyes, wondering if I knew something.

'They may be selling, but the gold price isn't falling,' I blurted out.

He grinned and held out his hand: 'That's a good answer. Name's Stanley Slimcop.'

'Jack Miner,' I replied, noticing that his newspaper was on the coffee table.

'Finished with the paper?' I asked.

'I'll give it to you on one condition.'

'What?'

'Do you think I should buy gold shares?'

'That's up to you. I did.'

I snatched the paper, picked up Jazz's lead and rushed out of the office.

*   *   *

Jazz and I raced from the broker towards the Heath. On the one hand I was on a high. I had sold my OilFinder and MineDeep shares before the crash and had bought gold shares. Dealing in thousands of pounds was better than wrapping up fish and chips and selling them for a fiver. But at the same time I was worried about the murder. It was big news and they were probably still looking for me. After passing some cottages and a white church, we came to The Freemasons Arms, a pub with a large garden. Successfully fooling them that I was older than eighteen, I bought a pint of lager and some crisps and asked for some water for Jazz. A blonde barmaid with an Australian accent accepted the order. She had a nice smile, so I chatted to her.

'I've got a friend who's from Perth,' I said. 'Where are you from? Sydney? Melbourne?'

'No ways. West Australian. Born in Kalgoorlie. Worked for Macquarie Bank in Perth.'

'Don't suppose you know Sandy Swann,' I said.

It was a long shot, but it was worth a try.

'Does she live in Hampstead? Quite a few Australians come here.'

'Her cousin's Mike Swann, the Australian fast bowler. She looks a bit like him.'

'Is that so? I'll look out for her. You can watch the cricket over there.'

She pointed to the TV screen in the corner of the room. The Australians were hitting the winning run.

'It's all over. You guys have won,' I said, passing her Martha's phone number. 'If you manage to spot Sandy, could you give this to her?'

Jazz pulled on his lead and led me into the pub garden. It had neat flowerbeds, a thick green lawn and dark brown wooden benches and tables. The lager tasted good. Two bearded authors were whinging about their publishers, complaining that they weren't earning enough money from their royalties.

I picked up the *Telegraph* and read the article about the collapse of Moscow Narodsky. Boris Yapolovitch, Moscow Narodsky's chief executive, was involved in a Russian mining scam. He had become friendly with directors of new Russian mining exploration companies. They were prospecting and drilling for gold, diamonds, platinum, aluminium and other minerals in the Siberian wastelands.

Yapolovitch persuaded Moscow Narodsky, a leading Russian bank, to make loans to the companies. The finance paid for the exploration. Soon afterwards, the directors announced that their companies had discovered exciting new gold, diamond and other resources. Russian, European and American investors were excited and Yapolovitch encouraged them to invest in the new mining companies. British, German, French and American banks were keen to lend the Russians hundreds of millions of dollars. The directors promised that the companies would soon develop substantial mines that would earn multi millions.

A few years passed by, but the mines produced hardly

anything. The companies spent a lot, continually requiring more money for drilling and other equipment. In most instances, the drills and tools never arrived. Losses grew and investors became impatient. The directors knew that their promises were empty, but the *Telegraph* was unsure about Yapolovitch. Did he know the full story, or was he in fantasyland? Yapolovitch remained full of confidence at various investor and banker meetings and enthusiastically backed the directors. Good times were around the corner, he claimed. Yapolovitch continually spun the optimistic story because he was no longer an objective, cautious banker. The directors were bribing him. The bank paid him an unexceptional salary, so his wealth came from backhanders. The bribes enabled him to enjoy the lifestyle of a jet set celebrity banker who owned a Moscow football club.

For a short while, Moscow Narodsky and other banks continued to lend money to the dud companies, but eventually the music stopped. Disenchanted investors and bankers at last decided that it was foolish to throw money down Siberian holes. Losses mounted. The corporations were doing so badly that they stopped paying their employees. The workers complained and the Russian police began to investigate. They found that the directors were fraudsters. Yapolovitch tried to wriggle out of his corner and decided that it was best to give State's Evidence. The deal was that he would receive a lenient sentence for his corruption, provided that he exposed the crooks behind the scam.

The company directors and Yapolovitch were the front men, but the *Telegraph* concluded that the true owners of the dud mines were the Russian mafia. When they found out that Yapolovitch was going to give evidence to the Moscow prosecutor, the mafia took out a contract on his life. He ran away to London, but couldn't escape the Russian criminal network. The public hanging was a message to others. Keep your mouths shut!

I held my breath as I recalled the struggling, twitching banker at the end of the rope and nervously paged through the newspaper. Relief! There was nothing about the police search for the key witness.

While I was looking, I came across another article. The story was about the death of a Russian journalist. Marcia Mirikover, freelance Moscow correspondent for the *Telegraph* and other foreign newspapers, had investigated the scandal. She had met with the angry workers. Most of the information in the *Telegraph's* Russian fraud article came from her reports. Mirikover had arrived in London the previous week to interview Yapolovitch. She had been a friend of his wife at university, so the refugee banker had decided that he could trust her. Her meeting with the Moscow banker proved to be fatal.

'Marcia Mirikover, a courageous journalist, died in mysterious circumstances last week,' the *Telegraph* said. 'She fell in front of a train at King's Cross.'

'The Railway Police first thought that it was yet another suicide on London's underground,' the article continued. 'After the body was recovered, British and Russian police cooperated. They concluded that it was very possible that someone had pushed Mirikover on to the railway line.'

The date of the death was scary. It was the very day I had arrived in London. I recalled the delay at King's Cross station and commuters saying someone had fallen in front of the train. Was the unfortunate person Mirikover?

I folded the *Telegraph* and noticed that the authors were grinning at the headline. One of them asked for the paper and laughed: 'Seems that Yapolovitch was yapping too much.'

I smiled weakly, held Jazz's lead tightly and quickly left the pub's garden. I was paranoid, fretting that I would be recognised by someone, anyone. I almost forgot Jazz, and holding his lead, sprinted across the road. A car almost hit us. I saw some shops in a place called South End Green, rushed inside a pharmacy and bought some sunglasses. Once we were on to the Heath, I let go of Jazz's lead. He struggled to keep up with me as I raced along a wide gravel track alongside a large duck pond. I hardly noticed mothers and children who were feeding ducks, swans and pigeons. We followed the track. It continued between the duck pond on the right and the family swimming pond on the left. I was running so fast that I could have pulled my calf or hamstring muscle. My body was tired, but I couldn't get the murders of Yapolovitch and Mirikover out of my mind. My feet were hot and uncomfortable. The sun beat down on my face and the sweat poured off me. At last we reached the top of a hill where there were some pine trees.

I rested on a bench under a tree and began to relax. Jazz panted furiously. Afterwards we jogged downhill to the southern tip of the Heath. I slowed down and began to walk as I neared the red brick wall of the Lido, the swimming pool. I needed a swim, so I tied Jazz to the bicycle railings, paid a few pounds and entered. I didn't want my money to be stolen again, so I carefully placed the notes in my socks, pushed them into my trainers and handed my belongings to the cloakroom attendant.

Still wearing my sunglasses, I rushed to the pool. It was about sixty metres long and about twenty five metres wide. I jumped in, using my dark blue boxers as a swimming costume; my glasses, still strapped around my head. The water was freezing. Colder than the ponds. I must have swum about thirty lengths, or more than a mile, without realising it. Afterwards I had a shower and felt a lot better, but I had selfishly left the exhausted and thirsty dog tied up for a long time. Anyone could have stolen Jazz. I had to calm down. How could they recognise me in my dark glasses? I would try to take it easy and carry on as normal.

8

THE SILVER FOX

I wandered about alone during the next few days, didn't read newspapers and switched TV channels to avoid the news. My dark glasses were on all the time except when I went to bed, or sneaked into the movies. Martha was bemused but didn't pry. My new mobile wasn't charged and I didn't bother phoning Wardle to find out how my shares were doing. That was another lesson that Manson had taught me. Don't get involved in daily dealings. Day traders who buy and sell shares every day, every hour, every minute, lose sight of the big picture. They make small profits, if they're lucky. Big events make the big money, he wrote.

Martha refused to take rent and fed me for free. To help out, I took her and the dogs out for breakfast and bought some groceries.

A welcome surprise. Martha told me that Sandy had phoned. I returned the call as soon as I was through the door.

'Hi Jack, got your number from an Australian barmaid,' said Sandy.

'Great. Didn't expect her to remember. Wanna have a drink? We can meet at the Freemasons Arms.'

'Sorry, Jack. I'm packing tonight. Flying back to Perth tomorrow. Maybe next time. You've got my address and email.'

So that was it. Sandy would be out of my life. Just like that. To think that she was the main reason why I had come all the way to London. She would soon be gone. What a letdown. I felt pretty flat.

'Plenty of fish in the sea,' said Martha, noticing my mood.

'No sea here, Martha. When I sell my shares, I'm skipping London.'

The next few days I jogged and swam in the ponds. Other than Martha and the dogs, I had no friends. So I went to Swiss Cottage Library and read more books about the stock market. I wasn't keen on the latest investment books. Most were full of jargon. Maths and stats that I couldn't understand. I preferred books that kept it simple. Traders' stories and good ideas. There were some funny old books like The *Money Game* by Adam Smith. He called fund managers 'gunslingers' – Wild West type guys who threw their weight about and dominated the market. *How To Trade in Stocks* by Jesse Livermore, the speculator, was one of my favorites. His trading methods were similar to Manson. Besides shares, he also traded commodities such as wheat. Made a fortune in the roaring twenties when there were bootleggers and gangsters such as Al Capone. In 1929 the market crashed and he lost everything. A few years later Jesse was so depressed that he blew his brains out. Jesse showed me that you could make a killing in shares and commodities. A fortune. But you had to know when to stop. If you didn't, the market would kill you.

Manson's book was still the best. It showed that you didn't have to be an expert to make money in the market. He was a performing actor and he did it. That's what I was going to do.

*   *   *

About ten days later, I arrived at Wardle's office, without knowing what had happened to my gold shares. But for the whirring printer, the office was dead quiet. They were observing me in silence. In the reception area, in the corner, the silver haired man was reading his newspaper.

'What's going on?' I asked.

'You should know. Your shares have gone through the roof,' said Drummond.

I looked at the screen on his terminal. The price of gold was $398 an ounce, a fifth higher than the day I had bought my gold shares. From my research in the library, I knew that if gold was up by about twenty per cent, gold shares were likely to be fifty to sixty per cent higher. I asked for the prices of my gold shares. Sure enough, their value had jumped from under £10,000 to more than £15,000.

Wardle walked in and shook my hand: 'Not bad, for beginners luck, my boy.'

'It wasn't luck,' I insisted.

'If you say so,' he said smiling, knowingly. 'Want to take profits?'

'Not sure,' I replied. 'Can I see some charts?'

I walked past the silver haired guy but couldn't remember his name.

He seemed to realise: 'Stanley Slimcop. Good to see you again. You can sit here.'

They were all watching me. I stared back and waited. Slimcop walked away and stood alongside Drummond's desk.

I sat down by the coffee table, examined the charts, took out my notepaper with the prices of the shares and updated the figures. I got hold of my aquarium drawing and drew a new level in the tank. With my orange crayon I drew gold fish swimming in the higher compartment. According to Manson, it was far too early to sell. There was a good chance that my gold fish would swim to the top of the water. This would happen if gold burst through $400.

'I think that I will hold on for awhile,' I told Wardle.

I was about to leave, when Slimcop called out to me: 'Want some lunch? Chinese?'

I turned to Wardle. He smiled and nodded his head: 'Silver Fox owes you one!'

I couldn't understand what he was getting at, but I felt like some Chinese.

*   *   *

It wasn't like the takeaways that I knew. This Chinese restaurant was real cool. The décor was white, the tables were white, the chairs were white and the waiters were in white. The restaurant was well above ground level. Our table next to the window overlooked Hampstead High Street below. The Community Centre was on the left and two banks and some mobile phone and clothes shops were across the road.

I looked at the menu and was at sea. I had never seen such a choice of fish, chicken, duck, meat and vegetarian dishes.

'Want a beer?'

'No thanks. Just a coke.'

Slimcop smiled: 'Anything you like?'

'Duck, anything, thanks.'

Slimcop and Wardle ordered and the waiters came with dishes ranging from crispy duck and pancakes to sizzling chicken and prawns. A waiter taught me how to smooth sweet plum sauce on the pancake, place duck, fresh strips of cucumbers and spring onion on it and then roll it up. I tried out chopsticks and when I dropped them, the waiter passed me a spoon and fork. I was so hungry that I didn't listen to the conversation. The food was so tasty that I picked up crumbs with my fingers and sipped coke in between mouthfuls. I looked up. Slimcop and Wardle were smiling. Wardle pointed at my chin. I wiped my face and some food fell off my serviette.

'What school do you go to?' asked Slimcop.

'Bridlington . . . Just finished my GCSEs'

'Going back to do your AS levels.'

'Dunno. Maybe.'

'You get your results in August don't you? How do you think you've done?'

'Not sure.'

I was beginning to get annoyed with this grilling. Slimcop seemed to realise it and he turned to Wardle and winked.

'He did me a good turn you know.'

Wardle smiled, as Slimcop stood up.

'Have to go. Tell him what I'm going to do,' whispered Slimcop.

The two shook hands. Slimcop, about six foot three in a sleek light grey suit, towered over Wardle. The broker, in his crumpled dark blue suit, looked sloppy in comparison. With full, longish silver grey hair and a white moustache, Slimcop could have been anywhere between sixty five and seventy five. Despite his age he was still handsome. The waiter brought the bill.

'You pay, old boy,' said Slimcop.

'Typical,' replied Wardle, but they grinned at each other as if it was a private joke.

I stood up and shook Slimcop's hand. He passed me a large plain white card with his name and address.

'Come and visit us.'

Wardle pulled my arm and made me sit down. I tried out Jasmine tea but found it bitter.

'What did he mean by good turn?' I asked.

'After you left the office last week, he bought a lot of gold shares.'

'He just asked me what I thought about gold. I didn't do anything for him.'

'He wasn't sure about gold. He knew that there was a big seller in the market. You helped him change his mind.'

'He bought just because I did?'

'Yes. He said that you made sense. Despite heavy selling, the price of gold didn't fall. That was a sign that there were informed investors who had started to buy.'

'I just said that I thought that gold was going to rise. That's all. I could have been wrong.'

'You were so sure of yourself that he was convinced you would win. We call him the Silver Fox, because he's canny.'

'Foxes are cunning.'

'No, canny is the word. He's not slippery. He's straight. I would trust him with my life. That's where you come in.'

'How?'

'He's going to give you a cut of his profits.'

'What do you mean?'

'You're going to get about £50,000. Ten per cent of the profits that he made on his gold shares.'

I was stunned. Some stranger asks me a question and then gives me 50K!

'You must be joking.'

'No, I'm serious. That's the sort of guy he is. He's the only one I know who does it. He helps people who he thinks need it. We have some extremely wealthy clients but none of them would give you a penny. They would just boast that they made a fortune from gold shares. They wouldn't even give you credit for the idea. They would brag that they thought of it themselves.'

'I'm not a charity case.'

'I know that you're not. But you helped make him some money, so why not? We brokers get commissions when clients buy and sell. He likes you, Jack. You remind him of his son.'

'His son?'

'He died. But when you see him again, don't talk about it.'

Wardle then told me Stanley Slimcop's story. His Dad died when he was fourteen. While he was at school he decorated houses on weekends to earn money and help his mum and sister. Hilton Safron, a stockbroker, owned one of the houses and offered him a job. Stanley, who was then sixteen, left school and went to work for the broker. He was so popular that new clients flocked to the firm and it became one of the biggest brokers in London. Slimcop became a senior partner and at the age of thirty five was rich. Safron and Slimcop became one of the most prestigious London brokers. It was a household name in the City. Members of the Royal Family were clients.

Safron and Slimcop were so busy, that they entrusted their accountant to bank money belonging to clients and the firm. Unfortunately Cecil Shweisder, the accountant, was a gambler. He speculated in the markets and bet on horses, football and golf. He also loved playing roulette and blackjack at casinos. To pay off his gambling debts and to make more bets, Shweisder began to steal cash from the firm. Stan and Hilton Safron were so busy with clients that they didn't know what was going on. Shweisder cooked the books, so they thought that they had plenty of cash. One day a client sold his shares and demanded immediate payment, but the firm couldn't pay. The clients' accounts were empty. In the early hours of the morning, Shweisder drove to a supermarket's parking lot, slammed a gun in his mouth and fired. The suicide was front page news and clients rushed to the firm to salvage their securities and cash. All gone. Safron and Slimcop were bust. Stan, his partners and clients lost everything.

'The courts cleared Stan, but he was in total disgrace,' Wardle went on. 'He could never be a broker again.'

'But he has money now. How did he recover?'

'Leila, his wife, is a sculptor and artist. She held an exhibition and sold virtually all her work. I bought one and that's how I first met them.'

They sold their house and went to Johannesburg, South Africa, Wardle continued. Slimcop became friendly with a geologist and learnt about the gold mining industry. Later there was a gold mining boom and Slimcop made a lot of money. He came back to London and bought a house in Hampstead.

'The Silver Fox is so canny that he bought the house at a fire sale price during a property depression,' said Wardle smiling. 'Leila has a studio there.'

Wardle continued: 'What I really like about Stan is that he went out of his way to find Safron and Slimcop clients who had lost money. He first paid back pensioners and other poor clients. Recently he settled his debts with the richer ones.'

'Some guy,' I said.

'I haven't come across another like him,' Wardle replied as we walked back to the office. 'You couldn't find a better friend.'

*   *   *

Dr Klugheim wants to see me again. Why the attention? What about the other cons? He's excited when I enter his room. His face, red from sunburn. Doesn't have his jacket on. A shirt button undone. Hairy and fat. I can't help but smile. He looks down and sorts out his shirt.

'Your book's getting really interesting,' he says keenly.

I know that look. Seen it many times before. Greed! I glance at file on desk. It says 'Portfolio'.

'What's that?' I ask, fully aware what this is all about.

'My shares.'

'O fuck, here we go again,' I whisper, loud enough for him to hear. 'What about the hypocritical oath?'

'The Hippocratic oath states that the doctor must do his best to take care of the patient. Any complaints, Jack?' he snaps.

'You scratch my back and I . . .'

'We're not going to get into that Jack. Doctors are entitled to make a living. Save for school fees, holidays, old age.'

'How your shares doing?'

'Not so good. We can talk about that later. First you.'

'What about me?'

'When you made your first few thousand, how did you feel?'

'Shit of course, what you expect?'

'Stop trying to be funny,' snaps Klugheim. 'I'm giving you extra time. I've got other patients. If you don't want to be here . . .'

'Obviously it felt good,' I reply, deciding I'd better play ball.

'I want to know how you really felt. Was it like gambling? Did you get a buzz when you beat the system? Was it a high?'

'Not like that. Never thought it was a gamble. Just made sense.'

'I'm not sure I understand,' says Klugheim, drawing me out.

'Dunno how to explain. When my gold shares did great, it was like slamming a ball into the goal post. Felt like doing high fives with the brokers.'

'Did you?'

'No. I could see they felt crap when I got it right. They were losing. I was winning.'

'How did you feel afterwards? When it sank in?'

'Pretty good. Funny though, it wasn't so much about the money. It was the respect. They began to take me seriously. Saw that I wasn't just a boy. Was someone.'

'Good. I want you to start feeling that way about yourself again. Regain your self-esteem,' says Klugheim, snapping his fingers. 'Time's up.'

He's smiling a genuine smile. I'm beginning to like him.

'The deal is that I take a look at your shares, right?'

'You'll continue with your book and we'll see each other again,' he says.

'Can I look?' I ask, as I open the portfolio file.

It shows that Klugheim owns shares in thirty companies. No wonder he doesn't know what's going on.

'What you reckon they're worth?'

'They've fallen from around 200K to 120K.'

'OK, get me stock prices and charts. Provided . . .'

'Provided what?'

'I get ten per cent of the profits.'

Klugheim smiles: 'Know what chutzpah means?'

'Got some idea.'

'This is between ourselves,' says Klugheim.

We shake on it. Not sure if I'll get my ten per cent, but maybe he'll get me out of here.

9

NEW FRIENDS

Reading a map that Wardle had given me, I crossed Hampstead High Street and walked through some narrow alleyways into Church Street. At the end of the road, I wandered into the church's shady graveyard. Tombstones, three to four hundred years old were in the shadows of beech and oak trees. John Constable's tombstone was there. He must have lived in Hampstead. Mum was a fan of his landscape paintings. We often walked in 'Constable Country' which was in Suffolk.

The church and graveyard were on a hill. Over the fence, about twenty metres below, I spotted the gravel road that Wardle had drawn on the map. I ambled out of the graveyard, turned right, walked down a path and reached the road. Iron railings surrounded a modern bungalow. I rang the security button and called out my name. The gate opened. Giant sunflowers and roses were on either side of a short, narrow, winding stone path that lead to the front door.

A large bronze sculpture of a bird was near the entrance. A boy and a girl opened the door. They were both blonde with freckles and looked about twelve. I guessed that they were twins.

'Hi Jack, I'm Tom,' said the boy in a broad South African accent. 'Stan told us you were coming.'

'I'm Tess. Are you going to swim with us?' asked the girl.

I followed them through a large open living room with wide windows and lots of light. The walls were covered with paintings and charcoal etchings of sparrows, eagles, vultures and other birds. Sculptures of birds, heads and torsos were on pedestals, bookcases and stools.

Slimcop was sitting on the patio with a woman dressed in white trousers and an emerald, silk, blouse. She was about seventy, with grey hair in a bun, lined but pretty, with lots of make-up. So much so that she looked like a painted doll. Slimcop stood up, came towards me and shook my hand and introduced the woman. He towered over her.

'Good to see you Jack . . . Leila, my wife.'

She held out a limp hand and I shook it softly as she looked me up and down. I felt a bit nervous.

'Take off your dark glasses, young man. Let's take a good look at you.' She turned to Slimcop: 'He's got an interesting face. You said he's sixteen. He looks older.'

'I turned sixteen on June 1,' I said.

'Marilyn Monroe's birthday.'

'Yes, my Mum always reminded me.'

'Gemini. Dual personality. Know what time you were born?' asks Leila, looking at the palms of my hands.

'Just before midnight,' I said.

I wondered if she was a mystic or something. She let my hands go.

'You could be a good subject, Jack. Want to sit for me?'

'Leila's an artist. A sculptor. Relax and sit down,' said Slimcop.

'You seem to like birds,' I said.

'Fascinating creatures. Did you ever see that Hitchcock film . . . The Birds?'

'No.'

'Flocks of birds attack families who are on holiday.'

'Wow!'

While we were chatting, Tom and Tess were running and jumping into the swimming pool, that was in the centre of the back garden.

'Come and join us Jack,' shouted Tess.

'Don't have any trunks,' I called.

'I'll lend you some . . . Let's talk first,' said Stanley.

Leila got up and came back soon afterwards with a drawing pad. She moved her chair to a spot where she could have full sight of my profile and started sketching.

'Don't take any notice of me,' she said.

'They're South Africans, aren't they,' I said, getting up to fetch a ball that Tom had thrown in our direction.

'Please sit down Jack. Don't move,' insisted Leila. 'The family immigrated here a year ago. They now live in Salisbury. Know many South Africans?'

'Only one. He was a friend of my Dad. I met him years ago. He was a prospector. Searched for gold, diamonds . . . that sort of stuff.'

'I know a few geologists. What's his name?' asked Stan.

'Fred Carrender.'

'Heard of him. The South African mining community is

small. Everyone knows each other,' said Stan.

Leila stopped drawing and looked up: 'Maybe he's a friend of Ivor. Tess, Tom come here, please.'

They grabbed their towels and ran to us.

'Did your Grandpa have a friend called Fred Carrender?'

'Yes, he used to come to our house sometimes,' said Tom.

'Brought lots of chocolate,' grinned Tess.

'You know Fred Carrender?' I asked amazed.

'Their grandfather's also a geologist,' said Stan.

'Grandpa's going to be here in a few days. We're going to Scotland,' said Tom excitedly.

'We have some cousins there. We're going to ride horses and walk in the Highlands,' said Tess.

'Then the Edinburgh festival and back to school,' said Leila.

Their faces dropped.

'Life always turns up with something interesting, Jack. Time for a celebration,' said Leila cheerfully. 'Perhaps you can meet Ivor and find out more about your Dad's friend.'

She went inside and a little later came out with some biscuits, beers and cold drinks.

'Want a beer, Jack?'

'Thanks,' I said, and quickly downed a bottle of Castle, a South African lager.

The children went off to change and Leila sat down again to etch me.

'I'll show you my drawing of Ivor later,' she said. 'He's a good friend. Helped us when we were down.'

I didn't want to tell the Slimcops everything, but it just

came out. It felt safe there. They were so open and friendly. I told them about Dad's letter, how he had saved Fred Carrender from drowning and that Fred had given Dad the OilFinder and MineDeep shares. How I sneaked out of Bridlington and kept the shares away from Mark Baton, the liquidator. I didn't tell them about Sandy. As far as I was concerned, she was history.

'Do you know how much your Dad owed his creditors?' asked Stan.

'Not sure. I think that Baton said it was around £25,000,' I said.

'I think Jim Wardle's right. Your Dad gave you his shares before he died,' said Stan thoughtfully. 'It doesn't belong to the insolvent estate, but that Baton sounds nasty. He could make your life uncomfortable.'

'Remember when we went under. The liquidators grabbed most for themselves,' said Leila bitterly. 'Get some legal advice, Jack.'

'I've got a better idea,' said Stan. 'Let's get shot of him. I'll settle your Dad's debts through my lawyer.'

His generosity was astounding. I didn't know what to say.

'You don't have to do that,' I stammered.

'The creditors will be happy. All they want is their money. My lawyer will act on behalf of an anonymous benefactor,' said Stan.

'What about Baton? He'll want to get his hands on it.'

'No way. My lawyer will obtain the list of creditors and pay them directly.'

'Mrs Derby. We owed her a lot of rent. She's a good woman,' I blurted out.

'Mrs Derby will be first on the list,' laughed Stan.

He was pacing up and down, walking up towards the swimming pool and back again. He seemed to be remembering something that had happened to him; possibly when he lost all his money.

'What if Baton wants more?' I asked.

'Baton will get a fee for his services,' said Slimcop.

'The lowest possible fee,' said Leila, clenching her teeth. 'We were insolvent once, Jack. We know what it's like. Liquidators scavenging, grabbing most for themselves.'

'Did Jim tell you that I'm giving you some money, Jack?'

'Yes . . . No need . . . You're doing more than . . .'

'You did me a good turn Jack . . . You helped me make my mind up. I've made a lot of money out of those gold shares. Will fifty thousand do?'

'You're already settling my Dad's debts . . . That's more than enough.'

'Fifty thousand pounds it is. What will you do with the money, Jack?'

'Not sure. Maybe I'll buy more shares.'

'Investing is a good idea. But so is education. What about finishing school and going to university?'

'I'll think about it. I'll see how I do in my GCSEs.'

'You get your results mid-August don't you?' said Leila. 'How do you think you've done?'

'Not sure. No point in guessing,' I said, thinking to myself that I would be lucky to get a few Cs.

*   *   *

I borrowed swimming trunks from Stan. They were too big for me, but I tied them as tight as I could. The pool seemed to be heated, as it was much warmer than the ponds on the Heath and the Lido at Gospel Oak. I had never swum in a private pool before, so I had to get used to it. With only a few strokes I was at the other side, turned and was back again. I must have done twenty or thirty lengths, but I reckon that I probably swam only three hundred metres. Pity Jazz wasn't around. He would have jumped in.

The pool was in the middle of a lawn that sloped down towards a fence about two and a half metres high. I climbed out and dried myself in the bright early evening sun and looked around me. Since the house and the pool were about midway up a hill, there was a good view below. To the left of the pool, which was eastwards, I could see a line of cars on the main road heading uphill towards the village. Further east were the green trees of the Heath. Southwards, through a heat haze, I managed to spot the dome of St Paul's, some five or six miles away. The pool and lawn dominated the garden. On the borders of the lawn were a variety of bushes and shrubs and multi-coloured flowers ranging from dahlias and marigolds to geraniums and fuschias. Sculptures of birds were placed in corners of the garden. They were elevated above large Grecian pots that were overrun by creepers. Nearby there was a large brass sculpture of a young boy with a ball in his right hand. I went up to it and when I was about to gently feel the clean-cut nose, I heard the voice of Tess.

'You mustn't touch him. He's their son.'

'Sorry . . . I didn't mean to,' I said. 'I just got carried away.'

'Beautiful, isn't he!' said Tess. 'He died two years ago, but they never talk about him.'

'What was his name?'

'Sean. He was twenty four. '

I turned around and observed the Slimcops on the patio. They seemed lonely, sitting there in front of their luxurious home.

'He must have been born when they were fairly old,' I said.

Tess had sat down on the lawn and was weeding out yellow dandelions and putting them in a neat bunch. 'Are there any other children?'

'No, he was the only one. Don't say anything,' she said, turning towards Leila, who was coming towards us.

'You seem to enjoy art Jack,' Leila said, putting her hand on Tess' shoulder. Tess presented the bunch of dandelions with a curtsy. We laughed.

'I've tried to paint, but I'm not very good. Mum used to take me to galleries. She liked Constable,' I said, pointing in the direction of the churchyard. 'Saw his tombstone. I didn't know that he lived here.'

'Hampstead used to be full of artists and writers, but bankers and brokers have moved in. It's now too expensive.'

'You're pretty good,' I said shyly, glancing at the sculptures. Leila smiled cautiously. She was obviously used to flattery, unsure whether it was genuine.

'Come let's go and eat. Do you like vegetarian food, Jack?'

* * *

I was no vegetarian, but I enjoyed the pitta bread, olives, hummus, mixed salad and cold pasta with green, red and yellow peppers. I could see that Tom and Tess hated the food and just nibbled the pitta. After supper, Stan took me to his study, which was at the end of the house. We walked along a wide hallway with walls made of thick reinforced glass, through which you could see the garden and the lights of London in the distance. The study had a wide window overlooking the garden, a bookshelf on one wall, an assortment of photographs and a charcoal etching of a blackbird on the other. Stan sat down behind a clear, clean, modern glass desk. On it were his laptop, several files stacked neatly on top of each other and a picture of him, Leila and Sean.

Stan clicked the laptop and glanced at the *Reuters* and *Bloomberg* sites. Gold and gold shares were up again. I was glad that I hadn't sold.

'We're doing well aren't we?' Stan said without any emotion in his voice. 'When are you going to take profits?'

'Not sure. I think I'll let my profits run.'

'I've learnt from experience that it's better to get out of gold shares when they're rising,' said Stan. 'They're volatile. When the market turns, their prices fall fast.'

'Have you started to sell?'

'I'm not greedy, so I've begun to take profits. I sold a few shares yesterday and I will sell some more next week. If I were you, I would do the same.'

'I'm expecting the gold price to go up a lot more. According to James Manson's book, it's natural for people to take profits. But the market can outsmart them. Gold and gold shares could go up a lot further than people think.'

'James Manson, the actor! I met him when I was a broker. A gentleman. Used to telex orders from all over the world. Well I never. I thought that his book was out of print.'

'I bought it in the Hampstead Community Centre,' I said. 'Why did you become interested in gold?'

'Something was happening. Moscow Narodsky was selling millions of ounces, but the gold price wasn't falling. In normal circumstances the price would have slumped,' said Stan. 'Then I met you. You showed me that there were enough buyers willing to buy the Russian gold. If the bank stopped selling, the price would rise.'

As soon as he mentioned Moscow Narodsky, I became nervous and wanted to leave.

'I think I better go now,' I said with a lame excuse. 'I have to take my dog for a walk.'

Stan was studying my reaction closely. I bit my lip, hoping that I hadn't given myself away. It was too late. I could see that he thought I was involved in some way.

'What do you know about Moscow Narodsky?' asked Stan.

'Nothing,' I lied, trying to bolt for the door. 'Thanks for today. I'll go and say goodbye to Leila and the children.'

Stan grabbed my arm. Despite his age he was pretty strong.

'When I talked about Moscow Narodsky at the broker last week, you ran out,' he said. 'You took my newspaper didn't you?'

'Don't remember . . . I wanted to read about the cricket match.'

'You're a bad liar, boy. Better tell the truth,' said Stan,

opening the middle drawer of his desk and pulling out a plastic folder with newspaper clippings. He took them out and put them on the desk. They were all about Moscow Narodsky. Stan went to the door and closed it. He then slowly flicked through the clippings.

'Why do you have all those articles about Moscow Narodsky?' I asked, trying to calm down.

'Russia is one of the world's biggest gold producers. The country has some big gold mines and refineries that melt the gold into bars. Moscow Narodsky is one of the Russian banks that stores the bars. It sells them on the London and Zurich gold markets.'

Stan picked out a few articles and laid them on the desk. They were about the murders of Boris Yapolovitch and the journalist, Marcia Mirikover. There was another article, which I hadn't read before. Paul Zibler, manager of Moscow Narodsky's Zurich branch, had had an accident. He was walking in the Alps and had fallen down a ravine. The Swiss police were investigating. I freaked.

'Coincidental, isn't it,' said Stan, reading and glancing at my reaction. I was trying to be as relaxed as possible, but I was shaking.

'Did you meet any of these people? Yapolovitch? Mirikover?' asked Stan softly.

I was silent. Stan half laughed to himself: 'Of course! Let me guess where you come in.'

He pushed an article in front of me and I felt his eyes on me as I read: 'Police are still looking for a youth who could be an important witness. He reported the Yapolovitch murder and then disappeared.'

'Now if I were the witness, what would I do?' Stan asked rhetorically without expecting me to answer. 'I could give myself up, but then I could be putting myself in danger. On the other hand I could run away and hope that all this will blow over.'

'What would you do if you were the witness, Jack?'

'I'm not sure. Do you think that Swiss banker was murdered as well?' I asked in a feeble attempt to change the subject. Stan laughed grimly.

'The Russian mafia is sending out a clear message. Accidents will happen to anyone who messes with them. Now if I were the witness, I would try and work out if they could convict these people. To do that the British and Swiss police would need co-operation from the Russian authorities. They would have to extradite the gangsters. Do you think that would happen Jack?'

'How should I know?'

'No chance. Perhaps it is a good idea that the witness should leave London. Let the storm blow over. Allow time to take its course and memories fade.'

He neatly collected all the clippings, put them in the folder and back into his drawer. The sharp shrewd look was replaced by a soft kindly smile. I knew I could trust him. He put his hand on my shoulder and we walked to the living room. Leila was playing scrabble with the twins. They were on a cream oblong sofa in the large living room with its wall of windows overlooking the illuminated garden. Numerous paintings and etchings were on its walls. There were a variety of smallish black and copper sculptures in the corners. Persian carpets covered the wooden floors.

'You guys had better start packing. Your grandpa is coming tomorrow,' Leila said as she shut the scrabble board while Tess counted the scores.

'I'm first, you second, Leila. Tom, last,' said Tess proudly.

'Too good for me, Tess. Tom you should read more. It will help your spelling,' said Leila.

'Would you like Jack to go on holiday with you?' asked Stan.

'Great!' shouted Tom. Tess nodded her head eagerly.

Both Leila and I were taken by surprise.

'Go to Scotland with Ivor Ensworth. Isn't it up to him?' asked Leila.

'We'll persuade him,' said Stan.

'Can I take my dog with me?' I asked.

'We'll see,' said Leila.

For the first time since Dad died I was really happy. I had been welcomed into a family. Would soon meet a guy who knew Fred, the man who unwittingly had changed my life.

10

THE LOCH

A few days later I was on my way to Scotland with Ivor Ensworth, Tom and Tess. Before we left, Leila took me shopping. She bought me some jeans, shirts, shoes, a jacket and the first suit that fitted me. A hairdresser gave me a spiky gel haircut. I looked in a shop mirror and seemed a bit older, maybe a bit taller.

Only one thing made me sad. I had to leave Jazz with Martha. Ivor didn't want to take the dog on the overnight journey from London.

We arrived in Scotland early in the morning and Ivor hired a car. About an hour later we were in our stone grey cottage in Crieff, a small Scottish town about twenty miles north of Perth.

Ivor was in his late seventies. He was medium height and stocky and had white hair and a red face. After years of prospecting and heavy work, his arms were thick. His hands were rough and his nails were broken from all the digging and sampling of minerals in the African outback.

During the train journey, I asked him about Fred Carrender.

'He's quite a lot younger than me, but we're good friends. Used to meet him sometimes when we were prospecting,' said Ivor. 'It can get lonely out there. Got to know him quite well. Told me that he had almost drowned.'

'He was sailing with my father.'

'Yes, Stan told me that Fred knew your Dad. They were caught in a storm off the east coast of Africa. The boat capsized and they clung on to the side of the boat. It was a battle to keep afloat.'

'Fred said that your Dad kept him going for almost twenty four hours. Had a great sense of humour. Told jokes and stories. They were terrified of sharks, but the hull was so slippery, they couldn't climb on. A fishing boat rescued them early the next morning.'

'Dad told me that they were in Mombasa.'

'You must go to Kenya sometime. Fascinating place. Fred's quite an adventurer, but he's never gone sailing again. When I first met him, he was broke. Then he struck it lucky. Discovered a rich diamond deposit in the Congo. From then onwards he never looked back.'

'It's because of Fred that I'm here,' I said.

'Stan told me that he gave your Dad OilFinder and MineDeep shares. Fred's a good guy. Always helps friends who help him.'

'Certainly did me a good turn,' I said.

'Carrender managed the diamond mine in the Congo for a time, but was soon bored,' Ivor went on. 'He's like me. Prospecting's our life. For months at a time, we leave our families and wander in south, west and east Africa, looking for diamonds, precious and base metals. I was going through a rough patch when I met him and he gave me luck.'

'How much luck?'

'We struck gold and found platinum and copper deposits in Namibia, southern Africa. Sold our claims to the Namibian government and South African mining companies.'

'I must go and see Fred sometime,' I said. 'Maybe I can repay him.'

'He won't want anything. He'll be just chuffed to see you. Come to South Africa. He's in Johannesburg. We'll both go and visit him,' laughed Ivor.

'I guess I also got lucky.'

'I heard about your dealings, young man. Win today, lose tomorrow. The trick is to know how to keep it.'

Ivor then told me a bit about himself. Some years previously, when Stan Slimcop was a wealthy broker, he had backed one of Ivor's prospecting ventures. That venture failed, but Stan never complained and continued to finance Ivor. By the time Ivor struck gold, Stan was bankrupt and struggling to make a living in South Africa. Leila was selling her sculptures and paintings to keep them going. Stan's stake in Ivor's mine put him on the path to recovery and they became fast friends.

*　　*　　*

The next week was great. The cottage was close to a big Victorian hotel called the Crieff Hydro. The twins and I went horse riding. We played tennis, cycled and swam in the indoor pool of the hotel. Early one morning, Ivor and I went for a long walk up a mountain.

'You go on,' said Ivor puffing. 'I need a rest.'

I walked through a wood to the top. It was a warm day and midges bit me, but when I finally reached the peak, I had a wonderful feeling of freedom. I could see the town below and in the distance the Scottish Highlands. I wondered what it was like to be Rob Roy, the outlaw, who fought against English aristocrats hundreds of years ago. He managed to beat the system.

Ivor and the kids went to visit relatives the next day. So I decided to cycle out of Crieff and visit a castle nearby. I cycled on the main road keeping well to the left as it was quite busy. Back in London I would have fretted that the Russian mafia were chasing me. Here I felt safe and a long way from it all. The road was winding with steep hills. I raced downhill and then puffed my way to the top of the next one before relaxing as I sped downhill again. I passed a farm and in the distance saw a small loch next to a wood. After cycling for about eleven miles, I felt hot and sweaty. So I turned onto a dirt track and peddled to the lake to see if it was clean enough for a swim. A stream flowed into the loch and then continued on its way through the wood. The light blue sky reflected on the loch's clear water. I took off the bag hanging on my back, stood behind some trees and changed into my trunks. Then I waded in and began to swim in the icy water towards the continuation of the stream on the other side. As I swam closer, I heard someone shouting. The voice came from some thick reeds about twenty metres from the edge of the lake. I swam closer but found that the water had become thick with lilies and reeds.

'Hi there, my ankle's stuck. Can you help me?'

It was a woman's voice, but I still couldn't see her.

I pushed my way through a clump of reeds. She had long blonde hair that gleamed in the sun and she was hopping about trying to get loose. The woman turned to face me, her blue eyes dominating a lovely delicate face. She was halfway into the water and the top of her bikini was navy blue with small white spots. She had a light tan and as she moved about I could see that she had an amazing figure. I gaped at her.

'Come on help me!' she cried in an American accent. 'I think that I'm caught in a rope or cord. I've tried to loosen my ankle, but it's slippery. When I pull, it gets tighter.'

'Let me take a look,' I said. I swam towards her and tried to stand, but the water was too deep for me. She must have been standing on higher ground or on a rock.

I was reluctant to duck my head under the water as her frantic efforts had made it muddy and dirty.

'I'll have to lean on your shoulder to find where you're caught,' I said. I pulled on the rope and she almost fell over.

'What the hell do you think you're doing,' she yelled.

'Take it easy, I'm doing my best.'

To avoid ducking my head into the dirty water I had to get closer to her. We were now very close, almost in a clutch. I moved my feet and realised that we were standing on the sunken keel of a boat. She must have been caught in one of its ropes. I found a foothold while I balanced myself by holding her hand and leaning against her shoulder. She slipped a few times, but I managed to stop her falling in. She was getting flustered, but I had to turn her in various directions to see if there was any slack in the rope.

In the end it was hopeless and I had to take a deep breath, close my eyes and go under. I felt her ankle and the rope and started to work on the slimy knot. It was too tight. So I came up for air and went down again with my eyes closed, clutching and following the length of the rope to find out where it was attached to the boat. It led to the end of the keel and was tied to the tip of what was once a rowing boat. I came up again, gasping for breath and went down again directly to the end of the boat. Luckily I managed to untie the rope from the boat and came up holding it in my hand.

'Free at last, free at last!' I shouted, mimicking Martin Luther King.

'Wise guy,' she muttered as we swam towards the middle of the loch with the rope still caught on her ankle. We dived into the clear water to get clean and then waded to a grassy bank. She sat down and struggled to get the rope off her ankle. I knelt down next to her long lanky legs, and tried to dig my nails into the knot. There was a sharp stick nearby and I carefully used it as a lever to loosen the rope. The sun was hot and my body dry, when at last I managed to pull the rope over her foot. I examined her ankle to see whether there were any cuts and while I was doing this, I had a funny feeling that she was looking at my body.

I stood up nervously and she got up as well. She was so lovely that I couldn't help myself and just gaped at her. I was about to say something when she kissed me on the mouth.

'That's to say thank you,' she said. She was about a half a head taller than me and I tilted my head upwards, stammering: 'You're welcome.'

Before I knew what was happening, she kissed me

passionately again. It was like a dream and I responded kissing her back, our mouths intermingling in a French kiss. My hand gravitated to the bikini top and loosened the straps. The bikini top fell to the ground and I felt a hard nipple. Her hand was in my costume now. I felt it turn hard as she felt and played with it.

She giggled as she pulled her hands out of my costume and then hugged and wrestled with me.

'Got anything with you,' she whispered into my ear. A shiver went down my spine. I was excited but nervous.

'A condom? Sorry, no.'

I was furious with myself. What an opportunity lost. But how could I have known that this would happen?

Amazingly she didn't seem to mind: 'Have you been fooling around?'

'No, I don't have a girlfriend at the moment,' I replied, feeling that I was a total loser.

'Good, you should be clean.'

She held my hand and pulled me towards a willow tree close to the loch's bank. I followed her through the leaves towards the trunk. It was a small enclosure and the surrounding hanging leaves made it a natural private room. She led me into another deep kiss and we sank to the ground. She pulled off my costume and untied the bottom of her bikini. I stroked and kissed her breasts and then tried to find my way into her. She guided me in expertly and I felt her warm slippery inside. I was so excited that it spurted out of me and I went limp. I didn't know what to say, I was so embarrassed. Would she realise that I was a virgin?

'Don't worry,' she said. 'It happens sometimes. Let's just

relax and have a cuddle. I forgot to ask you your name?'

'Jack . . . Jack Miner,' I said sheepishly.

'Just call me Maggie,' she said, stroking me gently and feeling my lower parts again. She kissed me again and I kissed and stroked her breasts and ventured down below with my left hand, feeling the rough hair and moisture. I felt myself go hard again, I then kissed her gently and stroked her firm breasts.

'You're beautiful,' I said. Maggie took control again and was now on top of me. I was inside her. I turned her around and I was on top. She was like an erupting volcano, moving up and down, then on top of me again, groaning and muffling her shouts. I was in charge this time and was on top of her, thrusting. She was moving so much that it felt as if I was on a trampoline. She yelped and subsided and I also came soon afterwards.

We lay beside each other in the shade of the tree. I looked up towards the branches and streams of light crept into our little hideaway between the leaves. She sat up and smiled, lifting my head towards her breasts and stroking my hair.

'You're gorgeous,' she said.

'You're lovely too,' I replied, kissing her arm. Now that I had cooled off I noticed that she was older than me. Quite a lot, in fact.

'Ah . . . what do you do?' I ventured.

'I teach at the American school in London.'

'I play the stock market,' I said, half telling her the truth. There was no way that I was going to tell her that I was still at school.

'If you're as good as being a lover then . . .'

She stopped talking, taking a long hard look at me. I wondered if she realised how young I was. I reckoned that she was in her late twenties, perhaps early thirties. She had tiny wrinkles in the corner of her eyes.

'Then what?' I murmured, kissing her gently. I was mad about her.

'Then I would follow you,' she said. 'Time to go. I must meet someone.'

She put on her bikini while I looked for my costume. When we were ready, we swam towards the middle of the loch. Treading water as we took off our costumes again, we cleaned ourselves. I swam up towards her and folded my arms around her.

'That's enough Jack, I'm not as good a swimmer as you,' she laughed.

'My clothes are on the other side with my bike. How did you get here?'

She didn't reply and swam back to the willow tree. I thought that she didn't hear, so I swam towards my bike, hurriedly dressed myself, climbed on and found a route round the loch towards our secret love nest. It must have taken about ten minutes. When I arrived she wasn't there. I found another cycle route and raced down it, but couldn't trace her. She had vanished and I didn't even know how to contact her. I was furious with myself for being so stupid.

I continued to follow the route and by chance came to the castle that I had intended visiting. Lots of people were wandering around an unusual garden. I found a maze and rushed through it, losing my way, fantasising that I would bump into Maggie. No such luck. The castle was closed, but the snack bar was open and I wolfed down two sandwiches. Sex sure makes you hungry.

I cycled, without stopping, all the way back to the cottage. All I could think about was Maggie, her blonde hair, blue eyes, luscious mouth and beautiful body. I was no longer a virgin and was in love again. Sandy was history. The only thing that bothered me was that I didn't know where to find Maggie. I would have to go back to the loch sometime. Hopefully she would be waiting.

*   *   *

Ivor and the twins arrived at our cottage late afternoon. I was relaxing in the small garden at the front of the house, reading a book about my Scottish hero, Rob Roy.

'Hello my boy. Had a good day?' shouted Ivor.

If only he had known!

'Pretty good. Was lost in a maze.'

Tess ran up to me and held my hand: 'We bought you some good luck presents.'

I had forgotten that my GCSE results were out in a few days. I grinned and followed them into the small dark living room with tiny windows. The smallest parcel had a mobile in it with a card from Tom. The second present, from Tess, was an iPod. Ivor gave me a red and black tartan kilt. 'Make sure you don't wear anything under it at the dance tonight,' said Ivor grinning.

It was like being part of a family. Ivor and the twins shook my hand warmly. He passed me a dram of whisky to get me going. I wasn't a whisky fan, but this was malt and felt and tasted smooth.

I changed into my kilt and wore a white shirt, Scottish style. We walked to the hotel, which was only a quarter of a mile away. Compared with the bed and breakfast places that my family went to, this was some establishment. The Hydro was a towering, huge Victorian hotel and the dining room overlooked a wide lawn where some guests were playing croquet and others, chess. Ivor ordered a red South African wine. I was ravenous and he and I had thick Scottish steaks while Tom and Tess chose hamburgers. Afterwards we had coffee in the lounge and soon the band began to play.

The guests drifted into a huge hall, which was empty but for chairs stacked in rows against the walls. Scots and others stood in groups of four, opposite their partners.

The Scottish music set the mood for the evening. Hotel entertainers dragged all of us onto the dance floor. Tess, who wore a light yellow dress, was my partner. A shy little girl, in pink, partnered Tom who was in a green and gold kilt. Ivor, in a smart cream suit, sat on the sidelines and looked on.

They taught us the steps and moves and then the music began. We were in squares. Tess and I danced towards each other, forwards and back again. We turned to the right, changing partners with the other three couples. They pushed me into the middle of our group and soon afterwards, Tess and the others followed. I did my best to keep up with the steps, but was in knots. Even so, it was great fun.

Just as the music stopped, she made her entrance. She was with a tall guy who looked about forty. Maggie looked stunning in a low cut black evening dress with a drop pearl necklace. I couldn't take my eyes off her.

'Oh no! They've gone to sit near Ivor,' I whispered to myself.

Tess overheard and noticed me gazing at them.

'Do you know her?' Tess asked. 'Are they film stars?'

I didn't know what to do. I wanted to rush up and say hello. On the other hand who was the guy with her? Ivor began to talk to him, but I grabbed Tess and Tom. There was no way that I was going to go up and speak to them.

Couples got ready for the next dance in 'long sets'. Eight couples were placed in each row and there were several sets across the hall. Our set was one couple short. Before I could escape, one of the dance instructors rushed over to Maggie and her partner, grabbed their hands and pulled them towards us. Fortunately for me, Tess and I were second in the row. Tom and his partner were third, but my eyes avoided the eighth couple. Each couple faced each other and the music began:

> Step it gaily, on we go
> Heel for heel and toe for toe,
> Arm in arm and row on row
> All for Mairi's wedding.

After a few steps, the couples held their arms up and formed an arch. The first couple ran around with the boy turning to the left and the girl to the right. Then they came back together, joined hands and ducked under the archway formed by the other seven couples. Tess and I went next, we danced a few steps again and then Tom with his partner. Finally Maggie and her man followed. By far the tallest, they struggled to get under the arms of smaller couples such as us.

During the next dance we changed partners and eventually Maggie stood facing me.

'You look great,' I mumbled with a shy grin.

She smiled but gave no indication that she knew me, let alone had made love to me that very morning. I looked at her left hand and saw the diamond engagement and gold wedding rings. I flushed. The beat of the music was faster and faster and although I was devastated, I did my best to keep going. The music stopped and the band announced that they were taking a break. Ivor called Maggie and her partner and ordered a drink. I tried to get away, but the moment that I dreaded had arrived. Tess and Tom, excited and happy, dragged me towards Ivor.

'These are my grandchildren, Tom and Tess,' said Ivor proudly.

He put his arm around me and laughed: 'Mr Jack Miner, their minder and companion!'

'Good to meet you, I'm Hal,' said Maggie's husband with an American drawl. 'My wife Maggie.'

She shook the twin's hands warmly and smiled. Then held mine briefly but glanced at me with a cool vacant expression. I felt the size of an ant.

'Are you actors?' asked Tess shyly.

'Not as exciting as that,' grinned Hal. 'I'm a banker, but Maggie teaches drama.'

'Then you must be an actress,' said Tom.

'Yes I've acted in plays and done some radio work and TV,

but nothing special,' said Maggie softly. 'I'm teaching now.'

'I want to be an actress!' said Tess. 'I was in "The Sound of Music" at school!'

'One of the Von Trapp kids. Not Tom, he was a nun,' joked Ivor, playfully punching the boy.

Ivor ordered whisky for Hal and himself, a beer for me, wine for Maggie and juice for the twins.

'Toast to you Jack,' beamed Ivor. 'Good luck for the GCSEs!'

I felt my face going deep red and glanced at Maggie to see how she was reacting. For the first time she let down her guard and was looking uncomfortable. The room with its chandeliers was bright. Now that Maggie was made up and looking very sophisticated, she looked twice my age.

'What do you want to do, Jack? Thought about it yet?' asked Hal.

'I'm interested in the markets. Stocks and shares, that sort of stuff,' I said, trying to cover the lie that I had told Maggie earlier in the day.

'First he must finish school. Another two years, right Jack?' said Tom.

'If I pass I can go to work,' I said, glaring at Tom.

'You need AS and A levels before you can go to university,' said Ivor. 'Can't understand the system in this country. Exam after exam. It's much simpler in South Africa.'

'Same in America,' said Maggie without looking at me.

'Are you staying here for long?' asked Ivor.

'Three days. It's our tenth anniversary,' said Hal. 'But we have to go home tomorrow.'

'Are your children with their grandparents?' asked Ivor.

That question hit a raw spot.

'We don't have children,' said Hal, playing around with his hands nervously and then blurting out: 'Maggie, can't . . . We can't have children.'

Ivor was put off guard by the indiscrete confession to new acquaintances. He did the best thing and tried to change the subject.

'Did you go touring or did you spend all your time here?'

'We've tried IVF several times, but nothing works,' continued Hal who wasn't listening to Ivor. He was downing another double whisky and was beginning to look drunk. He was obviously obsessed with their problem.

'What an idiot!' I thought to myself, looking across to Maggie and now understanding why she didn't insist that I wear a condom when we had made love. She just sat there silently, hoping that the moment would pass.

'What's IV . . .?' Tess couldn't finish the question, as I gently bumped her with my elbow. She looked at me crossly, but then noticed me put a finger to my mouth and quickly withdraw it again.

'I'm going to the rest room,' mumbled Maggie and she hurried out of the hall.

The music started again and I made my way to the dance floor with Tom and Tess. This time I didn't join in.

'I have to go to the loo,' I said. 'You guys begin.'

'What's IVF?' Tess insisted.

'It's fertility treatment to help you have babies,' I said.

I slipped out of the room, noticing from the corner of my eye that Hal was drinking and shouting as he chatted to Ivor. He didn't seem to notice me leaving. I rushed towards the toilets, feeling the thick carpets sink under me. I opened the door of the women's loo and slipped in. Three furious women glared at me.

'Sorry, wrong place,' I murmured, swiftly glancing at the cubicles and then withdrawing. I waited, but Maggie didn't come out. So I ran towards the reception room, up the hall to the lifts, but still couldn't find her. She must have escaped to their room. At the entrance of the dance hall I bumped into Hal.

His eyes were glazed and he swayed a bit.

'You OK?' I asked. 'You better see if Maggie's all right.'

He half lent towards me, but said nothing and made his way to the lift.

Back in the dance hall, I went to sit with Ivor again. He was looking at Hal's business card.

'Mergers and acquisitions guy. Bank Janderson,' said Ivor. 'Could be a good contact. He's quite knowledgeable about the mining business.'

I looked at the big white card and saw the name, 'Harold Humford'. Ivor put the card into his front pocket.

'He's pathetic!' I said angrily. I was still in love with Maggie, even though I knew that she was unattainable.

'Wasn't terribly discreet for a banker, was he?' said Ivor. 'That's what booze can do.'

Sets were forming on the dance floor again and this time, Tess and Tom pulled both Ivor and I onto the crowded floor. The tempo was fast, the band and laughter loud. Maggie and Hal were leaving tomorrow. As I danced thoughts kept whirling in my head. Maggie married? Would I ever see her again?

*   *   *

The next week we toured the Highlands and the West coast of Scotland. A few days later we were in Edinburgh for the annual summer festival. We watched the Military Tattoo within the grounds of Edinburgh Castle. It was a full moon. Scottish bands marched up and down blowing their bagpipes. Military bands from the West Indies, Australia and the US marched in different formations. The show continued and as the summer evening drew to a close, the castle lights went on and cannons boomed in a glorious finale. The thick crowd slowly shuffled towards the exits and down a cobbled narrow road towards the 'Royal Mile' and the City below.

During the next few days we saw lots of plays and shows. Big crowds watched musicians, comedians, acrobats and jugglers in the Royal Mile, the street that runs from Edinburgh Castle down to Holyrood Palace. Some sat high up on saddles of one wheel cycles and juggled balls and flaming torches. Actors pushed their way through the audiences and passed around leaflets advertising their shows.

The day before we left, Ivor put on his light linen suit to meet a business contact. We walked from the hotel to the Edinburgh International Book Festival. It was in the garden of Charlotte Square, which is surrounded by grey, stone, terraced town houses built about two hundred years ago.

'Fund managers control billions in those buildings,' said Ivor who was off to a meeting with one of them.

The twins and I wandered into tents in the garden where

authors were signing books and giving talks. A bookshop was in one of the tents and we were buying some books when my mobile rang. Ivor wanted me to meet him at the offices of Hastings & Murray, 15 Charlotte Square.

*   *   *

The Charlotte Square offices of Hastings & Murray were in a modest house at the corner of one of the terraces. Inside, thick beige carpets seemed to make the place soundproof. The twins sat down and read their new books and a receptionist took me through a narrow passageway into a small room. Ivor and the fund manager were chatting and sipping whisky.

'This is the boy,' said Ivor. 'It might be beginners luck, but he seems to have a feel for the market.'

The money manager rose. He was medium height and stocky with a small beard.

'Rob Hastings,' he said.

'Jack Miner,' I replied as he squeezed my hand tightly.

'I gather you've been doing well in the market, Jack,' said Hastings in a thick Scottish accent. He was studying me closely and I felt a bit uncomfortable.

'Tell him what you've bought Jack . . . It won't harm you if he knows.'

I had been having such a good holiday that I hadn't even thought about the market.

A computer terminal was on a table nearby.

'Can I take a look?' I asked.

'Sure,' replied Hastings.

I scrolled down the screen and glanced at the prices of my shares.

'They're going mad!' I cried.

'It's some boom isn't it?' smiled Ivor.

It sure was. Before I had left for Scotland, I had taken £1000 to pay for my holiday and had invested the remaining £49,000 that Stan had given me in bank shares. My gold shares had more than doubled and the bank shares were up about 30 per cent.

I looked at charts of my shares on the screen.

'Can I print off these charts?' I asked.

'Anything else?' asked Hastings.

'I don't have my share price stats with me. I need them.'

Hastings smiled, walked over to the computer, asked for the names of my shares and worked the keyboard. Charts and prices were soon running off the printer.

'Wow! Thanks,' I said. 'Do you mind if I look at these for a bit?'

'If it doesn't take too long,' said Hastings.

I sat down at the table grabbed some paper and quickly drew my aquarium. My gold fish were jumping out of the water. I drew my black bank fish. They had broken into the second level of the tank.

'Can I call Wardle to sell my gold shares?' I asked turning to Ivor.

'Go ahead,' said Hastings. He called his secretary, got the number and I was soon speaking to David Drummond.

'The gold market is going crazy,' shouted Drummond. 'Everyone's buying. You want some more?'

'No, I want to sell.'

'But . . . but, they could go higher!'

'Maybe, maybe not. If you don't want to sell them, can I speak to Jim?'

'No problem, Jack. I'll sell at best right away,' said Drummond. 'By the way Stan Slimcop is here. Do you want to speak to him?'

'Yes please.'

'Hi Stan, how's Leila?' I asked.

'She's fine. Are you selling your gold shares?'

'Yes.'

'The market's gone mad. I've also been selling. I'll get rid of my last ones today. What about your bank shares?'

'I'll keep them for the time being. See you in London, Stan. Thanks for the holiday. It's been great.'

I turned to Hastings: 'Sorry for taking your time.'

Hastings smiled: 'Thought about a career yet?'

'Not sure, but I like the stock market,' I said.

Hastings and Ivor grinned.

'He's still got two more years in school and then university,' said Ivor. 'He could contact you when he finishes.'

'About five years ago, they had a competition. A team of school girls versus fund managers,' said Hastings.

'No doubt the girls won,' chuckled Ivor.

'Not just once. Everytime!'

'So you're going to sack your fund managers and replace them with school girls,' said Ivor, laughing.

'Sounds like a good idea,' smiled Hastings. 'If Jack's interested, he could join us in London right away. It would be an interesting experiment for us.'

'Me?'

'It's up to you Jack. In Edinburgh we manage about £10 billion. We invest most of the money for pensions, charities and wealthy people mainly in Scotland, America and France,' Hastings said.

'French people? Has this got something to do with the history of the Scots and the French? Back to Mary Queen of Scots?'

'That's right. Did you learn that at school Jack?'

'No, I read about it and watched a history series on TV,' I said.

'There you go, Ivor. This young man reads and has general knowledge. Just what we want.'

I looked at Ivor, who was ruffling his white hair. I wasn't sure what to do.

'It's your life, Jack. Two years more at school and then a great time at university. Do you really want to work now? You've got more than enough money.'

Drummond phoned back. The shares were sold. I calculated quickly. Ivor was right. My bank shares and money in the bank were worth more than £100,000.

'Think about it Jack,' said Hastings. 'We have a small hedge fund business in London. My partner, Ronald Ruffish, can teach you a lot.'

'Hedge fund?'

'Hedge funds trade everything that moves – shares, commodities and currencies. Anything that goes up or down.'

He gave me his business card and a booklet about Hastings & Murray.

*   *   *

That night Ivor took us to a clown show that had come all the way from Moscow. They mimed, danced, jumped on trampolines and climbed high poles. There were eight in the show. I thought that I had seen one of them before, maybe on the Royal Mile. As the show continued and he somersaulted into the light, I felt a chill in my bones. His body seemed to be identical to the small wiry guy who had chased me on Charing Cross Bridge. But with clown makeup on, I couldn't be sure.

At one time in the act he was a statue. We were sitting in the third row and he seemed to gaze straight at me. They were the same piercing black eyes. I would never forget them. Could it be him? I shivered and wondered whether he had recognised me. I wanted to run out of the theatre, but that would have been stupid. He would then have noticed me. In any event, I had forgotten that I was in the audience and the lights were off. He was facing spotlights and couldn't see the faces of the audience properly. The show went on and the acrobat caught bottles and knives that were thrown at him. It was as if he was made of rubber, the way he quickly somersaulted backwards and then forwards. He tied another mime artist up, climbed a high bar and hanging onto the bar with his feet, pulled the artist upwards. He then held the rope with his teeth and loosened the knot with his hands, grabbing his partner by his legs when he was about to fall on to the floor.

'So that's how they managed to hang Yapolovitch from the bridge,' I thought to myself. I was now almost certain that the mime artist was one of the killers.

The show came to an end and the lights came on. The

audience clapped and I noticed in the front row a group of noisy and drunk Russians. They were clapping and cheering in their own language. One of them had a bottle of vodka. It was against the house rules to drink inside the theatre, but they were swigging from the bottle. The men wore smart casual clothes. They were with beautiful girls, with huge diamond earrings and massive ruby and sapphire rings.

The actors bowed time and time again and waved to the Russians. I held up the programme in front of my face and peeped with one eye. The snake tattoo was on his right forearm. The same one I had seen when I was running away from them. It was definitely him. I read the biographies in the programme and found that the man's name was Boris Krepolovitch. He was an acrobat, clown and mime artist in Russian circuses and shows.

We gradually made our way towards the exit and when we were outside we passed the stage door. The group of drunk Russians were there. Krepolovitch came out the door and a tall handsome Russian with thick blond hair, shook his hand. I felt sick. Krepolovitch turned towards us, but I had slipped behind Ivor, so that he couldn't see me.

Later, we had tea and cakes at a posh hotel and the Russian group and groupies walked in with some of the mime artists. They sat around the bar and ordered champagne. I breathed a sigh of relief because Krepolovitch wasn't with them. The tall guy with blond hair, combed backwards, was the centre of attention. The others seemed to be sucking up to him.

'Some Russians have become mega rich,' said Ivor.

'I thought that the Russian people were poor,' I said.

'How did these people make their money?'

'Russia has huge natural resources. After the Soviet Union collapsed around 1990, Russia became independent. Boris Yeltsin who was then the Russian president sold stakes in oil, natural gas, aluminium and other raw materials for a song.'

'Why?'

'Russia had huge debts. People were poverty stricken and the government needed the money. The country off-loaded large quantities of its metals on the market and prices collapsed. Mining companies were doing badly. Yeltsin was drunk most of the time and there was a lot of corruption. To cut a long story short, a few shrewd Russians backed by Western banks and other firms, bought the mines very cheaply.'

'And then prices recovered,' I said.

'Yes. Within a few years Yeltsin had created billionaires, let alone millionaires,' said Ivor with a hollow laugh. 'They call those Russians, oligarchs.'

'The guys who are buying football clubs, that sort of thing,' I said.

'That's right. Below the oligarchs are other rich Russians who have been doing all sorts of deals. Some are criminals operating in gangs. They're the Russian mafia.'

'Have you come across any of these people?'

'Yes. I was a consultant on some of their gold and diamond exploration ventures. They pay well, but I would never invest in their projects. They made me feel uneasy.'

'I know the feeling,' I said.

'You've come across them?' asked Ivor.

I shook my head. Stan was keeping his word. He had kept my awful secret.

'Do you know any of these people?' I asked looking in the direction of the bar where the Russians were laughing and drinking.'

'The tall blond guy, with girls hanging on to him, is Yevgeny Faramazov. I've seen him at mining conferences. I've never met him personally, but I've heard that he invests a lot of money in mines in Russia, Africa and South America. I'm not sure whether he's a goody or baddy.'

There was no way I was going to tell Ivor what I thought. Here, there, everywhere, how was I to escape them. Just keep my head down, I guess. Hope that Stan was right and they would forget what I looked like. I was very glad that I was returning to London, the next day. I would be far away from Krepolovitch. The Edinburgh festival was continuing for another three weeks. Hopefully, he would remain there and then go back to Russia.

11

THE INCUBATOR

I walked out of Green Park Station into the sun and fresh breeze. It was the beginning of September and after much rain in the past week, the park was lush. A sign showed that one of the paths led to Buckingham Palace, but I turned around and climbed the stairs and was on Piccadilly, a West End thoroughfare. On my right, overlooking the park, was the Ritz Hotel. I wanted to walk in and take a peek. Mum used to daydream that she would take me for tea there one day. Unfortunately, no time. I was on my way to have lunch with Ronald Ruffish, head of Hastings & Ruffish, the London division of Hastings & Murray. We would be meeting at Brown's Hotel in Albemarle Street, across the road from the Ritz.

The weeks since the Scottish holiday had gone fast. My GCSE results were out and had amazed me. I got As for English, history, maths and IT, Bs for physics and chemistry and Cs for French and Spanish. The only blot was a D for religious studies, but that didn't bother me as I had found the subject boring and didn't revise much.

I phoned my old friends in Bridlington and found that

most of them had done OK. Jack Miner was the surprise. Results far better than expected. James Horsely, the headmaster wanted me to do my AS levels, but there was no way I was going back to Bridlington. A London school was a possibility. Stan, Leila and Martha tried to persuade me to continue, but I decided to phone Jim Hastings in Edinburgh and he arranged a meeting with Mr Ruffish. They were serious about offering me a job.

I flopped down in one of the leather armchairs of Brown's, a posh, discreet 19th century Georgian hotel and glanced at the brochure. Rudyard Kipling wrote "Jungle Book" while he stayed there and Winston Churchill was a visitor. If only Mum and Dad could have seen me. Yorkshire boy, in my fancy dark blue suit, opposite some rich, maybe famous people, who were chatting on a huge pink sofa.

I felt relaxed. If Ruffish didn't like me, or I decided not to take the job, I could still finish school and go to university. There was nothing to lose. Ruffish walked into the hotel. I recognised him from his picture in the Hastings & Murray information pack. He stooped slightly, but I think he was only mid-fifties. I could see that he was wearing a toupee. I had expected Ruffish to be in an expensive suit. That is what city guys were supposed to wear. Instead he had a brown suede jacket over an open neck shirt. I stood up and he walked towards me with a slight limp. His skin was sallow and he had tired, kindly, sunken brown eyes.

'Ron Ruffish,' he said, shaking my hand. 'Sorry I'm late. Let's have something to eat.'

We went into a large half empty dining room and sat down at a table in the corner.

After ordering some soft drinks, and talking a bit about school, Ruffish got to the point quickly.

'Rob Hastings told me that you turned ten thousand into a hundred in only three months!'

'It wasn't all my money, Mr Ruffish,' I said. 'A friend followed my trades and gave me a cut of his profits.'

'That's against market regulations! You have to be a registered advisor.'

'No, no! I didn't ask him for anything, Mr Ruffish. He gave it to me after he made a killing in gold shares.'

'Do you think he'll back you again?'

'Dunno. I told him that I bought bank shares.'

'Completely different businesses. Why did you choose them?'

'They looked as if they were going up.'

'That's all? You didn't study the gold market? What about banking?'

'I just read a few books about investing, decided that prices were heading higher and bought.'

'So you follow a system. Technical analysis? Momentum?'

'Nothing fancy. I just look at what happened in the past and what's happening now. If I think the shares are beginning to rise, I buy.'

He studied my face closely, but it was difficult to gauge what he was thinking. I guessed that he was sceptical. A waiter came up and I ordered steak and chips and he Dover sole, vegetables and a salad.

'Ivor Ensworth speaks highly of you. Do you have another reference?'

'I met him through Stanley Slimcop.'

'That's a name from the past! When I first came to the City about forty years ago, I applied for a job at Safron and Slimcop. It was one of the biggest brokers in London. They were about to take me on board when . . .'

'The firm went bust.'

'Yes, that's right. Then he recovered. They call him the Silver Fox. Well I never! Is he the one who's backing you?'

I didn't answer.

'I like discretion. Our business is confidential. That's a very strict rule.'

Our food arrived. The steak was OK and the chips were almost as good as the fat tasty ones that we used to sell at "Our Plaice". Ruffish chatted about the good times in the City. Those were the bull markets when shares kept rising and he was paid big bonuses and made lots of money. Then he spoke about the bear markets when shares kept falling. Thousands of City people, including him, lost their jobs.

'When the bad days seemed to continue forever and everyone was gloomy, the market would always bottom out,' said Ruffish. 'The newspapers were another sign. When the front page carried stories about financial crises, the worst was always over.'

'Just like the bank crisis a few weeks ago?' I said.

He seemed impressed that I had followed the news. But he didn't know the real reason.

'Never fails. When there's extreme pessimism, close your eyes and buy. You had the right idea and bought bank shares. I like that,' he said.

'Luck helps,' I said modestly.

'I was tired of relying on a bull market to earn my living,' said Ruffish continuing with his own story. 'So about three years ago, I decided to open a hedge fund business. The good thing about hedge funds is that they can make money when the market rises and falls.'

'How do you do that?'

'I'll explain later.'

'So when did you start managing hedge funds?' I asked.

'About two years ago. I approached Hastings & Murray and they backed me. They own the business, but I've got a stake in it,' said Ruffish. 'Hastings & Ruffish only manage around two hundred million, but we're growing fast.'

'Mr Hastings said that you might have a job for me.'

'Maybe. By the way, what did your father do?'

'He had a fish and chip shop. I helped him.'

'You went to school and served in a fish and chip shop?'

'Sometimes I woke up early and went to the fish market with him. He haggled over prices. They liked him and gave him good deals. I didn't like cleaning fish. I preferred serving behind the counter.'

'Did you ever mind the shop on your own?'

'When Dad was sick, I went to the market to buy fish. Sometimes my friends gave me a hand. We had a good trade on Fridays and weekends, but our prices were too low.'

'Was the business doing badly?'

'Expenses were high, Mr Ruffish. We went down. My Dad died in June.'

'Call me Ruff,' he said sympathetically, 'Must have been hard for your family.'

'Mum died a few years before my Dad. I don't have brothers and sisters.'

There was silence for a moment. I felt uncomfortable. His questions were bringing back memories. I turned away from him and he called the waiter and asked for the bill.

'You grew up quickly didn't you,' said Ruffish thoughtfully. 'Fish and chips! You've been buying and selling since you were a little boy. I think Rob's right. You're a natural trader. Want to join us or go back to school?'

'I'll have a go.'

*   *   *

Ruffish's office was in Charles Street, just off Berkeley Square. This was Mayfair, hedge fund land, home of some of the sharpest traders in the world. He had told me that hedge fund managers chose prestigious and expensive Mayfair to impress the rich and famous. The Ritz, Brown's, Claridges and other top hotels are close by and their clients can shop in Bond Street and Savile Row and be in walking distance from West End theatres and Soho restaurants. Some hedge funds also have offices in Knightsbridge near Harrods. Investment banks are in the ancient City of London and Canary Wharf, Docklands, on the east side of the River Thames. They are the prime brokers of hedge funds and earn billions in commissions from buying and selling their shares, bonds, currencies and commodities. The brokers also earn interest by lending the hedge funds huge amounts of money to do more deals that in turn bring them even more commissions. Some business!

I rang the bell and on the sound of the buzzer, the latch

opened. I entered a musty, dimly lit hallway. At the end of it, was one of those ancient lifts with black, crossed iron gratings. You had to clutch the brass handle to open the door. Inside the tiny space, I pulled the door closed and pressed the button for the fifth floor. The rickety lift went up slowly, making me wonder how often they had tested the cable. It felt as if it could fall at any moment. No way would I use that lift again.

I got out at the fifth floor and saw the 'Hastings & Ruffish' plate. A young brunette, in a low cut light blue summer dress, opened the door.

'I have an appointment with Mr Ruffish,' I said.

The office was completely different from the rest of the building. The walls had been knocked down, leaving a large room. In some ways it was like the Chinese restaurant in Hampstead. Everything was white. The walls were white. Fund managers and other staff were in their own working spaces that were bordered by white round bookcases. People sat on white chairs. White Apple laptops with large flat screens were on their white desks. Next to them were terminals showing prices, charts and news.

In the far distant corner there was a glass enclosure. Through the glass I saw Ruffish looking at his screen. I knocked on his glass door. He stood up, shook my hand and we both sat down on a large white leather sofa.

'Want some coffee, Jack?'

I nodded my head: 'Is this place an office or a hospital?'

'Sometimes an office. Other times a hospital. Depends how we're doing,' replied Ruffish chuckling, despite my cheek. 'Two coffees please Bess.'

She returned with two cups and he introduced us. Bess nodded and walked out.

'Let me explain what you'll be doing, Jack,' said Ruffish. 'We're going to incubate your own hedge fund.'

'Incubate my hedge fund?'

'Just like a chick, Jack. We look after independent fund managers in a warm friendly environment. We help them grow and lay golden eggs for themselves and us,' said Ruffish. 'They put in their own money and we also invest in the fund.'

'How much money must I invest in my incubator?'

'We talk in dollars here and the fund's going to start with $500,000. From what you've told me, you must put in half the money that you have in the stock market. That's about $100,000.'

'I might as well invest everything,' I said, converting my pounds to dollars. 'I've got about $200,000.'

Ruffish looked pleased with the response.

'OK we'll double the amount we're putting in. Your fund will start with $1 million. Hastings & Ruffish will invest $800,000 and you $200,000.'

'Am I going to manage this fund all on my own?'

'Eventually yes. But at first one of the fund managers will supervise you.'

'Do I sell my shares before we start?'

'Only if you think that the time is right. You're going to manage a macro hedge fund.'

'What's that?'

'You can use your trading system to buy or sell shares, currencies, commodities, bonds. Anything that you believe will make money on the way up or down.'

'How do I make money when the market is going down?'

'You sell short. You borrow shares and sell them. If their prices fall, you buy them back at a profit. If they go up you lose. You can also sell futures and options.'

He noticed my puzzled expression.

'Don't worry. I'll get one of the fund managers to explain how to do it. Our hedge funds charge a two per cent annual management fee and a twenty per cent performance fee. The only investors at this stage will be the firm and yourself. You must take investment exams before you are allowed to manage money for outside investors. We're going to pay you a small salary of $4,000 a month and you'll receive an annual bonus of five per cent on any profit. Are you happy with that?'

Happy? I was ecstatic. I would get $48,000 a year. That was about £30,000, about £10,000 more than Dad paid himself, before he died. If the fund went up I would make money on my own investments and get a bonus as well. What a deal! Some work experience!

'Come and meet the team,' said Ruffish. 'We have four fund managers here, each doing their own thing with emerging market funds. We incubated them and their funds have grown rapidly.'

'Emerging?'

'Stock markets in developing countries – China and the rest of Asia, Eastern Europe, Africa and South America.'

'What about Britain, Europe and America?'

'There are too many of those hedge funds. We can't compete. You'll see at our morning meeting that we have seriously smart guys who know their countries. One is a mathematician, another an astrophysicist, the third a barrister and the fourth an accountant.'

'And me with my mediocre GCSEs!' I thought. 'Maybe I should get the hell out of here.'

Ruffish seemed to read my mind: 'You're an experiment Jack! Just do your best.'

He led me to a door on the other side of the room. We entered a passage with an adjoining toilet and shower room on the one end and a fairly large meeting room on the other.

It had a large round table, a *Reuters* screen, a laptop and whiteboard on the wall at the far end. Soon after we sat down, the other fund managers filed in. Ruffish introduced me and asked them to explain what they did. They were casually dressed. No ties and jackets. I felt out of place and took off my suit jacket and tie. They looked at me curiously. The meeting was totally relaxed. Bess came in with a notebook and took notes. I noticed two of the men ogle her cleavage. She didn't let on whether they annoyed her.

Krishna Doomassamy, small and thin, with fine features and an open necked white shirt was the mathematician. He played the Asian markets, including India, Singapore, Malaysia, Indonesia, Thailand, Hong Kong and Taiwan. He looked as if he was in his early thirties. Tong Chong Ping, an astrophysicist, with black framed glasses, was a little taller, but just as slim. It was difficult to gauge his age. He could have been anywhere between twenty five and forty. Tong spoke with a thick Chinese accent and his speciality, unsurprisingly, was China and Hong Kong.

Aram Zabkian, shook my hand warmly, telling me that he came from Estonia in Eastern Europe. His light pink shirt was open at the top and exposed a hairy chest. He was an accountant, about forty, balding, stocky with bulging muscles and had a neat small beard. It was evident that he irritated Bess. He touched her arm when he asked her to pass him a glass of water and she pushed him away in disgust. Aram's fund covered Russia, the Czech Republic, Poland, Hungary, Estonia and other Eastern European markets. The final fund manager came in a little late. She was a big woman, who towered over the others. Her long black hair was braided and she wore a light cream suit. I assumed that she would have an African accent, but it was very British.

'Are you the barrister?' I asked meekly, guessing that she was the lawyer who Ruffish had talked about.

'Graduate from Oxford University, no less,' said Krishna. 'Themba Shaka Mafuta meet Jack Miner.'

I shook her hand.

'Call me Maffie for short,' she said smiling. 'I mainly cover resource shares in Southern Africa and South America.'

'Maffie is a descendant of the Zulu King Shaka. He conquered Southern Africa,' said Krishna smiling. 'Watch out for her! Shaka was a brute. If his soldiers were out of line, he would beat them with a "knob kierie".'

He stood up, clutched a long ruler and waved it around like a big stick.

'Knob kieries are thicker than that!' laughed Maffie, grabbing the ruler from Krishna and gently tapping him on his shoulder. 'My great, great, great, great, great granddad, used to hammer them on the head if they didn't perform.

How have you done this month, Krishna?'

'I think you'll reprieve him this month, Maffie,' said

Ruffish. 'He's doing pretty well. And you Maffie. Are you winning like, your great, great, great, whatever?'

'The market's doing OK, thanks Ruff.'

'What did you do at university, Jack?' asked Tong, looking me up and down.

I felt embarrassed and shuffled about restlessly.

'Jack's going to university later. We're trying out something. Raw talent against you geniuses,' said Ruffish.

'Is he doing work experience, Ruff?' asked Aram. He had obviously worked out that I was no more than sixteen or seventeen.

'We're incubating him. He's going to run a small fund,' replied Ruffish.

'The Schoolboy Fund?' scoffed Aram. The others looked at me sceptically.

I thought that I had better stand up to this lot. Otherwise they would ride all over me.

'The Aquarium Fund?' I suggested.

'Sounds a good name, Jack,' said Ruffish. 'Jack used to help his Dad in a fish and chip shop. He bought fish at the market. He knows value. Have any of you guys traded the real thing? Been in a real business?'

'I've traded tins of baked beans, sardines and sweets. We'll offer you a special discount at my Dad's grocery shop, Jack,' said Krishna, half joking.

'Don't laugh guys. I'm sure you've read in the papers about schoolboys and girls who beat fund managers,' said Maffie. 'Are you happy to supervise Jack, Maffie?' asked Ruffish.

'Sure. Schoolboy and Woman. Aquarium will surprise you bigots,' joked Maffie.

During the rest of the meeting they talked about various markets and how their funds were doing. Afterwards Ruffish and Maffie took me to my own working space. On the desk were a cordless phone, large laptop and a *Bloomberg* screen showing prices, charts and news reports.

'Do you have chart books here?' I asked.

'We run off charts on the printer, but we also subscribe to a chart service,' said Ruffish. 'I'm old-fashioned, I'm the only one that looks at them.'

'If Jack wants them, you're back in fashion,' grinned Maffie.

*   *   *

The days passed quickly and autumn and winter swiftly followed. Early in the morning I would go for a run with Jazz and Pattie, have a quick shower, climb on to a bus in Swains Lane, opposite the Heath, and be in the office by 9am. By December, it was too dark, cold and wet to go out for a run, so the dogs had to wait for Martha. I hated going to work in the grey pre-dawn light and coming back in the dark. Longed for the spring.

Ruffish insisted that I study for the Investment Management Institute examinations. It was a pain to wade through the boring text books in my free time. But Ruffish and Maffie said that I had to do it. If I didn't pass, the Financial Services Authority, the market regulator, wouldn't allow me to manage money for investors. In the meantime I could only trade on behalf of myself and the firm.

I kept in contact with Ivor Ensworth and Tom and Tess

by email. He invited me to go to South Africa for Christmas, but I decided to spend it with Martha. Occasionally I would go and visit the Slimcops or go out with them for dinner. I was grateful that Stan had paid off Dad's creditors and especially happy that Gill Derby had received her back rent plus interest. Bailey & Baton were at last off my back. Stan's solicitor was a tough negotiator and had pushed the furious Baton's fee down to a derisory £1,000. Even that was far too much!

Leila introduced me to quite a nice girl. Suzi, an artist, was plump and pretty, but not really my type. I went out with her a few times and I'm not sure who dumped who. She didn't seem to be terribly keen. I spent evenings at my local in Swains Lane and other pubs in Hampstead or Highgate and met a few girls. We went to restaurants and movies. But there was nothing serious. I played football on Sundays and had drinks with the players afterwards. I didn't have much in common with them other than joking about football teams we supported. None of them were interested in cricket. I was an outsider from Yorkshire and accepted it. I felt pretty relaxed and the bad times, including the bridge, became distant memories.

Newspapers no longer carried anything about the Yapolovitch murder. Case unsolved. Old news. I was no longer scared and money wasn't a problem. There was more than enough to keep me going. Sometimes I thought about Sandy and Maggie. Wondered what they were doing. Maffie was now the only girl who interested me, even though she was older. Unfortunately she only wanted me as a friend. We often went to lunch together and joked around.

I bought a book on Shaka, King of the Zulus. He was an exceptional military strategist. So much so that historians called him the 'Black Napoleon', after the brilliant, ruthless, French Emperor and Commander who dominated Europe around 1800. Shaka's favourite battle manoeuvre was the pincer movement, which he called the 'Horns of the Buffalo'. His Zulu impis, or regiments, would advance towards the enemy in the formation of a buffalo's horns. Shaka's main force was in the centre and there were regiments on the left and right, just like horns. The impis in the centre would run towards the enemy with their spears held high. As soon as they clashed, the regiments on the left and right horn would turn inwards and surround the enemy from the rear. Shaka never lost a battle. Dingaan, his jealous brother, murdered him.

'Maffie, do you think Shaka's tactics could work in the markets?' I asked when we were having a light lunch in a French brasserie, near the office. It was spring and for a change, the sun was shining. I enjoyed going there with her, as she spoke French and joked with the waiters.

'Shaka believed that the best form of defence was attack,' she said. 'I guess that's what I do. Research shares and without any hesitation, buy or sell. If you vacillate you lose.'

'You qualified as a barrister, why did you become a fund manager?'

'It's a long story. My father, Lucky Mafuta, was an anti-apartheid activist in the seventies and eighties. He spent time on Robben Island, when Nelson Mandela was there.'

'So you were a little girl when he was in prison?'

'Yes. Those were tough times. My mother had to bring

up four children in a hut with one room. We were very poor. She struggled to find enough money to visit him in prison. So we moved to Cape Town.'

'When did Lucky get out?'

'Soon after Nelson was released. When Lucky was young he was a socialist. But after South Africa became a democracy in 1994, Mandela wanted the blacks to share the whites' wealth. My father was a miner and the big mining companies made him a director and gave him shares. So he became a rich capitalist.'

'Why didn't you stay in South Africa?'

'To be quite frank, Jack, my Dad embarrassed me. From being a struggling activist with high ideals, he became a fat cat,' she continued. 'The government managed to spread some of the whites' wealth, but it landed in the pockets of elitist blacks. The rest of the people remained very poor. I felt guilty about that, so I decided to leave.'

'You're still privileged.'

She winced: 'I wanted to prove to myself that I could go it alone. So I studied hard and did well at school. For the hell of it, I applied to Oxford. I was amazed when they accepted me. I studied law because I was interested in human rights. But when I qualified as a barrister I couldn't get much work, so I became disenchanted.'

'You could have practised in South Africa.'

'I would have had to retake the exams. English law is different to South African. They practice Roman Dutch Law there.'

'That doesn't prevent you from taking the exams.'

'Too late, I've got used to earning a good living. I don't

have to rely on any money from Lucky,' she laughed. 'My fund allows me to keep an eye on Africa. I can monitor corruption. I'm a trustee and advisor of a human rights group.'

'What about your love life, Maffie?' I asked touching the back of her hand. She withdrew it quickly.

'How many times do I have to tell you, Jack? We're good friends. I don't want to spoil that.'

Maffie noticed the disappointment on my face. She knew that at work, things weren't going right for me. It seemed that my gold and bank stock winnings were just beginners luck. I had become frustrated with my trading. I had followed the Manson way, but the system wasn't working. It required patience, but hedge funds are supposed to perform consistently every month. If the shares aren't making profits, you have to close your positions. I wasn't used to that.

At first the shares that I had bought rose about five to ten per cent and then slipped back. Under the risk controls of the fund, I was 'stopped out'. This meant that my losses were limited to a maximum of ten per cent. Time and time again, I was forced to sell. Previously I would have waited. Indeed, several of the shares that I sold, went up a lot afterwards, but it was too late for me, as I was already out.

I had to follow the rules of the hedge fund game and rigidly follow Ruffish's risk controls. That was reasonable from his point of view. He was risking the company's money and couldn't take any chances. I made money some months, but March wasn't a good one. The $1 million fund had fallen to $900,000 and I had traded actively with no success, for six months. It seemed that the boy trader experiment was a flop.

I was having lunch with Maffie that day, because she cheered me up. I was miserable ahead of a meeting with Ruffish early afternoon and was sure that he would fire me. Maffie punched my arm gently.

'In South Africa they call me Themba. It means "Trust, Hope and Faith". That's what you should have Jack.'

'I have trusted myself, but it hasn't got me very far,' I said gloomily as we walked back to the office. 'I like Themba. Why do you call yourself Maffie?'

'Maffie's short for Mafuta. It means Fat. They used to call me fatty Maffie at school. The nickname stuck.'

I glanced at her, but couldn't tell what was hidden under her flowing dress.

'You're not fat, Maffie,' I lied.

She laughed: 'Really? I spend my life dieting. Exercise doesn't seem to work.'

'You could run with me this weekend, Maffie. I could be your personal trainer. My fee is . . .'

I lent over and gave her a kiss on her cheek.

'I think church will cool your ardour Jack. Did you know that I'm in a gospel choir? Come and hear us next Sunday.'

'Provided I see your Zulu war dance after Ruff fires me,' I said half joking.

She slapped me on the back cheerfully and we walked into the building and raced up the stairs.

Aram Zabkian was leaving Ruffish's office as I was about to enter.

'Caught any fish yet, Jack?' he sneered. 'Your aquarium must be almost empty by now.'

I bit my lip. It was best to ignore him. Ruffish was looking at the Aquarium Fund file, when I walked in. He pulled out the results for the end of March. I waited for the worst.

'You're struggling to get going, Jack. Any problems? Girlfriends? Family? Money? Tell me, I'm here to help.'

'I guess the incubator isn't working,' I replied glumly. 'Your chick hasn't hatched.'

'You've been here six months, trading like mad, but you're still down ten per cent. That's not terrible, but not terribly good either.'

'If I continue like this, we'll be down a lot more.'

'Yes, I'm afraid you're right,' sighed Ruffish.

He examined the results over the period; three months when the fund went up and three down months. Down overall, despite all the trading! Only the brokers did well.

'Maybe it's time you went back to school, Jack?'

'Too late. Must wait until September.'

Maffie knocked on the door. Ruffish waved her away. She ignored him and walked in.

'The other guys think that you're crazy to let him manage money. My view is that you should give him more time.'

'And lose more money?'

'You were going to try him out for a year, so stick to that Ruff,' Maffie insisted. 'The other funds are doing pretty well, but emerging markets turn quickly. Who knows? Our funds could slump. He could carry us one day.'

'What do you want to do, Jack?' asked Ruffish. 'You can't be enjoying this.'

'I dunno. I feel like a footballer who is out of form. I just need a good game.'

'Give him another game,' said Maffy. 'I'll back him. But

first he must pass his exams. If he does, I'll put $100,000 in Aquarium.'

'I know your fund's performed. But that's a fair whack from your Christmas bonus, Maffie. Sure you want to do this?'

'Sure. He's learnt a lot in the past six months. He'll come right. I'm sure of it.'

The next few weeks, I worked hard on the investment course. I sat the exams expecting to fail, but by some miracle, passed. I was now on the way to becoming a fully fledged fund manager. Maffie kept her word and put in $100,000 of her own money. The fund's capital was back to $1 million.

*   *   *

Maffie lived in Kennington, not far from the Imperial War Museum in south London. I was to meet her there at the museum at 10.30am, but I arrived earlier to wander around the place. I climbed up to the cockpit of a Lancaster bomber and looked inside. The plane was huge, but inside it looked cramped. It must have been a sitting duck for German Messerschmitt fighter planes. I walked over to the First World War Section where they simulated the trenches and watched a film about the Battle of the Somme. It put everything in perspective. Succeed or fail in the next few months, I was one of today's fortunate people. Teenagers in the trenches were lucky to reach their twentieth birthday. Many who lived, lost an arm, leg, or eye or eventually died from the effects of mustard gas poisoning. Most World War

I veterans were either shell-shocked or had nightmares for years afterwards.

I waited outside for Maffie. It was Sunday. The first week in April. The warm sun brought out the best in the red, pink, white, purple and black tulips that were swaying gently in the spring breeze. I hadn't felt as relaxed and good as this for a long time. Sitting on the stairs of the museum, next to the columns, I read a book about Christmas Day, 1914 when the British and the German soldiers played football. The next day they were killing each other again.

I looked up and saw her. She was all in white and looked beautiful. The braids were gone and long straight black thick hair, gleaming in the sun, fell over her shoulders. If only she wanted me as much as I wanted her.

Maffie came up and kissed me lightly on both cheeks: 'Hi there soldier! Ready for some gospel.'

She looked me up and down and said that I looked good.

I was going to be Maffie's escort at some fancy lunch after the service and was glad that she approved. We walked to the church, which was a short distance away from the museum. The traffic was dense and noisy, but in a quiet turning, it seemed as if we were slipping back a few centuries. The Georgian church with its white clean walls stood before us. Not far from the green lawn in front was its graveyard with tombstones going back three to four hundred years.

Maffie introduced me to a cheerful, young couple. I walked into the church with them and looked around. It was packed, with a dozen white faces at the most. The vicar of the church didn't deliver the normal boring sermon.

Instead he whipped his congregation into a frenzy. Praised God, Jesus and the community.

'Love your brothers and sisters be they Christian, Muslim or Jew,' he shouted, holding up his fist.

'Amen. Hallelujah,' cried the congregation in response.

The vicar went on making them more and more excited.

'When a man is down, what do you do?'

'Pick him up!' the congregation shouted. 'Jesus loves, Jesus forgives!'

The huge preacher beamed, white teeth shining. Dressed in a black, red and gold robe, he stood out from the choir, only a few feet behind him. All the women were in white. The men wore white shirts and black trousers. It wasn't a church service. It was more like a show and what a performance! Gospel music, moving and uplifting. Sopranos, bass and tenors in harmony. It was not much different from the soul music that my Dad liked so much. In the stifling cell where I'm writing this, I can still hear those wonderful sounds in my head.

Time passed by unnoticed, as members of the choir sang solo and the chorus and the congregation followed. I never thought that I had much of a voice, but I got carried away and sang along with them.

'Singing does a lot for your soul,' said Lettie, the pretty friend of Maffie. I nodded my head. For the first time in my life, I had a true religious experience and it felt good. We stepped out of the church into the bright spring sun. Maffie came up glowing and gave me a huge bear hug. She introduced me to the preacher who shook my hands warmly.

'God bless you young man. I could see that you enjoyed it. Come back any time.'

                              *   *   *

Later Maffie and I climbed into a taxi to go to the lunch. The cab got stuck in thick traffic. At the pace that we were going, we were likely to arrive at tea! As the cab crawled passed Elephant & Castle, we decided to get out and rush for the underground. Luckily there wasn't the usual weekend repair works on the line and within half an hour we arrived at Gloucester Road Station. The Coffee Board of India was hosting the lunch at the Bombay Brasserie, nearby.

We arrived about halfway through the buffet lunch. I was expecting a small number of people. But when we walked into the large conservatory in the courtyard at the back of the restaurant, there was a large crowd there. Maffie had told me that the lunch was being held ahead of talks at the International Coffee Organisation. She was meeting some contacts from South America and Africa to get some information about their economies and markets.

I felt small and out of place. These were top government officials from Brazil, Colombia, Costa Rica, Kenya, Ghana, Guatemala, Jamaica, India, Indonesia and other coffee producing nations. They were going to negotiate with delegates from the leading coffee consuming nations – the US, Germany, France, Britain, Italy, Japan and other countries.

We filled our plates with tandoories, curries and poppadoms and found two empty places on a large round table. Two Colombian delegates were at our table. Maffie spoke Spanish and I listened, admiring her. Maffie was not only a lawyer and fund manager, but a singer and linguist. Besides English, Zulu and Xhosa, she could speak French and Spanish. She could even converse with the Brazilians in Portuguese.

The Colombian on my left, realised that I couldn't understand a word.

'Louis Rondario,' he said, giving me his card. He was a top official of the Colombian Coffee Federation, based in Bogata.

'Jack Miner,' I replied. 'I'm afraid I know nothing about coffee. I just go to Starbucks and places like that.'

'A cup of coffee costs you about £1.50, right? That's almost $3,' said Rondario.

'Not sure, never think about the price.'

'No of course you don't. You buy coffee in the supermarket. It costs you about £2.80. That's almost $5, correct?'

'I think so. My landlady buys Fairtrade coffee. They say that they give the farmers a good deal.'

There was a hint of sarcasm in his chuckle: 'Really? Your packet at the supermarket weighs about half a pound. So they are selling you coffee for around $10 a pound. Guess the average price of coffee for farmers in the past six months.'

I thought about the fishing business and the price chain. The fishermen sell fish to the market, which in turn sells to the fishmonger and shops and then the customer. 'Around $3 to $4?'

By now a few around the table were listening.

'60 cents. That's what the Colombians and Brazilians get.

We Ghanaians, 48 cents,' shouted a big woman sporting a red and yellow African headdress.

'That's peanuts!' I said.

'They screw us on those as well!'

'Why is your price lower than the Colombians?'

'Colombia, Brazil and other South and Central American countries produce Arabica coffee. It's mild and more expensive than African Robusta coffee which is more bitter . . ..Just like we feel,' she said with a hollow laugh.

'And a year to two years ago, what price coffee?'

Rondario didn't wait for an answer: 'About a $1 a pound Arabica and about 90 cents Robusta. And in the shops? $10 a pound!'

'I know you guys think that you've been screwed,' said Maffie, itching for a good debate. 'But your green coffee beans from the trees must be stored in your warehouses and shipped to the US, Europe and Japan. Lorries must then take the coffee to the manufacturers that roast the coffee beans, so that they're ready for drinking. The coffee must be packaged and distributed to the retailers. They must advertise it. All that costs a lot of money. Labour, machinery, fuel, insurance, rent and marketing. I could go on. Aren't all these guys in the chain entitled to a profit? To a living?'

'We don't dispute that! All we're saying is that between 60 cents and $10 there is one a hell of a gap. Jack's guess is about right. Coffee farmers should be getting $3 to $4 a pound.'

'OK, you think that they're screwing you. So why can't you raise your prices? It's a free market,' argued Maffie.

'That's our big complaint. As an African you should

know that only too well, even with your Oxford accent,' said
the coffee delegate from Ghana, a little nastily.

Maffie shrugged and I defended her.

'Maffie's a lawyer. She believes in both sides of the story.
Why are your prices so low?'

'There used to be international coffee, cocoa and sugar
agreements to help poor farmers in developing countries,'
explained Rondario. 'The aim was to give the producers
a fair deal and consumers a fair stable price. There were
minimum prices to help farmers make a living and support
their families and a maximum price to protect buyers.'

I was puzzled: 'How did you manage that? If the farmers
had big crops, how could they prevent prices from falling?'

'Good question. Producers and consuming nations would
meet once or twice a year and thrash out an International
Coffee Agreement. The deal was that farmers around the
world were given production quotas. When there was a
glut of coffee, farmers around the world would plant less
to reduce the size of their crops. If there was a shortage,
quotas would be increased and producers would farm more
to supply the coffee manufacturers. The agreement was to
keep coffee in a price range to satisfy the farmers and Nestlé,
Maxwell, Lavazza and other manufacturers.'

'Why did the agreement fall apart?'

'Quite simple, you can't interfere with the free market,'
said Maffie. 'When there are crop failures, prices go through
the roof. The farmers always want more and the consumers
want lower prices. Those sorts of agreements always fail.'

'That's true to some extent. It sometimes took three
weeks into the early hours of the morning to come to an

agreement,' recalled Romario. 'Then the Americans, British and Germans decided that they had had enough.'

'That was the eighties and early nineties when President Reagan and Margaret Thatcher were in power. They believed in the free market,' Maffie said.

'And do you know what then happened? Prices of coffee collapsed,' said Romario angrily. 'Thousand upon thousands of coffee trees were left untended because the farmers were so poor. The land was eventually sold. Guess who bought it?'

He didn't wait for an answer.

'The Colombian drug barons. The land is now used to farm coca to make cocaine! So much for your free market!'

'OK, OK, I take your point,' said Maffie. 'So why are you bothering to meet this week?'

'We want to discuss how to increase consumption around the world. Then your free market should lift prices,' said Romario. 'If the price doesn't rise, more coffee farms will close down.'

'Where do you hold your meeting?' I asked.

'Berners Street, in the West End. You can't observe the meeting of course, but there's a visitor centre. It explains what coffee is all about. You can taste our coffee there.'

An idea began to germinate in my head.

12

THE COFFEE TRADER

On the way back from lunch, I decided to stop by the Swiss Cottage Library. I was now so interested in coffee that I wanted to read everything about the beverage and its market. A chart book showed coffee prices on the New York Coffee Exchange from the nineteen seventies onwards. The coffee price went up and down like a yo-yo. Fortunes must have been made and lost. During the mid seventies, the price had soared from around 50 cents a pound to 340 cents, an increase of almost 600 per cent! By the late seventies, the price had fallen to around 110 cents. In the eighties and nineties it tended to surge to around 300 cents a pound and then tumbled all the way down to below a dollar a pound. After 9/11, coffee was hovering around 40 cents to 50 cents a pound, but it revived to about 60 cents. Manson's trading rules stated that it was a waste of time to look for the reasons behind gyrations. Just monitor prices to decide when to buy and sell. I thought, however, that the Manson system had let me down in the past six months. I now wanted to investigate the forces behind the coffee market.

Brazil, which generally accounted for about a third of

worldwide coffee production, tended to be behind the major price fluctuations. The big price surges came when frosts or droughts damaged the Brazilian coffee crop. Anyone who could understand and predict weather changes in Brazil could make a fortune in the coffee market.

I made a decision. I would use the Manson method for timing purchases and sales. But I would not act on a buy signal unless I was virtually sure that there would be a poor Brazilian crop.

Other than my brief run with gold, I knew absolutely nothing about speculating in the commodities market. When I arrived at work on Monday, I asked Ruffish to explain.

'The share market is kids' stuff compared with commodities,' he said.

'I'm a kid, Ruff, try me.'

'I don't want the fund to go that route. Why commodities?'

'Coffee's looking interesting.'

'The Aquarium fund has already lost money. If you go into commodities, we could lose the lot.'

'Please Ruff. I won't put everything in coffee. Only a small amount.'

'All right then. A maximum of $100,000 in commodities, OK!'

'Thanks Ruff. I won't let you down.'

'You better not. I'll be watching you closely.'

Ruffish spent an hour showing me the risky aspects of commodity trading. Millions can be made or lost in a day, let alone a week. As a speculator, I could either buy coffee futures or options. I'm not going to explain the details on how the market works, but a single coffee futures contract is equivalent to 37,500 pounds of coffee. That's as much as 17 metric tons or 250 of the bags of coffee that they store in the warehouses. At the latest price of 60 cents a pound, the value of a contract was $22,500. To buy this contract, I had to deposit 'margin' of $2,250 or ten per cent of the value of the contract, with the broker. If the price of coffee fell by ten per cent, I would lose my deposit. If the price rose by only ten per cent, I would double my money.

Most speculators trade in and out of the commodity markets every day. I had no intention of playing that game. I was going to follow the Manson method and play for much larger winnings. I reckoned that coffee could recover to a fair price for producers. That price was above $3 a pound. If coffee rose to $3, the value of a coffee contract would surge to $112,500. The profit on that small $2250 deposit would be $110,250! Mind boggling, but true! I printed off prices from the firm's database and ran off charts going back thirty years. Slowly and carefully I calculated the key levels of my aquarium. I concluded that coffee, which had bottomed around 45 cents a pound about a year ago, was at the beginnings of a bull market. It would surprise everyone.

As a loser in the markets during the past six months, I had lost confidence. I had to be certain that I was right. I asked Ruffish for advice. He told me not to rush into the market.

'You're due some leave, why don't you go to Brazil for a holiday?' he said. 'Maybe you'll find out something there.'

'What about New York or Chicago? I could learn more about commodities?'

'Good idea!'

I was surprised. Never thought that he would agree: 'Will that be work or holiday?'

Ruff smiled ruefully: 'OK, two days extra in New York. Then back to London. But it's going to be work. Right! I'll contact Blaby & Co in New York. We do a lot of business with them. They owe us. One of their guys can show you the commodity exchange and you can also learn about Wall Street.'

Maffie walked in: 'What's going on?'

'Jack's off to Rio, then New York. He likes coffee. Wants to do some research on it.'

'Good stuff. My friend Sergio Vieira can take him to some coffee farms. Afterwards some good futures and options trading courses in New York. That's where it's all happening.'

Maffie phoned Sergio and arranged a lightening tour. Fly to Rio de Janeiro. Visit some coffee farms and then have a good time in the city. Then the New York Mercantile Exchange and observe first-hand, trading in coffee, gold, oil and other commodities.

*   *   *

I flew into Rio at night and my taxi was caught in a traffic jam on the way to the hotel overlooking Ipanema beach. Exhausted after the long economy class flight, I went straight up to the room and crashed out. The phone rang before dawn. It was Sergio Vieira, my guide and interpreter. Half asleep, I packed my bags and rushed downstairs to meet him.

Sergio, slight, with an olive coloured face, shook my hand warmly.

'Want a cigarette?' he asked.

'No thanks.'

'It's a long journey. Takes about six hours. We're going to Sul de Minas in southern Minas Gerais. You'll visit lots of coffee plantations there.'

'Thanks for your time.'

We climbed into Sergio's four wheeler and still tired from the flight and jet lag, I slept most of the way. At last, after a few stops, we arrived in Minas Gerais, north west of Rio. Thousands of green coffee trees were on a plateau and within a few days we visited several farms. It was early May and the Brazilian autumn air was chilly.

'You should come here in September and October, when it's spring. The trees are covered with beautiful white flowers,' said Sergio.

I noticed a long line of people in one of the villages. A truck arrived. They clamoured on to the back, pushing and shoving each other. The unlucky ones were left behind.

'They begin to harvest the coffee in May and continue during the winter,' said Sergio. 'They're desperate for work, despite a daily wage that is less than the price of a cup of coffee in London.'

'That's awful. How do they manage to live?'

'Who knows? They scrape by. The whole family works and they pool their money.'

The farms that I visited were small. Young and old men, women and children were picking red coffee cherries from the trees. Other workers soaked and dried the cherries and then extracted the green coffee beans. Mothers and kids worked alongside each other.

'Shouldn't they be at school?' I asked.

'Food and shelter is more important here than literacy and numeracy,' said Sergio, who spoke good English. 'Life's hard. Power and water are erratic. Roads are bad. These people rely on good crops and coffee prices. But crops are unpredictable and prices are ridiculously low.'

'I thought that the Fairtrade Foundation and other charities help these people.'

'They are doing their best, but Fairtrade has to spread its money and influence. Besides coffee farmers, the Foundation must help cocoa, cotton and other commodity producers.'

'Doesn't Fairtrade get them higher prices?'

'Yes. But even though some coffee companies pay premiums for Fairtrade coffee, prices are still ludicrously low.'

On the final day in Minas Gerais, Sergio took me to his uncle Fulvio, who worked on a small co-operative coffee farm. He lived in a tiny hut with a stone floor. The old man was wearing a dirty cream shirt with a frayed collar and torn trousers. Fulvio was small but upright, with taut, powerful arms. He had deep creases on his face and looked as if he was about eighty. I nearly fell over when Sergio told me that he had just turned sixty five.

Fulvio, through Sergio, the interpreter, explained in great detail what was happening to the coffee crop. There was a drought last September, at the start of the Brazilian spring. It rained late October, but the rain came too late.

'Our coffee trees normally have beautiful white flowers,' said Fulvio through his interpreter Sergio.

'But the spring drought damaged them. There were fewer flowers. The ones that managed to bloom were shrunken and small.'

'What have the flowers got to do with the crop?' I asked.

'Coffee cherries grow from each flower. So the crop was smaller this year.'

Fulvio was worried about erratic climate changes. Despite the drought, autumn was much colder than normal.

'It reminds me of the terrible frost we had in the mid seventies,' said Fulvio. 'At that time the autumn air was also cool. No one believed there would be a frost, but it happened and it was bad!'

'If the crop has already been harvested, how can a frost hurt it?' I asked.

'Frost damages coffee trees. When that happens, the harvest in the following year is poor,' replied Fulvio.

We drank Fulvio's mild coffee and talked for a long while about the dangers of droughts and frosts. A combination would be lethal for the Brazilian crop. It was catch twenty two for the poor peasant farmers. Yes, prices would rise, but poor harvests meant less work. Prices had to increase and remain high to encourage the planting of more coffee trees. Only then would their living standards improve.

'If your uncle is right, how come coffee prices haven't gone through the roof?' I asked Sergio on the way back to Rio.

'Prices jumped last October when Brazilian producers predicted that the crop would be lower,' said Sergio. 'But since then the market has gone to sleep. People think that there are sufficient bags of coffee in our warehouses.'

'Didn't Fulvio forecast a bad winter and frost?'

'The summer was so hot that no one believes that there can be a cold winter. But my uncle has a second sense about these things. The crucial months are June and July.'

'I suppose everyone thinks that global warming and droughts are the danger,' I said.

'Yes, they don't believe that a bad frost is possible. Everyone talks about hot weather, but this is the coldest spring for some years.'

'What happens if there's a frost?'

'We'll have to sell from our warehouses, but I'm not sure about the quality of the coffee. The bags have been there a long time.'

'So you think there will be a shortage?'

Sergio shrugged his shoulders: 'We'll have to wait and see. One thing's certain. Either way the farm workers lose. If the crop is OK, prices will remain low and they will struggle. If the price rises because of a bad crop, they won't have work.'

'Keep me informed, Sergio. I'll speak to my boss. I'm sure our company can help.'

When we arrived in Rio, fun was not on my mind. I could have had a great time. Walking around that evening, I noticed that the girls were gorgeous. I loved Latin American music and the dancing in the streets, but I was disciplined and the next morning concentrated on the coffee market. I sat at the table in my room, connected my laptop and searched for charts on the net. Coffee prices seemed ready to run. Should I spend all the $100,000 at once, or should I wait? It was Friday. I would place some orders today and buy more coffee later.

My four star hotel room was paradise compared to how people lived on the farms. The balcony of my room had a good sea view and looked down towards Ipanema Beach. Instead of sunny sandy beaches and the deep blue sea on posters and postcards, the sea looked as grey as the water in Yorkshire. For Brazil it was gloomy, overcast and wintry. Not a good time to be there on holiday. No time to lose. Morning Rio time, was afternoon in London. I phoned Ruffish. He had left for the weekend. Luckily Maffie, who was looking after my fund, was still there.

'Hi Jack, enjoying the sun? It's pouring here,' complained Maffie.

'It's cold here too.'

'In May? I was sunbathing in Rio last year!'

'Maffie, can you check the price of coffee futures in New York?'

'What's up Jack?'

'Haven't got time to explain.'

'62 cents. The price is up a cent today.'

'Can you buy ten contracts of coffee? The margin should be around $23,000. Don't tell the broker that I'm in Brazil. If he asks where I am, say that I'm sick or something.'

'Of course, I won't tell them that you're in Brazil, dummy. Give me the number of your hotel. I'll phone you in five minutes.'

'Sure. The room number is 404. If you can't get through, try my mobile.'

I went on to the balcony of my room and observed the beach. A mist had come down from the mountain. The beach and streets below were hardly visible. I paced up and down from the balcony into the room and back again. If this cold spell lasted, it would only be a matter of time before coffee spurted. The phone rang.

'Bought ten contracts at 62 cents,' said Maffie. 'Now forget about it and enjoy yourself.'

I slammed my fist into the palm of my hand: 'Yes! See you next week Maff. Thanks a million.'

I was on my way. With only a $23,250 margin deposit, Aquarium Fund had bought coffee futures equivalent to 375,000 pounds of coffee, worth $232,500.

I was so excited that I decided to go for a run and a swim, even though the weather was grim. For the first time since my gold share trading, I felt that I had read the market right. I had the weekend to enjoy Rio. Despite being on my own, I didn't feel at all lonely. Was in a good mood and happy with my own company. I toured the city and went up the cable car to Sugar Loaf Mountain. From there I could see the giant statue of Christ the Redeemer and the city and the beach below. Favelas, the crammed shanty towns, were a world apart from Ipanema with its fancy shops, apartments, restaurants and magnificent girls.

Made me think. It was awful when Dad couldn't make ends meet. The times we had to eat leftovers from the shop. Hardly ever went to a restaurant. Had to buy my clothes from the local Oxfam charity shop and market stalls. But compared to the poverty on the farms and in the favelas, we were well off. We had more than enough fish, chips and bread from the shop, had a roof over our heads, free National Health Service and I could get a reasonable education.

Later on I wandered through Rio's Botanical Gardens

and saw some magnificent electric blue Morphos and other butterflies. There were some amazing postcards and I posted some to Stan and Leila Slimcop, Martha, Ivor Ensworth, Gill Derby and the guys in the office. Unfortunately, time was running out. There was no time for a trip to the rainforest. Sunday was the best day. The concierge managed to get me into Maracana Football Stadium. Two of the best football clubs in the world. Huge crowd. Awesome atmosphere! The score Vasco 2, Botafogo, 1.

*   *   *

That Sunday evening I flew to the Big Apple and arrived at John F Kennedy airport in the early hours of the morning. Blaby & Co had arranged a room for me at the Princeton Club. I was fast asleep in the taxi when I arrived there, but managed to steal a few more hours of sleep in my tiny room, before the wake-up call. It was such a rush for my meeting, that I hardly noticed the décor of the club that catered for Princeton University alumni. The club had wooden panelling and a foyer that was dark and dingy. Instead of having breakfast there, I ran out into the street into West 43rd Street. It was between fifth and sixth avenues, only a few blocks away from Broadway and not too far from Central Park. Ruff was right. Princeton Club was an inexpensive prestigious base in a good area.

Wowee! New York City with its noise, smells and battered yellow taxis. The bright light, heat and humidity took me by surprise and within seconds my suit jacket was over my shoulder. A deli's breezy air conditioning was a relief and I wolfed down fruit salad, yoghurt and a bagel. Huge helpings compared to London and half the price. Then I rushed past people on their way to work and went down the subway. Sweat poured off my face and my shirt felt damp in the steamy subway. London's underground is tatty, but compared to this place, a lot better. Thousands of people crowding into battered old trains with ghastly graffiti. Inside, bare bucket seats with no upholstery.

Downtown New York at last. Huge buildings surrounded me. I cricked my neck looking upwards. The City of London, with its few tall buildings, was puny next to this lot. Then came the shock. Ground Zero, the huge cleanup operation of the World Trade Centre.

How could I forget 9/11? Back from school in the afternoon, I had switched on the TV to watch a soap. The pictures were so surreal that I had thought I was seeing a movie. Two planes hitting the buildings. People falling from sickening heights. Smoke and fire and then implosion.

In front of me now was a virtually empty site. Bulldozers busy. I wanted to linger and remember the dead and the dreadful luck for them and their families. But there was no time. I had only twenty minutes to get to my appointment.

Blaby & Co's offices were on the 30th floor at One World Financial Centre, a huge complex with four towering buildings, reaching for the sky. The fastest lift that I had ever been in, opened outside the reception room. Before long my contact, Danny Dovetail, was with me. He was a large, bald guy with dark glasses, a goatee beard and a big grin. Casually dressed in light blue trousers and a cream shirt, he gripped my hand like a vice.

'How ya doing, Jack? I'm Danny. Good to meet ya.'

'Hi,' I replied, a little nervously.

'Ruff asked me to show you the Exchange.'

'Sure you have time? What about your clients?'

'It's a break for me. The coffee market's dead. I might as well trade oil or gold.'

'Going to do that?'

'Nope. Don't want to draw attention to myself. We're losing money on coffee, cocoa and sugar. If they think that the market is going nowhere, they could do what other firms have done.'

'What's that?'

'Let people go.'

The lift took us down to the ground floor and we walked through the 'Winter Garden', an awesome atrium with a huge glass dome, twenty foot palm trees and other tropical plants. There were loads of cool shops, cafés and restaurants.

'You're lucky Jack. You wouldn't have been able to walk around this place, nine months ago. A total mess. Debris and glass all over the place. See that makeshift walkway there. Used to be a concrete bridge with windows. Connected this place with the World Trade Centre.'

'Amazing how quickly they restored it around here.'

'Coffee, sugar and cocoa used to be traded at the World Trade Center,' Danny continued. 'We were in a nine-storey building at the foot of the twin towers. When the plane hit the Towers, the building collapsed and tonnes of concrete, steel and other debris fell on our offices. Luckily they evacuated everyone from the trading floor before it happened.'

'Were you working there at the time?'

'Yeah, but I managed to get out, unscathed. Could hardly see where I was going; had to struggle through a cloud of thick dust. It was so bad that I was almost choking; covered my mouth with a handkerchief. I was terrified as I thought that another building would fall. Thousands were trying to get out of the place. It was remarkable that less than 3,000 people died.'

'How did you manage afterwards?'

'Used to wake up in the night, sweating; disturbed my wife. She helped me calm down and eventually life went on. Blaby & Co and other firms found temporary accommodation. The Cocoa, Sugar and Coffee Exchange now has to share space at NYMEX.

'We'll come back to the Winter Garden for lunch Jack. Lots of things happen here. Rock and jazz concerts, classical music that sort of stuff.'

'Wish my firm had an office here.'

'Ask them if you can open one.'

'Me? Must be joking. I'm a junior.'

'You must have a future if they sent you here.'

We walked through the World Financial Centre to the building of The New York Mercantile Exchange alongside the waterfront.

'The Exchange overlooks Hudson River. Over there you can see North Cove harbour and further down, Battery Park City,' said Danny, pointing. 'And there she is! The Statue of Liberty!'

Danny took me on to the NYMEX trading floor. It was crowded and chaotic. Guys in yellow, blue and red coloured jackets were shouting and gesticulating and throwing pieces of paper into the air and on to the floor. Only days ago, I was talking to struggling farmers and wandering through beautiful groves of green coffee trees; holding handfuls of red coffee cherries and pulling out some green beans. Now this madhouse!

'Do traders visit coffee or cocoa farms?'

'Not these guys. They trade gold, silver, platinum and copper,' laughed Danny.

'And those guys dealing like crazy?'

'Energy trading. Oil, natural gas. Our biggest market.'

'Where's the cocoa, sugar and coffee exchange?'

'Over there.'

He took me across to the coffee dealing section, which he called a 'trading pit'. Compared to energy and precious metals, very little was going on.

'You asked whether coffee traders go and visit the farms to find out what they trade. Well the straight answer is very few. I've been there, but these guys? They're dealers in pieces of paper. Futures and options contracts. They know how the weather affects coffee prices. That sort of stuff. But if they go to Brazil, they spend their time on the beach and at the Carnival.

'What about you Jack? How come you guys bought coffee on Friday? Think the market's bottoming out?'

'I'm just here to learn about commodities,' I half lied.

No way was I going to tell him where I had been the past week. I looked at the price on the screen. Coffee was trading at 61 cents a pound, slightly down from Friday's levels. I was still comfortable with that. To get a panoramic view of the exchange, Danny took me to the public gallery, grabbed hold of my camera and took some photos of me, with the market in the background.

'NYMEX and the Chicago markets are the largest commodity trading arenas in the world,' said Danny when we looked down from the gallery. 'From here it doesn't seem that chaotic.'

'See the gold and silver pit?' he said pointing. 'The guy sitting near the traders is inputting price changes. As he punches in the data, they are automatically visible on those big screens on the walls and are almost immediately sent to trading screens around the world. Gold and silver are taking off, but as you can see, hardly anything is happening in the cocoa, sugar and coffee pit.'

'What do those hand signals mean?' I asked.

'That trader there, drawing the palm of his hand towards his face. He's buying. The other guy pushing his palm outwards is selling. Those quick finger movements. They're prices. Notice them touch their chins and foreheads? Those are quantities. Ten, twenty, hundred contracts. It's their sign language. They know exactly what's going on.'

'Why are they throwing away bits of paper?'

'They're completed orders,' said Danny. 'It's a big cleaning job afterwards. Piles and piles of paper.'

'They tell me that computer dealing is going to replace these big exchanges,' I said when we were back in the Winter Garden having an early lunch. A band was playing Beatles numbers in the background.

'Yeah seems to be going that way. Floor trading is very expensive for the brokers and investment banks, but it works well. Face to face dealing gives traders a good feel for the market – where the flow of money is going. You're not sure you're reading the market right when you're trading from a computer screen. It's much more difficult to gauge the direction of prices.'

Later that day, I walked around Battery Park City watching kids run through the fountains, guessing when the water was going to spurt upwards. In some ways it was similar to the area surrounding the London Eye, the big wheel on the south bank of the Thames. Mime artists, painters, bands and buskers. People were having a great time in the park, alongside the waterfront. I had been on my own for almost ten days, but didn't feel lonely. Just felt that I was so lucky to be there as I drank a beer under a tree and listened to a jazz band. If only Dad and Mum had been alive. They never had the opportunity to travel. Just struggled to make a living and bring me up. With the money that I was making, I would have helped them. They could have been here in New York, with me.

Later, I did the tourist thing and went on a ferry to the Statue of Liberty; climbed the winding staircase on to her crown and looked all around me. A shiver went down my spine. Here was I on the symbol of freedom; Manhattan skyscrapers in front and behind, the Atlantic and thousands of miles to Southampton. My friends at school would never have believed it.

The tour went to Ellis Island, the first port of call for millions of immigrants to America. Hundreds of thousands of names were on a Wall of Honour. All had tried their luck in the American melting pot. To get the feel of New York,

I got hold of a map and decided to walk all the way from Downtown to Broadway. The scale on the map indicated that it was about four and a half miles, but it took forever because of all the roads and traffic lights. On I went from Battery Park, through China Town to Greenwich Village. Then the Jewish garment and fashion district and finally Times Square. If only I could have told my parents about New York, New York, home to all nationalities and religions, the rich, average and poor. Descendants of those hopeful immigrants who patiently waited their turn on Ellis Island.

On Broadway, I queued up to buy a half-price ticket for a show and got talking to a bubbly girl from out of town. Not that special to look at, but she did have lovely long black curly hair. May was from Chicago and was on holiday in New York.

'I love English accents. Staying long here?'

'Naw. Have to go baack to Loondon tomorrow,' I replied putting on a thick Yorkshire accent for fun.

She couldn't tell the difference: 'The English are so cultured. What do you do, Jack?'

'I'm a trader. What show do you recommend, May?'

'Heard that "Annie Get Your Gun" is a must see. I'm on my own. Want to join me?'

After we had bought our tickets we went to a restaurant nearby and had hamburgers. May was really into my accent, which I changed from well spoken English to thick Yorkshire dialect and back again. To her it was all the same. It was an amazing show, reminding me that I should make greater use of theatres in London. Mum would have loved me to do that. Afterwards we walked up 43rd Street towards

May's hotel on 5th Avenue and went into a bar and had a couple of beers. She started to stroke my arms. If May was an example, American girls were much less inhibited than the English ones I knew. She was even more relaxed than Sandy, who was an easy-going Australian!

On the way to her hotel, we passed the Princeton Club and we were about to say our goodbyes, when I decided to take a chance. Would she come in and have some coffee? No problem. Up we went to my room to put on the kettle for some instant coffee. There was no time for that. Before long we were kissing. The room was small but the bed was big. It was only my second time and almost a year since Maggie and the loch. We started kissing and rolling around. May shouted so loudly that the people in the room next to us banged on the wall.

The next morning, I got up early, double-checked that my money, passport and other valuables were locked away in the safe-deposit box and went for a run in Central Park. When I got back, May was gone. She left me a note saying that she hoped to see me again and had to rush back to her hotel and get a taxi to the airport. On the notepaper were her email address and mobile number.

The low point of my visit to the Americas was the futures and options derivatives course at NYMEX. It sure was boring and took most of the morning. When I managed to keep my eyes open, I learned about complex trading things such as straddles and butterflies. It was better to follow Manson and keep it simple. Trading was common sense. On a screen, coffee was trading around 61.50 cents. Indications were that the price was firmly underpinned.

There were only a few hours before my plane left for London. The New York Public Library, a huge building that looked about a hundred years old, was near the Princeton Club, so I went in there to do some research. What a place! The Swiss Cottage library was a closet compared to it. Sergio, who was knowledgeable about climate change, had told me that melting ice blocks in the Antarctic were cooling the Gulf Stream. The change was causing unpredictable weather; sometimes heat waves and drought; other times hurricanes. 'El Nino' also caused climatic havoc. El Nino originates near the equator when the Pacific Ocean becomes much warmer than normal. Hot humid air rises and the winds despatch El Nino to North and South America, Asia and other places, causing anything from terrible storms and floods to tornadoes and other climatic disasters.

Global warming would bring about all sorts of changes. There were going to be agricultural crop failures and violent moves in prices of sugar, cocoa, wheat, corn and soya beans. Insurance companies would incur huge losses.

*   *   *

Ruffish was still away when I returned to work on Wednesday. Prices on the London coffee market were rising, but I decided to stick to the New York exchange, where Brazilian and other Arabica coffees were traded. The market opened higher and I bought more coffee futures through Blaby and two other brokers. Aquarium now held 40 futures contracts, equal to 1.5 million pounds of coffee worth about $1 million. That coffee would be delivered in three months from the date of the contracts, unless we sold before then. They were 'three month futures'.

I also used the remaining $900,000 in the fund to buy shares in commodity and agricultural companies, which tended to rise and fall in line with cocoa, sugar, corn, wheat and soyabean quotes. Aquarium had gold shares too. If food prices rose, inflation would increase and gold would follow.

The charts of some insurance shares showed that they had risen to high levels. Insurance companies would incur large claims during any climatic disaster. Aquarium sold the shares short, aiming to profit by buying back the shares when they fell.

While I was doing all this, Ruffish was at a funeral in Ireland. When I arrived at the office on Friday morning, he was pacing up and down in his office furiously. He called me in. He was so agitated that he didn't even ask me about my trip.

'What do you think you're doing?' he said softly, in an attempt to disguise his anger.

Ruffish was one of those calm people. He was there to stop his fund managers from getting carried away and soothe them when they were losing. He seemed agitated and sloppier than usual. His striped pink shirt was creased and a bulging tissue was in his pocket. He couldn't stop sneezing.

He wiped his nose, glared at me, picked up the phone and asked Maffie to come in.

She walked in looking amazing in a coffee coloured designer suit.

'See what I've got with my winnings, Jack,' she laughed, mimicking a model catwalk. 'Note the colour. It's in honour of our coup.'

I started to laugh, but Ruffish didn't appreciate the joke.

'I put you in a position of trust and you allowed him to place almost $100,000 on margin for coffee speculation?' he snapped at Maffie. 'Are you out of your mind?'

'You told him to go to Brazil. Well, he's found out something Ruff,' said Maffie, holding up her hands in an effort to calm him down. 'So far he's right. Our position is already profitable.'

'Come off it Maffie! You know very well what can happen,' retorted Ruffish.

'I've stuck to the rules Ruff, I haven't invested more than $100,000 of the fund in coffee futures,' I ventured.

Ruffish had a sneezing fit and scrambled for the tissues on his desk. Maffie gave him one.

'Invested! You mean gambled! Coffee can fall by ten per cent and your entire margin will be wiped out,' he shouted, snapping his fingers: 'Just like that!'

'And a ten per cent rise will do the opposite,' said Maffie quietly. 'Take it easy Ruff, Jack knows what he's doing.'

'And what about the grain and other agricultural shares in the fund? Selling insurance companies short? Expecting a climatic apocalypse are you?'

'You must admit, the weather has been erratic,' I said. 'Fulvio, a wise old guy in Brazil told me that there's going to be a frost. He forecast droughts, hurricanes and crop failures. They call it El Nino. I found out what happens after doing some research in the New York Public Library.'

'Tragedy for others, but luck for you Jack. Is that what you're saying?' growled Ruffish. 'Now get out you two before I . . .'

Whether it was luck or not, coffee prices almost doubled to 120 cents a pound by the end of the month, raising the value of our coffee contracts to $1.8 million. The profit on the $100,000 margin deposit was $700,000! Aquarium's other investments also rose, raising the fund's value to around $2 million, twice the capital we had originally invested. The normal policy of fund managers is to take profits, especially in the dangerous, volatile commodity futures market. If Ruffish had been around, he would have insisted that I bank at least half the gains. But he and Maffie went off to an investment conference in Brighton and were away on Thursday and Friday.

I was studying my charts and price tables when the phone rang. Danny Dovetail, my new broker friend, was on the phone.

'Hi Jack, you guys seem to have turned the market around. It's looking good here. Wanna buy more coffee?'

'No thanks, Danny, I'm up to my limit.'

'No you're not. You're well into profit. That raises your collateral limit. You can use that collateral to put down more margin and buy more coffee. Anyone can see coffee's going up. You would be crazy to miss out.'

'I'll think about it. Speak to you later.'

I put down the phone, wrote down the latest quote on my price table and looked at my charts. Then I took out my coloured aquarium drawing. Sure enough, my coffee coloured fish were ready to swim into a higher level of the tank. I was excited. It was now the beginning of the Brazilian winter. There was already talk about a possible frost. Coffee prices could easily rise to $2 a pound. Nestlé, Sarah Lee, Kraft, Lavazza, Illy and other manufacturers that purchase green coffee from farmers and roast them, were worried. They could well decide to buy ahead of a further potential price rise. Commodity funds and other speculators were also jumping on the coffee wagon. The phone rang again. It was Danny on the phone. Forget Ruff. Coffee looked an easy winner. I had to go for it.

'OK Danny, buy another 60,' I whispered, sweating with excitement. Within minutes, he was back to me. Aquarium Fund now had 100 coffee futures contracts, controlling 3.75 million pounds of coffee worth $4.5 million. By then the word was out that Hastings Ruffish had taken sizeable positions and was making big profits in the coffee market. After I had bought more coffee, other people in the market followed. The price jumped.

'You're moving the coffee market, Jack,' said Danny. 'I underestimated you. Thought you were just a junior.'

Prices gyrated wildly on Friday. Profits up one minute and down the next.

The following Monday I told Ruffish what I had done. He went ballistic. Maffie was angry too.

'You promised us that you would not increase the position, Jack,' scolded Maffie. 'How can we trust you now?'

'Apologies, Maff. I got carried away. Danny said that the market looked good, so I bought.'

'Brokers always encourage you to trade, you idiot.

Makes no difference to them. Win or lose they get their commission.'

'Danny's a good guy. He wouldn't give me a bum steer.'

'Maybe not intentionally, but brokers also get carried away. It's not only your money, Jack. Krishna, Tong and Bess also have a stake in the fund. Ruff's now under pressure.'

'The charts look OK, Maffie. The price action feels good. We're into the Brazilian winter. Give me a chance. Promise you, I'll get out fast if the market turns.'

Ruffish and Maffie decided to take a calculated risk and leave me alone for a week or so. They were angry, but it was also a test to see how I could cope with stress. Some days when coffee was rising, the value of the margin deposit doubled or trebled. When the price fell, profits almost vanished and losses threatened. Despite the roller coaster, I followed Manson's advice and focused on the big picture. Watched what the coffee price was doing. Did my best to ignore the large profit and loss swings on the tiny margin deposit.

I guess I was lucky. More and more buyers were entering the market and were pushing prices up. Within a few weeks, coffee hit $2 even though the Brazilian coffee plantation was still intact.

Our coffee positions had made us almost $4 million on margin deposits of less than $400,000! Commodity and gold shares had also soared in hectic trade. The Aquarium fund, which had started with $1 million, was now worth around $6 million. I was a millionaire!

13

PEARL

'Does the Governor know about this third session? Other inmates see the psychiatrist once and that's if they're lucky.'

'I've told him that you're a very interesting case,' says Dr Klugheim.

'A loner, an outsider?'

'Highly intelligent and talented.'

'Really?'

'Yes, really.'

Silence. Waiting.

'Know anything about suppressing the unconscious?' asks Klugheim.

'Such as?'

'Memories. The Russians . . . The hanging. You've stopped writing about them.'

'Why are you interested?'

I'm wary. Something's going on. Is the Russian mafia using him to get to me? I shouldn't have written about them.

'You sure only you and Mrs Small are reading my stuff?' I whisper. 'The Governor? does he know?'

'Don't worry, I'm keeping the book strictly confidential,' says Klugheim.

'How can I be sure it won't get out? You know what they can do! They're everywhere.'

'Trust me! I'm here to help. Just write a few pages every week. I'll keep them safely here.'

'They have ways of finding out.'

'Only Mrs Small and I know about it. Promise! Keep on writing. You mustn't suppress it. Let it out. If you keep it hidden it will come back; disturb you.'

I'm unconvinced. Say nothing. Silent.

'So you went on living as if nothing had happened? Bad memories gone?' asks Klugheim while he observes me closely.

Better talk. I'll have to trust him. What else can I do?

'Stan Slimcop was right. Time's the best healer. I only had occasional dreams about the hanging,' I mumble. 'I was focusing on trading. That was my life. I decided that they wouldn't recognise me. Grew a moustache.'

'Think back. Try and remember. Are you sure there weren't any more bad dreams?'

'Very seldom. I began to feel more secure.'

'Any dreams about them now?'

'No.'

'Good.'

He gets up suddenly, losing his train of thought. Paces the room, agitated.

'What about my shrinking portfolio, Jack? I got hold of the charts and prices.'

'*Wanna retire now?*' I mumble sarcastically as I shuffle to the table next to the window.

'*I'll ignore that Jack. We've gone through this before. You should know by now that I'm doing my best for you.*'

'*Sorry. I'm a bit of a cynic.*'

'*A bit?*'

'*I know you see a lot of prisoners, Doc. But there's no way you can comprehend what this place's like. Guys like me are shit scared. Terrified of being beaten up or raped. The stink. Cells like saunas in the summer. Freezing in winter. Not enough exercise. Rubbish food.*'

'*Just keep your head down, Jack. I'll do my best to get you out of here.*'

On the table are a laptop, chart book and prices. We pull up some chairs and we look through them. I make some notes and quickly search the Internet for extra stuff.

'*You've got thirty shares, Dr Klugheim. Do you have time to follow them?*'

'*No. All I know is that I'm losing.*'

'*Not all of them. Some are doing OK. These seven.*'

'*Want me to sell twenty three shares?*'

'*That's what I would do. Put all the money in the shares that are doing well. The companies and charts seem OK.*'

'*Why don't you take off your shoes and lie down on the couch,*' says Klugheim.

'*Thought we were finished.*'

'*You've still got time. Close your eyes. Relax. Tell me about your commodities trading.*'

'*Sort of takes over. Coffee up and down. Big profits, then losses. Profits again.*'

'How did it feel?'

'I was a winner! It's like the races. Your horse coming in. You're on a buzz.'

'Like a gambler?'

'Yes and no. You leave the racetrack when it's over. You're in the casino when you play roulette or blackjack. But when you trade in the markets, it's in your head. You're thinking about it all the time. Should I stay in? Should I get out? Should I sell half? You get a kick when it goes up, but your stomach sinks when it's down. Why didn't I sell? Should I get out now? That sort of thing. You're always edgy, especially when you're losing. Then the market goes wild and you forget to eat. When you're hungry, you go through packets of crisps. Eyes always on the screen.'

'What about drink and drugs? Do they help or increase stress?'

No answer. He's not going to sucker me into that!

'Didn't you take a break? Go to a movie. Play sport. Go out with girls to wind down?'

'Sure. But trading dominated my life. You're playing with margin. A small fall can wipe you out. That's all you think about. You're phoning your broker. Looking at prices on your mobile. Searching for news. Early morning to late at night.'

'Greedy one day; fretting the next?'

'That's about it! You're working out numbers in your head. What you have now. What you could have. What you're going to do with it. Do you have enough for a flat, a house, a Ferrari, a holiday? In the end it's a game. You've got to score.'

'And when you lose?'

'You sweat. Depends how much you're down. If it's a lot, you feel sick. Really sick. But those days were good. Coffee was big time.'

*   *   *

Ruffish held a fund manager meeting to decide what we should do next. I could understand why he was worried. The coffee market was going crazy and we had a lot of money in it.

Ruffish put his hand on my shoulder in the meeting room: 'Told you a schoolboy could do it.'

'Luck,' grunted Aram Zabkian.

'What would you do if you were in young Miner's position?' asked Ruffish. He was dressed in a smart light grey Savile Row suit.

'Bank the money and go back to school,' said Aram who was sloppily dressed in a yellow shirt with white stripes and creased dark blue slacks. Obviously, he wasn't meeting any clients or brokers. If he was, he would have been in a Versace suit or another favourite designer. Aram irritated me. He had chronic halitosis. We could smell the garlic across the table.

'Envy will get you everywhere, Aram,' said Maffie sarcastically. 'Let's hear what our astrophysics and maths geniuses have got to say.'

Tong Chong Ping took off his black glasses and rubbed them. 'At the moment coffee's all about round numbers. It broke $2, so I reckon the market momentum could carry it to $2.40. After that, I'm not sure. If there isn't a crop failure, the price will crash!'

'Most traders underestimate the scale of moves,' said Krishna Doomassamy.

He was a quiet, likeable, modest guy, who kept to himself. Krishna was always helpful.

'When there's a run, prices go much further than people expect,' he suggested. 'What were the previous coffee peaks, Jack?'

'In the bad frost of the mid seventies, coffee soared to $3.40 a pound and then collapsed,' I replied, showing them my chart going back forty years. Throughout the period, prices climbed steep mountains and fell into deep ravines.

'If Aquarium were my fund, I tell you what I would do,' said Krishna thoughtfully. 'I would sell about a third of my coffee positions and put the money in the bank. Then I would switch the rest from futures into options.'

'That makes sense,' said Ruffish. 'That will protect our capital and guarantee a profit.'

'Why switch from futures to options?' I asked.

'Didn't that course in New York teach you anything?'

'Not much. We did lots of boring simulations. Not the same as the real thing.'

'You've been playing a very dangerous game, Jack,' said Krishna. 'You're lucky that the price ran up. With futures you can lose all your money and a lot more if the market goes against you. Gains on options are less than futures, but your loss is limited. You can only lose what you put in the market. Not more.'

'Yes Jack, options are the safer route,' said Ruffish.

Tong was right. Within a few days after coffee broke through the 'round number' of $2, it shot up to almost $2.50 a pound. Ruffish told me to sell a third of our positions. We banked over $3 million, more than treble the original money we had in the fund. The big profit relaxed me so that I was less obsessed with the market. The rest of the futures contracts, which were also pure profit and worth around $6 million, were converted into coffee options. The options gave us the right to buy coffee at a future point in time. If the options expired at a loss, we would lose the $6 million. But if prices rose, the options' prices would soar. We could make millions more. The game was far from over.

*　　　*　　　*

After working late one evening, Maffie and I had a quiet drink in our local near Berkeley Square. Maffie said that she had to meet a friend and left. I had never met this mystery man and wondered who he was. I tried to get it out of her, but she never told me. Maffie was a very private person.

I remained in the pub to finish my beer before going back to Martha's place. A swim and run with the dogs would be great.

'Hi there,' said a cheerful husky voice in an American accent.

I lifted my head and saw her. She was petite and pretty with a heart shaped freckled face, green eyes and short, cropped red hair. She was in her early twenties and was all in black.

'Hi,' I said, trying hard to remember her. Maybe we had met in a pub or club.

'Can I buy you a drink?' she asked.

'No thanks. I'm going to walk my dog and go for a swim.'

She put out her hand: 'Pearl Fleecer. Where do you swim?'

Her hand lingered as I shook it and felt a tingle down my spine.

'Jack Miner. I swim in Hampstead ponds.'

We went outside. She took out a pack of cigarettes from her handbag and lit a match.

'Want one?'

'No thanks. Don't smoke.'

'What do you do, Jack?'

'I'm a trader.'

'What do you trade?'

'All sorts of things. Shares, commodities.'

'That's interesting. Things like gold, oil, sugar, coffee, cocoa?'

'Yeah.'

'Markets are cool. Not the financial stuff. I haven't a clue. The people, sharp, decisive. Is that you, Jack?'

Her questions were flattering. Made me feel good. It was easy to talk to her. I had made millions and was feeling good about myself.

'The only thing I know about coffee is my Latte every morning,' she said grinning. 'If I don't have it, I can't work.'

'Starbucks, Costa or Nero?'

'Any place, provided the coffee's good. Depends how I feel, or where I'm going. Dealing in millions. Must be nerve-wracking. How do you go about it?'

'Give me a break. It's after hours. Your turn. What do you do?'

She took out a business card from a small white handbag and gave it to me. On it was: 'Pearl Fleecer, Consultant, AAPF Associates.'

'Who's AA?'

'Anne Arenby, my boss and partner. She's English.'

'What sort of consulting do you do?'

'We're a small company. Branding, image, that sort of thing. Want a lift? My car's parked nearby.'

'Do you drive to work?' I asked.

'No. My office is in St John's Wood. Had to see a client in Mayfair.'

Pearl took out another cigarette as we walked to her car.

'Tobacco company?'

She coughed out a laugh: 'No, wish they were. We don't only work on corporate brands and images. People too. Pop stars, sportsmen and models. Thought about your image, Jack?'

'Lost cause.'

She grinned. I couldn't help but like her.

We were in the parking garage by now and Pearl walked up to a small yellow MG sports car. We climbed in and before long we were in light traffic, driving from Mayfair, across Oxford Street and into Regent's Park. Pearl accelerated and I could feel the breeze.

'I'm not taking you out of your way, am I?'

'Nope. My apartment's in Chalk Farm. Not far from you. Whew, it's hot. Can I join you for a swim?'

'Sure.'

'We'll stop at my place. I need to change.'

She had a one bedroom flat on the third floor of a converted, grey Edwardian house.

'I like to keep things simple,' she said when she opened the door.

I saw what she meant. There were a couple of dark blue leather chairs and a glass table. In the corner there was a kitchenette with a microwave, toaster and kettle. Pearl slipped into her bedroom and came out wearing a black bikini. It was under a paper thin, light green kaftan. She threw me her towel and car keys.

'OK, let's go,' she said. 'Wanna drive?'

'No . . . no thanks,' I said throwing them back at her.

'What car do you have, Jack? Porsche?' she asked, as we passed the Royal Free Hospital on the way to my place.

'I'm thinking of getting a new one,' I lied. No way was I going to tell her that I didn't have a licence.

The dogs went wild when we arrived, jumping and licking us. Pearl didn't like them much and pushed them away. Martha walked in with shopping bags and offered us something to eat, but we declined. She quietly observed Pearl, while she patted the dogs and calmed them down.

I went upstairs to change. Martha knocked on the door and came in.

'Careful Jack! She's got a hard face.'

'Sure Mum,' I laughed.

We walked to the mixed pond on the southern part of the Heath. After tying up the dogs outside, we entered the swimming area, jumped into the pond and swam a few lengths. Afterwards we changed and ambled back towards some cafés and restaurants on the east side of the Heath.

'Are you a Londoner, Jack?'

'No. I'm from Bridlington in Yorkshire. Heard of it?'

'No. I've only been here two years.'

'From New York?'

'Yep, but I was brought up in Washington D.C.'

'Your Dad or Mum in politics?'

She laughed: 'People always assume that. My father is a consultant on international affairs. My mother is a designer.'

'I presume you've been to New York and Washington,' said Pearl.

'Yes, I was in New York, last week,' I glowed.

'Oh really! What were you doing there?'

'Learning about the markets. Saw "Annie Get Your Gun". You remind me of her.'

She gave me a gentle push.

'When did you come to London?'

'About a year ago.'

'And you're already a trader?'

'That's right.'

'They start them young don't they?'

I looked at her closely. Yes, she was older than me, but I couldn't tell by how much. Perhaps five years. Had to be. Partner in a business. I wondered whether she realised that I had just turned seventeen. Just as well that my moustache had grown.

'Who taught you to be a trader, Jack?'

'Learnt about it in my Dad's fish and chip shop.'

She smiled sceptically: 'Yeah. Sure.'

'Just joking. Taught myself. I'm still learning. My firm . . .'

'What firm?'

'Hastings & Ruffish. It manages hedge funds.'

'Wow! A hedge fund trader. That's really impressive. How come you trade commodities? A hedge fund friend told me that they mainly traded shares and bonds.'

'Went to Brazil on holiday. It's a big commodities producer.'

As soon as that came out, I regretted it. She had flattered me so much, that I had broken Ruffish's golden rule. Never discuss what the firm does in detail. The hedge fund business is very competitive. Their employees, associates and consultants vacuum information in all sorts of places.

'Rio or Sao Paulo. Great places for a holiday. Were you there recently? What was the weather like?'

I changed the subject.

'Weather's been great this summer, hasn't it? Come and swim with me any time.'

Pearl edged closer and tucked her hand under my arm. That made me feel good.

We chose an outside table at Kalendar, a restaurant close to the Heath and near Martha's place. The steak tasted good and Pearl drank most of the wine. Later we walked back to Martha's place and we made a date for the weekend. She kissed me on both my cheeks, climbed into her car and drove away. After Pearl had gone, I suddenly realised that she had told me very little about herself. She had a sports car and quite an expensive flat. Either her branding firm was doing well or her parents had money.

*   *   *

Pearl took me shopping in the West End the following Saturday. First I got a new haircut and a few highlights in some fancy hairdresser. Then we looked at some boutiques around Bond Street. Pearl said that she wanted to smarten me up a bit. I'm not a shopping sort of guy, but this was kind of fun. With my background, I wasn't exactly the world's biggest spender. Pearl assumed that I was rich and wasn't worried about money. My credit card worked overtime. Before long we were struggling to carry bags from Armani, Ralph Lauren and Hugo Boss. Later, we took a cab to Mayfair. I honoured my Mum's fantasy and we had tea at the Ritz. What a place! The hotel's Palm Court, where I had to wear a tie, was a huge ornate, golden room. Delicate cucumber sandwiches, scones and clotted cream with Earl Grey Tea.

'Mum would have loved it here,' I said, feeling my eyes get a bit watery. I let go a bit and it came out. How Dad and Mum had died, how my relatives turned their backs on me. How I had arrived in London.

'You're quite a guy Jack. Self-made. I like that,' she said, in a sympathetic, but insincere way. I vowed that I wouldn't pour out my heart again. Pearl was no agony aunt.

'So how's the trading going Jack? Made money last week? What's the best bet? Gold and silver or cocoa and coffee?'

'Want some advice, Pearl? Keep away. Professionals can lose, so what chance amateurs? The market is going nowhere for the moment. Up, down, up again. Nowhere. Most players are losing.'

Afterwards we walked through an arcade and I tried on some shoes at Church's. Embarrassingly, my credit card was declined at the till. The shop assistant looked at me suspiciously. Pearl giggled. She seemed to realise what had happened. Sure enough when I phoned the credit card company to find out what was going on, I had exceeded my credit card limit. Not only that, they suspected that the card had been stolen. Except for my trip to Rio and New York, my credit card statement had never exceeded £1,500.

'Time you started banking at Coutts, Jack,' said Pearl.

'That's the Queen's bank! I'm not made of money, you know.'

'You're an up-and-coming hedge fund manager, Jack. They'll open an account.'

'You're assuming that I'm rich Pearl. What if I'm not?'

'Don't be stupid, Jack.'

I wasn't sure what she meant. I wondered whether she knew more about me, than she let on. The word had got around in the market that a young trader had made millions in coffee. Reporters had phoned Hastings & Ruffish, but I wasn't allowed to speak to the press. That made it all the more intriguing.

'Hey Pearl. Am I a new client?' I asked.

'Worried about my fee? Think you can afford me?' she laughed.

I was a little concerned. Is this how she landed clients?

We walked into a jewellery shop and Pearl tried on some simple gold bangles.

'Sorry Pearl, I've run out of credit,' I said, winking at the shop assistant.

When she slipped off to the loo, I asked the assistant to put one aside. Pearl was giving me a great time and I was beginning to like her a lot.

*   *   *

That evening, I wore some of my designer stuff when I went with Pearl to a 'Save the Whale' charity ball. It was at the Grosvenor House Hotel in Park Lane. Numerous large round tables were scattered around the huge ballroom and I recognised a few celebrities. Cameras were flashing. This was some event and I felt a bit out of place. Pearl found our table and rushed up to meet her friends and clients.

Pearl in a short, backless, black dress and open toed silver stilettos, introduced me. Two of them were Premier League footballers with their girlfriends who were models. Another was Mark Arenby, their agent. He was the husband of Anne, Pearl's boss. She looked at me haughtily and shook my hand limply. Two guys, who were bankers, seemed to be together. The remaining couple were an actor and actress in a soap.

'Jack's a brilliant trader,' said Pearl proudly. 'Watch this space!'

It was remarkable how she could brand me with that mystique. How could she tell whether I had performed? Even so, it was a good guess and I loved the attention.

'Where do you think the market's going?' asked Mark, the football agent.

'Which market?'

'Shares of course.'

'Dunno, I don't have a crystal ball,' I replied facetiously.

Bill Fitting-Pleasewell, one of the bankers, began pontificating about the economy and the market, boring me and the others. I just nodded and turned to the football stars. Rayne Turner played for Chelsea and Terry Crosswell for Arsenal. Both clubs, along with Manchester United, were top of the table in the Premier League. These guys were seriously skilled and here I was, sitting next to them! I was tempted to ask for their autographs, I was so awestruck.

After clamming up for a while, I managed to blurt out: 'Saw Botafogo beat Vasco. Amazing football!'

'You saw them in Rio?' exclaimed Rayne excitedly. 'What was it like? I'm told that the crowds there are wild.'

'Nice place for a holiday Rayne,' said his girlfriend in a cockney accent.

'Sure sweetheart. Maybe, next year.'

'You're always promising but doing nothing,' she complained with a sulk.

After dinner and speeches, the band began to play. I grabbed Pearl and we were soon dancing in the middle of the sweaty throng. Later I spent about two hundred on lottery tickets and did my bit to save a whale.

By the end of the evening, Pearl was too drunk to drive home, so we climbed into a taxi. I dropped her at her place, but she didn't invite me in.

*   *   *

The next few weeks sped by quickly. Pearl liked to go clubbing, showing me off as a new boyfriend and telling people that I was a star dealer. One day I met her at her office in St John's Wood. We played the fool. She took me into a small studio and showed me how to handle TV and radio interviews.

'Smile, smile and smile. That's the key,' she said, giving me a peck on my cheek.

'Relax Jack! Come on! Smile into the camera. Be sincere. Genuine smile.'

I started laughing and pulling a face: 'How about this?'

She gave me a gentle slap: 'Keep a straight face and smile! Especially if an interviewer tries to rile you.'

'OK, Mr Miner, why have commodity prices been rising?'

'Demand is exceeding supply.'

'Typical dealer response. What factors Mr Miner? Take coffee as an example. Prices have shot up.'

'Really? By how much?' I replied, smiling into the camera.

'People are complaining about speculation? What's your role?'

'What do you do if it's a question you don't want to answer?'

'Change the subject. I think that you're well versed in that, Jack,' responded Pearl with an insincere smile.

Later that evening I stayed over for the first time. Instead of driving me back to my place, Pearl invited me in and we had a few drinks. She went into the bathroom and walked out with nothing on. Her pale white body contrasted with her freckled face. She had narrow shoulders and small pointy breasts and I could see that she was a genuine redhead.

She came up to me and started stripping off my shirt. For the first time we had a long French kiss. I could taste the mixture of toothpaste and tobacco. Then she dragged me into the bedroom. It was sex, not lovemaking. Didn't last very long. In fact, it was almost clinical. I felt bad as I thought that it was me who had failed. Pearl gave me a gentle pat on the head, pulled out her pack of cigarettes and had a smoke.

'Pearl you smoke twenty to thirty a day, why don't you give it up?'

'Nicotine. Tried, but I'm addicted. Want to try something else?'

She went to a cupboard in the corner of the room, rummaged through some clothes, took out a small bag and brought it to the bed. It was pot. She put some in tobacco paper, rolled it up and lit it. Dad had made me promise that I would never smoke, but having a few puffs of weed wasn't the same. It was quite strong and I coughed. I felt a bit dazed and found that I couldn't finish sentences properly. We giggled a lot.

Over the next few days Pearl helped me look for a flat in Hampstead. We found a modern one in a converted Victorian hospital. Across the road were a theatre and a pub and friendly locals. The flat had some good views of the village. Standing on the balcony and looking towards the southeast, we could see Parliament Hill Fields and the city in the far distance. I put in an offer for about half a million and it was accepted. Pearl said that she would help me fix up the apartment and we visited furniture stores in Tottenham Court Road.

*   *   *

I hadn't seen the Slimcops for quite a while and they were keen to meet Pearl. We arranged to meet in Villa Bianca, a homely Italian restaurant, in the centre of Hampstead. Pearl was on form, telling all sorts of jokes about branding campaigns that went wrong.

I noticed that Leila wasn't laughing with the rest of us. She had been acting rather strangely that evening. Forgot what she was talking about midway through sentences.

'How's the sculpturing going Leila?' I shouted, as she appeared to be a little deaf. 'Want me to model for you?'

'Maybe, maybe not,' she replied in an unnaturally happy tone, dropping her spoon and fork on the floor.

The waiter replaced them. Stan put the fork and spoon into her hands, but she pushed him away. We had fish and chicken, but Leila chose spaghetti and was struggling with it. In the end, she hardly ate any.

'Is Leila OK?' I asked Stan when we were washing our hands in the men's room.

'She's having one of her bad nights. I'm not sure what's going on. She has been getting forgetful for some time, but I guess that's normal for our age. In the past few months, she's been sketching more than sculpturing. Most of the sculptures haven't been completed. Her portraits and sketches are very different from her usual style. Instead of landscapes and birds, she does faces and torsos. The faces look depressed and some appear to be frightened. I asked her about them and she told me that she's worried about getting older.'

'The unfinished stuff. What do you think of it?'

'Remarkably good. Very different from her usual work. Why don't you come over now and take a look?'

'Sure, if it's OK with Pearl. What are you going to do?'

'Not quite sure. Maybe it's an aberration. She had flu recently and slept a lot. Will check with the doctor. He might give her some tests.'

'Hope it will be OK.'

'I'm sure it will. Pearl, your girlfriend. It's obvious that you're taken with her. Eyes on her all the time. Hanging on to her every word. You seem to be gone, young man. How old do you think she is?'

'Dunno. What's the difference?'

'I reckon that she's not a day younger than twenty four. What does a girl like that want to do with you Jack? You're not even eighteen. Haven't even got your driving licence!'

I flushed: 'She doesn't know that! So what if she's six or seven years older than me? I'm not the first guy who's gone for an older woman.'

'I'm not thinking of you, Jack. It's good to get experience. Will help you choose the right one when the time comes. It's her. Why you when there are lots of eligible, older men about?'

'She doesn't know how old I am,' I replied fingering my moustache. Anyway, so what if she does? She might prefer younger guys. She's into me. That's what counts.'

He noticed that I was getting irritated: 'Sorry Jack, I don't want to interfere. I just want you to be aware that she could be with you for a reason.'

'If she is, so what. I enjoy spending money and I'm not telling her anything confidential,' I insisted. 'She's giving me a great time. Teaching me about fashion, improving my image. I'm meeting exciting people. Footballers who are going to invest in Hastings' funds. She's even helped me buy my flat and furnish the place. Say what you want. Pearl's OK.'

Leila and Pearl were waiting for us outside.

'Come to our place and have some coffee, Pearl,' suggested Stan. 'Leila has some lovely pieces.'

'Thanks, Stan. Another time. It's getting late,' said Pearl, pulling me towards her.

I really wanted to go with them. Stan looked down. He needed company, but I could see from Pearl's expression that she wanted out. We waved as Stan gently held Leila's arm and helped her cross the street.

'Thinking what I am?' whispered Pearl. 'It happened to my aunt. It gets worse, slowly but surely.'

'Shut up Pearl,' I snapped. 'How do you know what's wrong with her? You're no doctor. She's probably having an off day. She's a very talented artist.'

'Really? I'll introduce you to some young ones. Maybe buy some of their paintings.'

'Come with me to see Leila's art sometime. The architecture of their house is amazing.'

'You should spend more time with people our age. Stop being an outsider. You don't owe the Slimcops anything. They're not your relatives. Same with Martha. Her house is filthy. She smells of dog.'

'Martha doesn't smell. She's always having baths.'

'With the dogs?'

'Ha. Ha. Martha's just sloppy. She's been very good to me. Same with Stan and Leila.'

'Sure, Jack, sure. If you don't want to be cool, that's your business.'

We got into her car silently, me sulking. Instead of inviting me to her place, she dropped me at Martha's house, pecked me on the cheek and drove off. I felt angry and depressed. Didn't feel sleepy, so I took out the dogs and we walked late into the night.

*   *   *

The next few days, I tried to phone Pearl on her mobile and at her office, but she didn't reply to my messages. Anne Arenby became annoyed about all the calls, but I couldn't help myself. The more Pearl ignored me, the more I wanted her. I had mixed feelings about Stan. He was worried about Leila and I felt for him. On the other hand, I resented him for putting doubts in my head about Pearl. Had he said nothing, I wouldn't have had a spat with her.

I had to buy a sports car to impress her. So I bought motor magazines to find out about the latest models and began taking driving lessons. Ruff recommended an instructor. Harry Honis with tattoos all over his arms, would take me to suburban roads until I got the hang of driving.

'Do you enjoy doing this, Harry?'

'What's wrong with it?' replied Harry.

'Was just asking. That's all.'

'Believe it or not, I was a trader like you, Jack. I went straight out of school into the City and was soon in foreign exchange, trading pounds, dollars and yen. I made a bit of money and headhunters were after me. After a few years, I suffered from burn out. I was no longer performing. They wanted to move me out of trading into some boring bank office job. Not for me. They gave me a good payout two years ago and here I am. I got divorced while I was in the City.

Now I have time for my boys. My ex-wife has a job, so I pick them up from school and take them to football. It's a good life. Stress free.'

'I suppose it is also a good way to pick up girls.'

'That's right sunshine. I'm going to meet two after this. Want to come?'

'Not interested, Harry. See that flower shop over there. Can I park and buy some?'

'Sure, good practice. Now take it easy. Drive slowly. Use the outside mirror . . .'

It was getting late and the shop was about to close. Since they wanted to keep their stock fresh, I got a bargain; a magnificent bouquet of red roses and white lilies in a modern, light blue vase. Just the right thing for Pearl.

My card was to the point: 'Sorry Pearl, love you, Jack xxx'

Harry extended the lesson and let me drive to Pearl's place. We arrived around 7pm and we parked nearby. I was about to get out of the car and walk to the entrance, when I noticed Pearl with a tall well-built guy with short blond hair. He put his hand over her shoulder. They opened the door and were soon inside. I felt angry, jealous and full of regret. Had I blown our relationship?

'Is that your girlfriend with another guy?'

'I guess so.'

'Look mate, it's none of my business, but I've gone through this sort of thing before.'

'He's probably just a friend.'

'Sure mate. Just a friend,' said Harry sarcastically. 'Don't you think that it's time to move on?'

'Harry, can you do me a favour? Can you deliver them for me?'

'Positive you want me to do that?'

'Yes.'

'You'll learn.'

14

THE PLAN

In the meantime, coffee prices were going nowhere on the New York and London exchanges. Our options were up one day and down the next. Most brokers, traders and coffee manufacturers thought that prices were about to fall. The Brazilian weather was fair and I heard that some hedge funds were bearish. They had sold lots of futures and options short, aiming to buy back the coffee at a lower price and make big profits.

Ruffish called a meeting. Tong and Aram were travelling. So it was just him, me, Maffie, Krishna and Bess, who was taking notes.

'We're losing money on our options, what now, Jack?' asked Ruffish. He looked at me carefully. He thought that I was in a bad mood because of the market, but it was really Pearl. I just sat there thinking about her and didn't respond.

Krishna intervened: 'We can play it safe. Sell now and pocket $5 million, or hold on for a bit longer.'

'Time's ticking against us. If the price doesn't rise, our options will expire worthless,' replied Ruffish impatiently.

Bess looked puzzled: 'You've lost me.'

'An option gives the buyer the right to buy coffee at a future date, Bess,' explained Krishna. 'If the price of coffee falls, the option price declines, OK?'

Bess nodded.

'There's also a time element in options,' continued Krishna. 'We're now in June and have the right to buy coffee any time before December. If the coffee price doesn't rise, as we get closer and closer to Christmas, the option price will steadily fall. By the end of December, the option will expire, worthless.'

'So we're going to come unstuck, unless Jack gets the price moving,' said Bess, playfully throwing a paper cup at me. 'What chance Jack?'

'I dunno . . . Fifty, fifty. It could go up or down,' I replied, throwing it back at her.

'Stop playing around and concentrate,' chided Ruff. 'You're not in a classroom.'

'We're on a knife edge. If coffee falls below its critical support line, its decline will accelerate. We'll be down another couple of million within a day,' warned Krishna. 'I think you should sell half, Jack. At least we'll be banking some big gains.'

'That's the most prudent thing to do,' agreed Ruffish.

'I think we should wait until Jack speaks to Sergio in Rio. Let's get an opinion from the ground,' suggested Maffie.

'You paid those guys didn't you Jack?' asked Ruffish.

I was embarrassed and shook my head. I was so involved with Pearl that I had done nothing for our friends in Brazil.

'What's the matter with you, Jack? They spent a lot of their time with you. Made us a lot of money,' scolded

Ruffish. 'We'll pay Sergio and that uncle $25,000 each. That's the least we can do.'

'OK, OK, take it easy. I forgot. Sorry!'

It was late afternoon London time and morning in Rio, when we phoned Sergio.

'Olá Sergio, Como vai?' shouted Maffie over the speaker-phone.

'Hi Maffie, how's my friend Jack?'

'Fine thanks Sergio, what's the weather like there?' I asked, putting my Pearl problems aside and focusing on the market again.

'You've probably seen the reports. It's quite warm. They think the winter will be mild. The crop will be OK.'

'How's Fulvio, Sergio? Visited him recently?'

'He's here in Rio. We're going to watch football this afternoon.'

Maffie whispered: 'What luck!'

'Is he in your apartment now? Can we speak to him?' I said loudly over the speaker phone.

'Fulvio!' called Sergio. 'He's here, Jack, I'll have to interpret.'

'Olá Fulvio, Bom dia. Como está?' I asked. That was about all the Portuguese that I knew.

'Hello Jack, me fine,' said Fulvio.

'Do you expect a mild winter?'

Sergio translated and Fulvio spoke for a lengthy time in Portuguese. We looked at each other and waited, the room full of tension.

'He said that in recent years the frosts were mild,' said Sergio. 'Most people think this winter will be the same. But something happened to him. Fulvio swims all year round. So we went to the beach yesterday. It was very sunny. Quite a hot day for this time of the year, but Fulvio felt that the sea was much colder than normal. It reminded him of the seventies.'

Again there was a conversation in Portuguese.

'He says that in 1975 people also thought that a bad frost was unlikely. Then it suddenly became very cold. Winter was terrible.'

'What are the weather people saying?'

'They say that a bad frost is highly unlikely, but he's sure that they'll be wrong. People are in for a nasty surprise.'

'Ask him what he thinks about the crop?'

Another Portuguese conversation and Sergio interpreted: 'He thinks that it could be even worse than the seventies.

A few months ago, the spring drought hit the crop. A frost will damage it even more. It's going to be very bad. He feels it in his bones.'

'What about Brazil's coffee inventories?'

'If Fulvio's right our warehouses will have to supply the market. But there's a problem.'

'What problem?'

'We opened a few of the bags and tested the coffee. The quality isn't good. I think the coffee-roasting companies will reject the bags.'

'So you think coffee is going to be scarce?' queried Maffie.

'If Fulvio's right, there won't be enough coffee to supply customers, Maffie.'

Ruffish wrote something on a piece of paper and passed it to Maffie.

'We want to send you and Fulvio a present. For all your help and time,' said Maffie. 'I want to make sure of your addresses. Can you email them to me?'

'I don't want anything. Send them to Fulvio and people on the farm.'

Sergio translated what Ruff had said and they were in deep conversation again.

'Is there a problem, Sergio?' Maffie asked.

'Our farmers need help. They tell us that drug barons have come to their farms and have put pressure on them. They want them to store coca. Use their coffee farms as a cover for cocaine production,' said Sergio. 'The farmers don't want to take that risk.'

'I thought that the drug barons were based in Colombia,' said Maffie.

'They're everywhere.'

'Your farmers don't need to be involved in the drugs trade. Coffee prices are now much higher,' said Maffie, angrily. 'Why put themselves at risk? They are beginning to make profits from coffee farming.'

'The gangsters have done a deal with the Russian mafia,' Sergio continued. 'The Russians are buying coca from farmers in Colombia, Bolivia and Peru and are converting it into cocaine. They're transporting coca and cocaine through Brazil and are selling it in America, Western and Eastern Europe.'

'Why don't the Colombian barons do that themselves?'

'I'm not sure. I think the Russians provide the money and the sales outlets. I've also heard that the Russians are trying to push down the price of coffee on the world market. It's part of the deal with the Colombians.'

Our room was silent as we tried to take it all in.

'We must go now, Sergio,' Maffie said. 'Thanks very much for your help. Please phone us if it gets colder. Good luck.'

'I'm not sure what all this means,' said Bess, pouring us cups of tea.

'Colombian and other South and Central American coffee farmers couldn't make a living in the past few years. Prices were far too low,' said Maffie. 'Cocaine dealers encouraged them to pull out coffee trees and plant coca instead. The drug barons paid them much higher prices for their coca and made cocaine. Low coffee prices suit the gangsters, as they encourage more farmers to grow coca.'

'Now it seems that the Russian mafia are involved,' said Ruff.

I felt nervous when they mentioned the Russian mafia and quickly called Danny Dovetail in New York to find out if he knew anything.

'Hi Jack, wanna sell some coffee? The market looks bad.'

'No thanks, Danny. Not now.'

'You shouldn't wait much longer, it's beginning to look sick. Some big boys are dumping it. They've built up huge short positions.'

'That's what I'm phoning you about. You mentioned something about hedge funds yesterday. Do you know who they are?'

'Two big ones. They trade through several brokers. I can't identify them, but I heard that they're Russian. Have offices in Moscow and New York. Every time coffee rallies, they hit it.'

'Are they using Blaby?'

'You know very well that I can't tell you that, Jack! But as it happens, no.'

'Thanks Danny.'

I put down the phone.

'Some coincidence,' said Maffie. 'Russian hedge funds dumping coffee and a Russian deal with Columbian cocaine traders who want lower prices.'

'I don't like the sound of it. I think we should get out,' I said. Anything involving the Russian mafia scared me witless.

Maffie patted my shoulder: 'Strange that Fulvio is staying with Sergio; that the sea has turned cold. Maybe it's a sign.'

'Getting into Zulu mysticism are we?' scoffed Ruffish.

'If the old man is right, the market's going to be caught on the wrong foot,' said Krishna who was looking at the screen.

'Let's vote on it. Go with the market and dump our positions, or listen to the Old Man and hold on,' said Ruffish. He voted 'out'. I put aside my Russian fears, followed the rest and voted 'in!'

'Let's take a break and mull it over. I want you guys to be completely sure. A lot's at stake,' said Ruffish.

We took out some beer and cold drinks from the fridge in the meeting room, opened a hatch in the ceiling with a pole and pulled down a ladder. On the roof terrace, that cloudless summer's day, I looked around at the view. To our left were the trees of Green Park and a glimpse of Buckingham Palace. The Hilton and Continental Hotels and Hyde Park were about centre and down below were Charles Street and Berkley Square. In the distance, to the right, Oxford and Bond Streets.

This was Mayfair, hedge fund land; home of the money managers who cater for the super rich. I was one of them and had just turned seventeen. How many guys had achieved that! Most of them were wasting time at school and university, scrambling for work experience for zero money. They were either getting into debt or living off their parents. Not me. I was a player. A serious player! Already a name in the market! A headhunter had even called me. As I finished off my beer, I observed the others.

Krishna, one of the nicest guys I had ever met, was throwing and catching a squash ball. He wasn't only brilliant, but a good sportsman, keen on tennis, squash and cricket. He came from a poor immigrant family in Rishikesh, close to the Ganges, in northern India. I would sometimes come up to the roof terrace with him. He would change into shorts, put down a mat and do some yoga exercises. He tried to teach me the 'asanas' and showed me how to meditate. Not for me. I was fairly spiritual before, but Pearl had drummed into me that it was better to get on with the practical things in life. Make money. With money came respect, power and largesse. When I told Krishna what Pearl had said, he just smiled and shook his head. Inner peace was his thing.

Krishna noticed when I was down the other day: 'There are plenty of girls around, Jack. Be patient. The right one will come along.'

Nice guy, Krishna, but what did he know about my

relationship with Pearl? When you're mad about someone and they don't feel the same about you? He had an arranged marriage. A baby was already on the way.

Ruffish was a mystery man, keeping his family life to himself. He lived in stockbroker land, near Maidenhead, Berkshire. He had a family photo in his office. His wife was quite attractive and seemed to be about his age and his son and daughter didn't look much older than me. Ruff was drinking sparkling water, as he had been on a diet in the past few months. He now looked fit and young for a guy in his mid fifties. Ruff was talking earnestly to Maffie, who looked great.

Maffie was another closed book. As far as I knew she didn't have a boyfriend. We had great fun together, going to the movies, shows and parties, but she never let me get near her. After all these months, our friendship was platonic. It was frustrating at first, but I got used to it. Anyway Pearl came along and filled the gap. That is until I screwed up our relationship!

Bess Trilingham-Marsh was not only pretty and nice, but highly intelligent. She was the daughter of a leading criminal lawyer, Maffie had told me. Bess had studied languages at Manchester University and was still going out with a guy who she had met there.

It was about 5pm on that Friday summer afternoon and the terrace was bathed in sunlight. Staff could relax and sometimes entertain clients in our very own office garden with pot plants and garden chairs. Completely at ease, I took off my shirt.

'You're not on holiday here,' grinned Ruffish, pulling up

a chair and raising the large umbrella. 'Thinking time is work time.'

We sat in a circle.

'The best form of defence is attack,' said Maffie.

'Chief Shaka again,' I mumbled, closing my eyes for a second.

'Yes Jack, Just what Shaka would do. We should buy coffee.'

'Have you gone mad, we're thinking of dumping the stuff and you want to buy?' sighed Ruffish.

'Not immediately. Only if Sergio and Fulvio warn us that a frost is imminent.'

'What happens if it gets warmer and the price falls a lot further? We're already down,' said Ruffish. 'The logical thing to do is to cut our losses and get out.'

'And the logical thing for the Russian bears, is to go with the momentum. Build up their short positions,' argued Maffie. 'Danny believes that they're already massive. Who are at greater risk? Them or us?'

'Them of course! Ruff,' said Krishna. 'We don't have to cut losses. We still have a large cushion of profits. We've already banked more than $3 million. We left excess profits in the options market. OK, so our options profit is down $1 million to $5 million and could fall further, but it is still profit. We're in a very comfortable position.'

'But aren't the bears also making money?' I asked.

'Yes some are, but they have also been building up big short positions, around current prices. Maffie's right. They must be on edge,' said Krishna.

'You've lost me. Can you explain what's going on,' said

Bess, who wanted to become a fund manager.

'Sure Bess. We're the bulls, the optimists,' explained Krishna. 'We bought coffee futures and options at low prices. The prices have gone up a lot and we have made money. The price has fallen from the top, but we still have a big profit.'

'And the bears?'

'They are the pessimists. They believe that coffee prices will fall. They have used futures and options to sell coffee short. They hope to buy it back at lower prices. They'll make profits if the price falls and lose if it rises,' Krishna continued.

'They are playing with highly leveraged futures and options,' said Maffie. 'If the price rises by ten per cent or more, they'll be big losers. They either have to put up more margin, or buy back the coffee at a loss.'

'So who's in greater danger, Bess, them or us?' smiled Krishna.

'It seems like a game of poker,' said Bess, who had card parties with her friends. 'Players with winnings are comfortable and can put more money on the table. Others who are even, or are losing, are nervous. To me it doesn't matter whether you are bulls or bears. It depends on your hand. I guess it also depends on how you bluff.'

'That's precisely what we should do, Bess, play a game of bluff. How do you bluff in poker?' asked Maffie.

'Well you need luck, of course, but you bluff when you have a bad hand. You want your opponents to think that you have a better hand than them. Then they will throw down their cards on the table and you take the winnings.'

'Or you bluff with a good hand, a great hand, a Straight

Flush,' said Maffie. 'That's a double bluff. You make the other guys feel that you are bluffing with a bad hand, so they put more money on the table. They ask to "see you" and you show your hand. It beats them all.'

'We must have luck, lots of luck, Maffie. One of the other players may have a Royal Flush and finish us,' cautioned Ruffish.

'Sure Ruff, I'm not saying we should move now. All I'm saying is that we shouldn't leave the table yet. We need just one more card, a card with frost on the edges. The game isn't over.'

*   *   *

The flowers worked. After a week or so, Pearl phoned me.

'I'm off to New York, Jack. Business. Want to join me?' she asked casually.

I was taken aback. I thought our affair was over and now this offer! Pearl certainly blew hot and cold.

'Sure, if my boss lets me.'

'Persuade him. Now! I'm flying in a few hours and will be there for a week.'

I bolted into Ruff's office while he was having a meeting with Maffie.

'Why don't you guys knock before you enter?' exclaimed Ruff.

'Because we can see you through the glass walls,' I said. 'Would you mind if I go to New York tonight? I'll be back next week.'

'What if coffee takes off?'

'I'll get on a plane straight away and be back the next morning.'

'What do you think Maffie?'

'Nothing's happening in the market at the moment. The Brazilian weather forecast is mild for the next fortnight. I can handle his fund for him.'

'How come you want to go to New York again? You were there in the spring,' said Ruff, suspiciously.

'Pearl is going there on business. She asked me to go along with her.'

'I thought that you had broken up with her Jack,' said Maffie, surprised.

'It's on with her again,' I grinned.

'Does your girl know what we do here?' asked Ruff with a stern face.

'No! Promise Ruff. Only general stuff. Told her that we manage hedge funds, but I've never gone into detail. She doesn't know anything about our trading.'

'It had better stay that way Jack. Especially now. We have very special information,' said Maffie.

'Promise you Maff, my lips are sealed.'

'OK. You can go to New York. But you're going to do some research for us,' said Ruff. 'Danny Dovetail is a broker who I can trust. Have dinner with him and ask him everything he knows about those Russian hedge fund managers.'

'Good idea, Ruff,' said Maffie. 'Jack should get more information in New York. We want to know who their brokers are. Where they are based, where they hang out. Everything! Do it as subtly as possible.'

'How do I introduce the subject?'

'Just say that we are thinking of getting out of the market, but we want to make sure what's going on.'

'OK.'

'If we need you here quickly, you'll be on the next plane, right!'

'Sure Maffie, I promise.'

*   *   *

With Pearl, air travel was nothing less than business class. Compared to my economy flights to Rio and New York, the trip was heaven. Champagne, seafood and easy on the legs. We arrived at the Peninsula Hotel on Fifth Avenue at 10pm, New York time. The place was so luxurious that I felt embarrassed to be there.

'Is this on expenses, Pearl?' I asked.

'No, of course not. You're paying, Jack.'

My mouth dropped: 'What! Our room costs almost $800 a night!'

'You can afford it Jack,' said Pearl grinning. 'Get used to it.'

'What!'

'Just joking, Jack, just joking. Of course it's on expenses. My client is paying.'

'Who is your client?'

'What are you doing in the markets?'

'Touché!'

A light meal was served in our room, which had awesome views of Manhattan. We had showers separately and that night Pearl wasn't interested in making love. Pity, it was a king sized bed and would have been great for sex. It was the wrong time of the month, she said. My luck! Pearl rushed off early in the morning and I tried out the fitness facilities on the rooftop. There was a gym and pool and I swam a few lengths. With Pearl busy, it was a good opportunity to meet with Danny. To keep it as discrete as possible, I suggested that we have a drink after the market closed and go for a walk in Battery Park.

To kill time, I dropped in at Tiffany's. One of the girls helped me choose some diamond studs for Pearl. Stan and Leila had encouraged me to visit the Museum of Modern Art. I was more interested in sport than culture, but I was learning fast and especially liked Kandinsky and the strange paintings of Dalí. I thought about the vast majority of artists who struggled and died in poverty, long before their works were sold for millions. No justice in this world. Those guys had serious talent whereas traders like me merely had to take bets on the market and make loads of money.

Danny was waiting in a café in the Winter Garden of the World Financial Centre.

'How ya doing Jack? What brings you to New York?'

'My girlfriend's here on business. Asked me to join her.'

'Where you staying?'

'Peninsula.'

'Wow! That must cost an arm and a leg.'

'She has a big expense account for branding and marketing. That sort of stuff. She has to impress people.'

'Are you going to do any work? Take another course?'

'Thought I would make use of my time and meet with you. Find out what's happening in the market.'

'Coffee's down again, Jack. It's looking bad for you guys. Maybe you should get out.'

'Maybe. Are those hedge funds still selling?'

'Big time. They wait for the market to rally and then dump the stuff.'

We left the café and walked past the yachts in North Cove harbour, alongside the waterfront, towards Battery Park.

'Who are these Russian hedge fund managers?'

'I got some more information since I last spoke to you. The funds are called Veruschka and Borodino. I'm told that they manage as much as $10 billion.'

'Wow! They must have massive positions with that kind of money.'

'That's not all. Some US and Swiss hedge funds are following them and are also selling coffee short. They're betting that the price will fall below $2.'

'We're not far from there now. It's a crucial support level. If it cracks two bucks, the price could collapse.'

'That's why I think you guys should get out.'

'Where are the Russians based? Moscow?'

'Yes. But they also have offices here. Heard of the Russian Samovar?'

'The contraption that brews tea?'

'No. Name of a restaurant and piano bar,' laughed Danny. 'It's near Broadway. If I remember, it's on West 52nd Street. Not far from the Sheraton.'

'Does it have Russian music and dancing?'

'Yeah. Lots of Russians frequent the place. Vodka and beer to wash down herring, smoked fish, borscht and caviar.'

'Do those Borodino and Veruschka guys go there?'

'I'm told that it's their drinking hole. Their office is about a block away. I think it's on West 51st Street.'

'Would you know them if you saw them?'

'Yeah. Someone pointed them out to me at a hedge fund conference last month.'

'If they're such big players, don't you want them as clients?'

'My boss was going to pitch for them, but we decided against it.'

'Why?'

'We've been told that they've got unsavoury connections.'

'Who?'

'We hear that the Russian mafia might have a stake in the funds.'

I turned away from him, looked towards the waterfront and adjusted my dark glasses.

'Have you come across them in London?' asked Danny, observing me closely.

'No, I haven't,' I lied, feeling uneasy.

'Tell you what Jack, I don't live very far from the Russian Samovar. We can have a drink and bite there and go for a walk in Central Park. Who knows we might find out something.'

I wasn't terribly happy with the idea, but went along with it. Maffie and Ruff were expecting me to find out as much as possible about the Russians.

After leaving a message on Pearl's mobile, suggesting that we meet in Broadway and see a show, we arrived at the Russian Samovar. A pianist was playing Russian melodies and several people were sitting by the bar chatting in a language which I assumed to be Russian. We sat down near the bar and sampled some vodka, caviar and smoked fish.

'That's them,' whispered Danny, nudging me.

Two fairly big guys, who were dressed in smart suits, but looked like gangsters, entered. They sat by the bar near to us.

'Are you sure that they're hedge fund managers?' I asked. 'They look like thugs.'

'Yes. The guy with a scar on his forehead runs Borodino and the one who limps, Veruschka. Should we introduce ourselves?'

Before I could reply in the negative, another man came up to the bar and joined them. He was well over six foot with a large flat broken nose and a thick black beard. To say that I freaked was an understatement. If he wasn't the same killer who I had encountered on Charing Cross Bridge, he was a pretty good double.

'I have to meet my girlfriend,' I mumbled, after swiftly downing my vodka. I put on my dark glasses and carefully made my way past the bar, making sure that I didn't disturb the hedge fund gang. By the time I was outside, I was in such a panic that I was breathing rapidly. I had chest pains and was feeling dizzy. It was all the more scary as I had read an article about sudden death syndrome that morning. Guys my age could have a heart attack and die! The more I thought about the possibilities, the faster the breathing and the greater the pain. Danny followed me outside, rushed up to me and rubbed my back gently.

'Jack, what's wrong? Do you have asthma? Are you allergic to anything?'

'I don't think Vodka agrees with me,' I fibbed, making sure that my dark glasses were on and trying to stop breathing rapidly.

'Let's have something to drink, Jack,' said Danny, pulling me into a café. He sat me down, swiftly purchased two bottles of water and grabbed a paper bag.

'You're hyperventilating. Breathe into the bag. Yes, that's right. Hold it by the neck. Breathe into it. Say "sh . . . sh . . ." That's it. Good. Go on! "Sh . . . sh". Feeling better. Good.'

He anxiously watched me drink some water and sat with me as I leaned over the table and coughed.

'Thanks Danny. Thanks a lot,' I gasped, feeling relieved.

'No sweat. Did a course in First Aid. Sure you're OK?'

'Sure.'

'Do you know any of those guys?'

'Promise me two things Danny. One for my sake and one for yours. Don't tell anyone about this and don't have anything to do with them.'

'Sure, Jack, don't worry. When you're ready sometime, maybe you'll tell me what's going on.'

My mobile rang. It was Pearl.

'Hi Jack. You're lucky. I've just finished work and I'm very close to Broadway. A show's a great idea.'

Danny gave her some directions and she was soon with us in the coffee shop.

She didn't seem to notice my distress. Didn't even kiss me hello.

'Jack's been a bit sick,' said Danny.

She looked at me casually. 'He seems OK now. Right Jack?'

'Pearl, this is Danny,' I whispered hoarsely.

'Didn't take you long to get here, Pearl,' said Danny.

'I was virtually around the corner. My client's offices are in West 51st Street. What do you do, Danny?'

'I'm a trader. Friend of Jack. A good friend,' he said, massaging my back.

'What do you trade?'

'All sorts of things. Your accent, Pearl, where do you come from?'

'America, of course. Washington D.C. My parents live in Annapolis.'

'Where were you born?'

'What's the difference? Ukraine. We came here when I was ten,' replied Pearl, irritated.

'Just interested. Must go Jack, will speak to you soon. Now take care!' said Danny, putting a hand on my shoulder.

We shook hands and off he went. That night we saw 'The Music Man'. It was a wonderful show with many trombones. Pity that I wasn't relaxed enough to enjoy it.

*　　*　　*

The next morning, I went for a run in Central Park. Running always helped me calm down. If I had had the chance to run the previous day, I probably wouldn't have hyperventilated and would have got rid of the tension. Anyway I felt strong and though I had briefly panicked, there was no way that I would have a heart attack, like Dad. He was a smoker and unfit. I was the opposite. Back at the hotel, I had a swim and felt a lot better. Pearl had a couple of days off. So later in the morning, we bought a suitcase and filled it with clothes chosen from Saks and Bergdorf Goodman.

The shopping spree made me forget myself and at the end of the day, after we unloaded the stuff in the room, I gave Pearl her earrings. To my surprise – because I didn't have much clue about these things – she liked them. She hugged and kissed me and then undressed herself and me. We were soon under the power shower with warm water crashing down on us. Afterwards we made love, with Pearl being much more tender than usual.

Later I bought iPods for both of us and we walked into Central Park, holding hands. It was the most romantic evening I had ever had with her. We ambled from the Zoo to Strawberry Fields, Yoko Ono's memorial to John Lennon. Afterwards we hired a boat, rowed to the centre of the lake and relaxed, enjoying the peaceful park and the Manhattan skyline.

My head was on Pearl's lap while we floated aimlessly. We were so wrapped up in each other that we hardly noticed other boats struggling to avoid us.

'That Danny guy, is he a coffee trader?' Pearl asked suddenly.

'Yes.'

'Where does he think the market's going? Up or down?'

'I have no idea, Pearl.'

'It's boring not knowing what you guys are doing. It must be exciting, but you keep me in the dark,' whispered Pearl, and kissing my ear

'I'm not allowed to discuss my firm's dealings,' I said firmly.

'What's so important about your trading? Why the confidentiality? You're not a doctor.'

No reply.

'OK. I'll bring you into my confidence and don't tell anyone about it. I have to know more about coffee because we're doing market research and branding for a new US and European coffee chain,' she said. 'They aim to beat Starbucks and Costa. To do that they need to have the best information on the market and qualities and have good supply sources.'

'That's an interesting job for you, Pearl. What's the name of the company?'

'We're still deciding on a suitable brand name.'

'And you want me to tell you about our deals?'

'There you go. Loyalty to your firm. If you don't perform, they'll hang you out to dry. How on earth can we have a good relationship if you don't trust me, Jack?'

'OK. Who was that big blond guy at your place a few weeks ago?'

'Are you stalking me, Jack?' she snapped, pushing me off her lap. 'He's just a good friend, if you really want to know. I help him with his image from time to time.'

'OK, OK. I know it sounds corny, but I really love you, Pearl.'

'So help me with my work.'

I felt that I was letting her down. A frost and price surge could happen at any time, but that would be on the wires almost immediately. The whole market would know about it. Would it really be a problem if my girlfriend knew a bit about my trading? Maybe she had some ideas. After all husbands tell their wives what's happening. Pearl and I were getting very close. Maybe we could go to Las Vegas and get married.

'OK Pearl, you're right. I'm being unreasonable. We think that . . .'

I was about to tell her, when my mobile rang. It was Danny on the phone.

'Jack, how are you? Feeling better?'

'Yeah, thanks Danny. Nice of you to phone.'

'Maffie's been trying to get hold of you. She can't get through. Wants you to phone her as soon as possible.'

'Really?'

'Yes. Where are you?'

'Lying in a boat on Central Park Lake. With Pearl. Fantastic day.'

'Jack, put the handset close to your ear. I want to tell you something.'

'What?'

'It's about Pearl . . .'

The phone went dead. I banged it. Tried to phone back Danny. Couldn't get a signal.

'What's going on Jack?' asked Pearl.

I was a bit confused. What was Danny trying to tell me about her? I stood up in the boat and nearly capsized it.

'What does he want, Jack?' insisted Pearl.

'He's worried about the wheat and corn markets,' I lied.

'You were going to talk to me about coffee.'

'Will have to do that later. I have to sort out our grain positions.'

Back in the hotel when Pearl was changing for dinner,

I sneaked out of the room, found a discrete place in the reception area and phoned Maffie.

'Hi Maffie. Any news?'

'Yep, Sergio called. The weather's beginning to turn in Brazil. The temperature is falling fast. He thinks there could be a frost.'

'Have you started buying?'

'No. He called after the market closed. You must be here tomorrow. Can you make it?'

'I'll do my best to get the last flight. I'll have to break the news to Pearl.'

'What are you going to say?'

'That you're ill and there's a big problem with the fund.'

Pearl was livid when I told her that I had to fly out that Wednesday night.

'Why are you going, when I need you Jack? It's them, always them. What about me?'

She was so angry that she gave me a punch on the arm, so hard that there was a flaming red mark.

'We were supposed to spend the weekend together.'

'Sorry Pearl, I have to go.'

'You were going to help me understand the coffee market.'

'Haven't got time, Pearl. Will tell you in London,' I said.

She looked hurt. Seriously upset. Had to say something, anything, but despite my feelings and guilt, couldn't tell her what was really going on.

'OK, I'll break our rules for you. We think that the coffee and other commodities are weak and that prices could fall.'

'What am I going to do here by myself?' she wailed.

'Why don't you fly to Washington? See your parents. You haven't seen them for ages.'

'My mother and father got divorced. She got re-married when I was a little girl. I can't stand my stepfather.'

'What about your Mum? Doesn't she miss you? Go on! Go and visit her. I tried to hug her, but she pushed me away.

15

A KILLING

After managing to get on the last flight, I landed in London late morning and rushed straight from the airport to the office. The coffee charts and price statistics showed that the trend was still down. Since the market had been weak in the past month, profits on our coffee options had halved to around $3 million. The price was hovering around $2.15 a pound. Danny had told me that Veruschka and Borodino had built up huge short positions in the coffee futures and options market. Some European and US hedge funds had trailed them and had also sold coffee short. The Russian bears and their allies were betting that the price would fall below $2 and for the moment, they were on top.

Before the New York trip, Maffie and Krishna had told me to take profits on Aquarium's gold and agricultural shares and other investments. We now had an extra $800,000 cash in the kitty to purchase more options. Our tiny Aquarium fund was about to fight back. David against the Russian Goliaths.

Ruffish was becoming increasingly edgy. I was also nervous, for a different reason. I was paranoid about the big bearded thug at the Russian Samovar and the likelihood that he had murdered Yapolovitch. It was dangerous to take on those guys.

'Come on Jack, block it out. Keep focused. Your head down,' I kept muttering to myself. 'They didn't see you there. They don't know what you look like.'

These thoughts kept whirling round and round in my head.

At last the call from Brazil came. It was 12.30pm in London and 7.30am in New York. The New York coffee market was due to start trading at 8.30am.

'Sergio on the phone for Maffie,' shouted Bess.

We all rushed to Maffie's work station. Compared to us, Maffie was calm and relaxed. She first spoke in Portuguese and then in English.

'You say that the temperature has dropped, Sergio. Are you quite sure there's going to be a cold front?'

She noticed all the anxious faces and put the phone on to speaker.

'The weather forecasters are warning that it could get a lot colder, but they are not that certain,' Sergio said.

'Fulvio believes that there will be a frost, right?'

'Yes, Fulvio says that a severe frost is on its way.'

'What do you think it's going to do to the crop?'

'It's not whether the crop is going to be bad, it's how bad.'

'How come coffee prices haven't started rising?' asked Maffie.

'I can't understand it. It doesn't make sense.'

'It's weak because the market is following two Russian

hedge funds that are big sellers,' I said. 'What does Fulvio think?'

'Fulvio hasn't changed his mind. He's now even more convinced. He's sure that it will be 1975 all over again. That frost surprised everyone.'

'Thanks Sergio . . . You're a good friend . . . If we win, you'll also do well,' said Maffie.

'I was going to write, Maffie. Please thank your boss. We all appreciate it. Fulvio, the farmers and me,' said Sergio. '$50,000! Bless you all!'

'I'll tell him . . . Wait, Sergio. If Fulvio's right, then . . .'

'Maffie, Maffie . . . Can't hear you . . . Bye.'

She put down the phone and I looked at my watch. It was 7.45am, New York Time.

'The market opens in forty five minutes,' shouted Maffie.

'Aquarium bulls against Russian bears,' shouted Krishna, slapping his hands against his thighs.

We rushed into the meeting room and sat around the table. Maffie stood before us in front of the whiteboard. She had blue and red felt pens.

'OK, General Shaka we're in your hands,' said Ruffish.

'We're ready, Ruff. Jack has $800,000 to buy another 100 coffee options,' said Maffie.

'Are you crazy? We'll then have 200 options! That's the right to purchase 7.5 million pounds of coffee,' shouted Ruff. 'At $2.20 a pound that comes to $16.5 million! The leverage is enormous. Our exposure to the market will be more than sixteen times the original capital of the Aquarium fund. If the price falls, the fund's finished.'

'Don't worry Ruff, we're not going to buy all the options

at once,' replied Maffie softly. 'We won't lose our original capital as that is safely in the kitty. We are playing with profits and as you know, options are far less risky than futures.'

'I've been studying the coffee statistics,' said Krishna. 'Consumer demand for coffee is far greater than supply. The shortage should squeeze the bears. Prices could go ballistic!

'What's a bear squeeze?' asked Bess.

'South American, African and Asian coffee production has declined. They cannot meet the orders from the manufacturers that roast the coffee and sell it to the shops,' Krishna explained. 'In normal circumstances prices should have risen. Instead they have fallen because the Russian hedge funds and other bearish speculators, have been heavy sellers.'

'The bears sold coffee futures and options short, hoping to buy them back at a profit when the price falls,' Krishna continued. 'Now imagine how they will feel if a frost causes prices to rise unexpectedly. They will be nervous. They know that they have sold coffee that they do not own. They know that they must buy back their positions quickly, if prices rise. If they don't they will lose a lot of money.'

'So they will panic and try and buy back the coffee,' said Bess. 'But you said there's a shortage, so who's going to sell to them?'

'They will have to bid up prices to encourage sellers. But the market will soon realise that the bears are desperate to buy. So players who own coffee will wait and demand even higher prices. The bears will be squeezed into a tight corner.'

'My money and the firm's money are at stake,' said Ruff. 'If you're that sure, are you prepared to back it with yours?'

'Jack already has money in Aquarium and Maffie and I are putting in another hundred thousand each,' said Krishna.

'Me too,' said Tong.

'And you Aram?'

'Can't take chances. I've got a family to support. School fees. I'll give it a miss,' said Aram Zabkian, the Eastern European specialist, who had just returned from visiting his mother in Estonia. He had always been sceptical about Aquarium.

'I'll double my chips,' said Bess.

Maffie went to the board in front of us and held up the blue and red felt pens.

'If you guys don't mind, I'm going to head operations,' said Maffie. 'I'll decide when to buy and sell.'

'Good on you General, what's Miner going to do?' asked Aram.

'Jack's going to be the front man. He'll execute the orders.'

'Will do,' I said.

I wasn't annoyed that Maffie was taking over. I was relieved. Since I had seen the Russians in New York, I had become so jittery that I wasn't thinking straight.

'Krishna will do the calculations and choose the best options for Jack,' Maffie continued. 'He and I will remain in the background.'

'I presume I'll buy as soon as the market opens this morning,' I said.

'That's right. But you're going to buy and sell simultaneously Jack. You're going to sell 20 coffee options through two or three brokers and ask Danny and another broker to buy 50.'

I was puzzled. 'Why can't I just buy 30, Maffie?'

'It's like poker, Jack. You'll be bluffing,' said Bess. 'Some people will think that you're buying; others that you're selling. They won't be sure of your hand.'

'Precisely, Bess,' said Maffie. 'We want to buy our coffee at the lowest possible prices, but also send a message to the bears that they could be wrong. The aim is to stop them selling. We want the price to first settle and then rise.'

'Do you seriously believe that this boy will influence the market?' scoffed Aram.

'What's Jack's age got to do with it? He's trading on the phone and they think that he's older. Anyway who cares?' retorted Maffie. 'Jack's already made money in the coffee market. He's now well known in the dealing community. His friends call him Trader Jack and jealous dealers and brokers gossip about the teen trader. Brokers will talk. All brokers do. The NYMEX trading pit will be rife with gossip.'

'Jack's been out of the coffee market for a few weeks. Believe me, when Trader Jack starts buying again, they'll take notice,' said Krishna.

'OK, so that's the start. What's the overall battle plan, Maffie?' I asked.

'We'll follow Shaka's strategy,' she said.

'Oh no! It's not going to sound like a computer game, is it?' groaned Ruffish.

Maffie laughed and then drew two thick horizontal lines on the whiteboard. The bottom blue line was Aquarium and the red line above, represented our enemy, the Russian bears.

'Similarly to Shaka's tactics we won't attack the Russian

hedge funds immediately,' explained Maffie. 'We will advance slowly by carefully building up our option positions. If prices rise we will attack in earnest and buy a lot more.'

To illustrate her plan, Maffie drew two vertical blue lines that rose from each side of the lower blue Aquarium line towards the red line. These were Shaka's 'horns of the buffalo' that advanced towards the right and left flanks of the enemy. Maffie then curved the blue horns inwards so that the red Russian bear battle line was totally surrounded. That action represented the final coffee purchases that would encircle and squeeze the bears.

'Seems so simple. Hope your military game plan works,' said Ruffish with a half laugh. 'If you're wrong? If there isn't a frost in Brazil?'

'Highly unlikely,' said Maffie confidently as she looked at the screen. 'But if we're wrong, we'll retreat with less profits, not a loss.'

'OK, so we begin to advance towards the red line. But we're small and they're big. Who will help us?' I asked.

'The market will provide our extra regiments. As soon as the coffee roasters and others notice that the price is rising, they will follow us and buy,' said Maffie confidently.

Carefully following Maffie's instructions, I phoned Danny at Blaby just before the opening of the New York market: 'Hi Danny, sorry about the other day, we were cut off.'

'I was going to tell you about . . .'

'No time. Thanks to you, I'm back in London, Danny. I really appreciate what you did for me. By the way where's most of the selling coming from? Which brokers?'

'Darlington and Halesburg. Thinking of selling Jack? The price was down another 5 cents yesterday.'

'No. We want to buy. Here's the order . . .'

'What the . . .!'

We bought a lot of coffee options through Blaby and another broker at the opening of the New York market and simultaneously sold fewer options through Darlington and Halesburg. At the close of trade our net option positions had risen to almost 5 million pounds of coffee worth $10 million. Maffie's plan was working. The coffee price bounced off the bottom, but wasn't running away yet. The wires reported that evening that there was a sudden cold front in Brazil and the coffee price rose at the opening on Friday morning. We steadily continued to buy more coffee options as the price turned around and began rising. The Russian bears and their allies tried to counter the price rally and sold even more coffee short. Prices slipped when they sold, but quickly rose again when we and some other firms bought. This was another sign that the battle was beginning to swing in our favour. At the end of the trading day, Aquarium fund owned 200 options, giving us the right to buy 7.5 million pounds or 50,000 bags of coffee in warehouses worth about $18 million. We had completed our buying. Now we had to wait and see what the market was going to do.

*   *   *

Fulvio was proven right. Brazil had another, more severe, cold front on Saturday. I was on edge on Sunday and to relax decided to take the dogs for a walk. My mobile rang. It was Pearl.

'Hi Jack, I'm back home. Sorry I lost my temper and hit you.'

'No problem, Pearl. It should be me who should apologise. I let you down. You were entitled to be angry.'

'Let's make up,' said Pearl. 'Why don't we meet in Primrose Hill?'

That evening we went for dinner at a Greek restaurant in Primrose Hill, a London village, just north of Regent's Park. Pearl looked great in skinny white jeans and a black camisole, but seemed down.

She had chicken and I had some mixed grilled fish. We finished a bottle of wine and were silent most of the time.

'How's your Mum, Pearl?'

'OK, I suppose. I found the visit depressing. She and my stepfather are oblivious to everyone else. I miss my own Dad.'

'Where is he?'

'Moscow . . .' she stopped, as if she had made a mistake.

'Moscow? I thought that you were Ukrainian. How come your Dad's in Moscow?'

'Ukrainians speak Russian, do business with Russians why shouldn't he be there?' she snapped.

'Stop being oversensitive, Pearl, I'm just interested,' I insisted, holding up my hands.

How would she know about my experience with Russians? My paranoia. There were many millions of good Russians. Only some were bad. Still, why had she never talked about her real father? We left the restaurant and went for a walk in Primrose Hill's park near the village. It was almost 9.30pm, but was still light that lovely mid summer's evening. At the top of the Hill we looked towards the Aviary in front of London Zoo, the greenery of Regent's Park, the Post Office Tower in the West End and St Paul's Cathedral and the City further to the east. We sat on a bench and I put my arm around Pearl and gave her a peck on the cheek. She turned towards me and kissed me. This time, thankfully, I tasted Turkish delights, mixed with coffee. Not cigarettes. Feeling romantic, I pulled her closer, but this time she pushed me away.

'You don't trust me Jack. You never tell me what you're doing. You also lied to me. You told me that coffee was going to go down. Instead the price has gone up a lot.'

Another fib was necessary: 'Sorry Pearl, we thought that the market was weak. The weather took us by surprise.'

'You've embarrassed me, Jack. My client's furious! I've had to do a lot of explaining.'

Aquarium had already completed all its purchases of coffee, so I could give her some information.

'We think that the coffee price is going to rise further. You can tell the client that.'

'So you're no longer bearish? You're now bulls? Thanks a lot, Jack,' she replied sarcastically.

'We have to be flexible in volatile markets, Pearl. You know that we have confidentiality rules.'

'I thought that I could trust you.'

'You can, Pearl, you can. I'll tell you all I know about coffee, except our trading strategies and details.'

Again sarcasm: 'Sure Jack, sure. You'll tell me all.'

I tried to put my arm around her, but she wriggled away

and walked along one of the paths down the hill. I followed, tried to grab her hand but she pulled it away. She didn't want any physical contact. Pearl now had a vacant expression. Wasn't interested in anything. This wasn't the extroverted Pearl, I knew. She was normally full of life, full of fun. But she wasn't faking this. She was down, really down. Was it her parents or me? I couldn't be certain. Should I tell her? Help her in her branding exercise? I felt guilty that I had let her down. All these mixed feelings. Part love, part distrust. Maybe tell her later next week. Not yet. On Friday, Maffie and Ruff had given me strict instructions yet again: 'Keep your mouth shut!'

On one of the paths, about two to three hundred yards below, I thought I recognised a couple. Looked like Maggie and her husband Hal. They walked into a shadow and were soon indistinct. Time had passed swiftly. Memories were becoming distant; Maggie and the loch; Ivor Ensworth and the twins; the Scottish dances.

'Want to go to Cape Town for Christmas, I've got some good friends there?' I suggested.

'Maybe . . . If we're still together,' mumbled Pearl.

That hurt me, but it served me right. If I had been in her position, I would have felt the same. We walked in silence for about half a mile. From the park, through Primrose Hill village again and over a railway bridge towards her Chalk Farm flat. That night, we had a few drinks. She wasn't interested in making love or even being cuddled. She smoked some pot in an attempt to cheer herself up and offered me some. Not for me! No way was I going to be spaced out ahead of trading, the next day.

The weed didn't change her mood. It made it worse. Pearl, even more vacant and depressed, walked out of the living room into her bedroom. I watched some football highlights on TV and about ten minutes later went into her bedroom. Pearl was fast asleep on her bed with her clothes on. She woke up briefly and turned away from me when I tried to undress her. No point. She didn't want me there, so I gloomily went home and scrolled the Internet until about midnight to get my mind off her. News about South America showed that a severe frost had enveloped Brazil. The market was going to go crazy.

*   *   *

Early Monday morning, Krishna was hard at work on his calculations while I examined my figures and charts and drew a new aquarium. The brown fish had risen from the bottom of the tank and were breaking through the membrane into a higher compartment. The turnaround had been rapid. We expected pandemonium in the market. A severe frost would destroy at least half of Brazil's crop and it was the biggest coffee producer in the world. There was going to be a global coffee shortage. Manufacturers like Nestlé, Kraft and Lavazza would be doing their utmost to buy as much coffee as they could to supply their customers. They were already bidding robusta coffee prices higher on the London market. Bess was busy scrolling the Net for weather and other news and calling out snippets and prices from Bloomberg trading screens.

Maffie and Ruffish entered the office together. They were talking excitedly.

'You're going to experience something unusual in the market today, Bess,' said Maffie. 'An acute bear squeeze.'

'Does this mean that the bears are now cornered and the horns of the bull are encircling them?' asked Bess.

'Yep, there's going to be one hell of a panic,' said Maffie. 'The bears have to buy back the multi million pounds of coffee futures and options that they've sold.'

'No one is going to be keen to sell,' I said.

'From my information and calculations, the Russian hedge funds and other bears must be already beginning to lose on their short positions,' said Krishna. 'They'll be forced to bid prices higher and higher to get out.'

We waited for the opening on the New York Coffee, Cocoa and Sugar Exchange.

Danny was on the speaker phone: 'Hey guys, they're filming the market on *CNBC*. Put your TV on. The Brazilian frost is the worst in years.'

We rushed to the TV and sure enough, the lead story was coffee. Traders and their clerks were huddling together. A few of them seemed tense. The bell rang and there was bedlam. Dealers shouted and screamed, signalling with their palms and fingers, 'Buy! Buy! Buy.' Two dealers who held up their palms to indicate that they were sellers, were overwhelmed. They disappeared under a heap of scrambling bodies and emerged severely shaken. Within minutes, the price was 'limit up' which meant that the market couldn't cope with the volume of buy orders. The price was frozen at $2.80 a pound, a new high for the year. The market had come to a halt.

'This isn't normal buying,' shouted the *CNBC* reporter. 'It appears to be coming from distressed bears. They sold short, hoping to profit from a price fall. But the price is surging and they are worried about losing. They're desperately trying to buy.'

'Aren't there enough sellers around?' asked the presenter.

'Never seen anything like it. It's a buying panic,' shouted the reporter.

'Do you think it's a bear squeeze?' asked the presenter.

'I'm not sure, but as you can see, dealers are frantic!'

'How are they going to get out?' asked Bess.

'It's going to be "limit up" for a few days and then selling will come in,' said Krishna. 'That means the exchange imposes a maximum price at the end of each day to try and calm the market. That could go on for a while, so it will have to raise the limit each day.'

'How much coffee do you think the Russian hedge funds sold short, Krishna?' I asked.

'I can only make a shrewd guess. They've been keeping the price down for months, selling the coffee to Nestlé and other manufacturers. They'll either have to cover their sales by buying on the futures and options market, or deliver the coffee. On actual global production and consumption figures, the shortage could be around 10 to 15 million bags of coffee.

That's about 50,000 contracts equivalent to around $5 billion at current prices.'

'Imagine being those guys! Their toilets will run out of paper.'

'We've doubled our money today, Jack. Let's not be smug,' chided Maffie.

'When do you think we should sell?'

'No hurry. The Russian hedge funds will be forced to bid prices higher and higher. We'll get well over three bucks, I guess.'

The predictions of Maffie and Krishna were spot on. During the next fortnight, roasters and cornered bears pushed coffee prices through the all time seventies peak of $3.50 a pound. Our phones didn't stop ringing. Brokers acting on behalf of desperate bears tried to buy back the coffee that they had sold short. They begged us to sell, but we decided to hang on.

*   *   *

Maffie and Krishna were the brains behind the operation, but since I was the front man, traders and the press concentrated on me. Rumours were rife that a young hedge fund trader had bought huge quantities of coffee. These purchases played a major part in causing the surge in coffee prices and an ultimate bear squeeze. Reporters from the wires and newspapers called Hastings & Ruffish in an attempt to talk to me. We all agreed that I should keep a low profile. That suited me because I feared the very real possibility of a Russian reaction. I knew what they could do. Bess blocked calls, but that policy encouraged the rumour mill to spew out even more stories. Some newspapers wrote articles saying that speculators had pushed up the price of coffee to ludicrous heights. Sure, farmers were entitled to a living, but prices were now excessive, they wrote.

Maffie and Ruffish eventually felt that Hastings &

Ruffish had to make a statement. It was simple and to the point: 'We're not commenting on our trading. All our dealings are above board. The severe Brazilian frost is responsible for the price surge. Coffee manufacturers can complain, but they have made large profits for years. Now at last, poverty stricken farmers can obtain a decent price for their coffee.'

That statement, which was altered slightly from time to time, did not stop market gossip about a mysterious teen trader. To keep away from reporters I slipped into the office very early in the morning and left late. I shaved off my military moustache and put on my designer dark glasses.

After profit taking, our remaining 170 options contracts controlled almost 6.5 million pounds, or 42,500 bags of coffee. That was small, relative to total world supplies, but the market thought that we had a lot more.

*　　*　　*

Big event in my life. My very own personal present to myself for passing my driving test. A red Ferrari F430 Scuderia with a V8 engine! Cost a packet. More than 200K, but it was worth waiting for. After going for a spin with Harry, it was time to test it on Pearl.

Whether it was work, mistrust on both sides, or Pearl's mood changes, our relationship was beginning to cool off. Pearl had become unreliable and even stood me up after I waited more than an hour at a new fashionable restaurant in Knightsbridge. In the end, I tried it out alone, eating exquisitely presented, but miserly portions. The people around me, according to the friendly waiter, were movie, sport and media celebrities. They were so into themselves that they didn't even notice me. On the one hand, I wanted to be incognito, on the other, I wished that I was well known.

It was no fun being alone and about a week later I called Pearl.

'Hi Pearl, how are you?'

'Fine Jack. Sorry I haven't been around. Too busy.'

'Busy on what? I haven't seen you for weeks.'

'Not that long? Surely?'

'I've got something to show you. A new car.'

'At last Jack. Maybe we can go for a spin in the country. Let me check out a few hotels and I'll get back to you. What is it?'

'Surprise. When should I pick you up?'

'This evening, after the traffic dies down. See you.'

That was hopeful. Maybe there would be a fresh start to our relationship.

That Friday, we were off on a weekend together. Pearl loved the Ferrari as we weaved in and out of the motorway traffic. Pity that there were so many speed traps, limiting our maximum speed to seventy miles an hour. We went off on a slip road and Pearl tried out the car and was mad about it. It was a beautiful evening and the roof was down as we entered a glorious country estate that had been converted into a hotel. There were a few Jags and Mercedes in the car park, but it was great to see that the only Ferrari was mine.

After checking in we went on to the terrace to have a drink. It was a lovely evening and we sat there silently taking in the view of the rolling hills of the Cotswolds between

Cheltenham and Oxford. A tall, tanned, smart, grey haired man sat down at a nearby table and ordered a bottle of red wine. A short, stocky guy joined him. After about half an hour a pretty blonde, went up to their table and sat down.

She turned around to take out some cigarettes from her handbag and spotted us: 'Hey Pearl, is that you? Haven't seen you for a long time. What you doing here?'

'Oh hi Carli! Nice place isn't it?'

'Why don't you guys come and join us?' asked Carli.

Pearl grabbed my hand and we went over to their table.

'Carli, this is Jack. I'm Pearl, she said, smiling at the two men.'

'Ivan Smeerneck. My partner, Baz Tristwell,' said the tall man, signalling the waiter for another bottle of wine.

We chatted a bit and it didn't take Pearl long before she boasted that we had been taking the Ferrari out for a spin.

'What do you do Jack?' said Smeerneck, with an American Southern States drawl.

'Jack's a hedge fund manager,' responded Pearl. 'He knows a lot about coffee.'

Smeerneck's eyes narrowed: 'Coffee. You're not that trader are you?'

'Yes that's him,' said Pearl proudly.

'We're in your line of business,' said Smeerneck, handing me his card. 'We specialise in energy. If ever you want to trade oil or gas, call us.'

'We've got a top team at Wynchmore Energy,' said Baz. 'Swift execution, excellent research.'

'Nice to meet you. We must get going. Booked a table at the restaurant,' I said breaking away.

It was Friday. No way did I wanted to talk business with brokers who were hustling for business. Smeerneck seemed OK but Baz looked like a City spiv.

While we were talking, Pearl slipped away with Carli. While they were smoking and chatting on the lawn nearby, I noticed Carli pass Pearl a small sachet.

Pearl was flushed and lively at dinner that evening and after we had finished two bottles of wine, I asked: 'Who are those guys Pearl?'

'Just friends.'

'You mean business friends. I know how you operate. We didn't meet them by accident, did we? Why didn't you just tell me?'

'OK, Jack, I know you don't like talking business out of hours. They're new clients. Thought I could do you both a turn. I checked them out before I took them on. Smeerneck runs one of the top energy teams in the City.'

Later when we were in our room, I caught her in the bathroom, pinching some white powder from the sachet and having a snort.

'Try some of this stuff. It makes you sexy.'

'I'm not into coke.'

'Come on Jack, just a bit.'

I was reluctant, but I thought that I had better not be boring. So I sniffed some cocaine and it gave me a kick. We rushed to bed. For the first time since I had met her, Pearl was passionate, shouting and clawing the back of my shoulders.

That weekend we toured the Cotswolds and visited Bath and other sites. It didn't bother me that she hadn't been totally straight about setting up the meeting with Smeerneck and his sidekick. Sex was so good now, that I was hooked on her.

*　　*　　*

During the next few weeks, the Brazilian frost worsened. Combined with the drought that occurred in the spring, the crop was down to a quarter of its normal size. Speculation in the coffee market was rampant. Hedge fund bears were slaughtered and three went bankrupt. According to the *Wall Street Journal*, estimated combined losses of Borodino and Veruschka, amounted to about $4 billion. A third of their entire investors' capital was in the trash bin. Over enthusiastic bullish speculators pushed coffee through the $4 a pound barrier and the price touched an all time peak of $4.80 by the end of September. During this time, Aquarium gradually off-loaded its coffee options. We finally sold our last batch of coffee options close to the top of the market. Our profit was around $25 million. Ruffish and Maffie made sure that Sergio and Fulvio each received $500,000. Another $1 million went to the Brazilian farmers who I had visited in May. They had lost their crop during the frost.

My share of the take, including gains on my own original $200,000 investment in Aquarium, plus performance fees, amounted to $7 million! After tax, I was left with around $5 million or around £3 million. I was rich and I had not even turned eighteen!

On a roll, I paid off the mortgage on my Hampstead flat and following Pearl's advice, employed an interior designer. I spent a fortune on some uncomfortable glass fibre furniture and some black and white canvasses from a gallery Pearl recommended. To top it all they installed a large fish tank, my very own aquarium, with exotic, tropical fish.

Weekends Pearl and I would jump into my red Ferrari and race to parties or go abroad.

We went on a quick trip to New York and I bought a one bedroomed apartment for around $1 million on West 70th Street near Strawberry Fields. The location was in memory of Dad and Mum who were fans of John Lennon and the Beatles.

*   *   *

My love affair with myself began in earnest after another trip to New York to sort out my new apartment. As soon as I walked into the office, Bess handed me a *Daily Mail*. Inside was a two page spread: 'Teen Trader Traps Coffee Bears'. The headline was seriously impressive and I blushed with pleasure. I had met Rae Rilling, the writer, at a party with Pearl, but we had only had a brief chat. When I read the article closely, I saw that it had all sorts of personal information. Quoting a 'friend', it described my 'boring life in Bridlington', the fish and chip shop and Mum and Dad dying young. There was a picture of our tatty block of flats and another with the caption: 'Trader Jack Makes it Good'. There I was in my red Ferrari with dark glasses and red frames to match. I wasn't terribly happy with another photo: me leaning sideways on a bar stool with glazed eyes. An empty glass was almost falling out of my hand. The caption:

'Teen Trader's Late Night Out'. I wasn't quite sure whether the article was praising or damning me.

'How did they get all this stuff?' I asked.

'Perhaps Pearl,' said Bess, picking up the paper and glancing at the feature.

Yes, Pearl! That's why the *Daily Mail* had all the details. I had told her a lot about myself. Pearl must have given Rae the photos. One of them came from the drunken time we had spent with the energy dealers at that hotel in the Cotswolds. Despite that, I was secretly pleased with Pearl, even though she gave the reporter personal stuff. It made me famous. A two pager in the *Mail!* I went to the nearest newsagent and bought half a dozen copies.

Ruff, Maffie and other colleagues had a different view. They concentrated on a throwaway line that I had glossed over: 'Jack's Dad warned him against smoking, but he enjoys a joint. A friend hinted that he's tried harder stuff.'

'You're not into drugs are you Jack?' scolded Ruff. 'What the matter with you?'

Lovely Bess who was always supportive, was scathing: 'You've changed since you've made money. When you first arrived at the office, you were really nice, Jack. Gentle, considerate, modest. But now there's an arrogance about you. I don't know whether it's the money, Pearl's influence, or both. Those photos . . . You look like a spiv.'

'I think that sums it up, Jack,' agreed Maffie. 'I can understand that money's gone to your head. But booze and drugs? Really! I thought you had more sense than that.'

'OK, OK, I'm sorry. Really guys! Pearl gave me some. It was only an experiment. I won't do it again. I promise,' I insisted, hurt by the vehemence of their comments.

'That's what they all say,' said Krishna.

Maffie and the other guys at Hastings & Ruffish were appalled for good reason. The Hastings & Murray group of fund managers had an excellent reputation. The firm was regarded as a serious, principled Scottish investment company that donated to charities. The $1 million donation to coffee farmers was one such example. The firm and managers didn't want to be tainted by drugs. I could be sacked.

I called Pearl to tell her that the *Daily Mail* article had embarrassed me and wanted to know her motives.

'Hi Pearl. You were obviously the *Daily Mail's* source. What's in it for you?'

'Come on Jack, it's given you great publicity. You now have celebrity status. When you open your fund to investors, you'll have a ready-made marketable brand.'

'My boss and colleagues don't think so. You could have told me that you were giving the *Mail* a story. Why didn't they contact me? Why were they quoting "a friend" which could only have been you.'

'They couldn't get hold of you, Jack. I thought it was best not to give them your number and you well know that your office blocks the press. Come to my place and let's talk about it. Take it easy. Be cool.'

'OK, I've been invited to Leila Slimcop's latest exhibition. You've never seen her work. You can come along with me.'

'Sure Jack, would love to.'

When I arrived at Pearl's place, she didn't give me time to complain. She pulled off my clothes and dragged me to her bed. Before I knew it we were making violent love. I was so exhausted that I fell asleep. When I woke up, I realised that we would be late for Leila's show. We had a quick shower and drove to the exhibition.

'Pearl, the article was good, except the stuff on drink and drugs.'

'Sorry, Jack. Rae dragged it out of me when she caught me in the rest room. Journalists have their ways.'

'OK, please don't do that to me again. I could have lost my job.'

When we arrived at the gallery in Flask Walk, Hampstead, almost everyone had left.

Despite being in their seventies, Stan and Leila stood tall and elegant; Leila in a long black dress with black high heels and Stan in a light grey suit.

'Haven't seen you for a long while, Jack, good of you to come,' said Stan, shaking my hand warmly. 'How are you, Pearl?'

'Fine thanks!' shouted Pearl who seemed to be hyper. She knocked back a couple of glasses of wine and started giggling. The Slimcops just stood there, perplexed.

Somewhat embarrassed, I quickly walked around the gallery admiring Leila's charcoal drawings of birds and nudes and her sculptures in the adjoining room. The last room displayed her unfinished work. One was a torso without a head. Pearl followed, but it seemed as if she wasn't very interested.

David Drummond and Jim Wardle were there. I hadn't seen them for more than a year. Wardle had put on weight and I noticed that Drummond had begun to go bald.

'Hi Jack, heard that you're doing OK. Thanks for all

the business,' said Drummond, sarcastically.

'No problem. David, Jack's a big guy now. He doesn't need us,' said Wardle.

'Come on you guys, you know it's not up to me. We have to deal with . . .'

'Sure, Jack, sure. Only the big boys,' said Wardle.

They made me a little angry because they were being unreasonable. They were a private client firm and I couldn't deal with them without Ruffish's permission.

'OK guys, I'll ask my boss.'

'Sure, Jack, I'm sure you will,' said Drummond sarcastically. 'Saw you in the *Mail* today.'

I flushed, but before justifying myself, I noticed Pearl wandering around the sculptures giggling and fingering them. I fretted that she could damage them. Fortunately she went to the loo and I hoped she would calm down. A little later Leila followed and came back shaking. She whispered something to Stan and he pulled me aside. I couldn't understand why Leila was so upset.

'Leila caught your girlfriend snorting coke,' Stan said.

'It's only a bit of Charlie,' I replied rather stupidly. 'Hasn't Leila seen it before?'

'She certainly has. Sean was an addict. He had a heart attack because of cocaine. It killed him.'

At first it didn't sink in that he was talking about their son. They had never spoken about Sean before.

'I read the *Mail* today. You're also taking drugs aren't you?' said Stan looking straight into my eyes.

'No, no I'm not,' I said. 'I experimented with the stuff, but I've stopped.'

'That's what drug addicts always say. What Sean used to tell us,' he said, getting heated up.

He was seriously upset. I had never seen him in that mood. Unwittingly, he touched one of my weaknesses. When people became angry, I became aggressive. After being lectured at the office and having drunk a few glasses of wine at the exhibition, I lost it.

'Who do you think you are?' I snapped. 'You're not my father. You can't tell me what to do.'

'You're like a second son to Leila, Jack. I'm also fond of you,' said Stan beginning to control himself. 'But that was before . . .'

'Before . . . before what? Before I stopped coming to visit you?' I said, raising my voice.

'We don't expect you to visit us, Jack. You're young. You're busy. You've done well. We know that. It's not a duty.'

'So what do you mean?'

'If you want to see us, Jack, you must give up drugs.'

'As I said, I'm not on drugs,' I snapped. 'I've smoked a bit of pot, but that can't be classified as hard stuff.'

'And coke? Where does it end, Jack?'

'OK, I've tried that too. But I've promised my boss and my colleagues that I'll never do it again.'

'You must stop, Sean,' insisted Leila.

'Sean? I'm Jack!'

'You must give up that girl, Sean, she's a bad influence on you.'

'Come on Jack,' shouted Pearl, grabbing my hand and pulling me out of the gallery.

She was furious and the coke seemed to increase her

strength as she dragged me down the road.

'Who do they think they are? Trying to break up our relationship!' she screamed.

Before I could say goodbye properly and make my peace, the Slimcops were left standing outside the gallery. The owner, a plump, middle-aged, smartly dressed woman, who was next to them, looked shocked.

Back at Pearl's place we both fell asleep almost immediately. It was Saturday and early in the morning we made love. Sex had become really good with Pearl.

She gave me scrambled eggs for breakfast and then started complaining about the Slimcops.

'I've never been so insulted in my life.'

'They have a point. You were high as a kite!'

'I'm feeling pretty clear-headed now. Time you grew up, Jack; stopped looking for father and mother figures. It's natural. Your parents died young, so you look to older people for guidance. The Slimcops can never be the same as your parents.'

'I'm well aware of that.'

'You may need them for security and advice, but they also need you.'

'So what's wrong with that?'

'Nothing, provided you don't owe them anything. You told me that Stan gave you fifty thousand for helping him make money on gold shares. That was a gift, but psychologically you feel that you owe him. It's a sort of debt. Wealthy people do that sort of thing. But generally there's some form of payback.'

'They're not those sort of people, Pearl.'

'Maybe, maybe not. Leila called you Sean. Don't you find it odd?'

'It was your fault. Your coke sniffing brought back memories of her son.'

'Yes. But she genuinely thought that you were Sean. Remember when we were with them at the restaurant? How she behaved?'

'Yes. She was a little strange.'

'And now she calls you Sean? Thinks you're her son.'

'So?'

'The exhibition. The latest work. Very different from her earlier pieces. They looked incomplete.'

'I thought that you were too high to notice.'

'I noticed. What's happening to her, Jack?'

'Dunno, I'm not a doctor.'

'You're just not prepared to admit it, Jack. It happened to my aunt. Steady deterioration. Alzheimer's.'

'You want me to cut them out now? When she's ill?'

'No. It's going to get a lot worse for Stan. You can remain friends. I just don't think that you should owe him. He'll want you to be there continuously. Why should you be there when it doesn't suit you? You're not his family.'

'But that's what friends are for.'

'Up to a point,' she sighed. 'Now let's sit down and write a letter. Do you have your chequebook on you?'

'Yes it's in my jacket.'

It was then that I did something that I have regretted to this very day. I wrote out a cheque for 75K, made it out to Stanley Slimcop and placed it in an envelope. Pearl virtually dictated the letter:

Dear Stan and Rena,
Thanks for yesterday. I really appreciate all the help you gave
me when I first came to London. Please accept this cheque for
£75,000.
Best regards
Jack.

When I posted the letter the next day, I instantly regretted it. I never received a reply.

16

A PRIZE SUCKER

The *Daily Mail* feature caused the market to focus its attention on me. Maffie, Ruff and I reluctantly decided that I would have to respond. We decided that the best way to put the record straight was to offer *Bloomberg* an interview. John Spittlefields, *Bloomberg's* commodities correspondent, was a reporter who wrote stories without any bias.

Maffie gave me practice sessions, drilling me on how to come up with the right replies: 'Be smart, cheerful and cool, regardless of the questions. Watch the politicians on TV. They rarely get ruffled.'

Soon after Spittlefields' piece was on the wires, newspapers, radio and TV stations pestered me for interviews. That made me feel seriously important. Jack Miner, who hadn't even finished school, in front of the cameras defending hedge funds and explaining that the Brazilian frost was to blame for soaring coffee prices. Saying that poverty-stricken South American and African farmers deserved higher prices. Wow!

Not long afterwards, when the coffee market and media

were off the boil, Maffie and I were relaxing in a Costa coffee shop. A lined and crumpled man with a white beard walked in.

'Are you Jack Miner?' the man asked.

'That's me.'

'Israel McTavish, special correspondent of *The Wall Street Journal*,' he said. 'I'm writing a feature on the coffee market. Do you mind if I ask you a few questions?'

'Israel? . . . McTavish?' queried Maffie, a bit perplexed.

'My father was a Scottish Methodist and my mother Jewish,' said McTavish, smiling and pulling up a chair. 'Call me Issie. And you?'

'I'm Maffie.'

'Do you work with Jack?'

'Yes.'

'Could you please give me your full name?' he asked politely, taking out his notebook.

'Themba Shaka Mafuta,' Maffie replied warily.

'Are you from KwaZulu-Natal, South Africa? I was there last year to write a feature on the Zulu wars,' said McTavish looking interested. 'Shaka? You're not from the same family are you?'

'Maffie's a descendant of Shaka. She knows all about his military tactics. Applies them to the markets,' I blurted out.

'So you were also involved in the coffee market,' said McTavish, latching on to a new story angle.

Maffie glared at me and shook her head, but it was too late. Issie McTavish, the veteran reporter, knew he was on to something. He wasn't going to let go. He looked me up and down. Self-conscious about a spot, I put my hand over my cheek and sat up straight. He noticed my reaction immediately.

'How old are you Jack? Seventeen, eighteen?'

'What about you? Seventy, eighty,' I retorted cheekily.

McTavish laughed: 'Close. Old enough to be your grandfather. I'm semi-retired, but I still enjoy doing my bit for the paper.'

'What's the story?' I asked. 'Isn't coffee old news?'

'I've been writing about commodities for years. From what they tell me, you guys ran a pretty sophisticated operation. It wasn't only you, Jack, was it?'

I shrugged my shoulders. McTavish laughed again.

'Are you trying to tell me that you did it on your own? They tell me that you were playing the options market. That requires experience and knowledge. I don't think your school taught you much about options.'

Maffie and I looked at each other and said nothing.

'You don't need to know that stuff to trade,' I snapped. 'So what if Maffie helped me? All organisations brainstorm.'

McTavish smiled and Maffie sighed. She had gathered that it was one of McTavish's tactics to rile people he interviewed. If they lost their cool, there was a good chance that they would forget themselves and divulge more information.

'I've spoken to a lot of people. This is what I think happened,' said McTavish. 'Someone told you that a frost in Brazil was likely. You knew that some hedge funds had sold coffee short and had to buy back their positions. You used Shaka's battle strategies to corner them.'

'Our Brazilian friends could have been wrong. We didn't

deliberately squeeze the bears,' I insisted. 'We just went along for the ride.'

Maffie looked at the ceiling in despair.

McTavish laughed: 'Thanks! You've confirmed my sources. Good to meet you.'

He finished his coffee and walked out.

'What was all that about?' I asked.

'You gifted him the full story, or most of it, you idiot.'

The following week, Maffie brought in a *Wall Street Journal*. The headline on the front page was: 'Zulu battle plan traps Russian bears'. The subheading underneath was: 'Shaka helps Jack corner coffee giants.' By and large, McTavish had the whole story. His only mistake was that he didn't identify Krishna as the options whiz.

The article had a paragraph and a quote that disturbed me: 'Veruschka and Borodino funds are estimated to have lost more than $4 billion in the coffee market.'

'Yes, Jack has climbed to the top of the beanstalk, but beware of the giant,' said Igor Hellvosovitch, of Veruschka. 'One wrong step and all the way down.'

That quote unnerved me for a day or so, but I soon decided that it was pointless to be worried about the Russians. The Yapolovitch murder was now history. Moreover, my profile was now so high that they would be reluctant to take revenge. We had beaten the Russian bears fair and square. If they were financing the Colombian drug barons, it was good that they lost all that money.

To make the front page of the *WSJ* was really something. I was now on the celebrity party circuit. Pearl and I went from event to event and pictures of us appeared in *Hello!*

and *OK!* magazines. I read them when my hairdresser put highlights in my hair.

Pearl was full of fun when we were at parties, but as the weeks passed by she seemed to become bored with me. The experience with the Slimcops had shaken me up and I was now completely off drugs. I was lucky because I had experimented with very little, so it was easy to withdraw. Unfortunately she was hooked. Her mood changes from hyper elation to gloom became more frequent.

It was late October and we were in New York furnishing my new apartment. I was searching for a credit card in a drawer when I found some coke and pot and confronted her: 'Pearl, you promised me that you would stop.'

'Give them to me, Jack!'

'No way, Pearl,' I insisted and went to the bathroom and flushed them down the toilet.

She was livid.

'Who do you think you are? All you've done is make money. It's because of me that you're a celeb. You were a nobody before.'

'I'm just trying to help. This stuff is doing you no good.'

'That's for me to decide. Not you.'

'I care for you Pearl. I love you. I've been reading up on coke. You need more and more to give you the same kick. It's dangerous stuff. It damages your heart. You mix it with booze. That's lethal.'

'OK, OK, I'll stop, I promise you. But you can't stop me smoking pot. That's not addictive,' she said, taking a cigarette out of a pack and lighting it.

I grabbed it and stubbed it out.

'Not in this place, Pearl. You know the rules. How many times have I asked you to give up smoking?'

'Nicotine's addictive. Not weed.'

'From what I read about pot, it's psychologically addictive. People need counselling to get off it. A London psychiatrist researched the stuff and found that if you took cannabis at age eighteen, there was a sixty per cent probability that you would become psychotic.'

'So you think I'm a psycho? You know what? I'm embarrassed to go out with you,' she retorted sneering. 'I'm nearly twenty five and you're not even eighteen.'

'We've talked about this before, Pearl. Who cares what people think? So long as we're happy. That's what counts.'

'Jack there's no future in it. Your age all over the newspapers. My friends and clients sniggering as soon as we turn our backs. Pearl the cradle snatcher! Toyboy Jack.'

'I'm not a toyboy. Women over forty go for toyboys. You're only in your twenties. The age difference is nothing.'

'Oh yeah? It might be great for you, but not for me.'

'Thanks, Pearl. Thanks a lot,' I said raising my voice. 'Remember when we first met. It was you who approached me. We never worried about our age difference before. It was just us. Our business. Now it's public and it's your fault. It was you who contacted the *Mail*, not me!'

'It was my jo . . .'

'Your job! What do you mean? Did you publicise me to help you get more clients? Get you more invitations? Stan Slimcop warned me about you. Thanks to you, Stan and Leila are no longer my friends. They're good, genuine people. Always there to help me. Thanks Pearl, thanks a lot.'

'You have to take responsibility for your own actions, Jack. I just advised you.'

'Advised me? Is that what you call it? You virtually wrote the letter. Got out the chequebook! I'm still trying to work out why you had it in for Stan. Maybe because you realised that he saw through you. Would turn me against you.'

'You're being mean to me. I think we should cool it Jack,' said Pearl, her eyes now tearful. 'I am fond of you, but it's now time for you go out with girls your own age.'

I didn't reply. Just put on my trainers and running vest and took off for Central Park, through Strawberry Fields, past the lake, fountains, statues of dogs and around the reservoir. Running, walking, running and walking again. Not as fit as I used to be. Too good a life. Sweating and exhausted, I lay down, closed my eyes and before I knew it, I was fast asleep. When I returned, it was nearly dark. The apartment was empty. Pearl had packed up and left.

* * *

After the long weekend in New York and the lonely flight back home, I arrived at the office late. It was empty, so I went to the meeting room. Rob Hastings from Scotland was addressing the whole staff, but Ruffish and Maffie weren't there.

'Good morning, what's going on?' I asked.

'Ruff and Maffie have eloped, Jack!' said Bess giggling. 'Who would have thought?'

At last it made sense. They always left the office late. Maffie and I went out a lot, but it had always been platonic.

She had told me that she preferred older men, but Ruff? Surely not him! He was far older than her. Married for years. A son and daughter at university. I looked at the others in the room. I guessed that they were thinking the same.

'Where are they, Rob?' I asked.

'Somewhere on the west coast of South Africa,' said Hastings. 'Ruff phoned me early last week and told me that they were going.'

'Why didn't they tell us? They could have at least said goodbye,' I mumbled, feeling hurt. I had thought that Maffie was my best friend.

'They wanted to keep it secret. I'm sure they will contact you when the time is right,' said Hastings.

'Who's going to run Hastings & Ruffish?'

'Ruff found a buyer for the business. We . . . Hastings & Murray are selling.'

'I thought that the business was going well,' I said. 'Ruff told me that he was going to open my fund to outside investors.'

'We've decided to concentrate on our business in Scotland. Hastings & Murray are now managing $20 billion. We prefer to invest conservatively for our clients.'

'Where do we go from here?' asked Krishna.

'You will all be paid good bonuses,' said Hastings. 'Hastings & Ruffish is a small, but profitable hedge fund business. I think you're good managers. You can join Hastings & Murray in Edinburgh, or you can remain in London.'

'Who's buying the firm?' asked Tong.

'Ruff put out feelers in the past year. He got a good price from LeashTrade Inc., a hedge fund business in New York.'

'I introduced them,' said Aram smiling proudly. 'About a month ago, Ruff said that he was thinking of retirement. I told him that LeashTrade wanted to expand in London.'

'How do you know them?' asked Tong.

'They invest in my fund. They're nice guys. Good friends. They're very interested in you, Jack,' said Aram.

'Why me?'

'They think you could go places. They've heard a lot about you.'

That was the first time that Aram had shown any admiration for me. I wondered what his role would be.

'You can come to Edinburgh, Jack, but you'll have to stick to the rules. We are traditional, conservative investment managers. We don't speculate,' said Hastings sternly.

I was flattered but wasn't sure what to do. I wished that Maffie was around to advise me. I shouldn't have discarded my friendship with Stan Slimcop. It was strange. I had made all this money and yet I felt insecure.

*   *   *

The International Coffee Organisation invited me to a Christmas cocktail party in Berners Street in the West End. Coffee prices had fallen from their heady peaks and were trading around $3 a pound.

'It suits us, Jack,' said Louis Rondario, Colombian Coffee delegate. 'We were uncomfortable with prices of more than $4 a pound. We don't want coffee to become too expensive.'

'You mean that you don't want us British to drink more tea,' I chuckled.

I wandered around the room, but without Maffie, I didn't have any contacts. It felt strange. I was an outsider in the crowd and it was lonesome without her. I stood in a corner, sipping my glass of wine, observing some young guys joking around. One of them was John Spittlefields of *Bloomberg*.

Spittlefields, about six foot tall with floppy brown hair and a cheerful friendly face, spotted me and came over. I liked him. He was straight and had reported the interview with me fairly.

'Hi, John, Sorry, don't have a story.' I said, glad to have company. 'Nothing much is happening in the markets.'

'No problem, come and join us.'

He introduced me to reporters from the *FT, The Times, Reuters, Dow Jones* and *Associated Press*. They were not much older than me. They were happy and cracked jokes. I wondered what it was like to be a journalist. On the outside, looking in. Scrambling for stories.

'Why isn't Pearl Fleecer with you tonight, Jack?' asked *Times* reporter, Max Radar, a skinny guy, with an annoying smile.

'We've broken up.'

'Surprise, surprise,' grinned the reporter.

'Surprise? What do you mean surprise?'

I was irritated. What did Pearl have to do with him?

'Horoshi Kofia Corp is Pearl's biggest client.'

I was puzzled: 'Never heard of it.'

'Come on Jack! Horoshi is one of Russia's biggest coffee manufacturers. Surely you know that Pearl worked for them?'

'No, really. It's news to me. Pearl told me that she was

doing market research and branding for a new chain of coffee shops.'

'That's news to us. Branding?' laughed Radar. 'Maybe a bit, but that's not her main line. Pearl's in public relations. She's a spin doctor.'

'She's been spinning for Horoshi,' said Spittlefields. 'She phones us regularly. Says her client supports fair trade.'

I was silent, thinking. What was Danny trying to tell me about Pearl? Why didn't I speak to him? Stupid!

'Pearl said that speculators like you disrupted the coffee market,' said Radar. 'She even mentioned manipulation.'

I shook my head: 'Rubbish! We never manipulated prices. You know that! Speak to Rondario. He'll confirm that coffee farmers are only now making a decent living.'

'Pearl said you were just interested in the money. Not the farmers.'

'Pearl and I had our differences, but she would never say that about me,' I growled. 'She knew very well that we gave money to the farmers. That we cared for them. OK, she did leak stuff to the *Daily Mail*, but it did me good. People now know who I am. Pearl brands companies and people. I was one of her clients.'

Two of the reporters started to snigger. Spittlefields shut them up: 'That's Pearl for you. The *Daily Mail* piece was meant to embarrass you Jack. That's why she fed them that information about drugs. Get you guys out of the market. The police to search your firm. Perhaps get you fired! Slick operator, that Pearl.'

'No doubt Horoshi Kofia Corp was using her to get information about you guys,' said the *Associated Press* reporter.

'OK, Pearl asked me questions. But that's because she was interested,' I insisted, still hoping that they were wrong, but in my heart of hearts, knowing that they were right.

They looked at me silently, probably wondering how a successful trader could be so naïve.

'Don't worry Jack, she's also fooled us,' said Spittlefields. 'They call journalists, reptiles, but spin doctors! They're alligators!'

'Pearl's very shrewd. She builds up relationships, milks them and then dumps them,' chirped the *Dow Jones* reporter.

And she gets paid twice, I thought to myself. All those presents. Jewellery and designer clothes. Five star hotels!

'Pillow secrets,' said Radar.

Sensing that I was getting angry and could hit him, he put up his hands: 'Take it easy Jack. It happened to me. I was busy on a big story. Pearl made a play for me and I foolishly showed her my article before it was published. I don't like saying this to you, but we were in bed at the time. She told her clients about it and they persuaded my editor to kill the story.'

It should have been obvious why Pearl questioned me about my coffee trading. It mostly happened after I had had a drink, smoked pot or we had made love. When I was most vulnerable and accessible. Branding! Coffee chain! How could I have been so stupid? My brains were in my balls and fame filled my head. A prize sucker.

'Can you excuse me guys, I have to phone someone in New York,' I said gloomily, walking to an empty corner of the room.

Danny Dovetail was on the phone swiftly: 'Hi Jack,

thinking of going back into coffee, it's come back a lot.'

'Danny, remember you were going to tell me something about Pearl?'

'Why are you only interested now? Bit late isn't it?'

'Some reporters have told me something. Maybe you can confirm it. They say that one of her major clients is Horoshi Kofia Corp.'

'I'm afraid they're right Jack. Remember when you were recovering from a panic attack outside the Russian Samovar?'

'How could I forget?'

'Pearl arrived quickly because she had been working around the corner.'

'So?'

'She said that her client was on West 51st Street.'

'I don't recall that. What's the significance?'

'Don't you remember what I told you? Veruschka and Borodino have their New York offices there.'

'Oh my God, no!'

'That's not all. I found out that Horoshi Kofia Corp also has offices in West 51st Street.'

'You think there's some link between Hiroshi and the Russian hedge funds?'

'Draw your own conclusions. They're in the very same building. There's something else . . .'

'What?'

'I don't believe that Pearl's Ukrainian. I think that she's Russian. I had a Russian girlfriend who lives in America. Her accent is exactly the same.'

'You think that she's some Russian Mata Hari?'

'Jack, tell me. Does Pearl question you about the coffee market? At odd times. Romantic moments. After sex, that sort of thing.'

'Not now. We've broken up. She did when we were involved.'

'Just as well you've broken up with her Jack. Watch your back, my friend.'

After he hung up I felt depressed. Yes, I had made lots of money, but my girlfriend had slept with the world and had knifed me. My good friends, Maffie and Stan, were no longer around to give me support. Why did I listen to Pearl and write that silly letter to Stan? Why did I let her influence me? I had to apologise as soon as possible. Feeling stupid and humiliated, I decided to go home.

Spittlefields, who could see that I was down, asked if he could accompany me. It was dark and chilly outside. We walked along to Goodge Street tube station, passing some homeless guy with a dog. He brought back memories and I gave him £100.

'How long have you been writing about the markets, John?'

'About five years.'

'Ever wanted to be in the game yourself? You make much more money.'

'No . . . Brokers offered me jobs. But I like to chase stories. You become addicted to it. Gives you a kick. It's fun being on the outside, looking in.'

'I suppose you know Issie McTavish.'

'Issie the veteran? Good guy. Top-notch journalist. Been doing it for years. Very helpful. Taught me a lot.'

'He certainly got the story out of us,' I said.

'Great story. Zulu battle plan corners bears.'

We continued to walk slowly and silently.

'Do you know that you've made enemies Jack?'

'My former boss warned me about that.'

'Watch your back Jack! The hedge fund managers who lost, are out to get you.'

'A friend of mine said the exact same thing. Who cares? If you play the markets, you have to lose sometimes. They know that.'

'Someone told me that the Russian mafia controls the funds, but I haven't confirmed it,' said Spittlefields. He suddenly stopped and looked straight at me. 'Former boss?'

Perhaps I was being indiscreet, but I liked John.

'Yes, I've got a story for you,' I said.

*   *   *

A few days later LeashTrade Inc. came to town. Through the glass walls, I could see my new boss, Leash Grobnick. He was sitting in Ruffish's chair with his feet on the table. I knocked on the door politely and entered his office. Grobnick stood up and shook my hand briskly. He was about fifty five, medium height with a powerful build, a red face, a grey moustache and thick black hair, tinged with grey on the sides. He was dressed in a smart pinstripe suit. On the sofa were two guys who looked as if they were in their late twenties or early thirties.

'Good to meet you Jack, we've heard a lot about you,' said

Grobnick with his New Yorker accent. 'Let me introduce you to my sons, Cy and Max.'

'I saw a picture of you in *Hello!* magazine with quite a girl,' grinned Cy. 'It must be fame, money or both. Certainly not your looks!'

He laughed at his own joke and I decided that I had better join in. Cy was taller than his father. He looked like Leash, except that his face was softer. Leash showed me a photograph of his son's little daughters.

'Cy has done me proud. Max I'm still waiting,' Leash scolded playfully.

I felt sorry for Max, who was about five foot four with a large crooked nose and a face scarred by acne. Instead of a suit, Max was sloppily dressed in a creased pink shirt and brown corduroys. His father and brother seemed to dominate him.

'We think that we have a good business here, Jack. Your fund has a lot of potential, so we have decided to merge it with the Eastern European and the Resources Fund.'

I could understand why he was combining Aquarium with Maffie's Resources Fund, but why Aram Zabkian's Eastern European Fund?

'We want Zabkian and you to be partners. We'll keep the name Aquarium and the merged fund will have $300 million under management,' said Leash. 'Our aim is to make Aquarium one of the biggest macro hedge funds, trading right across the spectrum – stocks, bonds, currencies and commodities.'

His decision took me by surprise. I liked Krishna and Tong, but Aram had never been helpful. He was no friend of mine.

'What about Krishna and Tong?'

'They're joining Hastings & Murray in Edinburgh.'

'What are you going to do with their funds?'

'We'll merge them as well. Our own team will manage them. This business is going places, Jack. The New York and London funds now manage around $1 billion,' said Leash. 'Cy is director of marketing and Max is systems manager. What about a basic salary of $300,000 and a 7.5 per cent profit share in Aquarium?'

The offer astounded me! For that sort of money I could work with anyone. Even Aram.

'That's just the start, Jack. We want to build up the business to $10 billion in the next few years,' said Cy. 'Max, can you go and get some coffee for us?'

'Where's Bess?' I asked.

'She wanted to be a trainee fund manager, but it didn't suit us,' said Leash, abruptly. 'We let her go.'

*　　*　　*

In the markets, decisiveness was the name of my game, but in life I procrastinated. At last I picked up courage to go and apologise to the Slimcops. It was better to see them face to face than to talk on the phone. On that cold, grey January day with Jazz alongside me, I struggled to think of the right words to say. The light drizzle turned into sleet, a contrast to that bright hot summer's day, when I first visited Constable's grave and walked down the pathway towards their home. This time I had to walk gingerly as the path was muddy and slippery and the dog was pulling on his lead.

No one responded to the security button at first, but I waited and then rang again. A woman answered. It was difficult to speak to her on the intercom as it wasn't functioning properly. She eventually opened the gate and we made our way to the entrance past the lone sculpture of the Eagle. In the winter it looked fairly menacing without sunflowers and roses surrounding it.

A middle-aged woman, in a blue nurse's uniform, opened the door.

'I'm Jack. Can I see Stan and Leila?' I asked.

'I told you they're not here.'

'I couldn't hear you properly. When do you think they'll be back?'

'You're wasting your time. They've gone away. I'm looking after the house.'

'Are they OK? How's Leila?'

She wouldn't answer.

'Can you tell me where they are? They're good friends, I want to talk to them about something.'

'What?'

'It's personal. Where can I reach them?'

The woman looked at me closely.

'You said you were Jack?'

'Yes.'

'They talked about you.'

'Is she still mixing me up with Sean? Their son?'

'You know about her problem?'

'I think so. I feel very bad. I've let them down. I've come to say sorry,' I replied beginning to feel tearful.

The woman softened: 'Come inside and have some tea.'

'What about the dog?'

'He seems friendly enough. Bring him in, but hold his lead. I don't want any mess.'

The woman, who's name was Sara, brought in some tea and biscuits. Through the large glass window, on the far edge of the lawn, near the covered swimming pool, was the statue of Sean. She noticed me look in his direction.

'Tragic for Mr Slimcop. Him dying so young and now her . . .'

'Are you helping Leila?'

'Yes. When they're here. They're in South Africa now. Mr Slimcop has rented a home in Fish Hoek, near Cape Town. They're going to stay there during the winter. He's got another carer for her.'

'How bad is she?'

'Deteriorating rapidly. Alzheimer's is a cruel sickness. Relentless.'

'Can you tell them I came to visit? That I'm very sorry for what I've done. For not being there, when they needed me.'

'Sure. When they next phone. Here's their address. He told me not to disclose his email.'

*   *   *

Winter came and went. Leash would alternate his working weeks between New York and London. Max was brilliant with systems. He asked me to explain my market strategy and spoke to Aram as well. Using our ideas, he built an automatic buy and sell trading program for us. As I got to know him, I began to like and trust Max, who was also in charge of risk controls and compliance, the internal regulation of traders and the business. I also got on with Cy. Leash, however, was very different from his sons. Beneath his charming veneer, he was a ruthless, nasty bit of work, who bullied the new secretary Matilda. She lasted a fortnight. Within six months he had four secretaries, until Maisie, a curvaceous, curly haired brunette, arrived. Leash was always touching her, but she didn't seem to mind.

Leash Grobnick seemed to thrive on conflict. Ruffish would have briefed him about his staff, before he sold the business. So Leash must have been aware that I wasn't exactly friendly with Aram. To make matters worse, Leash did away with the workspaces that gave us some privacy. He changed the office to open plan. So I constantly had to work alongside Aram with his dreadful halitosis, a mix of garlic and tobacco. Now that I was working in close quarters to Aram, I observed his yellow nicotine-stained teeth, some of which had turned black. To be fair, he did try and joke around a bit. But whenever he spoke, I had to turn my face away to avoid the full blast of his breath. I don't think that was very good for our relationship. We fought a lot and that amused Leash.

'That's what I like. Strong arguments. They bring results,' said Leash after observing a sharp difference of opinion at a meeting.

Aram enjoyed researching and getting tips from brokers. But I didn't want to put money in a stock or commodity, unless I was sure that the timing was right. We had Max's automatic system, why not just follow it?

Gradually I lost patience and interest. After about six months, I let Aram control the daily trading. I would just discuss our general strategy each week. After I made that decision, we began to get on. The Aquarium fund was doing well and we were making a lot of money.

I was anxious to get away from the office and jumped at the opportunity to join Cy on his marketing trips in Europe and the US. Our 'road shows' were informal seminars and gatherings where Cy would try and persuade investors to place money in LeashTrade funds. The road shows were gruelling. We would get the Eurostar to Paris, have two meetings there, sleep overnight and then travel to Luxembourg and Brussels. The following day we would fly to Geneva and then to Zurich. After that we would go to Frankfurt, Milan or Madrid.

Same with America; New York, Boston, Chicago, Houston, San Francisco, Los Angeles to Miami and then home. I didn't have any time to enjoy the cities, meet girls and go clubbing. All I saw were planes, airports, trains and stations, taxis, banks, offices, hotel rooms and conference halls. I enjoyed good restaurants, but on these trips, they were business lunches and dinners. I began to put on weight, as I was too tired to wake up early and go for a run. I found the gyms in hotels boring and their swimming pools, too small.

Cy Grobnick was a super salesman. He sold the Aquarium fund as a mix of youthful daring and experience. Before we went on the road shows, he asked me about my adventures in the gold and coffee markets. That helped him amuse our audiences with anecdotes.

'In one corner Jack the Yorkshire Youth had a sling full of coffee beans. In the other corner the City giants,' he boomed. 'You know how schoolboys and girls can beat the pros. Well here is an example. A young trader who has performed consistently.' The audiences tended to be sceptical at first, but Cy would continue: 'Yes, you can laugh. But how did a tiny island beat the Nazis in the Battle of Britain? Their fighter pilots were so young that they didn't know fear. That's what you need in today's markets, in today's battlegrounds – naked courage. The courage of youth.'

Cy knew how to embellish the facts. When we travelled, I read many books. One of them was about the Battle of Waterloo after I had visited the site near Brussels. On a trip to Pennsylvania, I found time to read Gore Vidal's *Lincoln* and over the weekend visited the Gettysburg battlefields. Cy told the audience that I was fascinated with military history. That Napoleon and Wellington were my heroes; that I had spent time at Waterloo and Gettysburg and was a fan of Abraham Lincoln.

Cy would then take out a copy of Lincoln's Gettysburg speech and solemnly pronounce that I strongly believed that emerging nations should be free from dictators. That 'government of the people, by the people, for the people, shall not perish from the earth'.

It was remarkable. They really seemed to love that stuff and became all the more interested in our fund. Cy also showed potential investors slides of Issie McTavish's *Wall Street Journal* article. Conveniently ignoring Maffie's role, he said that I had defeated the coffee bears with Shaka Zulu battle tactics.

'Shaka was known as the "Black Napoleon",' boomed Cy. 'He was brilliant in the art of war. Modern day markets are a war zone and only the best strategies become winners.'

By then, Cy had his audiences in the palm of his hand.

'Just in case you think this young trader is totally on his own, we have the hand of experience behind him.

Jack's partner is a fund manager who's been through bull and bear markets,' Cy would say. 'Yes, Aram Zabkian is the wise old General who steadies Captain Jack. Makes sure that the fund trades relatively conservatively. My brother Max, our compliance officer, is a PHD in computer science. He has set up a trading programme that seeks opportunities but applies strict stop loss limits to control risk.'

He would then pause to allow his speech to sink in. Normally the ploy was to have a sip of water.

'Jack is a young man who knows about charity,' Cy would then continue. 'He helped poverty stricken coffee farmers obtain a decent price for their crop. His fund made a big donation to Brazilian farmers.'

To close the sales pitch, I would follow Cy's talks with power point presentations. They had neat graphs showing the performance of Aquarium and the mix of its investments. I was nervous at first, but soon enjoyed it, learning from Cy how to gain the trust of investors by underplaying large gains. The trick was not to boast about performance. If you did, investors wouldn't take you seriously. Let the statistics speak for themselves. I explained that we had devised our own system to trade the markets. It wasn't infallible, but it had an excellent track record over time. I couldn't divulge details, otherwise our competitors would copy us, I stressed. In this way I added to Aquarium's mystique. Money poured into the fund.

*   *   *

About six months after the Grobnicks had taken over the business, Cy and I were in Switzerland, enjoying the Zurich spring sunshine. We were eating a light lunch outside a brasserie on Bahnhofstrasse, near Paradeplatz, the historic Swiss banking area.

'I want to introduce you to a potential new investor,' said Cy. 'Some of his biggest clients have already placed money in our US funds. He's considering investing in Aquarium.'

A tall man in a smart light brown summer suit walked towards us. Cy stood up and rushed towards him. He brought the man to the table and introduced me. I was taken aback. It was Hal Humford, who I had last seen in Edinburgh, two years previously. Humford looked at me casually. He didn't remember me.

'Hal Humford, Banque Discretione,' he said shaking my hand. I decided not to let on that I had met him and his wife Maggie.

'Jack Miner, LeashTrade,' I said.

'Sit down Hal and have something to eat.'

'No thanks Mr Grobnick. I'm on my way to a meeting. I look forward to hearing your presentation later.'

'Please call me Cy. Hal is investment chief at Banque Discretione, Jack.

Humford looked me straight in the eye and nodded. I

was amazed that there was no recognition. What an irony. A fling with his wife and now he might advise his clients to invest in my fund!

17

Pumping Prices

'*Trader Jack's girl elopes with Boss,*' By Sheila Shellhoff.

The headline in the News on Sunday startled me. I picked up the newspaper and read the story:

Maffie Mafuta, who made millions in coffee trading with Jack Miner, has run away with his former boss.

'Jack is furious with Ronald "Ruff" Ruffish,' a friend revealed.

The love nest is in the dense forest of Knysna, in the middle of South Africa's beautiful Garden Route.

'They keep to themselves,' said Tokkie Van der Merwe, who owns a curio shop on the waterfront. 'Knysna is a good place for secrets.' Ruffish's wife, Sandra, is seeking a multi million pound divorce settlement from her super rich spouse. 'He made £20 million as hedge fund boss of Jack and Maffie,' a source says. Sandra and their two children are living in their £2 million Surrey country house, but she deserves a lot more, the friend believes.

'I'm used to Ruff having a bit of rough on the side,' complained Sandra. 'But he's left me without a fair settlement.'

Ruff fled to South Africa to escape his wife's lawyers, a friend confided. Maffie, also a former hedge fund manager, is a descendant of Shaka, a ruthless Zulu chieftain. She's now a family lawyer who acts for abused women and children.

Jack insists that he and Maffie are 'just friends', our source said, but he's clearly angry with Miss Mafuta, which means 'fat' in Zulu.

The story had a picture of Maffie towering over me at an International Coffee Organisation function. The caption for the picture was *Jack and his Giant Ex*. There was also a picture of Ruff and his family and a sketch of Shaka with his shield and 'Ikiwa', a short sharp spear.

It was Sunday and I phoned *Bloomberg* to speak to John Spittlefields. When I had tipped him off that LeashTrade had bought the Hastings & Ruffish hedge fund business, I had disclosed that Ruff and Maffie had eloped. He was supposed to keep that snippet confidential. I wanted to find out whether he had sold the story to the News on Sunday. Spittlefields wasn't on duty, but a colleague said that he would pass on the message.

My mobile rang. It was Spittlefields.

'Hi, Jack, what's up?'

'John, have you seen the News on Sunday Story? How did they get all that stuff. They made out that Maffie was my girlfriend. That's a load of rubbish!'

'I've never met Sheila Shellhoff,' insisted Spittlefield. 'I played the story straight, Jack. I just wrote that Ruffish left for personal reasons . . . Maybe . . .'

'Maybe what?'

'Pearl's the source. She phoned me after she saw my piece. Tried to find out more. I think she's still spinning against you, Jack. Yes, it must be Pearl.'

It was Sunday, after a long week on the road. We had pitched Aquarium in three European cities. After breakfast, lunch and dinner meetings and presentations around the clock, I wasn't in the mood for this. Needed to wind down. Take the dog for a walk. I hadn't seen Jazz for weeks. Martha's place had virtually become his home.

Still seething, I put on my sunglasses, climbed into my Ferrari and furiously drove down Hampstead's East Heath Road on the way to Martha. I slammed my foot down on the accelerator and revved up the car. Waste of time. As usual there was a traffic jam. A four wheeler was ahead of me. Some silly mother was trying to drive and control her screaming kids, while she was speaking on a mobile. I hooted. She took no notice. I hooted again. She stopped her car at a pedestrian crossing and got out.

'Shut up,' she screamed. 'You don't own this road.'

'You're not supposed to talk on your mobile while you're driving!' I shouted back.

'Nice Ferrari! Pity that death, taxes and traffic jams make us all equal!'

By now there was a long line behind us. Other drivers were hooting, so she rushed back to her car and turned into the next side road.

Without her slowing me down, the rest of the journey was easy. I picked up speed and raced towards Martha's place.

Jazz and Pattie went wild when I arrived, but Martha,

dressed in dirty dungarees, with straggly greasy greying hair, wasn't terribly keen to see me.

'You should have phoned, Jack. I would have tidied up,' Martha chided.

I nodded my head. The house was a mess and badly in need of refurbishment. I had given Martha 5K to get the house decorated, but she had done nothing.

I scolded her: 'How can you live like this Martha? Why didn't you get hold of the Polish painters I told you about?'

She shook her head and went into her messy kitchen, opened a jar and brought out a brown envelope: 'Here I don't want this! I'll paint my place in my own good time.'

I opened up the envelope and saw that she hadn't touched the money.

'This place isn't fit for my dog, let alone you.'

'Who do you think you are Jack?' said Martha in a soft, but angry voice. 'You think that money can buy me? Buy you control?'

'All I'm trying to say . . .'

'I don't need your charity, Jack. I don't want it. I like looking after Jazz. He's our friend, isn't he Pattie?'

The dogs were wagging their tails as she patted him: 'Nasty Jack, silly Jack.'

'Look Martha, I'm grateful to you. You've been good to Jazz. Just keep the money for a rainy day . . .'

'Look Martha, look Martha,' she said mimicking me, opening a big jar on the table and pulling out photographs and showing them to the dogs. 'Look at Jack! Quite a celebrity isn't he?'

Suddenly, something occurred to me: 'Was my ex-girlfriend here?'

'The red-haired one with a hard face? Yes, she was here. Came for a cup of tea. Was in tears. She said that you had dumped her. Had some photos of her. I let her take a look at them and she took some.'

'That's my private property, Martha. Why did you give them to her?' I shouted.

'Because they were hers, that's why!' Martha shouted back, trying to be heard over the din of dogs, who were now in a barking frenzy.

'They were mine and they're now in the News on Sunday!' I fumed, storming to the car, running back and throwing the paper on the table. Martha read the article and burst out laughing.

'You've made it Jack . . . The News on Sunday! You're a real celeb!'

The dogs wagged their tails, stopped barking and brushed against her. I couldn't help myself and began to laugh so much that I fell backwards on to the sofa. A loose spring jabbed my neck: 'Ouch!'

'That's you, Jack. A pain in the neck,' said Martha grinning.

I put the leads on the dogs and we ran to the Heath. Martha was Martha. How could I be angry with her?

*   *   *

I phoned Pearl several times but she didn't return my calls. So I went to her flat about 10pm that Sunday night. From the street, the lights were on and I could see that there was movement in the apartment. I rang her phone and her mobile. Again no answer. There was no way that Pearl could avoid me. I still had the outside door key. Luckily Pearl hadn't changed it and it worked. I rushed up the stairs and banged on the door.

'Pearl I know you're there. Open the door please!'

No reply. I banged again. This time the door opened. Before me stood a tall, well-built guy, with short blond hair. The same guy I had seen when I had brought Pearl flowers, during the spring a year ago. His grey eyes were cold. A gold chain was around his neck and he had a gold Rolex watch imbedded with diamonds.

'What do you want?' the man asked in a heavy Russian accent.

'I want to see Pearl. Is she here?'

'Let him in Yevgeny, he's Jack,' shouted Pearl from the bedroom.

I walked into the living room. A half-full bottle of champagne, two glasses and leftovers from a Chinese takeaway, were on the table. Pearl, her hair wet and with no make-up on, came out of the bedroom in a white gown. Through the open door of the bedroom, I could see an unmade bed with her clothes strewn on the floor. It did not require a stroke of genius to guess what had been going on. Even though we had broken up months before and she had spun against me, I was a bit jealous. I couldn't get rid of my feelings for her.

Pearl noticed me turn red and smiled wickedly. She introduced us casually.

'Yevgeny Faramazov . . . Jack Miner.'

We shook hands warily. Faramazov seemed familiar, but I had come across so many people, that I couldn't be sure that I had met him.

'Jack's the trader I told you about, Yevgeny. He's a good friend.'

'Oh yes,' said Faramazov with a suspicious look on his face.

'He's brilliant, Yevgeny. Maybe he could do something for you.'

Pearl was always on the lookout for opportunities. The only problem was that you were never sure whether she was genuine; whether she was working for the other guy. I had learnt a hard lesson.

'Thanks for the News on Sunday article, Pearl,' I said sarcastically, pulling the page out of my pocket.

'Can I read it?' asked Faramazov.

I passed it to him.

'I can't understand what Maffie and Ruff's romance has to do with me,' I said, doing my best to restrain myself. 'You are well aware that Maffie and I were just good friends.'

'That's exactly what they quoted me as saying,' said Pearl grinning.

'Very funny! Since when did you become my spokeswoman?'

'I thought that we still had an arrangement, Jack,' replied Pearl, naughtily fingering an emerald ring that I had bought her. Faramazov noticed and narrowed his eyes.

'Finished long ago, Pearl,' I hissed.

'Don't worry Jack, the paper's ready for fish and chips.

You must admit that it does keep you in the public eye.'

'Come off it Pearl. I know how you network to build your business. You met Sheila Shellhoff at a party. She needed a story and I was a target.'

'Wrong again Jack. Sandra Ruffish is my client. She wants her money. You were the news peg.'

By now I was getting seriously agitated. I was tired and confused. Faramazov intervened.

'No point in weeping over wet milk,' he said, unsure of the idiom. 'Give me your address Jack. I'm having a party in the country next Saturday. You're welcome.'

I gave him the office address and left, wondering why on earth he was inviting me. Perhaps he was curious. Maybe he wanted to take Pearl's advice, get to know me and offer me a job.

*   *   *

Leash Grobnick was in one of his moods when I entered the office on Monday morning. Through the glass walls of his office I could see him having a go at Cy. He was gesticulating, walking up and down and shouting. Named after his Lithuanian grandfather Lazer, the young man decided that it would be more American and original if he changed his name to Leash. Little did Leash know that his employees would mockingly pull imaginary dog leads when they heard their boss bark like a vicious pit bull terrier. I had a fair idea why Leash was annoyed. He was complaining about the expenses for our trip and that Cy had not chased more potential investors. Cy, in fact, had raised a lot of money for Aquarium. We had twenty large investors, including two pension funds. The fund was now managing $600 million. Leash complained that Cy was behind budget. He wanted the fund to have a billion dollars by the end of summer. That meant road shows and more road shows. It would be a tedious treadmill.

Leash was brought up in New York. His father had worked in a sweatshop and the family of five were poor. He had pulled himself up by his bootstraps, selling clothes in markets, buying property cheaply and doing deals. Eventually he had enough money to start a fund management business. His childhood poverty had never left him. Money was everything. It kept him secure.

I knew all about Leash's tough childhood because of my meetings with him, Cy and Max. He never let them forget about his upbringing, saying that they were brought up with silver spoons in their mouths. He was constantly complaining, taunting them and pushing them. Leash was totally insensitive about people's feelings and humiliated his sons in front of me and other staff.

One day we were having a working lunch in the board-room. Max was eating slowly.

'Slow eaters are slow workers,' sneered Leash. Max walked out. Max had recently decided to go back to New York. I thought that he wanted to get away from his Dad, who was spending more time in London. The real reason was that Max had a boyfriend who lived in Greenwich Village. He had kept it secret from Leash.

After his sons escaped to their own desks, Leash called me in with Aram. The News on Sunday was on his desk. I was hoping that Leash did not read the tabloids. Unfortunately Maisie, his secretary and girlfriend, enjoyed them.

'What's this all about, Jack?' snarled Leash. 'Our business is discreet, but here you are talking to the press.'

'If you read the story closely you'll see that they didn't speak to me,' I insisted. 'How could they? I was in Zurich.'

'Don't be insolent with me young man!' shouted Leash.

I was livid. I wasn't going to let him get away with it. No way was I going to be his whipping boy.

'Sure old thing,' I said smiling.

Leash, narrowed his eyes, looked straight at me and said nothing. I stared back at him, looking him right in the eye. Realising that it was pointless to fight me, he opened a file on our fund and started questioning our performance. Leash wasn't interested in medium and long term gains; whether the fund had risen over a year or two. The fund had to do well every month. If there were losses he would rant. Fortunately the fund was consistently in profit in the six months ended March.

'You can see that we've been positive. That's why we've got more investors,' said Aram, who nervously shuffled about when he spoke to Leash.

'The markets have been up and down, how did you achieve that?' asked Leash.

'Good trading,' said Aram, trying to smile. 'We're up 3.5 per cent in the past six months.'

'That's gross,' said Leash. 'Net it is around 2.7 per cent. Your investors won't be satisfied with that.'

Leash was referring to the large fees that we and other hedge funds charged investors. Each year investors had to pay a hefty 2 per cent annual management fee, whether the fund rose or fell. There was also a performance fee of 20 per cent on any gains of the fund. On the figures in the first half of the year, the net annualised gains after all the fees, were around 5.4 per cent. This was a profit, but given the risks of trading in the markets, the net return was not that much higher than interest on a secure government bond.

'Got any ideas, Jack?' asked Leash, taking off his glasses and looking me up and down.

'I've been on the road, Leash. I haven't been looking at our portfolio closely. But the market's been difficult and Aram has done OK'.

'That's for me to decide, young man,' he said. Grobnick was always patronising; always reminding me of my age.

'We should be getting another $100 million from the latest road shows,' I said. 'Max has a good program. It should help us find something that will make big money.'

'We'll put it in oil and natural gas,' said Aram.

'Oil I can understand, but why gas?' Leash asked.

'It's been depressed since 9/11. It's only around $3 a British Thermal Unit. Production can't keep up with demand. China and India are consuming huge amounts of energy and the war in Iraq has raised concerns about supply disruptions,' said Aram. 'It's only a matter of time before prices rise.'

'Check your charts and numbers, Jack,' instructed Leash. 'If you think gas and oil will run, we'll pull in more investors.'

I walked back with Aram to his working space. He looked dejected.

'Why do you let him push you around, Aram?' I asked

sympathetically, keeping my distance. The halitosis was as bad as ever.

'Jack, I've got a wife, four kids at private schools and an expensive girlfriend. That costs a lot of money,' said Aram, sighing.

'Mistress? You wanna be like Ruff? Get into the News on Sunday?' I laughed. 'By the way, how come we haven't lost any money in the past two months?'

'What do you mean?' replied Aram defensively.

'From what I can tell, the shares and commodities that we've been trading were mostly down in February and March, but we're up.'

'Don't worry, Jack. While you've been away, I've been going long and short. I've also rolled our options and futures positions forward.'

'What do you mean?'

'I've carried some of the loss making positions from March into April. That keeps March positive.'

'Are we allowed to do that?'

'Why not? Oil and especially gas should do well this month. Our April profits will exceed the losses in March. We'll still be able to show Leash and our investors good results.'

'And if they fall, what then?'

'We'll think of a plan, Jack, we'll think of a plan. But energy prices won't fall. I'm convinced they won't. I know that some big knowledgeable players have been buying.'

I went back to my seat near Aram and pulled out all the prices, trading volumes and charts. He was right. During the recession after 9/11, oil prices had languished around $20 a barrel and gas had traded around $2.50 a British Thermal Unit, but in recent weeks they had begun to increase. I sketched black fish for oil and grey fish for gas and both had definitely broken into a higher level of the aquarium.

I was a little uneasy about Aram's policy of postponing losses, but Bank Kaboom, the independent administrator of the fund, had not complained. We managed the fund in London, but it was registered and legally based in the offshore, tax-free Cayman Islands. Every month we sent our fund's performance results and other information to Bank Kaboom. If the bank accepted the figures, investors were happy.

Aram brought me the latest monthly report for Aquarium and noticed me examining the charts.

'See what I mean,' he said. 'They're going to move, Jack. They will boom like coffee. We can invest in energy futures and options and in oil and gas stocks.'

I nodded my head. As usual, I approved the latest monthly returns by placing my signature next to his. The results were then despatched to Bank Kaboom and the investors in the fund.

Just before lunch, Cy tapped me on my shoulder: 'Don't forget our presentation at the Armourers' Hall at 4pm.'

'Cy, are we definitely getting another $100 million? Aram wants to put it in oil and gas.'

'He told me that he's already bought them.'

'What! He never told me that!'

'He's used the fund's loan facility,' said Cy. 'It should be OK. Hal Humford of Banque Discretione called me from Zurich. He told me that his bank intended investing more in Aquarium. That will give us more leeway to borrow more.'

I rushed over to Aram.

'We're supposed to be partners. Why didn't you tell me that you were going ahead?'

'I had to move fast Jack. Prices are beginning to move. Best to get in now. Remember coffee?'

'We did that in stages, Aram. First a bit. When the market confirmed that we were right, we bought some more coffee. If we were wrong we could get out with a small loss.'

'That's what I'm doing Jack. This is just the start. Take a look at the screen. Oil's trading around $30 and gas is $3.10.'

'You've borrowed $100 million and also bought options and futures,' I said angrily. 'That's dangerous. Borrowing to speculate on margin. One hell of a risk!'

'Take it easy, Jack. That's what leverage is all about. Borrow to lever profits upwards. We'll have enough capital. When oil and gas take off, more investors will come in.'

'What about the interest on the borrowings?'

'That's in hand. Besides buying shares in oil and gas companies, I'm purchasing their bonds as well. The interest on their bonds is offsetting the interest on our loans.'

'Corporate loans? What if the companies are risky?'

'Why not Jack? They're solid companies with either large oil and gas resources or seriously exciting exploration rights. The income from the bonds is much higher than the interest on our loans.'

My fund manager course in investments had taught me about bonds, a multi trillion dollar market, far bigger than equities and commodities. US Treasury, British, German and French government bonds, i.e. major nation loan issues, are regarded as top notch safe havens. Companies issue bonds to borrow money. So corporate bonds are dependent on the financial strength of the company and long term profit prospects. A start-up company or oil or mining business is generally regarded as a higher credit risk as the business could fail. So the market demands much higher yields or interest from their bonds, than from government securities. In some instances the yields are so high that the market calls them 'junk bonds'. Despite these risks, a shrewd investor can make big gains if companies do better than expected. The price of their junk bonds rise and the investor receives better interest. The downside is if the companies get into trouble. In those instances, the prices of their bonds fall.

I wondered if I should brief Leash about Aram's investment and trading strategy, but decided against it. The Aquarium drawing showed that oil and gas prices were breaking through to higher levels of the tank. The shares and bonds seemed OK as Aram, a qualified accountant, had made shrewd investments in the past. There was a good chance that he would be proved right and we would make it big time.

*   *   *

That afternoon, Cy, Maisie and I climbed into a taxi and went on our way to a seminar at the Armourers' Hall. Cy shuffled through the papers for the presentation. Relaxed, I sat back and looked out the window. The taxi wound its way through the traffic to Piccadilly Circus, then down Haymarket past a night club and Georgian theatre, towards

Trafalgar Square. Tourists were happily taking pictures of each other next to the fountains and Nelson's Column. South Africa House overlooks the square and I thought of Maffie and Ruff. Wondered what they were doing and decided that I would go to South Africa at Christmas to find them. See Ivor Ensworth and the twins again. We had kept in contact with emails at first, but that had petered out. I continued to daydream, absently observing us drive up The Strand and past Bush House, where the *BBC Overseas Service* had interviewed me about coffee. The taxi trundled through the traffic on Fleet Street, passed the old *Telegraph* Building, which housed Goldman Sachs and the old *Reuters* building on the right. Then it accelerated up Ludgate Hill towards St Paul's Cathedral, which still looked magnificent on that grey, cloudy day. We continued on our way past the Bank of England, turned left towards Moorgate and into a narrow street, stopping outside the Armourers' Hall.

On one side of the stairs were medieval suits of armour that the city Armourers' Guild used to make. At the top of the stairs was a room full of bankers, pension fund managers and men and women who managed money for the super rich. Cy began to network.

At the seminar, three different hedge fund managers would present their funds to potential investors. We were giving the final presentation, a psychological ploy of Cy. It would be brief and to the point and since we were last, it would be fresh in the minds of the audience. When the delegates left, Maisie would stand at the exit and pass them folders about Aquarium. I wasn't interested in listening to the boring presentations of the other fund managers. So I sat down on a chair in the cocktail room and paged through the *Guardian*.

'Hello you, long time no see.'

The voice and Australian twang were unmistakeable. I looked up. It was Sandy, her brown hair much shorter than when I last saw her. Her dark eyes, lively and enticing; face and arms bronzed. Her light blue suit by coincidence matched mine. Looking at her again, it wasn't surprising that I was once crazy about her. Yes, Sandy, who I had followed to London; who had changed my life, without knowing it.

'Sandy! What are you doing here? Thought that you were at University in Perth,' I said trying to be casual.

I felt myself blushing. She noticed, laughed and touched my face.

'Decided to travel with my mates,' she said. 'You know. The Australian thing. Through Thailand, India, then Europe. If we make enough money, the States as well.'

'Sounds great.'

'Wow Jack! I saw your name on the programme. Didn't dream it was you.'

Some coincidence. She had probably spotted my name on the Net. Read the articles on how I had made it. Saw that I was to speak at conference and applied for a job as an organiser. Very convenient. I decided to play along with her.

'How's that friend of yours? The guy who drove the Golf convertible?'

'Come on Jack! He's history. You've just reminded me of him. Time sure flies. What's been happening with you, Jack?'

'As you see, I'm a hedge fund manager,' I replied, with a smile that had a deliberate touch of superiority.

'What a hedge fund?'

I did my best to explain the arcane world of hedge funds. She touched my hand and I felt a tingle up my spine. Two years had passed and though she had hurt me, I still couldn't help but fancy her. She looked at me with that knowing, mischievous, grin of hers: 'I'm not sure what you're talking about, Jack, but it sounds that you take punts on the market. Guess you win some and lose some, right!'

'That's about it.'

She looked at my Savile Row suit, my silk, dark blue Hermes tie and Gucci shoes: 'Seems you're up at the moment, Jack. The last time I saw you . . .'

'I was down and out. Broke! One of the cleaners at Lord's.'

Sandy shook her head in mock amazement and noticed her agitated boss beckoning.

'Do you want to come to a fancy dress party with me on Saturday?' I blurted out.

Her number was ready and she pressed it into my hand: 'Sure Jack, see you later.'

Despite my cynicism, I floated into the conference room. Cy described my presentation as a brilliant performance. Sandy slipped in, waved and slipped out.

'Jack, you had them in the palm of your hand,' said Cy when I'd finished. 'An energy and commodities boom! You really think there's going to be one?'

'Who knows? Oil and gas are already rising. Long may it continue, we're up to our necks in the stuff.'

'I think those guys are going to give us a lot of money,' Cy said. 'You sounded like a natural gas evangelist. From what I could tell, you converted them. They went out believing that demand will soar because it is much cheaper than oil and it is clean energy.'

'They believed me because I believe it,' I said. 'It won't stop global warming, but it will help curb pollution.'

18

GOLDEN DAYS

Later that week, Sandy and I were on our way to Angels, a fancy dress hire specialist, not far from Soho. We had to choose a costume from the eighteenth or nineteenth century. I spotted a Nelson costume and tried on the white breeches and navy blue jacket with tarnished medals. The costume was tight. Not surprising. I was a lot heavier. Luckily there was a bigger Nelson costume and I fitted easily into that. The Admiral's famous hat fitted perfectly. It was much easier for Sandy. As Emma Hamilton, Nelson's mistress, she looked ravishing. The full-length, white, early nineteenth century dress clung to her sensuous curves and showed off her perfect cleavage.

I decided to leave the Ferrari outside the shop and didn't bother if there was yet another parking fine. Sandy tucked her hand under my arm as we walked about a quarter of a mile towards Soho. We chose a Moroccan Restaurant, ordered chicken couscous and caught up on the last two years. The meal lasted for hours, but was over too soon. I decided not to tell Sandy that it was she who had originally motivated me to make money. After being dumped before,

I wasn't going to make a fool of myself again.

I drove her to her place in Bayswater and parked outside a decaying Edwardian building. The paint had faded and the walls were dirty grey. She didn't want me to go inside, but I insisted. Sandy turned the key of the front door and we entered a dusky passage, with poor lighting and a shabby dirty carpet. We climbed two floors on rickety, squeaky stairs. Sandy unlocked the door of her bedsit and put on the light. Clothes were strewn on the floor. The armchair, with two pairs of knickers hanging over its back, was decrepit and the bed was roughly made. Her kitchenette was shabby with unwashed dishes in the sink. I went into the bathroom to relieve myself and wash my hands. Both the toilet and bath were dirty and stained. The place smelt musty.

'How can you live in this dump, Sandy?' I asked.

She was busy picking up clothes in a desperate attempt to tidy up the place.

'You can't imagine rents in London these days, Jack. It's just temporary. I'm waiting to get a proper job.'

Money makes you fussy. The untidy filth turned me off Sandy and I decided not to stay. Instead of making a pass, I gave Sandy a kiss on the cheek and told her that I would pick her up early Saturday afternoon.

* * *

Saturday was a perfect spring day; sunshine and blue skies. The Ferrari's hood was down. While I was driving, I touched Sandy's knee by mistake. She pushed aside my hand and looked at me warily. Thinking that she was playing hard to get and my date would go nowhere, I acted out a sulk. It mostly worked with others. I put on some reggae and stopped talking for about an hour, drumming my hand on the wheel in time to the loud music. Sandy was unfazed and ignored me. When we reached the open highway and the speed restrictions were raised, I stepped on the accelerator and the car took off. My eyes were mostly on the road. But I managed to glance at Sandy as she ruffled her hair, leaned back, closed her eyes and relaxed. I could see why I was mad about her when I was sixteen.

We arrived at Yevgeny Faramazov's mansion late in the afternoon. The house looked as if it was once a gothic nunnery. A tower was on each corner of the house, which appeared to have thirty to forty rooms. Farmland surrounded the large garden and in the distance I could see cows, calves, bulls and horses. Several hundred people, looking like eighteenth and nineteenth century aristocrats were milling about. The garden was magnificent with thousands of daffodils and tulips in full bloom. It led down to the Thames where I could see a motorboat and a ferry full of guests.

Yevgeny Faramazov, as Tsar Alexander, and his wife, as Catherine the Great, were in the centre of the garden. They received their guests who bowed and kissed their hands. This was part of the fun, but I couldn't help thinking that people were fawning over them. We went up to introduce ourselves. Instead of kissing his hand I shook it. He looked at me warily, knowing that I knew about him and Pearl. He introduced us to his wife, Katya. She was beautiful and for the life of me I couldn't understand why he needed to stray.

Since we had left without any breakfast or lunch, we were both starving. Sandy grabbed some smoked salmon and caviar canapes. We then rushed for the punch, finished our drinks quickly, pulled out the sodden apples and grapes and ate them. They had absorbed lots of alcohol and after allowing my glass to be filled again with champagne, it was not long before I was drunk.

Late afternoon, guests moved towards a stage that was in front of a tent. Two miming artists came out. The show began and straight away I recognised the artist. Boris Krepolovitch was demonstrating his acrobatic and juggling skills. It then came back to me. I had seen Faramazov before I met him at Pearl's place. It was at the Edinburgh festival when I was with Ivor Ensworth and the twins, after we had seen Krepolovitch's performance there. Another figure was at the back of the stage helping with props. It could have been the drink, but I don't think so. It was the big bearded thug who I had seen at the Russian Samovar. Since he was with Krepolovitch, there was now no mistaking. He was definitely one of the murderers on Charing Cross Bridge. He was dressed as a Victorian undertaker, all in black. An apt costume! There they were, the two hangmen together again.

It was twilight, but I put on my dark glasses and clasped Sandy's hand so tightly that I felt the sweat. She tried to pull it loose.

'Hey Jack, your nails are digging into me,' Sandy cried, as she used her right hand in an attempt to free herself. She managed to pull her hand away, as I felt myself hyperventilating. Following Danny's advice, I blew slowly into the side of my fist using the closed fingers as a tunnel; 'Sh . . . sh . . . sh . . . relax, relax.'

Sandy, not realising what was happening to me, angrily slapped me hard on my back.

'What's wrong with you, Jack?' she said, shaking her hand in pain. 'Are you a sadist or something? Look what you've done to my hand.'

I took my eyes off the thug and saw the nail marks on her left hand. They had drawn blood.

'I'm sorry Sandy, I don't know what got into me. It was a bad memory,' I gasped, trying to kiss her hand.

She pulled it away: 'What happened, Jack?'

'Never mind,' I said, swiftly dragging her away from the makeshift stage and crowd of eighteenth century dandies and their ladies. We went to the buffet table, where I filled a glass up with iced water, wet a table napkin and gently placed it on Sandy's hand. By now, I was breathing normally and was in control of myself. Since most of the other guests were watching the show, we were virtually first in line to choose from the assortment of delicacies on the buffet table. We chose lobster, asparagus and artichoke hearts and we sat down at one of the round tables. Sandy tucked in, but I just picked at mine. Didn't feel like eating. Afterwards, when I was more relaxed, I took off my dark glasses. They made me more noticeable, especially in the Nelson costume. It was unlikely that the murderers would remotely recognise me. Other people joined us, but they spoke Russian and some other Eastern European languages, so it was difficult to mix. That suited me.

Pearl, dressed as Marie Antoinette, came up.

'Hello, Jack, glad you could make it,' said Pearl. She carefully studied Sandy. 'Who's your friend?'

I introduced them. Pearl didn't show that she was jealous, but I suspected that she was more than curious. Sandy was looking really pretty.

'Thought you were coming alone, Jack,' said Pearl ruefully.

Perhaps that was Faramazov's motive for inviting me to his party. I would be a cover for his mistress.

By this time the party was beginning to hum. The band was good and people were dancing. We joined them. Sandy was having a great time and when the music was slower, we danced closely and kissed for the first time since Bridlington beach. Around midnight, rockets went off and the fireworks display began.

There was no way that we could drive back to London. Instead, given the amount of alcohol in me, we found a cosy bed and breakfast near Pangbourne, a village not far from Faramazov's place. We went up the stairs into the room and collapsed on the bed, undressing each other at the same time. There wasn't much of a shower, so I filled up the bath and climbed in. Sandy followed and sat facing my back, using soap and a cloth to wash and massage it. We shuffled around in the tight space, splashing water while I washed her back as well. Then we faced each other, kissed and with the smooth soap, I ran my hands over her breasts down to her belly button, while she did the same with my chest and tummy. We stood up in the full bath, embraced, grabbed some towels, dried each other and then rushed to bed.

The last time I had experienced such passion was with Maggie, alongside the Scottish loch. Very different from

Pearl's cocaine-fuelled sex that had left me with bruises and scratches.

Sandy was all over me, murmuring and shouting with pleasure. When it was all over we fell asleep in each other's arms, before breaking away later into more comfortable positions.

She was still asleep when I woke up early in the morning. I took out my trainers from my overnight bag, put on some shorts and carefully closed the door. I was soon on the road, running on a narrow path until I came to a toll bridge across the Thames. All the memories had come back, but instead of panicking, I wondered what was going on. Ivor Ensworth had hinted that Faramazov had made a lot of money doing dubious deals, but was unsure whether he was one of the Russian mafia. The presence of Boris Krepolovitch and that bearded brute at the party, indicated that they were somehow connected. Had he just employed them for the show, or was there more to it? Pearl Fleecer. Here there and everywhere. Was she working for Faramazov? The presence of the bearded thug indicated that Faramazov could be linked to the Russian hedge fund managers. They were resentful because, through me, they had lost fortunes on coffee and had threatened revenge.

I had become careless about my personal safety. Back in London, I installed an expensive alarm that would receive an almost instant response from the police.

*　　*　　*

On Monday, Leash held a meeting with Cy, Aram and myself.

'You guys have done well so far this year,' said Leash, smiling.

'We're up 11 per cent this month and the energy market is only beginning to take off,' said Aram.

'There's another source of demand that the market hasn't noticed yet,' said Cy.

'What's that?' asked Leash.

'Pension funds. That's why I suggested we have a meeting.'

'Explain.'

'I've been reading that the buzz words for pension managers are now alternative investments such as hedge funds and commodities. Aquarium is now in fashion as it's a macro hedge fund that mainly specialises in commodities and resource stocks and bonds.'

'Brilliant, Cy. Never thought you had it in you,' shouted Leash, excitedly.

That was typical Leash. A slap on the back and then put-down. Cy, used to his father, smiled wryly. I really liked Cy. He was smart and a decent, nice guy. A highly successful salesman, he genuinely believed in LeashTrade funds, which was easy, as they were all doing well.

'If pension funds intend buying raw materials, a lot of money is going to pour into oil, gas and alternative energy,' I said. 'The market is going to be surprised by the boom. It happened with gold and coffee.'

'It's going to be win, win. Prices going up and money coming in,' shouted Aram enthusiastically.

'We must pitch to as many large American and Canadian

pensions as possible before July 4,' insisted Cy. 'It will be much more difficult to get hold of the decision makers during summer vacations. Later we can try the European pensions.'

'Can Jack accompany me, Leash? His fund presentations are excellent.'

'Will you be able to manage the fund alone, Aram?' asked Leash.

'Sure, I'm already running the fund on a day to day basis. Jack's been on the road for some time.'

'He would be based in the New York office for most of the summer. Don't you want him to be in London with you?'

'We'll make a plan, Leash. We'll have transatlantic conference calls.'

The transfer to New York couldn't have come at a better time. My paranoia about the Russians had returned and I wanted to be far away from them. Of course that was illogical as they could follow me anywhere in the world, but that was the way I felt.

*   *   *

I couldn't wait to tell Sandy, who had moved into my Hampstead flat: 'I'm off to the States for a few months. Want to come?'

'Wow, Jack, of course,' she said as she fed my fish in the living room's large aquarium. 'We must get someone to look after our pets.'

'Get packed, I've already sorted out the servicing of the tank. You'll love my New York apartment. It's close to Central Park.'

Those were golden summer days. The guys at LeashTrade's offices in Park Avenue were fun. There were two New York funds. Their managers and analysts were friendly and smart. They concentrated in large and small companies, going 'long and short' by being bullish on some stocks and bearish on other shares. On Sundays we joined them in Central Park and played softball. Sandy was a great antidote to Pearl, who had hurt me a lot.

'Come on, wake up! Time to meditate,' she insisted at the ludicrous hour of 5am. Bleary eyed, I would sit with her and try to rid my mind from random thoughts that kept rushing into my head. Eventually my mind was empty and I would see all sorts of wonderful colours. It was restful, invigorating and the best anti-stress medicine anyone could hope for.

'You're getting there, Jack! The Sivananda Ashram gurus and devotees keep still for hours.'

The Yoga ashram in India had changed Sandy. She was good for me as she was not money mad.

'You've got more than enough, Jack. Why don't you quit your job and travel? We can teach poor kids in India, Asia or Africa.'

'You've already dropped out of your history of art degree, Sandy,' I said as we walked around Whitney Museum of American Art.

We were in Washington DC, as Cy and I had given a presentation to a global investment expert at the World Bank. He advised Third World nations on establishing pensions. Since these nations were raw materials producers, investment in oil rigs, mines and commodities came naturally.

'I'm learning far more here,' laughed Sandy. 'Jackson Pollock, Mark Rothko, Andy Warhol, Edward Hopper. We get scraps in Australia!'

'That's my point. You're touring North America with me. While I'm pitching to those boring pension managers in New York, Philadelphia and Boston, you're having a great time. We were in the Art Institute of Chicago a couple of days ago. We might as well pitch tents in museums.'

'The Art Institute was awesome, Jack! Not in my wildest dreams did I expect a Midwest city to have such a place. I love Frank Lloyd Wright architecture.'

'Maybe I should buy some art. You can be my expert.'

She squeezed my hand and kissed me.

'Jazz and the Chicago Merc and Board of Trade? What about them?' I asked.

'Loved the Jazz. But the commodity exchanges! Human animals, shouting and screaming in their own self-made pit.'

'We're off to the West Coast, next week. Seattle, San Francisco, Los Angeles and San Diego. The pensions treadmill, but there will be plenty of sites for you to see. Shopping for you and me?'

'Who cares about shopping, Jack? I've got enough clothes and trinkets. I'll be waiting for you outside the offices to make sure you see something interesting.'

'You could do with some clothes, Sandy. Aren't you bored with the ones you are wearing?'

'Thanks, but no thanks, Jack. Time you went to Macy's and got a decent pair of jeans. That designer stuff you're wearing. Big rip-off. Indian and Chinese textile workers earning almost nothing and living in poverty. It costs about

$5 to make a shirt there and the celebrity designer shops are selling them for $200!'

'The chains also buy from India and China. They provide people there with jobs. Yeah, they're paid peanuts, but the cost of living is much lower and at least they work,' I said gently. 'Let's go to the vegetarian restaurant I told you about.'

* * *

The American tour was so packed and busy, that it was over all too quickly. It was late summer and a letter was waiting for me at the London office. Michael Braggens, Mayor of Bridlington, was inviting me back to my 'home town' to discuss redevelopment of the town.

We left early Friday for a long weekend with Jazz in the back of the car. I left Sandy at her cousin Sue's house. Sue had changed a lot since I had last seen her. She was still living with her Mum and Dad. But she was now a single parent. Sandy and Sue hugged each other and Sue's Mum gave us all a cup of tea.

'It would be good to see Tom and Joe. Do you know where I can find them?' I asked.

'Tom is making good money. He's a plumber and is working in York. Joe's at Leeds University,' replied Sue. She phoned their parents, but they were both away. Pity, but I doubted if I now had anything in common with my old mates.

I left Jazz with Sue. He was terrified of the toddler and crept under a table.

Later I arrived at Bridlington Town Hall, a wide brown

Edwardian brick building with a clock tower. Braggens, overweight and balding with a fixed smile, came up and shook my hand. He took me into the Mayor's meeting room where five other councillors were around a table. One of them jumped up and rushed over to me, shaking my hand warmly. It was Martin Miner, my uncle. His beer belly was now so big that it bulged over his trousers and he looked like a prime candidate for a heart attack.

'I oope you doon't mind, Jack, but I arranged family reoonion for you,' he said in his thick Yorkshire accent.

I remembered the last time I had seen him and tried to be as civil as possible. Martin, my Dad's brother, had totally rejected me when Bill died. I had just turned sixteen and not a single one of my relatives was prepared to look after me. I was to leave school, get another job in a fish and chip shop and take care of myself. How could I forget such 'generosity'?

'Sure, I'll come,' I said without any enthusiasm: 'Where is it?'

'Loonchtime tomorrow a' Cook's Tavern . . . Just ootside Filey,' he said, smiling sheepishly. He seemed to know what I was thinking.

'Yep, I know it . . . the place where Sheila and Mike got married,' I said.

'I've been reading aboot you in newspapers,' said Uncle Martin, pompously. 'Told me colleagues that a Miner would put sommet back into town.'

'Come on, let's get on with the meeting,' said Braggens, clearly irritated with Uncle Martin. 'We've got a long agenda.'

I cannot understand why people go into politics, especially local politics. I was wearing a red Lacoste T-shirt, but the stuffy councillors kept their jackets on during that hot summer's day. They sweated like crazy while they argued about boring issues. Planning permission, road signs, one-way systems, pedestrian crossings, nurseries and school budgets.

The main topic, which was why I was there, was the fundraising campaign. When they finally came to the Bridlington development item on the agenda, they asked me if I knew any potential sponsors. That was as broad a hint as any. I pulled out my Coutts chequebook and wrote out a cheque for £80,000, insisting that the money had to go towards the development of Bridlington's tatty seafront. From the way they sucked up to me, the donation must have been the biggest that they had ever received.

'Oonly eighteen and look what ee's achieved,' beamed Martin. 'That's a Miner for you!'

*   *   *

Later that afternoon I picked up Sandy and Jazz at Sue's place, a small terraced house overlooking the beach.

'I want you to meet an old friend, Sandy,' I said as we drove off. I found a parking place near the harbour and we walked o the seafront. All sorts of memories flooded back. The fish and chip shop was gone and a tatty tourist shop was in its place. The block of flats where I used to live, looked much whiter and cleaner. Major renovations of the harbour were taking place, reducing the space to squeeze through the crowd. The fairground, nearby, was as popular as ever. Jazz pulled like mad. I let him off the lead and he led the way, rushing up the stairs towards our old flat. He stood outside one of the doors waiting and panting.

Gill Derby opened the door and cried: 'Jack Miner! What a surprise!'

Before she had time to hug me, Jazz got in first. He broke away from me and jumped on her, licking her face and vigorously wagging his tail. It was as if he had found his long lost owner. When Jazz was finished, Gill grabbed me and gave me a long tearful hug. The soapy smell of her skin came back to me and I enjoyed her warmth. I was embarrassingly emotional and turned away from Sandy, so that she couldn't see my tears.

'Jack, thanks for the Christmas cards, but why haven't I heard from you?'

'No excuses, Gill . . . This is Sandy.'

She looked at both of us and beamed: 'Hello Sandy. What a lovely girl, Jack! Let me take a good look at you. You've filled out Jack . . . taller too.'

We went into her living room where there was a framed photograph of us, just after my sixteenth birthday. I was thin as a reed. I peered into the large oval mirror in the centre of the room. Yes, I had filled out, I thought, as I admired my muscles. Gill had hardly changed.

We talked about the old times. Jazz ran around the flat sniffing, wagging his tail and then waiting in the kitchen for the biscuit that Gill always gave him. It was something like a time warp. Nothing had changed, except that Bill, my Dad, was no longer there. Gill was like a substitute Mum to me. I was sorry that I hadn't been in contact with her.

'I see that the flats have had a coat of paint,' I said.

'Yes, Jack . . . Thanks so much, we were all paid out in full,' Gill said. 'Your friend gave me something extra. That paid for the decoration.'

'My friend?'

'I forget his name. He came all the way from London to the creditors meeting. It was so funny,' she recalled. 'Baton . . . Remember that horrible man! He tried to get a higher fee. Your friend made some great jokes about liquidators and undertakers. All the creditors laughed and Baton backed down.'

'What did he look like?'

'Distinguished. Tall, long grey-white hair and moustache.'

'Stan Slimcop? He came to Bridlington?'

'Yes, that's him. He was very fond of you, Jack. After the meeting he came back here and wanted to know all about you, your Dad and Mum. I showed him the album you left here and he poured over the family pictures. I hope you don't mind Jack, he took one. I think that he regarded you as a surrogate son.'

I was flabbergasted. I had no idea that Stan had felt that strongly about me. I thought that he was just a good friend and wished that I hadn't sent that stupid letter. Maybe I was some sort of replacement for Sean. I know Leila mixed us up. Despite my letter of apology, I still hadn't heard from them. Why had I been so arrogant, so thoughtless? Stupid! It was bad enough losing parents, but losing a son? I put my head in my hands. Had to find them. Apologise face to face.

'Are you OK, Jack?' said Sandy, coming up and holding my hand.

'Yes I'm fine I'm just an idiot, Sandy.'

Later we left Jazz in the flat and the three of us went out for dinner at the Captain's Table, the pub restaurant that I used to go to with Dad and Mum. It was at the end of the harbour and our table had a view of the sea. One by one, the pleasure cruisers came in; the Yorkshire Belle, the Pirate Ship, some sailing boats and an occasional speedboat. I tucked into my Yorkshire Pudding. As I tasted each mouthful, I realised how much I had missed Yorkshire food. The sun was setting and it was now difficult to spot the boats on the orange reddish sea. We talked and talked until it was dark outside, but for a lighthouse in the distance. Time was still. I was home again.

*   *   *

We spent the night in a small hotel that overlooked Filey beach and sneaked Jazz into the room. Early morning we went for a run and later we drove to Cook's Tavern.

'It was named after Captain Cook,' I said.

'Really, Jack?' replied Sandy sarcastically. 'Was he the guy who founded New South Wales? Didn't know he had anything to do with Australia.'

'Something you don't know, Sandy,' I retorted. 'His voyage began in Whitby, just north of here.'

She gave me a kiss on the cheek. Sandy made me feel good. I wished that I loved her as much as she loved me. I couldn't help myself, I kept thinking about Pearl. It was ridiculous, but she still had a hold on me.

'What's up Jack, what are you thinking about?' asked Sandy who seemed to sense what was going on in my head.

We arrived a little late and I parked the Ferrari next to the tavern garden. We got out of our car, tied Jazz to the fence and walked through the gate. I reckon all my relatives were there – old, young, teenagers, toddlers and babies. It seemed as if there were a hundred there, very different from the few relatives who had turned up at Bill's funeral. They waved when we arrived, but before I could talk to any of them, about twenty men and boys rushed to the car, crying: 'Wow a Ferrari!' Within seconds, the Miners and the Upworths, on my Mum's side, were pushing and shoving each other to get a glimpse of the car. Two boys, who I had never seen before, jumped over the sides and sat in the driver and passenger seats. Jazz began to bark like crazy, but no one took any notice of him. All I could hear were chants of: 'What do you think it cost? 100,000 . . . 200,000??'

'Come on Jack, give us a spin!' shouted the boys.

Uncle Martin and Aunty Peggy came up to me and she gave me the dreaded hug. Peggy was now so fat that she had to cover herself with a tent like pink dress. As she enveloped me, I was reminded of her smell. Pungent stale sweat and cheap perfume. She tried to kiss me, but I avoided her ashtray mouth.

Peggy offered me a cigarette, but I shook my head.

'Still don't smoke, Jack?'We really missed you,' said Peggy who was a shameful liar. 'We were going to take you in, but you disappeared.'

'And coom back with red Ferrari,' grinned Uncle Martin.

'The Council were impressed with doonation, Jack. Mighty impressed.'

Uncle John, another 'generous' member of the family came up. He hadn't changed. His face still looked pinched and mean. Small hands and thin arms protruded from a plain white shirt that was tucked into shiny black trousers. His wife Alice awkwardly mumbled that she was sorry that she hadn't made Dad's funeral.

'That was ages ago,' said Sandy.

'It was like yesterday,' said John Upworth glumly. 'Jack's Mum was my sister. Also died young.'

I pulled Sandy away from these ghastly relatives and we went up to my cousins Mike and Sheila who I liked.

'You probably saw that piece in the *Daily Mail*, Jack. A reporter came round asking all sorts of questions about you,' said Mike.

'So you were one of the sources?'

'We just told her about the fish and chip shop, the school, that sort of thing. Took us out for a drink. Was very nice.'

'Sure, charming very charming,' I replied, gritting my teeth.

Other relatives interrupted our conversation. There were so many of them that it became a blur. I can't remember their names nor what they looked like. Didn't have a single drink as I spent most of the time taking kids for a spin in the car. Just before we left, Martin called me over. He was sitting in a quiet spot under a tree.

'You're doing very well, lad. We always knew you were gooing places, but this? Beyond our wildest dreams.'

'Thanks Martin,' I said abruptly.

'Wish could say same for my business. Times are hard.'

I knew where this was heading.

'How can a construction business struggle in a property boom? You're a councillor. Didn't they give you any contracts for the redevelopment?'

'Tha' would be coorruption, Jack. No. Haad to rely on other business. Can I coom see you soom time? With your contacts you could raise capital. It's a good business. Just needs finance.'

I stood over him and looked down. This time I had the money, the upper hand. This was my Dad's brother who wouldn't take me in when I lost both my parents. What a nerve!

'Sure Martin, give me a call. Maybe we can get together,' I said insincerely.

Soon afterwards, we said our goodbyes, got in the car, gave the royal wave and sped away.

19

MONEY AND CONTROL

During the autumn, winter and spring natural gas prices soared to around $9 a British Thermal Unit while crude oil surged to $40 a barrel. Heating oil, gasoline and other oil products followed while platinum and palladium also jumped as the metals could be used in fuel cells, an alternative energy source. The market began to worry about inflation and gold, silver and other commodity prices rose. Aquarium's money under management rose to $800 million. The fund was making huge gains and growing numbers of pension funds, wealthy investors and banks were pouring in money. We charged two per cent for annual management services. Regardless of whether the fund went up or down we were paid as much as $16 million. We also earned almost $50 million on our twenty per cent performance fees. My combined salary and profit share came to more than $5 million. I was only eighteen, but with my own money in Aquarium, I was now worth almost $15 million or around £9 million. The way life was going, I would soon have enough to buy a football club!

It was a funny thing about money. I had apartments

worth more than £1 million, a Ferrari, holidays in five star hotels and a lovely girlfriend. Everything that I could possibly want. Yet I still wasn't satisfied. Trader publications rated me as one of the top thirty traders of the year. But I wanted to be in the top five. I read the Forbes and Sunday Times rich lists. Compared to those people, I was poor! I would get to the top, buy Newcastle United, my favourite football club, and choose players. For the moment, I had to do with a Chelsea season ticket.

I now understood Leash, who had also started with no money. In fact, I had begun to get on with Leash Grobnick. He shouted and screamed at everyone but left me alone. Maybe because I stood up to him and gave him cheek. Maybe he saw a bit of himself in me.

Sometimes he would take me to Dino's, an Italian restaurant in Mayfair, near our office. He would eat simply. A mixed salad, spring chicken and sparkling water. He was in his mid fifties, but looked ten years younger. He could be very charming when it suited him.

One day we were at Dino's where Leash was eating his usual while I had spaghetti bolognese. I was eating as rapidly as him. Leash did not believe in long relaxed meals.

Leash was always direct and to the point: 'If you eat all that, you'll get fat, Jack! Are you getting enough exercise?'

'Yeah. I go to the gym and have a swim afterwards. On the weekends I go for a run with my dog.'

'Then you must cut down eating and drinking. Exercise is good but it's an inefficient way to lose weight.'

'I suppose you're right. When I'm finished in the gym I

can have two or three beers, fish and chips, chocolate. I love chocolate, Leash.'

'Cut them out, Jack, cut them out. You know there's something funny about being rich.'

'What?'

'The more you have, the less you eat.'

We laughed.

'Don't worry Jack. Just keep fit and thin. Work hard; enjoy life. Don't be like me. Don't get married too soon.'

Silence. Me thinking.

'What about that pretty girlfriend of yours? Is she going to hook you, Jack?'

'Not yet, but she would like to,' I replied.

'You've got money; you're not bad looking. You can get as many as you want. Live Jack, live!'

He laughed for a few seconds and then became serious again. 'You and I know what it's like to be poor. People think that I'm greedy, but they're wrong.'

I observed him, quietly, as he sipped his sparkling water.

'I want more money because I have this awful feeling . . . That I could lose it all.'

I nearly fell over. The rich lists showed that Leash was worth around around $400 million, perhaps even more. The way LeashTrade and his investments were going, his fortune was growing even larger.

'You wonder why I worry? Why I push my sons? Fund managers like you? My grandfather was a rich man, but he lost everything in the 1929 crash. The family moved from a big Manhattan apartment to a boarding house in Brooklyn.'

'Something like Arthur Miller?'

'Almost identical. My father didn't finish school and became a tailor in a sweatshop. We had no money. Roast chicken was a luxury. My father tried, but he couldn't come back. His old friends ignored him and he couldn't get finance for any new business ideas. My mother left us. How can you respect women after that?'

So that's why he went through three wives and umpteen girlfriends, I thought to myself.

'How did you make your money, Leash?'

'I'll tell you someday,' he said, sipping some more water. 'You know what I like about money most?'

'What?'

'Control. My father and his family were always living on the edge. Me? I'm in control of my life, my family, my sons . . . everyone.'

'Everyone?'

'Try it someday, Jack. If someone works for you; wants to borrow some money; wants you to invest some capital; buy something, you're in control. It's like walking into a five star hotel in Bangkok. They're all over you. Clean the floor in front and behind you. Feels good, doesn't it? You've got the money. They want it. What about you, Jack? Come across anyone who wants something from you?'

Leash had the knack of drawing out resentments.

'My Uncle Martin. He's asked me to lend him some money. Bit of a cheek. He didn't help me when my Dad died.'

'If you don't like him, keep him waiting a little longer. Then see him . . . I'll tell you what to do.'

He leaned across the table and whispered his plan.

*   *   *

A few days later, I put Leash's advice into practice. I emailed Uncle Martin and told him to come to London to meet me. Maisie booked a table at Tony Jay's, the celebrity chef's Soho restaurant. It was intimate and expensive. Actors, directors, writers, agents, politicians, editors and top business people went there.

Martin arrived ten minutes late, flustered and puffing. After being in the train for several hours his dark grey suit was creased. He was sweating and stressed. I stood up and was as gracious as possible, but deliberately looked at my watch to embarrass him.

'Leeds to London train. Always late,' he muttered. 'The traffic . . .'

'Sit down, Martin. Relax, we don't want you to have a heart attack do we?'

I knew that I had immediately found a weak spot. He flinched and touched his chest with his left hand, breathing rapidly. I was sure that his doctor had warned him about his heart. He was overweight and had smoked all his life. I smiled insincerely.

'Have a drink, Martin. Some wine?'

The waiter took a bottle of Chablis out of an ice bucket and poured some wine into his glass. Martin swallowed so quickly that he didn't have time to savour it. Philistine! I looked on, following Leash's advice, smiling superciliously. Showed him that I was totally in control. Martin looked around and noticed a couple of TV stars.

'Did you see . . .?'

I nodded, knowingly.

'You've become soophisticated, Jack. Remember when we kicked ball on lawn.'

'I'm sorry, I don't remember,' I said, feigning a yawn. 'Let's eat. It's getting late.'

I called the waiter and let Martin order first. Leash had bet that he would order the cheapest item. That would show that he wasn't taking advantage of me. Leash won. Martin ordered chilli con carne. I promptly chose lobster and waited for the reaction, making another bet with myself.

'You doon't mind if I change mind, do you?'

'Of course not, lobster for two,' I told the waiter.

As so often happens in fancy restaurants, there was more sauce than food. We talked about everything, except the real reason for our meeting. I waited for the right moment, a time when the noise level in the restaurant had died down and shouted loudly: 'You're struggling aren't you, Martin?'

Taken completely by surprise, he looked distinctly uncomfortable. He turned his eyes downwards, deeply embarrassed. He knew from the silence in the restaurant that people had heard me. He knew that tables nearby, were waiting, listening.

'How much do you need Martin? How much?' I asked loudly again.

Martin said nothing. He was humiliated. I could see that he wanted to run out of the restaurant, tear himself away from these people. Get away from me. But he couldn't. He couldn't afford to antagonise me.

Martin, I want to help,' I said gloating in a booming voice. 'Your business is going down, isn't it?'

Martin sat there silently. Not a word. I wondered what was going through his head. Perhaps he remembered Bill's funeral; when he said that he and Peggy couldn't take care of me. Perhaps he was regretting that he had come to London. By now the restaurant was noisy again. There were more interesting things to gossip about.

'Let me pay,' offered Martin, when the waiter brought the hefty bill. He made a mock attempt to put down his credit card, but I got in first. That's what control was all about, Leash had said. Be generous and hard at the same time. Keep them wondering.

Martin, leading the way, pushed through the narrow gaps between the tables with his eyes down and rushed for the exit. Outside he adjusted his tie and did his best to stand tall.

'Thanks for lunch and your time, Jack,' he said shaking my hand.

'Just tell me how much you want, Martin,' I said.

He shook his head and smiled sadly, as he climbed on to a bus. This time it was me who felt uncomfortable and I regretted that I had played Leash's silly game. What was the point? I had the money, but it was Martin who kept his self respect. I never heard from him again.

*   *   *

Some weeks later, I arrived in the office and found that Aram was in a panic. Oil and gas prices were gyrating and Aquarium was down. Aram, terrified of Leash, asked me for my opinion.

'We've made a lot of money in the past two years. It doesn't matter if we've lost some,' I said.

'But investors will withdraw their money,' he said nervously. 'Leash won't like that.'

'That's not for us to worry about. It's Cy's department,' I said. 'The question for us is whether we should get out of the market.'

I went to my desk and pulled out all the statistics and charts. There were some unusual patterns. As soon as prices fell by a few percentage points, they bounced back swiftly. My stats backed the market gossip. There were some big buyers out there who kept entering the market as soon as prices dropped.

'I think we should hold on, Aram. It's probably just a short term setback. The bull market seems to be intact.'

'Should we follow the Zulu strategy and buy some more?'

'We don't have enough money.'

'We can borrow,' said Aram.

'We've already borrowed $400 million, Aram.'

'The rules of our prospectus allow us to borrow as much as investor's capital in the fund. Investor funds under management are $800 million. So we can increase our loans to $800 million.'

'And have $1.6 billion in the market?'

'Not all of it. But it gives us plenty of leeway, if the market goes our way.'

I knew that such a move would be extremely risky, but Aram assured me that many hedge funds were doing it. Making fortunes out of leverage.

'The trick is to lever performance and fees with loans,' he said.

I wasn't impressed, but to make sure, went to my desk and did a calculation on a simple, but telling example. No point in going into details, but after paying interest on the borrowings and hefty hedge fund fees, investors only do well if the hedge fund manager makes exceptional profits in the markets. If the hedge fund manager loses, the leverage goes into reverse with a vengeance. Investors can easily lose a quarter or half of the money invested, sometimes even more.

Aram's plan was even more risky that! He intended to deposit a quarter of the $1.6 billion as margin to buy oil and gas futures and options. The remaining money would be placed in oil, gas and mining shares and high yield junk bonds and the money market to earn dividends and interest. Generally our margin was about 10 per cent of the value of oil and gas futures. Some $400 million placed on margin for futures and in options, would enable us to control oil and gas worth around $4 billion. A price rise of only 10 per cent would make us $400 million and push the value of our fund from $800 million to $1.2 billion. If prices were to fall, however, Aquarium could lose half its capital and if they fell further, we could be wiped out. That was far too dangerous for me.

'I don't think Leash will accept your proposal,' I said tactfully, sure that our boss wouldn't accept that extent of risk.

'Don't worry Jack, I've got all sorts of trading tactics to protect us from losses. It means that we won't get as much profit, but it will be a lot safer.'

Aram then explained several complex futures and options trades with weird and wonderful names such as 'butterflies and wingspreads', 'straddles and strangles', 'caps and collars' and Delta, Gamma, Theta and Vega. I tried my best to follow him as he wrote down all the formulae, but I'm afraid it was Greek to me. I had always thought that Krishna and Tong were the mathematicians, but Aram was pretty good too. All this mathematical quantitative derivatives trading in the energy market was impressive stuff. It seemed that Aram had closed all the gaps.

'That's not all,' said Aram, noticing that I had a glazed expression. 'I know who's buying.'

'I heard that there are four to five hedge funds,' I said.

'Yes, some hedge funds have been big buyers, but they're small fry compared to the ones I know.'

'Who are they?'

'I'm sworn to secrecy. It's confidential. All I can tell you is that they are operating through Swiss banks. They're worth multi billions.'

'Aram if you're so certain, why are you nervous?' I asked.

'It's been a bad couple of days. That's when your nerves are tested,' Aram said. 'I'm worried because I have to explain all this to Leash. He's a difficult guy.'

Aram was very secretive, but after working with him for a long time, I now respected and trusted him. We didn't joke around or go out for a drink. But I didn't mind. He was smart and worked very hard for his family and mistress; had lots of good ideas. He watched the market all the time, was always on his mobile, always dealing. Aram was committed. The best thing of all was that he found a new dentist and had got rid of his halitosis.

We walked over to Leash's office. Through the glass walls we could see the boss having yet another row with Cy. This one looked terrible and we wondered if we should enter. We knocked on the door and Leash stopped screaming. I was amazed when I saw Cy. He seemed so relaxed and happy. He smiled at us as he left the office.

Leash sat there silently. He looked shattered. We waited for a while before Aram showed him the file of Aquarium and explained what he intended to do. Instead of grilling us about the fund and high risk trading strategy, as I had hoped, Leash merely nodded his head absently. Aram was given the go ahead. Leash wasn't concentrating. His mind was elsewhere and when I tried to warn him about the risks, Aram swiftly dragged me to the door.

After wild swings, the market recovered during the next few weeks and I felt more comfortable. Prices took off again and Aquarium's assets jumped through the magical mark of $1 billion towards $1.5 billion. Some investors, who were uneasy about the boom and our trading tactics, took profits and withdrew their money from the fund. Aquarium's investor capital was back to $800 million again. I went to several presentations to help Cy raise money. Despite all our efforts we weren't succeeding, but even though it was disappointing, and Aram's strategy was very risky, I was relaxed. We had banked lots of money and our performance fees were enormous. Moreover, under the Aquarium system, oil, gas and several other commodities were still pushing upwards. They were penetrating the upper membranes of the tank. Our computer system picked up the signals and Aram borrowed and invested. The following months, Aquarium made huge gains and Leash was more than satisfied with the profits and his booming business.

*   *   *

Cy's mother died suddenly and he and Leash returned to the States to attend her funeral. I sent Cy's family a sympathy card and flowers. Cy was touched and called me.

'Jack, some Boston pension fund consultants are interested in our fund. Can you meet me there?'

'Sure, Cy.'

'I've got a great idea. We can see them after Labor Day. My wife and girls are in Martha's Vineyard. Fly to Boston on Friday and I'll pick you up at Logan International Airport. You and Sandy can come with me to the island and spend the long weekend with us.'

'Wow, thanks Cy. Must be a great place. Do you have room for us? We can book a hotel.'

'No way. The girls want to meet you. We've got more than enough space.'

'What flight should I get?'

'Get the early one. You should arrive soon after lunch. It's less than a two hour drive to Hyannis, Cape Cod and we then take the ferry to Martha's Vineyard. You'll love it.'

On Friday afternoon we were on the ferry to Oak Bluffs, one of the island's ports.

'We cycle here. No cars. Think you'll be OK with those backpacks?' said Cy when we arrived.

'You must be joking!' murmured Sandy.

'Sure am. We'll hire a taxi. But after that, you guys are going to cycle or walk. OK? The Vineyard has lots of cycle paths.'

'Sounds fun.'

The house overlooked a long beach, not far from Edgartown, a former whaling port. The sea was darkening and the sky was already changing from yellow to orange red; the sun a sphere to the naked eye. The house was modern with massive windows and skylights, very different from the quaint buildings in Oak Bluffs and Edgartown. Cy's wife gave him a big hug when we arrived. Elaine, pretty with dark hair and a long elegant nose, shook our hands warmly.

'Cy's told me a lot about you,' said Elaine in a light American accent. 'Lucy, Nikki, come meet Jack and Sandy.'

Their two daughters ran down the stairs and Cy went down on his knees as they rushed into his arms. Nikki shook my hand tentatively, but Lucy was shy and kept close to her Mum. She ran into another room, opened a door and their white Highland Terrier, with a red ribbon on her neck, ran up barking. I bent down and tickled the dog under her neck. She lay on her back as Lucy petted her.

'What's her name?' I asked.

'Polly. I asked for a parrot and got her instead,' giggled Lucy.

'Come downstairs into the basement Jack, I'll show you your room,' said Cy. 'I hope you like it.'

We certainly did. There were some amazing seascapes and Shaker furniture. After freshening up, we joined them downstairs. It was the first time that Sandy and I had experienced the homely warmth of a traditional Jewish

Friday night meal. Nikki blessed the wine in Hebrew, had a sip from the goblet and passed it to me. The red wine tasted sweet and warm. Lucy then blessed the bread that they called challah and we ate some. I preferred the chopped liver to the herring. The next courses were chicken soup and a large roast chicken, with lots of potatoes and green vegetables. They chatted about all sorts of things, especially school and art, Elaine's favourite subject. The paintings in the guest room were hers. We ended the meal with apple meringue. No wonder Cy found it difficult to lose weight.

'Daddy, what's going to happen to Polly when we go to San Francisco?' asked Lucy.

'Dogs aren't like cats,' said Sandy, smiling and leaning down to pet the dog. 'They don't run away and try and go back to the old house. Polly will get used to the smell of the new home and new walks. I'm sure that she'll love it there.'

'Are we opening up a branch in California?' I asked, wondering why I wasn't told about an important change in the business.

Cy looked at Elaine and I could see from his expression that he didn't want her to say anything more.

'I'll talk to you about it later,' said Cy.

Sandy and the children picked up some dishes and took them to the kitchen. I offered to help clear the table, but Cy pulled my arm and we went into the TV room. He poured out some twelve year old malt whisky and we sat down on a largish pink sofa.

'I'm leaving the firm,' he said. 'Leash told me to keep it quiet until September.'

I virtually swallowed the entire contents of my glass in one gulp. 'Why?'

'I've had enough; commuting between Europe and New York; the constant treadmill; being away from the family. I want to do something else.'

'So that's what that big row with Leash was all about a couple of weeks ago,' I said thoughtfully. 'When are you leaving?'

'After I finish training the new marketing manager. She arrives in a fortnight.'

Elaine, Sandy and the girls came in and Sandy snuggled up to me while we watched a movie on TV.

*   *   *

Cy woke me up early the next morning to go for a walk and a swim. It was the end of August and the weather had already become fresh and cool. The house's garden was fairly small, with a gate leading to a sandy narrow path that went down a bank towards the beach. The dog ran ahead of us, chasing some seagulls. We took off our trainers and left them with our towels alongside some rocks and started our long walk, half paddling in the shallows.

'I hope Max is OK.'

'He took it badly. It was a stroke. Took us completely by surprise. Max is like Mum, a gentle soul,' said Cy softly. 'He also resigned from the firm and is going to teach. Leash is looking for a good compliance and risk officer.'

'Both sons out of the firm! Must be a big letdown for Leash.'

'Death is awful, but it makes you reassess your life.'

'Is that why you are leaving the firm?'

'Yes. There's more to life than money.'

'That's if you have enough of it. Your father is obviously upset that you're leaving.'

'If he is, he hasn't told me. We've never really got on,' said Cy, sadly. 'He likes you Jack.'

'He keeps giving me lots of advice.'

'Leash likes controlling people. Not just being a boss. Changing them; moulding them.'

'You argue a lot with him, don't you?'

'Yes. My father's a strange mix. He has some good points but there are lots of things I dislike. He made Max's life a misery. Max is shy and sensitive and Leash can't accept his way of life.'

'He found out at he's gay?'

'He must have always known. Just didn't let on.'

'And you?'

'You've heard all the rows Jack. I stand up to Leash, or I think I do. But he likes belittling me. He seems to enjoy that.'

'You've worked for him for a long time. How many years? Ten?'

Cy didn't reply. We walked silently for a few hundred yards. Compared with Bridlington and Filey, the beach was wide, with steep embankments at the end and few houses in sight.

After a while, Cy told me his story for the first time. He and Max were sons of Leash's first wife, Adele. They lived in New York when Leash was a stockbroker. He travelled a lot and had lots of affairs. Cy and Max first realised this when they were small and heard their mother and father having a row. When Cy was eight and Max six, Adele decided to get divorced. The divorce became very bitter because of arguments about money. Leash tried to force Adele to accept a less favourable settlement. She refused. In an attempt to avoid lawyers, he came home one evening and made an offer. When Adele still didn't give in, he lost his temper. Frightened that he was going to hit her, the boys ran in and stood between him and their mother.

He tried to turn them against Adele, but he failed. From that time, Leash's attitude to Cy and Max changed. Adele never got remarried and she and the boys continued to live in Manhattan, where they went to school. After about three years, Leash moved to Florida, got married again and had two girls. When Leash came to New York on business, he would see the boys. Once the boys went to Leash's home in Florida, but Leash's second wife didn't get on with them. That didn't matter, as Leash soon divorced her and a few years later married a model about twenty years younger than him. As the boys got older, they saw less and less of their father, but he was making a lot of money. He paid for their college education and they were never short.

By now, Leash had started a fund management business and had moved back to New York. He first offered Cy a job and later, Max. He was depressed and lonely at the time, as the model had left him for a younger man. Leash told the boys that he wanted to get closer to them. He had given the boys everything materially, but his psychoanalyst had told him that there wasn't an emotional bond.

'I want to get close to you,' Leash would say continuously, but he would blame Cy and Max, rather than himself for the distance between them. He made the brothers feel guilty, so instead of looking for other jobs, they joined him. They could easily have found good jobs, as both of them went to Yale.

We had walked for a fairly long time by now and were feeling fairly hot. So we ran into the water and had a quick dip. The dog tried to follow but retreated when the waves hit her.

We turned back towards the house again. Cy, stroking his wet hair, looked at me directly: 'Leash sees a lot of himself in you, Jack.'

'I can understand why you and Max are bitter, but he's been pretty good to me.'

'He's domineering Jack. Be careful! If you're constantly with someone like that, you can become like him. You and I have gotten to know each other. You've seen me get nasty sometimes, but I always regretted it afterwards. I reckon that my bad side comes from Leash. Like it or not he's influenced me.'

By now the sun was beating down, swiftly drying the water off our shoulders and backs. There had been a drought that summer. My mind wandered and I absently thought it could be a good time to buy wheat and corn. Cy, a little impatient with me, broke the silence again.

'Leash takes to you because you also come from a poor family and you're self-made, Jack.'

'Guess you're right. He's taught me a lot.'

'That money gives you the power to control people, right Jack!'

I nodded my head and told him how Leash had told me to handle Uncle Martin. Cy's laugh was bitter.

'My father could write a thesis on Schadenfreude.'

'Schadenfreude?'

'Getting a kick out of someone else's misfortune.'

'Did you experience that?'

'When I first started working for Leash, he told me that I should be hard,' said Cy. 'A friend of mine lost a lot of money and needed a loan. I got him to pour out his heart to me. Gave him the impression that I was going to help, but did nothing. At first I felt the power, but afterwards I didn't feel good.'

He bent down and stroked the now soaking Polly.

'I guess I felt the same when my uncle left,' I said.

'Good! There's hope for you. The problem with my father is that he doesn't have a conscience. If he does something bad to someone, he forgets about it. He puts it behind him. When he sees them again, he carries on as if nothing has ever happened.'

'But isn't that because of his quick temper?'

'No, much more than that. I can't recall the last time he hugged me, put his arm on my shoulder, made me feel warm. He didn't even do that at Adele's funeral. He lacks emotion; lacks warmth.'

I didn't show it, but I was beginning to get annoyed with Cy. He was wealthy because of his Dad. He had nothing to worry about. Whether Cy liked it or not, money had given him the power to control his life. That's why he could leave the business and do what he liked; the same with Max. I thought that I would stick up for Leash.

'Come on Cy, your father isn't all bad. You shouldn't knock him. He's done a lot for you guys.'

'You're quite right, Jack. Leash has some good in him. He gives to charities. Yes, he makes sure that everyone knows about it, but he still gives. He keeps in contact with old people; went to my mother's funeral, even though he couldn't stand her. I'm just trying to help you, Jack. You're a nice guy and I'm worried that Leash will influence you. Try and make you become like him. Money mad.'

'Money mad? Not with Sandy around!'

'Good. She's a lovely girl; watched her do yoga on the beach. Stick to her! She seems to love you and she'll help you keep things in perspective. Money dominates Leash's life. It is everything to him. He's got so much that it has become meaningless. He has become a big art collector. Not out of love of art, but because he wants to show off his wealth. Meet important people. There are genuine art collectors out there who can't stand hedge fund managers.'

'He's entitled to spend his money and enjoy art. What's wrong with that?'

Cy looked at me and shook his head. He was realising that I was getting tired of hearing all this personal stuff; the outpouring of emotion. On the other hand, his mother had just died and I could understand that he needed someone to talk to.

'Sorry Jack, I can tell what you're thinking. All I'm saying is don't end up like my father. Yes, I've got "stuff you money". I don't have to grovel to employers or anyone else. Enough to keep my family going without working again, I can do what I like. I can travel, teach, become a writer, run a charity.'

'Yes, but give Leash his due. It's because of him.'

'I appreciate that. But Leash and others like him can't stop. For them, money's an obsession. They think that they're in control, but their money controls them. They have multi millions but if the market falls by 10 per cent, they fret. They fall out over business deals. Fight over divorces, over wills, over money that doesn't make the slightest difference to their lives.'

'That's exactly what Sandy says.'

'You're lucky to have her, Jack. My Dad was rich, seriously rich, when he divorced my mother. It would have made no difference to him if he had settled for another million or two. But she was taking his money. That's how he saw it. He lost all sense of proportion. Didn't realise or care that the fight was damaging his little boys. That Adele had been good to him for years, gave him children, looked after him when he was sick, supported him when he was down. The threat of losing money totally coloured his judgement. He even fell out with his brother and sister. He was totally obsessed with money then and he's totally obsessed by money now. Don't become like him, Jack. Don't!'

He patted me on my back and we walked back to our towels, had another swim and joined the girls. Later we all cycled to Edgartown, wandered through the quaint streets and had crab and lobster at a tasty seafood restaurant. That afternoon, a children's author was reading his book in the garden of Edgartown's bookstore. Lucy sat on Sandy's lap and Nikki and I licked our ice cream cones. Elaine and Cy held hands and looked on with pleasure. A lovely family. The big question: Should I marry Sandy? Were we too young?

Much later when she was snuggling against me on the flight back home, Sandy broached the subject.

'It's great to have a family, Jack.'

'Yes, they are close aren't they.'

'Cy and Elaine have got the right idea. Escape from the rats and do your own thing.'

'I'm not ready to drop out, Pear . . . It's not just money. I like what I'm doing.'

'You were about to call me Pearl! You still think of her, don't you?' snapped Sandy, sitting upright in her seat. 'You miss the celebrity circuit, don't you, Jack? The buzz, the fame.'

'No I don't Sandy, promise.'

'I've heard you call her in your sleep. I'm asking you again. Come to Perth and meet my family. My Dad and Mum would love to see you. Same with my brother and sister. We'll ask my cousin, Mike Swann, to come around. You love cricket. Australia is playing England in Perth in December. Mike could get you a ticket.'

'Next year, Sandy. It's inconvenient now. Aquarium is beginning to take off.'

Sandy was right. As much as I was fond of her and loved her company, I couldn't get Pearl out of my mind.

* * *

Back in London, I did something underhand, I broke Cy's confidence. Curiosity got the better of me. I wanted to hear Leash's side of the story. He seemed to know exactly how Cy and Max felt. There must have been some awful rows with all the resentment coming out.

'My ex-wife was by no means an angel,' Leash responded. 'Adele turned the boys against me even though I made sure that they were never short. Yes, I'm not the "love you", touchy, feely type. But that doesn't mean that I don't care for Cy and Max. I gave them an expensive, outstanding education and brought them into my business. They've never had to worry about money.'

I listened silently, not knowing what to think. There were, as usual, two sides of the story.

'When we separated, Adele – God rest her soul – proved to be a greedy bitch,' continued Leash. 'Be careful of women, Jack. They'll clean you out. I should know. I've been through divorce three times. What's the worst investment in the world, Jack?'

'Divorce?'

Leash laughed: 'You're learning. Don't let that girl push you into marriage! You'll regret it.'

*   *   *

A few days later, not long after my nineteenth birthday, I had some awful luck. Sandy decided to go on a Stratford-upon-Avon Shakespeare Tour and see a production of Anthony and Cleopatra. After all the travelling, I preferred to relax and stay in London.

Whether it was telepathy or not, I don't know, but that Saturday at about 11pm, Pearl buzzed the intercom: 'Jack, I have to see you. Please! If I don't see a friend now, I might do something to myself.'

'Take it easy Pearl. Stop the histrionics. You're not the type.'

'Please Jack, let me in, I'm feeling terrible. I need you.'

When I opened the door, she looked an absolute wreck. She had lost weight, looked pale and her nose looked odd. Evidently her promise to stop taking cocaine was just that.

'Pearl what the . . .?'

'Jack, do you think I'm manic?'

'Bipolar? I'm not a therapist, Pearl. I've noticed you get depressed sometimes. But that happens to most people.'

'Yevgeny says I'm a manic depressive,' she cried. 'He's left me.'

'He's married, Pearl. You can now move on. You should be glad, not depressed.'

'He was going to leave Katya. We were going to get married.'

'Don't most married guys say that?'

'Hold me Jack . . . please,' she murmured as she threw her arms around me. 'I should never have left you.'

'But you did, Pearl. Was it for Faramazov?'

'No Jack, I tried to leave Yevgeny for you. Believe me Jack. You grew on me. I loved you.'

'Are you saying that you were Yevgeny's lover before you met me?'

'Yes! I've been with him for more than five years. Before and after he was married.'

'And me on the side in between. Did he know?'

'Yes, he accepted it.'

'Why don't you have something to eat,' I sighed.

Pearl struggled to swallow some carrot soup that Sandy had made and picked at some bread and cheese.

'Are you still with that pretty Australian?'

'Yes. She's in Stratford-upon-Avon. Loves the theatre.'

'Can I sleep here tonight?'

'Better not, Pearl. What would I say to Sandy?'

'Please Jack, she'll never know. I feel desperate. I don't want to be by myself.'

I was really worried that she might do something stupid. So I let her stay. She had a shower, climbed into our bed and was soon asleep. I watched TV and then went to the bathroom. I heard the door open. Fearing an intruder, I crept towards the phone in the bedroom to set off the response alarm. The bedroom light went on, just as I was leaning over the bed.

It was Sandy, her expression, a mixture of shock, grief and anger.

'Sandy what are you doing here?'

'That's a question I should be asking,' she shouted, throwing her bag at me and then pummelling me on my chest.

'How come you're back so early?'

'I missed you. Wanted to be here, you bastard. The play finished early and I felt lonely, so I came home.'

'Hey what's going on?' shouted Pearl, who had just woken up. 'It's not what you think.'

That was the worst thing Pearl could have said. Sandy was out of the door. I went searching for her, but it was a waste of time. She probably found a taxi and went to some hotel. The next morning I made sure that Pearl was soon out of the flat, changed the sheets, cleaned up the place and went to the various hotels in the area to find Sandy. Nothing. When I returned later I found a note on the bed with a box full of the jewellery and gifts that I had given her.

Dear Jack,
We've both known for some time that it's not working. Good
luck with Pearl. I've decided to go back home to finish Uni.
Take care
Love
Sandy

That's all it said. I opened the cupboards and drawers.
Her clothes were gone. Dazed, I phoned the airport about
flights to Perth, but couldn't trace her. Maybe it would be a
good idea to get in a taxi and rush to the airport. We would
kiss and make up. I went to the fridge, opened a bottle of
beer and thought about it. I would do nothing. That would
put Sandy off guard. Make her regret that she had left me.
She would probably phone me. I waited for her call for a
couple of hours and phoned the airport. Then at last I tried
her mobile but there was no response. So I went to a movie
on my own and a pub later. She would be home when I
returned. That's how deluded I was.

*   *   *

Dr Klugheim is pacing up and down his room when I come in.
I haven't seen him for months. He's lean, with a flat tummy and
a thinner face. Also has a very short haircut. Makes him look
younger. He's pensive, as he pages through my manuscript: 'Leash
Grobnick. What do you really think about him?
 'He was a sociopath.'
 'Beware of labelling people, Jack.'
 'I'm not saying that he's a psychopath who injures or kills

people, without any conscience . I've come across plenty of those guys in this place. He didn't beat people up. Far too cunning for that. He sought and found weaknesses in people and played on them.'

'That doesn't necessarily mean he's a sociopath,' says Klugheim, half smiling. Personalities are far more complex than that.'

'From what I understand, sociopaths are superficially charming, until you annoy or anger them, or are of no use to them.' I respond, getting carried away .'They enjoy the power to control and humiliate people. Some are exponents of "Schadenfreude". They gloat when people are in trouble. Take pleasure in people's misery.'

'Aren't you really talking about a bully, Jack? Wasn't Leash a corporate bully? Many bosses are like that.'

'He didn't have any empathy; didn't care about anyone or have genuine feelings. He was cold and contemptuous. The more money he made, the worse he became.'

'From what you wrote Leash wasn't all bad. He genuinely wanted to help his children.'

'OK, nobody is all bad,' I say, standing up and looking outside the window .' Do you see any parallels with me?'

'I'm not sure, Jack. Is this something you would like to talk about?'

'Let me tell you what happened . . .'

20

PERFORATED PRIDE

It was a virtual car show. Lamborghinis, Ferraris, Porches, Aston Martins, Daimlers and convertible Mercedes, drove into the circular entrance of London's Dorchester hotel. Hotel drivers took the keys and went off to park the cars.

The hedge fund crowd flowed into the foyer and shuffled down the passage to a huge, ornate room where cocktails were served. Later they moved into the ballroom and took their places around the tables. The stock and commodities boom was in full swing. This was the Hedge Fund Autumn Awards evening.

Each firm paid £100,000 for a round table and the money would go to charity. The biggest hedge fund managers had several tables and the smaller ones, such as ours, one. I had booked a room at the hotel, so that I could have as many drinks as I wanted. Jane Lazenby-Faulks, a daughter of one of our clients, was with me. She was a lingerie model and wore a tight black cocktail dress that showed off her curves. She towered over me and everyone stared at her. The organisers of the event had found a brilliant band and I looked forward to dancing with Jane until the early hours. It was our second date and she had already indicated that she would spend the night with me.

I had taken out a string of girls since Sandy had left me; had phoned her in Perth, pleading with her. I sent her long emails swearing that it was she who I loved; even offered to go to Perth, but she wasn't interested. So I decided to move on and find another girl, but so far no-one matched Sandy.

Jane and I sat between Elaine and Cy. It was his last function with the firm. He and his family were leaving for their new home in Sausalito, across San Francisco's Golden Gate Bridge. Leash was across the table with a much younger woman. He had dropped poor Maisie, who had left the firm. It was the first time that I had met Aram's wife, Annushka. She was Russian, with dark eyes and curly black hair. Both were in their late forties, but she looked younger. The new marketing director, who was replacing Cy, was also there.

Amanda Brockenspruit, who was in her mid thirties, was striking rather than beautiful. She had dyed red hair and a great figure. Amanda was a multilingual career woman from Amsterdam and Leash was over the moon that she had joined LeashTrade.

The food was standard hotel stuff. After the coffee and liqueurs, the awards ceremony began. The market had soared in the previous year. Hedge funds had done brilliantly and investors had placed multi billions in them.

Hedge funds that performed the best in the past twelve months were given awards. The editor of AlphaBeta Plus magazine and her panel of judges chose Aquarium as the top commodities and resource macro hedge fund. The citation was 'Outstanding consistent performance'. Aram and I strutted up to the podium and accepted our certificate and bottles of champagne. When we came back to the table, Leash was beaming.

'Pity you aren't staying with us, Cy. This will help Aquarium go well over a billion,' said Leash.

Cy shrugged his shoulders. I hadn't seen him for a while. He had gone to California to help Elaine buy a house and find a school for their girls.

'What are you going to do Cy?' I asked.

'I've formed a foundation to educate disadvantaged kids,' said Cy.

'Your charity can invest in our funds,' shouted Leash across the table.

Cy ignored him: 'We're starting small. Expenses will be low. We want to make sure that almost all the money goes to the kids.'

'Surely that is what charity is all about,' said Jane snootily.

'Yes, but many charities have huge expenses. Their executives get large salaries. Lots of money is wasted on expensive events, advertising, mailshots and administration,' said Cy. 'The people who need the money are left with a small proportion of donors' cash.'

'So you think that this event is a waste of time?' snapped Jane.

'No. It's a means to an end. Unfortunately many of those charities have high expenses and as I've said the beneficiaries can receive very little,' Cy said. 'Money for African charities, for example. Africa is rife with corruption. There's no guarantee that most of the money won't land in Liechtenstein bank accounts.'

The awards were finally over and the charity fundraisers started an auction. Sponsors offered a Harley Davidson motorcycle, holidays in the Caribbean, South Africa, Mexico and Australia. Other items on the list were jewellery, paintings, tickets for Chelsea and Arsenal football games and the SuperBowl. The bidding began with each table doing their best to beat the others. Eventually a trumpet blared and the charity organisers announced that more than £5 million had been raised. There was a loud cheer and the hedge fund crowd thumped their tables.

I glanced at Cy and Elaine. They weren't enjoying themselves.

When the noise abated a few decibels, Jane turned to Cy: 'Come on! They'll probably raise ten to twenty million. Maybe even more. Even if the children get half of that, it's still a a lot of money!'

'Yes you're right,' replied Cy. 'But look around you and take a guess. How much do you think all the people in this room are worth?'

'I haven't a clue,' said Jane.

'Several billion. You still think that they're denting their bank balances?'

'Yes I do, actually,' said Jane. 'I'm sure that they give to other charities. I've helped organise events. A lot of time and effort goes into them. They do a lot of good.'

'I'm not disputing that,' argued Cy. 'All I'm saying is that everything is relative. A poor person who's donating twenty pounds can be sacrificing a lot more than a wealthy guy. Others spend hours each day, helping the sick and old. Thankless tasks, for low wages or no money. They don't get their names in the paper. Photos in *Hello!*'

'Come off it Cy. It's the amount of money that counts,' shouted Leash across the table. 'Are you seriously saying that a hundred bucks counts for as much as a million? I'm sick and tired of people who envy and preach to the rich. The British media in particular are always having a go at us, cynical about these events. It's nothing less than bigotry. Prejudice against the wealthy. People here are doing good. That's all that counts. If they're enjoying themselves, good on them.'

'Are you a priest or a hedge fund manager, Cy?' laughed Linda, Leash's girlfriend.

'You mean, rabbi,' I joked.

'Rabbi? He doesn't have a beard,' said Jane puzzled.

'Promise you, Jane, he's the real thing,' I said in an attempt to lighten the conversation.

'I agree with you Leash. This event will help the poor,' said Cy. 'How could I possibly think that it's a show, a big ego trip, a public relations exercise for hedgies?'

'I knew we were on the same wave length!' exclaimed Jane eagerly, failing to detect the sarcasm. Cy and I smiled at each other.

'You should have stayed with Sandy,' said Cy, shaking his head.

'I blew it Cy,' and I told him the whole sorry story.

'Why don't you go to Perth and propose to her.'

'Doubt if she'll trust me now.'

Aram had slipped away, when we were talking about charities. I noticed that he went to a table at the far end of the room. He was joking around with someone who had his back to me. Aram waved to me. I walked over to the table and the man he was facing, turned around. It was Yevgeny Faramazov. Pearl Fleecer was at the same table. I knew that Faramazov was involved in mining, oil and other Russian raw materials businesses. What was he doing at a hedge fund event? I shook hands with Faramazov and Pearl jumped up and kissed me on both cheeks. She looked a lot better. Hopefully she had sorted herself out.

Faramazov introduced the others on the table. They looked like gangsters and I soon realised who they were. Managers of Borodino and Veruschka, the Russian hedge funds! Suddenly the room started spinning. I couldn't focus properly and almost lost my balance. They pulled up a chair for me and I sat down to re-orientate myself as soon as possible.

'I'm OK, just slipped,' I lied as I sipped some water and did my best to relax. 'What's your view on the markets?'

They were smart and very knowledgeable about oil and gas and the mining industry. The boom would continue for at least another year, they said.

I wanted to get away as soon as possible and swiftly took the opportunity when the band began playing: 'I better go and dance with my girlfriend.'

When I was about to leave Faramazov's table, someone tapped me on my shoulder.

'You're sitting in my chair, Mr Miner,' said the voice.

I turned around. It was Hal Humford. I thought of asking him whether he was happy with his investments in our fund. Instead he turned away from me and began talking to Faramazov.

'Why didn't you tell me that you knew those guys?' I asked Aram, when Jane and I returned to our table during a band break.

'How was I to know that you were interested?' replied Aram. 'Yevgeny has been a client of mine for years. He doesn't want everyone to know what he's doing.'

'Is he in the hedge fund business?'

'Yevgeny has his fingers in all sorts of pies: mining, energy, banking, funds, anything that makes money.'

'You seemed to be speaking Russian to them?'

'Yes, when I was at school in Estonia, we had to learn Russian.'

'And Hal Humford of Banque Discretione? Why's he with them?'

'He's a banker. Yevgeny knows a lot of bankers.'

I was a little concerned. Discretione was a big investor in Aquarium and Humford was friendly with Faramazov. Jane grabbed my hand and pulled me on to the dance floor. We danced until two thirty in the morning and then fell into bed.

*　*　*

I was so busy during the next two months that I lost track of time. Pearl went into rehab and I lost contact with her. Jane took me to some celebrity functions and introduced me to some of her friends, but our relationship was fairly superficial.

The energy boom continued and oil and natural gas soared far beyond the wildest expectations of dealers and analysts. Aram was in charge of Aquarium's trading, with a little input from me. I had meetings with him twice a week, when we discussed what we would do in the market. At the end of each month, I co-signed the monthly returns showing how the fund had performed. Everything was going well. We were making big money.

The roadshows with Cy had given me experience in marketing. So Leash told me to help Amanda Brocken-spruit. We not only sold Aquarium to investors, but other LeashTrade funds as well. I found Amanda quite sexy. One evening in Paris, I made an advance. She enjoyed the attention, but wasn't interested. Amanda later told me that she lived in Camden Town with her partner Carol, an accountant.

A superb saleswoman, Amanda was almost as good as Cy. She got on with everyone, was full of fun and had a great sense of humour. The Aquarium fund now had more than $1 billion of investors' cash. Leash's entire fund management business managed more than $5 billion, compared with about $500 million, five years previously. The firm was making more than $100 million a year on annual management charges alone and another $200 million in performance fees. We were becoming seriously rich. I had learnt Leash's lesson. It takes as much time to manage a big amount of money, as a small sum, but the rewards are far greater. That was why he kept on driving us to push Aquarium and the other funds.

Trader Jack was the guy with the golden touch. The image attracted investors and girls. I wanted to contact old friends like the Slimcops and Gill Derby, but whenever I was about to phone or write a letter, something else came up. Stan and Leila would have been very pleased that I had given up coke and weed. I was into healthy eating and went to the gym.

*   *   *

October came and natural gas, which was as low as $2.50 a British Thermal Unit soon after 9/11, suddenly surged to almost $15. It gyrated, falling back to $11 and then recovered to $12. Crude oil, as low as $20 a barrel in the bear market, soared past $100 and moved swiftly to almost $150, before tumbling back to $120. Gold broke through $1,000 an ounce before retreating. Silver, platinum, copper, aluminium, zinc, nickel, wheat, sugar, cocoa and coffee also fluctuated wildly, rising when the US dollar sank and falling when it rallied. Energy and mining shares followed suit, playing a major role in causing global stock markets to rise and fall. Our attention was focused on the most exciting of all the markets, notably energy. Gas was fluctuating at prices 300 to 400 per cent above the levels it had been when we first entered the market. Aram traded in and out the market, piling up the gains. Whenever gas fell, it seemed to be supported by big buying.

Aram, Amanda and I had several meetings on whether we should take most of our money off the table. Aram, our energy expert, thought that there would be a final burst. The price would soar past the magical $15 round number and race to $20 or more, he predicted. Oil could reach $180 a barrel; possibly top $200! A gold price of $2,000 was also possible, he said. That would be the time to sell and bank serious money. Aram emphasised that in the past year we had had only two poor months. The percentage declines in those months were small, while profits of the other ten months were outstanding.

One day, early December, Amanda took me out for a drink. She was worried.

'Banque Discretione, our biggest investor, is taking profits,' she said. 'At the end of November they redeemed $200 million and have given us notice to take out their remaining $200 million at the end of December.'

'Have you spoken to Hal Humford, the chief investment officer?'

'He told me that it was the clients' decision. Discretione is still bullish on energy and commodities.'

'We'll have to sell some positions to pay them their money. I'll speak to Aram,' I said.

I also promised Amanda that I would contact Humford before I left for my Christmas holiday in Cape Town. Hopefully I could discourage him from withdrawing more money. Unfortunately I couldn't get hold of Humford. His London and Zurich offices said that he had gone skiing in Aspen, Colorado. He had given instructions that no one should contact him.

Despite Amanda's worries, Aram was relaxed. He told her that in January we would have a big presentation at a Florida hedge fund conference. Aram believed that oil and gas would reach new heights within weeks. Money would then pour into our fund. My charts indicated that it was very possible. My gold and coffee experiences showed that in the final phases of bull markets, prices rocketed. The crowd was following Aquarium. We and our investors would make pots of money.

*   *   *

A few days before the Christmas rush, I relaxed in my British Airways First Class seat, on my way to Cape Town. Maybe I would meet someone there. I shouldn't have messed up with Sandy. I kept thinking of Maffie, the gospel choir and her flowing white robe. Just over two years had passed, but it seemed much longer. I really missed Maffie. She was my best friend. I had to find her.

Mount Nelson, Cape Town's historic hotel, was a short walk from Table Mountain and I went halfway up to see the wonderful view. Ivor Ensworth was pleased to hear from me when I phoned him after the walk and he invited me to a Christmas barbeque. Ivor lived in a white washed bungalow with a small garden. It was in Rondebosch, a scenic suburb near the memorial of Cecil John Rhodes, who founded De Beers, the giant diamond company. It was almost four years since we were in Edinburgh. Ivor was now over eighty and looked frail. It was a small party. William, Ivor's tall tanned son, was busy 'braaiing' meat and chicken on the barbeque. His wife, Gail, was helping him.

'Tom, Tess! Jack's here,' yelled Ivor.

What a change! I had remembered them as children. Now they were teenagers, almost as old as I was when I first met them. They greeted me much more formally than I had expected and we shook hands.

A middle-aged man, about six foot two, with short grey hair and a ruddy face, rang the bell and entered. He was wearing a khaki shirt and shorts, as if he had just returned from the bush.

'Hello Fred. Great to see you. I've got a surprise,' shouted Ivor, calling me. 'Meet young Jack Miner.'

'Bill Miner's son? Well I never. Glad to meet you, Jack. I'm Fred Carrender. Your Dad was a great friend of mine. He saved my life.'

'I know, Mr Carrender. You've changed mine.'

'Call me Fred. Ivor told me how you've done. Remarkable! Maybe I should touch you for a loan!'

We laughed and sat down to eat. Fred regaled us with stories about him and Bill.

'I had no idea that my Dad was so wild,' I said cheerfully.

'Quite a ladies' man, your Dad. He even came prospecting with me once. I'm afraid we didn't find any gold and diamonds, but I made him jump when I found a dead scorpion and left it close to his pillow.'

I helped Gail clear the table. An old servant was washing the dishes. Gail looked embarrassed.

'I'm afraid my parents-in-law still live in the past. Apartheid's finished but the master-servant relationship remains,' she whispered.

'Jack, this is Thandi.'

I shook Thandi's hand, after she'd dried it.

'Thandi has worked for Ivor for thirty years,' said Gail. 'She's part of the family. You've looked after Ivor, since Helen died. Right Thandi?'

'We've both grown old together,' laughed Thandi.

'Have you heard of Themba Shaka Mafuta?' I asked. 'She's a family lawyer for the black community. She lives in a place called Knysna. Is it far from Cape Town?'

'You know Miss Mafuta?' shouted Thandi excitedly. 'She's very active in Khayelitsha township. Helps women when their husbands and boyfriends beat them up; when they do bad things to children. Miss Mafuta takes them to court.'

'Is she in Cape Town now?'

'I don't know, but I'm friendly with a woman who she's helping. When I see her I can pass on your message.'

'Please! I'll write a note. I must see her. She's a very good friend.'

'Have you visited Stan and Leila Slimcop?' asked Ivor.

'No. Could you tell me where they're staying?'

'In Fish Hoek, about an hour from here.'

'Have you apologised to them, Jack?'

'You know what I did?'

'Yes. You hurt them badly. Leila's getting worse. Stan's having a tough time, poor guy. He's now employing a carer.'

'I went to their home a year ago to apologise. A woman, who was looking after the house, said that she would tell them that I was sorry. I also wrote to them. They still haven't responded. Makes me feel really bad.'

'They've heard nothing.'

'You had better write another letter of apology to Stan now,' Ivor insisted. 'Phone him in a few days time.'

Afterwards, Gail took a photograph of all of us and put it in the envelope with the letter.

*   *   *

It was the first week of the New Year and she walked into the hotel foyer in a smart grey suit. Not the Maffie I knew. She was now fairly slim and had short, curly hair, African style. I rushed to hug her, but she withdrew. Instead she shook my hand in a cold, businesslike way. We ambled to a table on the patio and ordered some soft drinks and a light lunch.

'How's Ruff?' I asked.

'He's fine,' Maffie replied. 'He's in Knysna.'

'Say hello from me. I heard that you're back in law again.'

'Yes there's a group of us helping vulnerable women and children. Tourists visit the beautiful parts of the country, but few witness the poverty.'

She went on describing the new South Africa. Many blacks had advanced and had rapidly caught up with the whites. That was good. Unfortunately there was a very wide income differential between the wealthy black elite, the growing black middle class and the poor. The vast majority of blacks still lived in shanty towns, with primitive facilities and inadequate health, water and education. AIDS was a huge burden on the country. Unemployment was high and crime was rife. Abused women and children needed help.

'What about you, Jack? I've heard that you've made a lot of money. Won a hedge fund award. Become a fully-fledged member of the celebrity circus. Pictures in *OK!* magazine with models.'

'Who told you that?'

'Two people. Bess and I regularly email each other. She was here a few months ago, completing a PHD in sociology. She wrote a thesis on our legal foundation.'

'And the other?'

'Remember Issie McTavish of the *Wall Street Journal*. He was in Knysna during the Christmas holidays. We bumped into each other.'

'There's nothing accidental about McTavish, Maffie. You should know that!'

'Maybe, maybe not. Anyway, Issie got nothing from me. I told him that Ruff and I were no longer involved in the markets. Our money's invested conservatively. A major proportion finances the foundation. He was more interested in you, Jack.'

'Why me?'

'He told me that he tried to contact you several times, but you were always unavailable. He believes that you have caught the hedge fund manager disease. Too much money, self-indulgence and arrogance.'

'That's not quite true. I've been busy, Maffie. Really! Aquarium went past the billion mark. Leash Grobnick, my boss, pushes us. He gives us strict instructions not to talk to the press.'

'You had better speak to Issie when you get back, Jack. He's busy on an article on unusual trading activity in the oil and gas markets and alleged ramping of energy shares. He attended Africa Oil Week in Cape Town and sources there told him that American and British regulators have been investigating allegations of market manipulation and falsification of results. Some sources allege that with prices swinging up and down in unpredictable markets, your results are too good to be true. According to his information, Aquarium is under the spotlight and could be acting in concert with two or three other hedge funds.'

I was dumbfounded that the US Commodity Futures Trading Commission and the UK Financial Services Authority had suspected our fund and responded to the allegation angrily: 'Aquarium has bought a lot of oil, gas and other commodities, Maffie. We have also invested in energy and mining shares. I'm not denying that, but manipulation? No way!'

'You're aware that this commodity boom is causing untold misery for poverty-stricken people in Africa, India, Pakistan, Bangladesh and some Latin American countries. Prices are so high that they can't afford to buy staples like wheat, maize and rice. It is now extremely costly for them to heat themselves in winter because of soaring energy prices. Doesn't that bother you?'

'Come off it Maffie. If we didn't do it, someone else would. It's a free market. You can't curb that,' I insisted. 'When you were a hedge fund manager, did you feel guilty?'

'That was then and I did feel guilty. That's why I got out and am now doing something useful. Come with me to some of the townships. Malnutrition. No water and electricity. Freezing cold in winter.'

'I donate to charities.'

'Really? You never struck me as being altruistic. Why have you been buying oil and gas, Jack?'

'Similar reasons to coffee, Maffie. Demand is well in excess of supply and prices are going up. Aram has good information.'

'Aram Zabkian? What's he got to do with it?'

'He's my partner, Maffie. We both manage Aquarium.'

She shook her head and laughed: 'Jack, you and Aram never got on. Why on earth are you partners?'

'We get on OK now, Maffie. It's a good arrangement. He's in charge of the portfolio and I spend most of my time marketing the fund.'

'You have nothing to do with the portfolio?'

'I discuss strategy with him and check the charts and prices. He runs the fund day-to-day. He knows what's going on in the market.'

'Have you heard rumours about market manipulation?'

'Sure, Maffie. But wasn't that the same with coffee? The price is rising and we're making money. We'll sell oil at more than $100, gas somewhere between $15 and $20 and the other stuff too. Nothing illegal about that.'

'What's been happening this week, Jack?'

'I have no idea. When I go on holiday, I cut myself off from the market. Aram's in charge. Aram's done well.'

'Oil and gas prices fell sharply yesterday and some more this morning. Oil's around $70 and gas $11. That's a long way from $100 and $15, Jack. I'm glad to say that grain prices are also falling. It will be a relief for poor people and the aid charities that buy them food.'

I was startled. It was evident that something was wrong. I felt my pockets for my mobile. It wasn't there.

'You said that you don't follow the markets anymore, so how do you know what's happening?' I asked.

'McTavish called me. Your office told him that you were in Cape Town. He asked me whether I had seen you. All I want from you, Jack, is the truth. Are you involved in market manipulation and any other wrongdoing?'

I gulped. So that's why Maffie was so cool to me. She hated dishonesty and corruption and suspected me.

'I swear Maffie. I have not manipulated any market,' I responded.

'What about Aram?'

'I can't be sure, but from what he told me, his trades have been above board.'

Maffie disclosed what McTavish had learnt from his sources. The Russian mafia had ramped oil and gas prices and Aquarium and other hedge funds were also involved. The Russians had pushed prices higher to boost shares of their oil and gas exploration companies on Russian and London stock exchanges. I was worried because McTavish's information rang true. Shares of newly listed energy and other resource shares had soared on AIM, London's junior exchange. Large and small investors had piled in. The Russian directors had made fortunes. Indeed, virtually all resource shares listed on exchanges in London, New York, Toronto, Sydney, Johannesburg and elsewhere had surged. They had leapt on the back of the commodities boom.

'It has been a carefully controlled operation,' continued Maffie. 'The market has been conned into thinking that there is a shortage of oil and gas, when in fact, there's a massive glut. There are extensive commercial inventories in tankers on the sea and in harbours, in depots and else-where. This is over and above huge Government strategic stockpiles.'

I remained sceptical: 'I think McTavish has got it badly wrong. All the brokers I know are writing bullish reports. They say that China and India are big buyers and energy is scarce. There is a war in Iraq and the Middle East is unstable.'

'Issie knows about that view. He says that brokers and analysts are sanguine. There are now huge holdings on the books of hedge funds such as yours and also pension funds. This is another energy stockpile overhanging the market. The same applies to several other commodities.'

'I'm not quite sure how the Russians are involved in pushing up oil and gas prices,' I ventured nervously.

Maffie sipped her sparkling water. 'A group of Moscow controlled hedge funds have been big buyers through a Swiss bank. Rising prices attracted other hedge funds and speculators. So they also bought.'

'Just like us,' I said, getting agitated.

'According to Issie's sources, the huge speculative commodity inventories will have to be sold one day and since there is a glut elsewhere, buyers will withdraw. When that happens, prices will crash,' warned Maffie.

'Why does McTavish believe that I could be involved?' I asked beginning to feel distinctly queasy.

'A *Wall Street Journal* reporter saw you with Russian hedge fund managers at a charity event. You were sitting with them.'

'I only spoke to them for a moment,' I snapped. 'Aram introduced me to them. I do not do business with those hedge funds, I swear I don't.'

I was not just angry about the accusations. I was very worried. Aram insisted on building up our positions and Aram knew the Russians.

'Maffie, please don't go, my mobile is in my room,' I said

nervously. 'I swear I'm not involved in any irregularity. I just agreed with Aram that oil and gas were good buys and believed that other commodities would follow.'

I rushed into the hotel foyer to get the key. The receptionist handed me five messages. I opened them. They were all from Amanda. She wanted me to phone her urgently. I ran up three flights of stairs to my room, opened the door and rushed to the toilet. I parted with my breakfast and lunch within seconds. The mobile was in my suitcase. It had been a bad idea to cut myself off. I connected the mobile to the charger and switched it on. There were six messages from Amanda. I phoned back and left a voicemail. I took some deep breaths, composed myself and walked slowly down the stairs to Maffie.

'Are you OK, Jack? You look terrible. Don't worry, I believe you. You wouldn't lie to me, would you?'

'No Maffie, I swear it.'

My mobile rang. Amanda was on the phone.

'Jack, we need you back urgently. Aram's mother is ill. He had to go to Estonia today.'

'How's Aquarium doing?'

'Bad news Jack. Banque Discretione has withdrawn all its money. Aram had to cut positions and other investments to repay them. The market got wind of our sales, so oil and gas prices are falling. Our shares followed suit and unfortunately Aram couldn't get buyers for our bonds. He tried to borrow more from the banks, but they refused. I don't want to sound alarmist Jack, but it's a sort of meltdown.'

'What caused prices to tumble?'

'The CFTC announced that they had opened an

investigation into the cause of unusual price movements in the energy market,' she said, her voice becoming shrill on the phone.

'The FSA called to speak to our compliance officer. Since Max is no longer with us, I told them that Leash was responsible and that he's in Florida.'

I was beginning to panic. The US Commodity Futures Trading Commission and the UK Financial Services Authority!

McTavish was right. The regulators were concerned that something was going wrong. I tried to be calm.

'Don't worry Amanda, I'll get on the next plane and will think of a strategy. How much did Discretione withdraw?'

'$400 million in total. The fund's investor capital is down to $600 million.'

Maffie looked at me quizzically. 'Aram's gone to Estonia. Bit of a coincidence isn't it?'

'Maffie, you said that those Russians are operating through a Swiss bank. Did McTavish give you the name?'

'Let me think . . . Banque Dis . . . Banque Des or something . . . Sorry, I can't remember.'

'Banque Discretione?'

'Yes, that's right. A small private bank. He told me that a Russian bank owns it.'

That queasy feeling came back again, but this time I felt really sick. I kissed Maffie on her cheek quickly and sent my regards to Ruff. Then I rushed back to my room and the toilet and vomited until I had severe stomach cramps, a sore throat and the taste of bile in my mouth. Afterwards, I brushed my teeth, stripped, switched on the shower and sat on the floor of the cubicle. As the water poured over me, all sorts of things passed through my head, some bad, some worse than bad.

I had to get on a flight that night. Later that afternoon I was at the airport waiting in the standby queue. The airline had overbooked first and business class tickets, but I managed to get in economy class. I squeezed into a seat between two large people. The three of us didn't sleep much on the long trip. I remembered how Sandy had taught me to meditate and I closed my eyes and tried to empty my mind and think of nothing. 'Om Shanti, Om Shanti, peace, peace,' I whispered. As much as I tried, I couldn't slip into meditation. Throughout that long horrible journey I had to continually squeeze my way past my unfortunate fellow passengers to get to the toilet.

21

FALLING APART

The plane landed in London early Friday morning. As soon as I was through Customs, I ran out of the airport, jumped in a taxi and tried to reach Aram on his mobile. No answer. I went straight to the office, tired, dirty and unshaven. It was early and those who were there, stared at me. After a shower and shave in the office cloakroom, I felt better, but still had to put on a creased shirt.

Sitting at my desk I gulped down a cup of coffee, glanced at my terminal and saw that energy and share prices were sliding. Charts showed that the fish were falling back into lower levels of the proverbial Aquarium tank. This was a bad sign. I opened my post and found nothing important. Lots of envelopes were on Aram's desk. I tore them open. They were mostly brokers' notes, with purchases and sales of futures and options. I didn't have Aram's password, so I couldn't access his computer. His desk was locked. Jenny, Leash's latest secretary, didn't have the key. Leash was in Palm Beach, Florida on vacation. It was too early to call him. Around 9am, Amanda walked in. She looked stressed.

'Hi Jack, sorry to cut short your holiday.'

'It's OK, Amanda. Did Aram give you the key of his desk? His password?'

'No. He didn't come in yesterday. I still can't reach him.'

'What about his wife?'

'His family is skiing in Switzerland.'

'How's Aram's mother?'

'Don't know. I'm still waiting for his call.'

We struggled to open Aram's drawer, but failed. Tried again to access his computer, but without his password, couldn't see his emails and dealing records. A locksmith arrived and opened the desk. Piles and piles of unopened envelopes were inside the drawers. We took them out, but there were so many, that we decided to sort out the mess in the meeting room. We called the office's IT consultant to come and access Aram's computer data. He also failed. We were relaxed about Aram's secrecy when the fund was doing well. Now we cursed him.

Amanda and I silently opened all the envelopes. Inside were brokers' notes and statements going back two months. Aram, who hadn't taken a holiday for more than a year, had accounts with three brokers, two in London and one in New York. We carefully sorted out the brokers' notes and statements into three piles. Once we had done so, we tried to make sense of them. The brokers' notes, showing Aram's futures and options transactions, were incomprehensible. There were so many buy and sell orders, that only he would know what was going on. We called him again. No answer. Jenny managed to find Annushka, Aram's wife. She was at their chalet in Gstaad, Switzerland. Annushka had also tried to speak to Aram at his mother's house in Estonia. The phone lines were down and his mobile wasn't working.

The statements of brokers Jamieson & Co and Blaby & Co, showed that Aquarium had made a profit until the end of December. But we couldn't understand what had happened at the New York office of Gallopy & Co. Aquarium had two accounts at Gallopy. The "Aquarium Account" showed that at the end of December the fund had made a profit of $55.1 million on its transactions. But "Aquarium Volatility Account" had a loss of $241.2 million. Amanda and I checked again and again, but the statements clearly showed that the net loss at Gallopy & Co was $186.1 million. Since there was a combined profit of $18.1 million at the two other brokers, Aquarium's total net losses appeared to be $168 million.

Amanda was puzzled: 'I thought that Aquarium was in profit at the end of December. Our investors believe that they are doing well. What's going on?'

We both sprinted out of the meeting room to our desks and brought back our own files of Aquarium's monthly statements. We compared the separate statements that Aram had given us. They were identical. They showed that at the December 31 year end, Aquarium had made a profit of $73.2 million. Aram had conveniently added the $55.1 million of the profitable Aquarium account at Gallopy and the $18.1 million profits at the other two brokers. We had no record of Gallopy's "Aquarium Volatility Account". Until now, we had no idea that this account existed, let alone the massive loss of $241.2 million.

We sat there silently for a few seconds before Amanda spoke: 'There must be a mistake. There has to be a mistake!'

'I'll call Gallopy and Bank Kaboom, our Cayman Islands administrator,' I said grimly. 'Maybe they've got some answers.'

'Surely you knew what was happening, Jack? You're the co-manager! I'm just a saleswoman. What the hell do I know?' shouted Amanda.

'Take it easy Amanda. Aram's in charge of trading. We just discuss strategy,' I said trying to calm her.

'Some strategy! You don't know what the f*** he's been doing!'

'You've missed another F word, Amanda.'

'What?'

'Fraud!'

Amanda freaked. She jumped up, clutched her hair, opened her mouth to scream and then put her hand over it. She lowered her hand. It was shaking. I was worried that she was beginning to lose it. It was a mistake to mention the possibility of a scam.

'What should we do? What can we do? Where's Leash when we need him?' she shrieked. 'Since Max has left, he's been in charge of compliance. If he didn't have the time, why didn't he hire someone? Why didn't he know what was going on?'

I put my hand on her shoulder, but she tensed up and shrank away. It was as if I had some horrible contagious disease.

'Don't worry, Amanda. No problem,' I lied. 'I'm sure there's a mistake. I know Aram. He's straight.'

Unfortunately I knew Amanda was right. I didn't know what had happened, but who would believe me? In the eyes of the world I was the co-manager, the co-trader and co-signatory of the fund. Investors, who had received positive, profitable statements during the past year, would be furious if their profits turned out to be losses. And that was when the market was booming! With prices falling, what losses now?

I had to sort this out quickly. I phoned the London head office of Gallopy and told them that I had to speak to the London managing director. We needed Aquarium's New York records urgently. As far back as possible. Jenny contacted Jamieson and Blaby for brokers' notes and statements going back twelve months. Gallopy's manager phoned back and said that I could see him in the afternoon. Amanda phoned Annushka for permission to enter their house in Eton Square and open Aram's business post. Jenny was to get hold of Leash and tell him to fly to London.

* * *

Gallopy and several other large investment banks were based in Canary Wharf, in London's Docklands. I was soon on the Docklands Light Railway train speeding towards the financial centre. In the distance, through the glass front window of the train, the huge tall buildings came into view, overshadowing the pale winter sunshine. I got out of the train, went up the escalators, turned past the shops and gave my details to the security guards of Canary Wharf Tower. It is one of Europe's tallest buildings and Gallopy was near the top floor.

I had an appointment with James Whistfield, managing

director of the commodities division. The receptionist pointed towards his office. It was on the other side of a trading floor that was about the size of two football fields. Hundreds of traders, sales people and analysts were sitting in front of computer screens, dealing, shouting and talking to clients. I walked across the floor and knocked on the door of Whistfield's office. He was busy on the phone and indicated that I should come in. While he was talking, I walked over to the window. Far below, I could see the Thames winding its way through London's eastern Docklands, westwards towards the ancient City of London and St Paul's. Further west, the Thames shimmered alongside the Millennium Wheel and Houses of Parliament, on the way to Chelsea.

Whistfield stood up and shook my hand. The office was cold because the heating wasn't working properly. I tightened up the buttons of my jacket. Unlike his traders with their shirts and braces, Whistfield wore a smart, dark blue suit and a plain, silk, light blue tie. He was about three or four inches taller than me. He had thick brown hair and eyebrows and a strong jaw; an ideal trading manager to rein in wild dealers. Whistfield looked me up and down. I was quite a sight. After being in a suitcase the previous night, my clothes were creased. He noticed me putting my hand over a stain, just below my left trouser pocket.

'I flew in from Cape Town this morning,' I said in an attempt to excuse myself. Unsmiling, he picked up a file on his desk and placed it on a table close to the window. At last he invited me to sit down. It was obvious what was going to happen. He would try to bully me.

'I see that you have some problems with Aquarium's account,' he said.

'I think that we both have problems with the account,' I answered, showing him that I was no pushover. 'My partner dealt with your New York office. Who was his broker there?'

'Ivan Smeerneck. You should know him. You're co-manager of the fund.'

'I've never traded with him. Smeerneck? I met him some time ago. He headed an energy firm. It was Wynchmore Energy, wasn't it?'

'We took them over at the beginning of last year,' said Whistfield. 'Surely you dealt with him?'

'No I didn't. I just met him once. I must have given his card to my partner. Aram Zabkian is the day-to-day trader. I'm involved in strategy and marketing. I leave all the details to him.'

'What happens when he's away?'

'He hasn't taken a holiday for a year.'

'So where is he now?' asked Whistfield, suspiciously.

'He's in Estonia. His mother is ill. Can I speak to Smeerneck?'

'He left the firm a few days before Christmas.'

The broker who handled Aram's trades gone? Something was wrong. I stared straight into Whistfield's eyes, saying nothing. If he was concerned – and he should have been – he was certainly not showing it. I didn't trust him. Whistfield opened the file and pulled out Aquarium's trading records.

'Fortunately our system allows us to swiftly obtain duplicates from our New York office,' he said.

He picked up a phone. 'Mr Miner's here. Can you join us?'

There was a knock on the door and another executive walked in. He was a small, worried looking Asian guy with a slight squint. He introduced himself as Sachin Menon.

'Mr Menon has been going through the records and has found a large loss on your account,' said Whistfield.

'That's why I'm here,' I snapped.

I examined the papers and saw that the losses on "Aquarium Volatility Account" had begun last summer, while the "Aquarium Account" was consistently profitable.

'Were you aware of these losses?' I asked, deciding to be aggressive and put the blame on them.

'Our New York office acts as an independent unit,' said Whistfield. 'They sent you the brokers' notes and statements.'

'Not to me . . . to my partner Aram,' I insisted. 'Had I known what was happening, I would have cut the losses immediately.'

I could see that they didn't believe me.

'In June the losses were only $10 million. Of course I would have cut them,' I insisted. 'At the end of December they had mounted to $241 million! Didn't your New York office know about it?'

'We're trying to find out. Smeerneck was in charge.'

'Why didn't your firm contact Leash Grobnick, my boss? You guys have made huge commissions out of Aquarium's dealings. Aquarium's a big fund. We're an important client!'

'Are you seriously trying to tell us that you were unaware of these losses, Mr Miner,' said Whistfield, countering my attack and showing me several statements. 'Take a look!

"Aram Zabkian and Jack Miner, Managers, Aquarium Fund". If your partner was doing anything wrong, you must have known about it. Who do you think you're kidding?'

They had me there. No way to escape that fact. The statements were addressed to both Aram and me. I had to think fast.

'You guys must have known too,' I said. 'Now you tell me that Smeerneck has left? Why? On Aquarium's trading alone, he made Gallopy a fortune in commissions.'

They glanced at each other. I could tell that they suspected that Smeerneck was implicated.

'He's been suspended. For legal reasons we can't divulge the details,' said Whistfield. 'We're conducting an investigation.'

For the next couple of hours I sat in the office with Sachin Menon, doing our best to clear up Aram's mess. The deals were complicated. All sorts of sophisticated futures and options trades that were now mostly losses. Buying natural gas, selling oil, 'butterflies, straddles, collars and caps'. If only Aram had kept it simple. Menon was bright and he began to unravel the trades. The upshot was that Aram had concentrated on the natural gas and oil markets and had bought huge amounts on margin. We had to cut our positions drastically. Whistfield and Menon advised that we should sell our gas, oil, other commodities, shares and bonds gradually. Only a few at a time. Otherwise prices would slump.

Gallopy began to sell on that awful Friday. We hoped it would take a few weeks at the most; that prices wouldn't fall much. Maybe there would be a crisis in the Middle East or a hurricane that would cause prices to jump. Then, perhaps, we could get out at a small profit. The problem would then be solved and Aquarium investors would not lose money. On the other hand, if prices fell further, over-borrowed Aquarium would collapse.

Hopes of a price revival turned out to be fantasy. By the time I was back in the office late afternoon, oil had fallen to $55 and gas was below $8. Our positions were in the red. Our shares were tumbling and it was impossible to sell the junk bonds. Other investors were not prepared to buy securities of companies that could be damaged by a commodities slump. There was a risk that some companies could fail and their bonds could be worthless. Aquarium was trapped in the market quicksand.

I now had all the copies of the brokers' notes and statements and phoned Bank Kaboom, the Caymans administrator of Aquarium. They emailed me copies of the papers that they had received from Aram. They were the same as the ones that Aram had passed on to Amanda and I. Bank Kaboom was also unaware of the huge losses. Aram had kept them in the dark. The bank hadn't received any brokers' notes and statements of the "Aquarium Volatility Account". They had no idea that the account existed, let alone that Aram had parked $241 million losses in it. I don't know how Aram and Smeerneck managed to fool Kaboom, but that was the bank's problem.

Jenny called Florida, but Leash must have been on his yacht. She couldn't get hold of him on his mobile. I phoned him and also left a message, saying that he should contact me urgently.

I calmed Amanda, saying that everything was in hand. The brokers were helping.

Aram's housekeeper had refused to allow her to take away any post, but she had opened his business mail. There were no signs that he had dealt with more brokers. I told Amanda that I would try and figure out Aram's chaotic dealings over the weekend. She was relieved and left to go to a wedding in Shropshire.

After everyone had departed from the office, I went into the meeting room where there were now several large piles of brokers' notes and statements. I placed each pile into separate black bags.

*   *   *

Later, in the dark winter gloom, I loaded a taxi with my luggage and four black bags. It was Friday and Cape Town was already a distant memory. When I arrived in Hampstead, the taxi driver helped me drag the bags and baggage into my apartment. It was freezing and I switched on the heating system. Another shock; the water of my Aquarium in the living room was clouded. My magnificent tropical fish were floating under ice, dead. I had forgotten to arrange servicing of the tank when I went on holiday.

Periodically hitting my chest in tearful anger and frustration, I arranged the paperwork in neat piles on the living room carpet. Each pile was in date order in an attempt to match the deals of Gallopy, with those of Jamieson & Co and Blaby. I hoped that Aram had sold futures, options, shares and bonds through Jamieson and Blaby. They would then offset the purchases at Gallopy. I had to make Aquarium Fund profitable again, but I couldn't do so until I understood what Aram had done.

I tried to reach Aram yet again. No reply. Then I phoned Annushka and made contact, but could hardly make out what she was saying. She was crying, trying to tell me something in her Russian accent, but her mobile kept fading. Eventually I understood. The house of Aram's mother had burnt down. Both Aram and his mother had been killed in the fire.

I let the phone go and slumped on to the floor. Aram dead! Impossible! I rushed to the fridge and grabbed a bottle of Chablis, opened it and drank the lot. Feeling sick, I rushed to the loo and vomited.

I came back, switched on my laptop and googled 'fire in Estonia', not expecting to find much in English. An Associated Press report from Tallinn, the capital of Estonia, had the story of the tragedy. Mirska Zabkian, widow of Indisius Zabkian, former Mayor of Tallinn, had died in a house fire. Aram, her son, had attempted to drag her out of the burning home. He died later in hospital from burns and asphyxiation. The report added that fires in Estonia had killed almost 11,000 people the previous year. The country had one of the worst fire safety records in Eastern Europe. Shell-shocked, I continued to scroll the Internet, not concentrating on what I was doing.

I tried to calm down; best to throw myself back into work and try to put Aram out of my mind. So I sat down on the carpet again and waded through the broker notes and statements to try and sort out Aram's complex deals. About half the positions were with Gallopy. But Jamieson & Co and Blaby also showed that Aquarium had extensive futures deals on margin and numerous options that could expire worthless. If prices tumbled further, resource shares would slump, especially the relatively unknown Eastern European, African, Asian and South American energy shares that Aram had bought. I would have to contact the brokers on Monday. Oil and gas had to rise or at the least remain steady. If they didn't Aquarium would be in big trouble.

A bank statement showed that the fund had borrowed $1 billion. Aquarium was leveraged to the hilt. It had bought futures and options on margin and had also borrowed extensively to buy shares and bonds. Losses would compound rapidly if prices continued to fall. Billions could be lost. I struggled on, trying to figure out the deals. In the end I had to admit to myself that I didn't have a clue what Aram had done. His dealings were unfathomable.

I wasn't functioning very well given the lethal mix of wine, jet lag, lack of sleep, sickness and stress. How could we drag ourselves out of this mess? Then it dawned on me. There was little point in pretending, or being in denial. It wasn't we who had to surface and recover. It was me! I was now responsible. Aram was dead. I felt sick again, ran to the loo and tried to vomit, but nothing came out. I threw off my clothes and sat down naked. The runny tummy and stomach cramps returned. Feeling sick and dirty inside and out, I remembered what Mum had told me: 'The best thing when you're feeling bad, is a hot bath'.

I turned on the taps and when the bath was full, slid in, dipped my head under the water, came up again and just lay there without washing myself. I switched on the hot tap again and felt drowsy from the steam. Memories and dreams floated in my head. I was a little boy, playing football with Dad and Mum on the beach. Then I was in the sea swimming far from shore. A wave, swiftly building up into a giant curved monster, crashed and overwhelmed me. I was twirling and whirling in uncontrollable cartwheels down, down into the deep. It was freezing cold, so cold that I was losing my breath and desperately clawing the water; struggling to swim upwards. I awoke with a start and pushed myself upright in the bath, gasping for breath. I must have been there for at least an hour. The water was cold. I had fallen asleep in the bath, without realising it and had slipped under water for a moment.

That would have made some headline: 'Fraudulent Fund Managers Die in Fire and Water.'

Shivering, I dragged myself out, ran into my bedroom, jumped into bed and pulled the covers over my freezing body. Gradually I felt warmer and I fell into a deep sleep.

*   *   *

It was about noon when I woke up that Saturday and looked at the mirror. My dull eyes were half closed and ugly dark hairs sprouted from unshaven cheeks and chin. My unkempt hair was like a matted dog's coat. Stumbling into the living room and easing my way through the paper piles to the kitchen, I thought of Aram. Why had he continued to buy after prices had risen so far? Why didn't he take profits? He never struck me as being that greedy and he certainly wasn't stupid. His death could have been an accident. More likely, it was murder. He must have made a deal with the Russian mafia and they wanted him out of the way. The big question, what deal?

I phoned Annushka to see how she and the kids were coping. Her mobile was on voicemail, so I left a sympathetic message telling her to call me. Sitting in the kitchen, drinking a cup of coffee, I missed the company and comfort of my dog. I had a shave, felt fresher and drove to Martha's place to pick up Jazz. Martha wasn't there, so I decided to leave Pattie, in case she wanted to walk her own dog.

It was a cold, misty, January day. Black corduroys, a thick black jumper and a dark blue ski jacket and gloves, suited my mood and the weather. We walked past the ponds up a hill towards a clump of trees near Kenwood. Then we turned left and ambled along a wide path that was parallel to the wood. No running this time. I was too sick and weak.

After walking about a quarter of a mile, we turned left again, down a sandy hill into the open and through another wood. In front of us was Parliament Hill. The nausea that had bugged me in the past two days had gone and I felt a lot better. We walked slowly, ever so slowly, to the top. The sky had turned dark grey and specs of snow floated onto my jacket. The gloomy mist was so thick that I could hardly see the City. The Barbican, the Gherkin, St Paul's and Canary Wharf were barely visible. It was now almost four years since I had first seen the City from this hill. Then it was a bright summer day of hopes and dreams

Now I was super rich, going super broke. The light winter sleet started again and we shuffled slowly down the hill to a café where other dog owners were sitting. Instead of joining them, I sat alone, sipped my coffee and picked at my breakfast.

*　*　*

The sleet stopped and the brighter light made me feel a bit better. We walked towards the bleak, reddish brown brick wall surrounding the Lido swimming pool. Memories again. I had my first swim there after my first deals. Today, payback time. I couldn't bear to imagine what was going to happen. I had checked Friday's closing New York prices on my laptop and they had slid further.

We continued our walk along a pathway around the southern tip of the heath, past a railtrack on the left and an obstacle course and children's playground on the right. I went over to watch the children playing. Despite the cold, parents and kids were having a good time.

A tall blonde, in a beige trench coat and brown suede boots, was with a little girl. The woman turned and my heart stopped. It was Maggie Humford. I shuffled around the playground observing them for about ten to twenty minutes, building up courage to go up to her. Finally I tied Jazz's lead to the fence and walked into the playground. Maggie pushed the child on a swing for a time, pulled her from the seat and led her to a slide. Slowly and nervously, I walked up and said softly: 'Hi Maggie, how are you?'

'Jack! What are you doing here?' she asked, turning around, startled.

'Walking my dog.'

The little girl slid down the slide, ran up to us and partially hid herself behind Maggie's legs.

'Hi, what's your name?' I asked.

'Jacqui,' she replied.

'How old are you Jacqui?'

The little girl was silent.

'She's three in May.'

Her thick black hair and blue eyes jolted my memory, but I couldn't pinpoint what it was.

'She's cute,' I said.

Maggie smiled and Jacqui ran off to a climbing frame with us following. I was puzzled, remembering what had happened at the Crieff Hydro in Scotland. Hal Humford was drunk and had complained that Maggie couldn't have children. Perhaps they had adopted Jacqui. On the other hand, she looked a bit like Maggie.

'How's Hal?' I asked.

'We've split. I'm getting a divorce,' she whispered. 'Jacqui and I are leaving for Boston tomorrow evening. We'll stay with my parents for a while.'

I was surprised: 'I'm sorry . . . What about Jacqui? Doesn't she want to be with Hal? Doesn't he want to see her?'

'Of course! He's crazy about her. He'll have to come to Boston.'

'Where's Hal?'

'He's in Mayfair. He moved into his bank's apartment. He's coming to visit tomorrow, before we go to the airport.'

Maggie went up to Jacqui and helped her climb to the top of the climbing frame. Then it came back to me. Jacqui reminded me of some photographs of my mother as a child.

I wished I had a photo on me to confirm it, but they were at home. Yes, Jacqui did look a bit like Maggie, but Maggie was blonde and fair skinned. The child's hair was black. The light blue eyes, small mouth and delicate nose; very similar to those pictures of Mum.

Jacqui climbed down and ran towards a little boy who was alone on a see-saw. She jumped on to the other side.

'Your daughter's lovely. Is she . . .?'

'Adopted? No!'

Silence for a while. Maggie, wary, turned away from me. Seemed to want to get away. She went towards Jacqui, as if she wanted to protect her. I wasn't going to let go. Had to know regardless.

'Jacqui's your own child? But in Crieff, Hal said . . .'

'That I couldn't have children. I also thought so. But it isn't me, it's him!' she suddenly exclaimed with a bitter laugh. 'All our problems, the trauma. Him not me.'

'Whatever, she's yours. That's wonderful!'

I watched Jacqui on the see-saw, up, down, up again. Laughing with the little boy. His mother close by, making sure that they didn't fall. Maggie was less fearful, helping Jacqui become more independent. The surface of the playground was rubber and the see-saw wasn't very high. It was quite safe. I made a simple calculation on my fingers. If Jacqui was turning three in May, she was conceived in August when Maggie and I were in Scotland. Maggie noticed me counting my fingers.

'The loch, the willow tree?' I blurted out.

'Yes Jack, you, but she's mine,' confessed Maggie, at last.

My feelings were a mixture of wonder, relief, joy and pain

that this was the very first time that I knew I was a father and had never seen Jacqui as a baby.

Maggie noticed and said firmly with a determined smile: 'Hal's her father.'

I could see why I had once fallen in love with Maggie. She was beautiful. I wanted to rush over to Jacqui, hug her and hold her high above my head. I stared at Jacqui mesmerised. Her eyes, my Mum's eyes. Jacqui was my daughter, my own daughter. I couldn't believe it! Maggie came up to me and held Jacqui's hand.

'Time to go, Jack. Say goodbye, Jacqui.'

'Can't I take you to the nice cake shop in South End Green? It's not far from here,' I pleaded.

'No thanks, we have to get going,' said Maggie.

'Please Mummy, I want some cake,' shouted Jacqui excitedly.

*   *   *

The mid January winter light was fading fast when we left the café in South End Green. Jacqui had a lovely time there and for the first time in days, I felt happy. Maggie, however was tense. Jacqui wanted me to go to their house to see her new rocking horse. Maggie had reservations, but she agreed at last.

'OK Jacqui, but Jack and Jazz will only stay for a short time,' she said firmly.

It was a short walk to Maggie's home in Parliament Hill Fields. The large terraced Edwardian house was only a couple of hundred yards away from the café. Jacqui helped me pull in Jazz and she proudly showed me her dolls and horse which were in the living room. I read her a story while Maggie cooked her some pasta. Jacqui stroked Jazz and he wagged his tail happily. After she went to bed, Maggie gave me some French bread and cheese in the kitchen and Jazz some scraps.

'You mustn't let her know who you are, Jack,' Maggie said softly. 'Hal's her father. They are mad about each other.'

I looked around the living room and saw the suitcases.

'But you've split. You're going to America. How often will she see Hal?'

'I don't know. We'll be with my parents. She'll have a family.'

'Can I keep in contact? Maybe I can be her godfather?'

'Not a good idea. Hal and I split because of you. It just got worse and worse.'

'Because of me? Why?'

'When I fell pregnant, we were amazed,' explained Maggie. 'We had tried for years. Fertility treatment, again and again. Nothing worked. Then it suddenly happened.'

'Didn't he think that it was him?'

'He knew that it was impossible. We hadn't made love for three months. The IVF treatment had became such a routine that it put us off sex. We also weren't getting on that well.'

'So what did you tell him?'

'Hal forced it out of me. I told him about our fling by the loch.'

'Surely you told him that it happened by chance? That it wasn't serious.'

'Of course, but Hal is jealous, very jealous' she replied.

'He resented me right through the pregnancy. Then, when Jacqui was born, he was mad about the baby.'

'If you didn't want to antagonise Hal, why did you call her Jacqui? After me?'

'Hal chose the name.'

'Really?'

'He wanted me to feel guilty. Remind me what I had done. He changed. Gave the child everything. All his love. Continued to resent me. We argued constantly. Hal would tail me sometimes. Thought that you and I were having an affair, or I was sleeping with someone else. He didn't believe me. Except for you, Jack, I have always been faithful.'

'I can't understand it. When I met him in Zurich, he didn't seem to remember me.'

'Oh yes he did Jack! Once when I was cleaning his study, I found a file with newspaper articles about you. How you made a fortune in the coffee market. Of course he remembered you. We had lots of arguments and it would always come back to you. He was obsessed. I think it was more than jealousy. As crazy as it seems, I think you undermined his manhood.'

'But I came across him several times and he seemed relaxed with me. His bank was the biggest investor in our fund.'

'He never told me that . . . You said "was".'

'They pulled out in December. He's given us a bad headache.'

'That was revenge, Jack. Revenge!'

'It doesn't make sense. Why get involved with me?'

'He hates you Jack. I can't tell you how much he hates

you. Our arguments became violent and he tried to throttle me twice. That's why I decided to leave.'

I couldn't help myself and put my arm around Maggie. She was first tense and then relaxed. She seemed to need the comfort, allowed me to hug her softly and kiss her gently. It was late afternoon, but it was already dark, so she took me up to her bedroom. Instead of making love, we just cuddled. I was so exhausted from the trauma of the past few days that I fell asleep. Something woke me up. It was Jacqui who came in and snuggled up to Maggie on her side of the bed. She was soon sleeping, her thumb in her mouth.

I lay there looking into the darkness and began to think of Hal Humford. I had to see him and find out what was happening. The chances were that I was going down. He had to help me put the pieces together. If he wouldn't tell me, I would threaten him. Bring him down with me.

Maggie had told me that Hal was living in the flat above Banque Discretione's London branch, Mayfair. I slowly got out of the bed and without disturbing them, quietly picked up my clothes and sneaked down the stairs. Jazz and I were soon out of the house. It seemed very late in the winter darkness, but it was only 7pm. I found a taxi driver who was prepared to take the dog. There was hardly any traffic and we were soon in the West End.

22

CONSEQUENCES

Banque Discretione was near the American Embassy in Grosvenor Square, but I wasn't sure of the address. I asked the cab to drop me off at Claridge's, one of the luxury hotels where we had given presentations to investors. The concierge found the address and I gave him a pound. No more fivers. I had to economise.

It began to drizzle again and I ran a few hundred metres from Claridge's to Grosvenor Street. The bank was in a discreet, nondescript building. I rang the bell several times. Eventually the security guard answered.

'Is Mr Humford in?' I asked.

'Do you have an appointment?' replied the burly security guard, who had a thick East European accent. I shook my head, but insisted that Humford knew me. He phoned Hal and let me in with the dog.

Hal's flat was directly opposite the lift on the first floor. I was shocked when he opened the door. Hal had always been immaculate. Not so this time. He was unshaven in a white shirt that had a large yellow stain. He smelt of whisky, his trousers were dirty and his fly was open.

'Hello Jack Miner, long time no see,' he slurred, staggering back to a large leather chair in the spacious living room. On a table next to it, was a glass of whisky. The bottle was almost empty.

'Wanna drink?'

'No thanks. I need some questions answered,' I said, walking across the room. It had ceiling to floor curtains right across the windows. I pulled one of the curtains and peered outside. The flat had a balcony and nearby there were some bare trees. No one was outside. The street, in eerie, misty, yellow lamplight, was empty.

I asked Hal for a glass of sparkling water. He staggered to the kitchen, returned with a small bottle and gave it to me. His eyes were red. It wasn't only the booze. It looked as if he had been crying. Once again he slumped into the chair, his back facing the curtains.

'What are you going to do about Jacqui when she's in the States?' I asked.

'How did you find out about Jacqueline?' he growled, glaring at me.

'I saw Maggie with her in the playground today. Found out that I'm Jacqui's father.'

'I'm her father, not you. I've done everything for her since she was a tiny baby. I love my daughter. You have no claim whatsoever.'

'Maggie's left you. They're going to live in America. It's Maggie's decision, not yours,' I snapped.

Humford pulled himself out of the chair and tried to be as threatening as possible. Jazz began to bark viciously. I held back the dog and changed the subject.

'Maggie told me that you couldn't stand me. Why did you invest in our fund?'

'Take your dog away. I can't talk with all that barking.'

I pulled Jazz's lead and put him in the bedroom. Two open suitcases, filled with clothes, were on the bed. I closed the door and went back to my chair and sat directly in front of him.

'Going somewhere?' I asked aggressively as I faced him eye to eye.

'They could get me.'

'Who are they? Did they kill Aram Zabkian?'

Hal's face froze when I mentioned Aram. He tried to get up, but I pushed him down. His hands were shaking.

'Now I'm certain. Unless I get away, they'll kill me too.'

'Why Aram? What did he do to them?'

He didn't reply. Instead he picked up his glass and gulped down more whisky. The bottle was now empty. Hal went to a cupboard and took out another Jack Daniels. I snatched it from him, took hold of his arm, dragged him to the kitchen, put on the kettle and poured him a cup of coffee. I had to make him as sober as possible, get some sense out of him. Back in the living room he slumped in his chair and sipped his coffee.

'You screwed my wife. You were a boy. Sixteen! Imagine how I felt.'

'It happened only once. It was a chance meeting.'

'Quite a coincidence that you know about Jacqui.'

'It was the first time I had seen Maggie since Scotland. I swear it.'

'When I found out that you were the father, I decided

to teach you a lesson. I couldn't find where you were. Then I read about your coffee trading. Trader Jack, the Teen Trader. *Daily Mail, Wall Street Journal*. A celebrity. Not for long! I would crush you.'

He then told me about his bizarre revenge.

'I joined Banque Discretione about the time you made money in the coffee market,' he said. 'Yevgeny Faramazov has a major stake in the Russian bank that owns Discretione.

'Faramazov is a major investor in the Russian hedge funds that lost billions in the coffee market. His company owns Horoshi Kofia, the Russian coffee manufacturer that also lost a lot of money.'

'Borodino and Veruschka? It's not my fault that the Russians sold short and lost. We were bullish on coffee so we bought. What's wrong with that?' I said.

'They weren't terribly pleased with you, Miner.'

'Why didn't they bump me off then?' I asked, trying to joke about the possibility, though the thought terrified me.

'They needed you.'

'Why?'

'I told them that you would be useful. That they should use you.'

'How?'

'Russian and foreign natural resource companies in oil, gas and mining are their main investments. Faramazov and his friends wanted to make the companies profitable and list them on international stock exchanges. Faramazov's hedge funds also had big bull positions in oil, gas and other commodities. But prices were depressed at the time. My plan was to push up those prices. If we could do so, it would be win for the resource companies, win for their hedge funds, win for Faramazov and win for Banque Discretione.'

'And win for you!' I muttered. 'What was the plan?'

'First spread the word to banks, analysts and others that major shortages were on the way. That demand from China, India and emerging nations would overwhelm production.'

'So where did I come in?' I asked.

'When prices were depressed few believed us. So the second phase of our strategy was to encourage international hedge funds and other big time punters to push up the prices of oil, natural gas, metals and other commodities. Make prices treble, even quadruple. Aquarium would lead the way.'

'Why Aquarium? There are much bigger funds. Why me?'

'You made a name for yourself in the coffee market,' said Humford, glaring at me. 'You also gave excellent presentations to pension funds and other investors, telling them that energy, other commodities and natural resource shares would boom. We passed the word around that Trader Jack, the coffee star, was buying oil and gas. That encouraged others to follow and prices took off.'

'You mentioned Aram. What about him?'

Hal's smile looked more like a sneer. I could tell that he thought I was naïve.

'I had met Aram some time ago. So I approached him and encouraged him to be your partner, even though the two of you didn't get on. I promised that Discretione would put a lot of money in Aquarium on one condition. The fund had to keep buying to keep the momentum going, keep prices on an upward trend.'

'I thought that it was Cy Grobnick who persuaded you to invest.'

Hal sniggered: 'That Jew! No way. We made a deal with Aram.'

'I suppose you are anti Blacks and Muslims also,' I said with disgust.

He seemed to find that funny. Coffee dribbled on to his chin while he giggled stupidly.

The racist. Made me feel sick.

Wiping the bottom of his face with his hand, Humford continued: 'Poor Aram! At first he bought in good faith when I told him that energy prices were cheap and they were at the time.'.'

'Discretione put hundreds of millions into Aquarium. You were our biggest investor! Why?'

'Our clients were the investors. Not the bank. The more investor money you had, the more gas and oil you could buy.'

'Did you encourage Aram to borrow money as well?' I asked, biting my lip.

'Yes. I helped him get credit lines from American and French banks. This enabled Aquarium to buy even more commodities and securities.'

'What was your deal with Aram?'

'We made him financially secure. Aram had money problems when I first approached him.'

Hal staggered to the bathroom and I did some serious thinking. Whether I liked it or not, I was caught in a scam. A scheme that encouraged investors to climb aboard a hot-air balloon that would inevitably burst. Pension funds and other investors were going to get badly hurt. Companies would fail and workers would lose their jobs. Worse still, Humford had succeeded in tainting me. He had associated me with the Russian mafia.

Hal came out of the bathroom. He looked a bit better, now that he had washed his face. He went to the liquor cabinet, opened a bottle of red wine and filled two glasses. Several newspapers were in a magazine rack. He pulled out a *Wall Street Journal* and passed me a glass of wine.

'What was Faramazov's role in all this?'

'Faramazov headed the operation.'

I thought about the Russian mafia coffee deal with the Colombian cocaine barons.

'Is Faramazov involved in drugs?'

'I don't know anything about that side of the business,' said Hal.

I didn't believe him. The drug chain probably laundered money through Discretione.

'Pearl Fleecer. How did she figure?'

'You mean Petrovna Fleshnikov. She changed her name. She's an employee and former lover of Faramazov. He owns her public relations company. Useful. Your own private, apparently independent, spin doctor. Faramazov and her father Ivan Fleshnikov were former KGB officers. Their association goes back a long way.'

'Petrovna Fleshnikov! Talk about sleeping with the enemy,' I whispered to myself.

'Surely you now realise that Pearl didn't meet you by accident,' said Humford sneering. 'You're probably bitter, but the irony is that she saved you. Believe it or not, she was very fond of you. You're still alive because of her and me!'

I shuddered. Pearl – Petrovna Fleshnikov – the girl I once loved. A daughter of a KGB officer! It beggared belief. I downed my wine quickly and glanced at the *Wall Street Journal*. On the front page was the headline: 'Oil & natural gas slump – Manipulation fears.' The article was by Israel McTavish. I snatched the paper from Hal to see whether McTavish had written about me.

'The Commodity Futures Trading Commission and the UK Financial Services Authority are investigating unusual activity in the oil and natural gas markets. Jack Miner's Aquarium Fund and other hedge funds were big buyers, but Miner was unavailable for comment,' it said.

The article didn't mention any connection with the Russians. I sighed with relief.

'After Aquarium and other suckers bought, what was the next phase of your operation?' I asked.

'When prices rose to satisfactory levels, Faramazov listed his companies on the Russian and London stock exchanges. Their shares trebled within months. Faramazov and his friends made a lot of money. Our clients did well too. Soon there was such euphoria that prices rose way above our expectations. Naturally Faramazov's hedge funds began to take profits.'

'And Aquarium and other foolish managers were the buyers,' I said, becoming increasingly angry.

'Precisely! We had to sell our holdings to someone. Aram had an agreement with us. He had to keep on buying from us until we instructed him to stop. If he didn't obey . . .'

'Faramazov would put on the financial pressure and threaten him and his family,' I whispered.

Aram's complex deals began to make sense. Instead of taking profits, the scared sucker had bought. Prices began to fluctuate wildly while they were peaking. Our losses mounted, so he hid them away in the 'Aquarium Volatility Account'.

'I suppose Ivan Smeerneck was also on the payroll.'

'Yes. Smeerneck is an old friend of mine. Very useful. You met him through Pearl didn't you? Faramazov set that up. Pearl encouraged you to pass on Smeerneck's details to Aram so that he could be broker to Aquarium. Smeerneck helped us in two ways. First he built a relationship with Aram and helped us offload our positions. Second, you met Smeerneck and his senior dealer before Aram. This would convince a judge and jury that you were the instigator of the fraud.'

'Very thorough!' I hissed. 'One thing I can't understand. If you wanted Aquarium to keep on buying, why did Discretione withdraw hundreds of millions of dollars from the fund in November and December? Why didn't you get out gradually? Sell bit by bit?'

'Three reasons. If Discretione's investors had lost large amounts of money, we would lose them as clients. Second the Swiss National Bank would have held an enquiry. That would not have suited us. I had to get them out quickly.'

'And the third reason?'

'I decided that it was time to break you, Miner,' laughed Humford hysterically.

'We have to dump our oil, gas, gold, shares and bonds. Everything to repay $1 billion loans,' I said. 'If we sell in a weak market, prices will fall further and we'll be left with massive losses. We could owe billions!'

'You're on the road to financial hell, Miner. Ruined! They're going to lock you up and throw the key in a sewer!'

With some difficulty, I controlled my anger.

'You're also caught in the whirlpool, Humford. You've gone too far. Sure your Russian bosses made big money, but they are still committed to the raw materials market. What about their energy and mining companies? If prices crash, they could be in big trouble. Their shares and bonds will slump. Some of the companies might fail and lay off workers. The Russian government would then be involved.'

'You're right. I realised that before you came. I went too far. That's why I'm packing. Booked on a plane to South America. They wanted me to withdraw money in stages, but I decided to protect our clients and finish you.'

I looked at him closely. He had a wild look in his eyes and it wasn't the booze. It wasn't just because he had an irrational hatred for me. He had also lost Maggie and Jacqui. He was over the edge. To pull me down, Humford had deliberately screwed up his devious plan. After building Faramazov a model energy and resources castle, he had grabbed a sledgehammer and knocked it down.

'What about Aram?' I asked.

'He came here, just like you; complained that we had put him under unbearable pressure. Couldn't understand why Discretione had pulled money out of Aquarium. Why I reneged on my deal. He threatened to tell the authorities. I warned him that my bosses didn't play games.'

'And you? What about you?'

'Now he's gone and I'm next,' said Humford, pouring

some more wine into his glass. 'I lost them money and I know too much.'

He had a look of despair and I began to feel nervous. How could I forget Yapolovitch of Moscow Narodsky, hanging from Charing Cross Bridge; Journalist Marcia Mirikover, pushed under a train; Aram and his mother, caught in a fire.

'Is your bank connected to Moscow Narodsky?' I asked.

'Moscow Narodsky merged with Faramazov's bank after Yapolovitch died. It became Narodsky Faramon and it owns Banque Discretione.'

At last all the pieces fitted together. We sat quietly for a minute or so.

'You had a good life. Why did you do this?' I asked.

'Because you're going down. You're finished, you bastard. You screwed my wife. Now that you know everything, you'll be watching your back for the rest of your life.'

During his 'confession' I was boiling inside and now I lost it. Shouting and swearing, I jumped up from my seat, grabbed his shirt collar and pulled him up. He was bigger than me, but I had done a lot of weight training. I shook him, put my arm around his neck in a wrestling lock until he was red in his face and was choking. I wanted to finish him off.

Then I thought of Jacqui and regained control of myself. I let go, slapped him and pushed him back into his chair. I must have hit his nose as blood started pouring out of it. I rushed to the bathroom pulled out some toilet paper and gave it to him. He mopped up the blood on his face, held his nose tight and tilted his head to stop bleeding.

'Why don't you do it?' he said in a rasping voice. 'Come on! Finish me off!'

'You're a nothing,' I growled. 'I'm not going down because of you. I'll fight back.'

Despite my tough talk I knew I was finished.

I had some blood on me, so I went to the bathroom to wash it off. I just kept washing and washing. The taps were on at full blast. Water was all over the place, over my clothes, the floor, everything. I calmed down and switched off the water and stood there for a few minutes, eyes closed, silent.

The dog barked suddenly and scratched the door of the bedroom. I opened the bathroom and saw a stranger in the living room. His hood was down and he was wearing a black tracksuit and black gloves. His forearm was locked around Humford's neck. He was dragging him towards the balcony. It was clear what he was going to do. He would push Hal over the railings; make it look like suicide.

'Stop!' I shouted, rushing over to them.

Jazz, who was still in the other room, was barking like crazy, but I didn't have time to let him out. I grabbed Hal's legs and pulled. The man was in a mask, but I could see his eyes. They glared at me. I recognised those eyes. How could I forget them? I had first seen them on Charing Cross Bridge. The nightmare bridge. I looked down at Hal. He was unconscious. In that instant the man loosened his grip and sprinted to the balcony. I rushed after him, but he was too swift for me. He balanced himself on the railings and then dived towards the tree. It was about ten to fifteen metres from the balcony. The yellow light of the streetlamp shone on him as he reached out and clung on to a branch. He let go and as he fell, clutched a lower branch, then another and finally landed softly on his feet. Then he sprinted into the darkness. The remarkable acrobatic skills were the same as that show in Edinburgh. At Faramazov's party. It was Krepolovitch. It could only be Krepolovitch.

I went back inside to see whether Hal was breathing. He was still on the floor, unconscious.

I had taken a few lessons in martial arts and my instructor had told me about the 'carotid sleeper'. If you lock your opponent's neck in a tight enough vice, you can block the carotid artery. If you hold it there for only twenty to thirty seconds, the victim can die of heart failure. I prayed that Krepolovitch hadn't killed him, for Jacqui's sake.

Jazz was still in the bedroom, barking, so I let him out to calm him down and stop the noise. He rushed to Humford and sniffed him. I was about to try mouth-to-mouth resuscitation, when I heard banging on the door. The security guard, who had his own key, let himself in and saw Hal. The guard was a six-footer with thick powerful arms. He soon had me in a bear hug, so tight that I could hardly breathe. I tried to explain about the intruder, but he didn't listen. Jazz was barking and growling. The brute kicked the poor dog so hard that he landed three to four metres from us with a yelp and remained there whimpering. The guard relaxed the bear hug and searched me for possible weapons. He pinned both my arms behind me, pulled out the wires from the TV equipment and used them to tie my hands and legs. He called 999 and then placed his mouth on Hal's lips and pumped his chest. By then it was too late.

* * *

Hal was covered with my finger prints and my DNA. His blood was on me. They took me for questioning at Charing Cross Police Station. The last time I was there, I had left a note reporting Yapolovitch's murder.

It was hardly surprising that I was the prime suspect. Before Krepolovitch had arrived, I had almost strangled Hal myself. Given him a bloody nose. I had plenty motives, Maggie, Jacqui and financial. I asked the police if I could search my mobile for friends who could help. Bess's name came up. I remembered that her Dad was a criminal lawyer. Thanks to Bess, Jeremy Trilingham-Marsh agreed to act for me.

I had a lucky break. The forensic pathologist found two hairs that belonged neither to Hal nor me. Krepolovitch was wearing a hood when I saw him, but Hal might have pulled it off in the struggle. I had told the detectives that Krepolovitch performed as an acrobat. They found that he was in a show at a theatre in Islington. Performers told them that Krepolovitch had left for Moscow late Saturday night because his father was ill. The forensic pathologist tested some hairs in the dressing room and the DNA matched the hair found on Hal's body. Unfortunately they couldn't extradite Krepolovitch from Russia. The police investigation would continue, but for a time I was off the hook.

They let me out on bail. The entrance of the police station was crowded with reporters and photographers. I was big news. Two police officers escorted me, but they weren't in the murder team. They were the fraud squad. They took me to my flat in Hampstead and gaped at the piles of brokers' notes and statements on the living room floor. They put the papers in separate boxes and we went to the office. Amanda and other members of staff turned their backs on me when I walked in with handcuffs. The fraud squad put the papers on the meeting room table and started going through them. One of their staff accessed Aram's computer. They also examined all our personal records. Leash Grobnick wasn't there. He had decided to remain in America until the crisis blew over. The UK-American commercial crime agreement was unfair. They could only extradite people from Britain to the US. Not the other way round.

The officers asked me a lot of questions and I did my best to tell them what I knew. I blamed Aram, but they didn't believe me. By then oil had slumped to $35 from around $148 a barrel at its top. Natural gas, which had peaked around $15 British Thermal Unit, a few weeks before and was $10 on Friday, had tumbled to $3. Oil and natural gas shares and bonds were in free fall and there were already reports that some companies could fail.

Wire and press articles estimated that Aquarium's losses could easily be $5 billion and were mounting. The losses were well in excess of the money that investors had placed in the fund. They had lost everything. Aquarium was finished. Other funds that were caught in the crash would also fail, the reports said.

*   *   *

An anonymous friend put up bail. I guessed it was Stanley Slimcop. I wrote a third letter to him and Leila, apologised once again and thanked him for the help. Martha, who remained a good friend, let me stay with her. I jogged and walked Jazz and Pattie, wearing dark glasses. Aquarium ended up with losses of $7 billion. The banks sold my flat in London, apartment in New York, my Ferrari and everything else that they could get their hands on. I was broke. Leash Grobnick's LeashTrade closed down, but he, Amanda and other staff members were not charged. The Financial Services Authority fined LeashTrade and Leash $5 million each, record penalties at the time. Lots of investors sued Leash and the firm, but so far they haven't been able to recover much money.

I lost contact with all my former colleagues, although I received letters from Cy and Maffie. As expected, Cy came up with the obvious: 'You will come out of this stronger'. Maffie wrote that she was disappointed in me; that I had lied to her. I replied that I hoped she would forgive me one day. I haven't heard from either Pearl or Sandy.

After building me up as a celebrity when I was doing well, the media now trashed me as a rogue trader. The paparazzi followed me everywhere. One of the photos of me jogging had the caption, *Teen Trickster Still Running*.

Jeremy advised me to plead guilty to fraud. He tried to persuade the judge that Aram was the main player and that I wasn't fully aware of all the details. The judge wasn't convinced and gave me seven years. I had expected that I would get three to four years at the most. Jeremy thought that the judge gave me a long sentence as I was the catalyst for the global financial crash. I wondered whether the judge had lost money.

Gains from the bull market during the previous few

years were wiped out. Several hedge funds, investment banks and pension funds lost billions of dollars. Hedge funds had to sell shares, bonds and other assets to meet their debts and repay investors who wanted to withdraw their money. The vicious circle widened. Share prices slid further, leading to more sales and financial bankruptcies. Global stock markets slumped. I used to play dominos with my Dad. Neatly stack them up on their edges and then flick one. They would collapse like a concertina. Aquarium was the single domino that caused what they called the 'The Teen Crash'. Governments, the US Federal Reserve Bank, the Bank of England, and the European Central Bank bailed out banks that had lent hundreds of billions to hedge funds and companies. Despite that, some small banks failed. Hundreds of stockbrokers, fund managers and businessmen were forced to sell their art, jewellery and homes to meet their losses. Property prices fell, causing further problems and financial grief for owners with big mortgages.

A few people made money. No prize for guessing. They were Faramazov and his crowd. Issie McTavish came to visit me. He had heard that the Russians had hedged against losses on the commodity and stock market, by selling futures and options short. They had managed to extricate themselves from the turmoil and were not prosecuted for fraud.

The financial slump hit the economy. During the boom there were huge takeover deals that were financed with borrowed money. Some companies overburdened with debt had to lay off their workers. People spent less, so shops and factories struggled or closed. By the time I was inside, there was a recession. Many people lost their jobs and the numbers of homeless grew. This time I wasn't one of the unfortunates who sought shelter under Queen Elizabeth Hall. I had a roof over my head, a bed and three meals a day.

A year ago the markets settled down and the economy improved. Lower energy and commodity prices helped as they lowered inflation and costs of businesses. Central banks pumped trillions of cash into the system and share prices soared. The crisis was over for the time being, but unfortunately I couldn't buy the bargains.

Martha, my steadfast 'Mum', brought me a book a few weeks ago: 'The Teen Crash' by Israel McTavish. Most of the chapters were about the fraud, but the book blamed the crash on the banks, brokers, hedge funds and other institutions. McTavish wondered how supposedly skilled fund managers and sophisticated wealthy investors could bet big money on a boy; a teenager who had not even completed school. The deluded market crowd had followed me because they thought that once a winner, always a winner.

'It's all about greed and the fear of being left behind,' wrote McTavish. 'Greed of investors, greed of fund managers and greed of brokers and bankers who rake in commissions and bonuses.

'From the South Sea Bubble and Tulip Mania to the 1929 crash, booms and busts in the 1970s and today; markets haven't changed, only the participants do. Lawyers and accountants, pension fund trustees, doctors, scientists, professors, business people, artists, actors, writers and journalists. Intelligent, qualified, skilled and talented individuals, all floating in a bubble, all fools in a crowd. A crowd that believes that one and one makes three, perhaps four or five.'

The book quotes a scene from Thomas Hardy's *Far from the Madding Crowd*. A dog herds the sheep over a cliff and ruins the farmer. In 'Teen Crash', the dog went over with the sheep.

'Greed makes fools of us all.'

My Story

Jack Miner

EPILOGUE

Months have passed since I gave Dr Klugheim the final chapters of my book. Mrs Small has edited it and cut out the swearing. I've done nearly three years in this hole. Four years left! I often think of Jacqui and wonder how she is.

Martha, who is still looking after Jazz, visits regularly. Gill Derby makes the long journey from Yorkshire whenever she can. Stan is in contact and says that he will help me when I get out. Leila is now a lot worse and doesn't even recognise him.

The police are still investigating the murder and I remain a suspect. They are struggling to extradite Krepolovitch, as the Russian government prefers to try its villains through its own courts. Faramazov is in the clear. There's even talk that he's about to bid for a premier club.

It's summer and it's boiling hot in the cell. The prison is overcrowded, but I can regard myself as lucky. I'm sharing a cell with only one guy. My new cellmate, Jake, arrived recently. He's a quiet, nice guy and leaves me in peace. Reads a lot. Doesn't talk much. I don't even know why he's inside. We swap books. He's keen on Dickens and Russian literature. Gave me Bleak House, *which is about the useless legal system and Dostoevsky's*

Crime and Punishment. *Jake was fascinated with McTavish's book and lent me* Extraordinary Popular Delusions and the Madness of Crowds.

Today I'm seeing Dr Klugheim again. The market's recovered and he's made lots of money. My Aquarium methods worked well for him. It would be great if he would give me ten per cent of the profits! Anyway, it's thanks to Mrs Small and Klugheim that I wrote the book. It helped me get through here. Maybe it's the start of something else. I could be a journalist when I get out. A reptile who knows what it's like inside. Maybe write a best seller.

*   *   *

I knock on Klugheim's door and am surprised. Jeremy Trilingham-Marsh is there with some other guy. Klugheim, in a dark blue suede jacket looks very prosperous indeed!

I've never seen his office so tidy; books stacked neatly in the bookshelf; files in the filing cabinet; an empty desk with in and out trays.

Wow, it must be parole time! They're going to let me out for good behaviour. Maybe I'll get an electronic tag; at worst, Ford Open Prison. Maybe the guy with Jeremy will be my parole officer,

'Jack, I want you to meet John Primeheart,' says Jeremy. 'He's Detective Chief Superintendent of Scotland Yard, International Branch.'

'Thanks for allowing Dr Klugheim to show us your book, Miner,' says Primeheart. 'It helped us considerably.'

'How? I'm in here, but the guy behind the fraud is about to buy the football club I support!'

'It's well down the league. Bound to lose more matches if he takes over,' says Klugheim with a wry grin.

Primeheart, who has been looking at me warily, attempts a smile: 'We've been watching them for some time. Your book confirms a lot. We'll get them.'

'The Russian mafia? Fat chance! If they get hold of the book . . .'

'They won't.'

'You better be right. If you aren't, there'll be another suicide here; except it won't be a suicide.'

I turn to Klugheim: 'Are they letting me out?'

'I don't know,' he says. 'It's up to you, them and the Governor.'

'Thanks Dr Klugheim. Thanks a lot. You promised that if you showed them the book . . .'

'You're lucky Dr Klugheim took an interest in you,' says Primeheart, in a quiet cold voice. 'That's why I'm here.'

He puts on a tape recorder and states the time and date. Jeremy sits next to me.

'Now let's get down to business,' says Primeheart in a flat tone. 'When the police interviewed you before the trial, why didn't you tell them the full story?'

He peers at me with his ice blue eyes. He seems to see right through me. I don't reply.

Klugheim opens the door and looks outside to make sure that no one is behind it. When he closes it, Primeheart continues to grill me.

'Let me ask you again, Miner. Why didn't you tell the police everything you knew? You know very well that you're not out of the loop. The Humford case is still unsolved.'

'Put yourself in my position. You know that the Russian mafia

*murdered at least five people: Yapolovitch, a Moscow journalist,
a Swiss banker, Aram Zabkian and Hal Humford. What about
me? You cops don't earn much money. Faramazov has a thick
chequebook. If you were in my position wouldn't you keep quiet?'*

*'We don't take bribes,' snaps Primeheart. 'If you're that
worried, why did you write about it?'*

*'Yes, I took a big risk. I trusted Mrs Small and Dr Klugheim.
They don't have an agenda. Anyway, I thought we had a deal. I
would write the truth and get out sooner.'*

*'You did the right thing. We want you to tell us all you know
Jack,' says Klugheim.*

*'Yes, we must question these people and prosecute them,'
adds Primeheart. 'A quarter of a million Russians now live in
London. New York has a big Russian population. They're all over
the world. Moscow crime syndicates are operating everywhere.
Russian crime has also become our problem.'*

*'What's in it for me? So far you're just offering me a short
life!'*

*'I don't believe that you murdered Humford,' says Primeheart
casually. 'I never did. One sentence in your book confirms it.'*

'Jacqui,' says Klugheim. 'No way would you kill her father.'

'I'm her father,' I protest.

*'Biological father. Her mother and her grandparents look
after her,' says Klugheim. 'You have to accept that, Jack. We can
talk about it later.'*

'Are you prepared to help us?' asks Primeheart.

'It depends. If you're talking about the Russians, no way.'

'He can remain silent if he wishes,' says Jeremy.

*Primeheart ignores him:'Do you get on with your cellmate,
Jack?*

'Yeah. *They put him inside a few months ago. Nice guy. Keeps to himself. Don't know what he did. Probably fraud. Clever. Swaps books with me. Knows I'm interested in Russia so he's lending me books by Dostoevsky.* Brothers Karamazov. *Father murdered. The wild brother who didn't do it, is sent to Siberia. Bit like me.'*

Then it occurs to me: 'He's one of you lot, isn't he? He's my minder!'

'*You know of five people who the Russian mafia murdered,' says Primeheart. 'Do you want to know about a sixth?'*

'*No way.'*

'*From someone who believes your story, has been working behind the scenes?'*

'*All right, then.'*

Primeheart speaks on his mobile: '*You can come in now.'*

'*Detective Sergeant Sasha Melnikov,' says Primeheart, as she enters.*

Instead of a uniform, she's in a smart dark blue suit. She's a stunner!

'*Tell Mr Miner why he can trust you.'*

'*Because you're a cop?' I say sarcastically.*

She stares straight at me. Steely, grey blue eyes.

'*My father was the manager of a diamond mine. They wanted to take it over. He opposed them. He's now dead. We believe that he's been murdered.'*

'*That's terrible. I'm . . .I'm sorry,' I say, embarrassed. 'I suppose they own the mine now.'*

'*Yes. Do you know anything about diamond mining, Jack?' asks Primeheart.*

'*No, but I can learn,' I reply eagerly. 'Fred Carrender, the prospector I wrote about. He knows everything about diamonds. He can teach me.'*

Primeheart seems interested. My hopes soar. If I'm prepared to help, will they let me out?

'I've got something for you, Jack,' says Melnikov, opening her handbag. She pulls out a CD, a ring and a photograph and passes them to me. The CD is the same one that belonged to Dad with his favourite numbers, Louis Armstrong and Ella Fitzgerald. I kiss Mum's engagement ring and turn away and stare at the picture of the three of us in Cornwall.

'How did you get hold of these?' I say, rubbing my eyes with the back of my hand.

When I'm ready, I look at Melnikov closely. She's Sasha! The homeless girl I had met years before. Left her and her friend before I saw Yapolovitch hanging from the bridge. What a transformation!

'The police questioned us early in the morning and asked us whether we had seen you,' Sasha explains. 'You left your backpack, Jack. Remember? We waited and when you didn't come, we had to leave it behind. I took out these things and kept them for you.'

'Melnikov told the officers that she was Russian and that she wanted to join the police force,' says Primeheart. 'Unfortunately she didn't know where you came from, so there was no way of linking the photograph with Yorkshire, let alone Bridlington.'

'They were starting a Russian unit so they recruited me for training ,' says Sasha.

'She passed with excellent results,' continues Primeheart in his matter of fact tone. 'When we read your book, we put her on to the Yapolovitch case immediately. Your DNA fitted the ones on

the Yapolovitch rope and your mementoes. It was proof that you were the witness.'

I look at Dad and Mum's things, turn away, blink my eyes and face them again. They're sympathetic, except for Primeheart.

'You wouldn't mind getting out of here would you, Miner? Open prison with plenty of privileges. Five star hotel compared to this place.'

My hopes soar: 'Yes, of course.'

'Your book. A virtual hagiography isn't it?'

'Hagiography? What's that?'

'An autobiography that spins in favour of the author,' says Primeheart. 'You blamed Aram Zabkian for the fraud. Are you seriously claiming that you had nothing to do with it? That he ran the fund all the time? A wife and four kids, but never went on holiday? Had a mistress to entertain? Just sat there in front of the screen day after day, without spending his money? That you were set up? Come on! I read the court records. It's very convenient that Zabkian's dead, that we can't hear his side of the story.'

'I pleaded guilty didn't I?' I reply, doing my best to remain cool.

'But you want to get out now don't you? Well before time.'

'Is that unreasonable?'

'Tell me what you think about this: A highly intelligent, cunning young villain writes a book showing that he's basically a nice decent guy. He includes sob stories about his parents and friends. The prison believes him, agrees that he's hard done by and gives him parole. Now what if he were the same as the other super rich fraudsters?'

'I didn't just write about my good points. I showed my flaws as well,' I protest.

'Hah! That's why this sociopath is so clever. He needs to show that he's three dimensional; that he isn't Mr Perfect.'

I look straight at Klugheim. He has to counter that. He owes me big time.

'Jack's trying hard to become a better person,' says Klugheim, swiftly. 'He's a model prisoner. I've got to know him. I think he was naïve and got caught up in it.'

Relief! That might do it.

No way. Primeheart ignores him and irritatingly continues to refer to me in the third person:'As I said, what if he's another wealthy sociopath who has enough money to get the best lawyer?'

'Jack was awarded legal aid,' insists Jeremy.

'What a joke,' says Primeheart with a sarcastic laugh. 'A sharp young speculator who becomes a wealthy multi millionaire loses billions, causing ordinary people like you and me to lose their money, jobs and pensions. He's such a deserving cause that he gets legal aid at the taxpayer's expense! How do you know he hasn't got money stashed away in Liechtenstein or some other funk hole? That he didn't steal from Aquarium; hasn't made deals with other crooks?'

I'm boiling inside. Typical cop! He's used me. Got what he needs from the book and is now throwing away the key.

Klugheim tries to come to my rescue: 'He's really benefitted from therapy. He's very bright, you could use him in the force. You know very well that the villains are ten steps ahead of the fraud squad.'

Primeheart looks Klugheim straight in the eye, at his designer clothes and points at the book shelf: 'Hah! 'How I made $5 million in the stock market'. You two look out for each other, do you?'

Klugheim wincing, retreats and cowers in the corner.

As much as I hate him, I cannot but admire Primeheart. He's a smart operator.

'I've come across plenty of these people,' he continues. 'Most of them escape prosecution because of their lawyers and shredding of evidence; few, like this young man, do time. Others rip off the greedy, unsuspecting, and other suckers within the legal boundaries.

'This is what they generally say: "Me? How can you possibly think that? I'm innocent. OK, I'm no paragon of virtue, but who is? I'm a straight sort of guy. Have a family, educate my children; I'm on the school board. Give to charities. It's them, not me!" Well, Miner, is that you?'

Am not bothering to reply. What's the point? No chance for parole.

'It will pay you to tell the truth, Jack. We know it's over, what the judge and jury decided. That you're doing time,' says Sasha, giving me some hope again. 'Do you still claim that you were not complicit in the fraud? That you were set up? That you were innocent?'

I remain silent for a while, rubbing the photo against my cheek and kissing Mum's ring. They wait silently as I look out the window and then vacantly peer at a wide beam of sunshine, full of dust and microbes, across the room.

'You won't believe me, but the truth is . . .'

'The truth is what?' asks Sasha.

'I really don't know.'

THE END

NEIL BEHRMANN

About The Author

NEIL BEHRMANN, is a journalist and author based in London, Neil was a prolific London-based special correspondent of the *Wall Street Journal* for more than two decades, concentrating on commodity markets and mining. He also wrote *WSJ* features on hedge funds, personal finance, property, sports business and travel. Neil is London correspondent and columnist of *Business Times, Singapore*, a leading Asian business publication. He also writes for other UK and international publications.

Neil's major scoops and investigative stories and features include billion dollar scandals, notably the $3 billion Sumitomo copper fraud in 1996; rogue trader, Nick Leeson; international coffee market crises; the hidden hoard of former Philippines dictator Ferdinand Marcos; Madoff, Bayou and other major hedge fund scams and dealings in the diamond trade. He's been interviewed on radio and TV.

'I love reading and writing fiction, says Neil, 'When I write, I wake up early in the morning, meditate and let my imagination take over.'

Neil's articles can be found on *neilbehrmann.net*. Other sites are: *thestoryofjackminer.com* and *readmore-books.com*

Due for release in 2012

JACK OF DIAMONDS

The Story of Jack Miner continues with Jack entering the murky world of diamond smuggling and double dealing.

More details about this highly original and unusual page turner next year.

BUTTERFLY BATTLE

'Butterfly Battle – The Story of the Great Insect War', Neil Behrmann's anti-war children's book has been relaunched.

Butterfly Battle is aimed at children between the ages of nine to eleven, but crosses the age borders. Children of six to eight enjoyed the exciting fantasy when it was read to them at school. Adults have been captivated by the story. The book is vigorously anti-war, but also shows that war is sometimes forced on us. Superwasps invade Leponea, a peaceful butterfly paradise. Robert and his sister Kim enter the insect world and join in the fight for freedom.

The Superwasp characters symbolise Nazis and other fascists. The butterfly characters and their insect allies are like our grand parents and great grand parents, who had to make a stand and fight Hitler.

Then the anti-war message: Robert who is fascinated with computer war games, soon discovers the awful reality of an actual war. The soldiers are insects but behave like human soldiers. They fret and struggle to fall asleep before the battle. When the action begins, they fight bravely, but panic when the battle goes against them. The inhabitants of Leponea suffer alongside the many wounded soldiers.

The book promotes conservation and sparks an interest in insects. It delves into the mystery of life and death.

Illustrator **Oscar Chichoni's** art ranks amongst the top in the genre of Science Fiction/Fantastic Realism. He has received numerous awards.

Review from the *School Librarian*, magazine of the UK School Librarian Association:

'This is a highly original and exciting book. It tells the story of a war between the insects: the Superwasps versus the rest. Two pre-pubescent children, Kim and Robert, find themselves shrunken down to insect size and drafted in to help. We follow their adventures and the saving of Leponea, the land of the butterflies, and meet some wonderful characters on the way: Morpho, the brave, resourceful daughter of the emperor of all the butterflies and her husband, Morphan. We also meet the demonical dictator, Wreka, leader of the superwasps. The book is masterly in its interweaving or the lifestyles of various insects with the demands of a modern war story: and Robert's understanding of military strategy which he learned from his computer games is handled with assurance and effect. Description is a strong point of the book, especially the battle scenes which are magnificently conveyed. They are realistic and convincing, and will allow children to begin to understand something of the horror, as well as the heroism, of all wars. The black and white drawings are sensitive, well researched and detailed, adding a great deal to the visualisation of the text.' — 'An exciting, fast-paced book which will appeal to children between 8 and 14': Irene Babsky

The London Parents' Guide: titles for 9–14 yrs

Computer-mad Robert spends his time playing electronic war games. His sister loves the outdoor life and longs to help endangered species. Outside their doors, there's very real danger in the insect world – superwasps want to take control and are killing every insect in their way. The children get drawn into the Great Insect War and Robert finds his war strategy skills are the key to survival. He also learns that wars are not just about winning. A gripping fantasy on one level, there are many deep messages within the story. My 10yr old loved it.

Butterfly Battle – The Story of the Great Insect War
by Neil Behrmann

available from

Readmore Books ISBN 978-0-9533843-0-3

www.readmore-books.com

Readmore Books is an imprint of New End
Books

Commodities

Price Slump Despite Lower Interest Rates Raises Fears of Deeper Global Recession

By NEIL BEHRMANN
Special to THE WALL STREET JOURNAL

Commodity prices have slumped despite a sharp fall in interest rates, raising fears that the international recession will be much deeper than originally believed.

"The decline in commodity prices could be indicating that the recession will be as deep as the one in the mid seventies and it could even be the steepest slump in the post-

Coffee Producer In Past 12 Mont.

By NEIL BEHRMANN
Special to THE WALL STREET JOURNAL

LONDON—Coffee-producing nations incurred losses of around $4 billion during the past 12 months, following the collapse of an agreement to support prices, International Coffee Organization officials say.

"The economic situation of African countries, notably Uganda, Cameroon, Rwanda, Burundi and Ethiopia, is critical," says Owusu Akoto, chief economist of the organization, which acts on behalf of producing and consuming nations.

The bulk of these African countries' total exports come from coffee sales, and they are suffering under a huge foreign debt burden, he says. South and Central American producers such as Colombia, Guatemala, Costa Rica and El Salvador are also hurting, Mr. Akoto says. But they managed to pare their losses to some ex-

Alleged Rogue Transactions Dwarf Barings Scandal; Powerful Trader Is Cited

TOKYO — Sumitomo Corp., the giant Japanese trading company, said unauthorized trades by its former head of copper trading over the past decade caused it huge losses that may total $1.8 billion.

If Sumitomo's estimate pans out, the trading loss would be one of the largest in

corporate history—dwarfing the $1.3 billion lost by Nick Leeson of Britain's Barings PLC and the $1.1 billion lost by a trader at Japan's Daiwa Bank Ltd. And the fiasco adds a new name to the roll of all-time rogue traders: the flamboyant Yasuo Hamanaka, who until recently was the world's most powerful copper trader—and the one most feared

Yasuo Hamanaka